Damn. Tro

women were aro[illegible]

It came to him in a flash. Missy remained. Yet that couldn't be. She didn't fit the description of the woman Hans had chosen on paper two months ago. Hell, he lacked too much sleep to play guessing games. "So, spit it out. What happened?"

Luke watched Missy lean against the wagon. Lean? It looked as if she wanted to burrow into the wood.

Hans pulled his hands out of his pockets, gestured with them in front of him. "I chose my bride, and Albert claimed Lila." Lila. Ah yes, Hans had raved about her. "Tom chose Sarah instead of Roberta, and Peter wanted Roberta."

Was anything ever simple? After an exhausting day of catastrophes, and this hopscotch of brides, a headache threatened.

"And now the last two don't match, is that it?"

Hans studied his boots, drove his hands back into his pockets then glanced at Missy. "We don't know if they'll match. They've...just met."

It took a split second for Hans' words to register, to become crystal clear. No. Hans knew why Luke had picked Rosie. He wouldn't intentionally turn the tables on him. But lust and love would, by damn. It made men commit worse crimes.

He swallowed the lump in his throat. "You chose Rosie." His words almost gagged him. He dreaded to hear Hans' confirmation. Hans nodded.

Acid churned in his stomach, and a sour taste spiraled up to his mouth. He'd purposely picked a voluptuous dance hall woman who'd have no problem finding another man after he'd finished here. One who most likely would go along with his scheme and the proposition he offered.

Jesus! He was in a world of shit.

Praise for Beverly Wells

Beverly Wells is an award-winning author whose writing took third place in the Inland Valley RWA *Put Your Best Hook Forward* Contest.

Only When the Loon Sings

by

Beverly Wells

Kathy,
Hope you enjoy your step back in time as you journey with Morgan.
Always,
Bev

This is a work of fiction. Names, characters, places, and incidents are either the product of the author's imagination or are used fictitiously, and any resemblance to actual persons living or dead, business establishments, events, or locales, is entirely coincidental.

Only When the Loon Sings

Contact Information: info@thewildrosepress.com

Cover Art by *Kim Mendoza*

The Wild Rose Press
PO Box 706
Adams Basin, NY 14410-0706
Visit us at www.thewildrosepress.com

Publishing History
First Cactus Rose Edition, 2012
Print ISBN 1-60154-986-5

Published in the United States of America

Author's Note

This story is a tribute to all who have become victim to the devastating, vise-like clutches of ALS (Lou Gehrig's Disease). For years, research has battled to discover the cause, seeking a cure against this horrific and debilitating disease. The future looks bright, great strides are being achieved—and I thank all the workforces who strive to gain answers—but there still remains a tremendously long journey before any true help can be offered. Yet those who suffer this affliction are the ones I truly admire, for their courage, their diligent fight, their perseverance to face each day with every ounce of strength and hope they possess.

I've used writer's liberty here, as ALS was not officially diagnosed nor named until circa 1889. I apologize to anyone who may find this offensive.

A big thank you to all at LCRW for supporting me through the years—you kept me inspired. To Vincent Bedient for his video on pioneering logging, Glenn Miller at Yates County Emergency Services for his expertise regarding cabins and fires, and to Nancy Sproule for introducing me to the world of Romance fiction.

To my own hero, Kent, you're the best.

A sincere thanks to Eve Mallory for my first edits, and a very special thank you to my editor, Nan Swanson, for having the patience of a saint and believing in me. My gratitude to Kim Mendoza for her fantastic cover, and all those at TWRP.

And most of all I'm thankful and honored to have known Claudia, who fought ALS's grueling battle to the very end with dignity, perseverance, and a zest for life that still holds me in awe. May your child, born through a C-section, walk in your footsteps and be your legacy.

Chapter One

Washington Territory, 1880

"Where are you, Mr. Luke Kincaid?" Morgan Prescott hissed through clenched teeth. "If you order a bride, you should be here to meet her."

Morgan's ire was so festered from stewing over her future husband's long-delayed arrival she was surprised her hair hadn't smoldered by now. Her backside prickled unmercifully, and she squirmed for the hundredth time on the hard bench outside the weathered general store. Stretching her back, she flexed her shoulders and ground the tips of her high-laced black shoes into the dirt. All failed to release her frustration.

Nearly every man in this logging town had praised Luke Kincaid up and down for his exemplary leadership, backbreaking hard work, and infinite wisdom. Well, if he possessed all they claimed—it seemed mighty darn hard to believe, from her standpoint—the paragon definitely lacked being punctual or considerate.

"And my tongue will tell you as much, Mr. Not-So-Perfect," she vowed to the waning sunlight, as if it might agree. By God, she'd give him a lashing when the rude man showed his face. How embarrassing to be so blatantly neglected!

For the first hour or so, she and the women she'd befriended on the ship had chatted while the men sorted through the list of names. Once each had staked his claim, so to speak, he rushed his bride-to-be into the saloon to become better acquainted. Most would have the traveling preacher tie the knot tonight, Morgan figured.

And here she sat. Alone, discouraged, uncomfortable. Darn well offended. A loud creak rent the air as the saloon door opened, its harsh sound nearly drowned out by the boisterous laughter from within.

"Ho, there, Missy," Hans called, stepping past the doorway, not thirty feet away. "Ya sure ya won't come inside, have something ta warm yur innards? It's turnin' a mite chilly out. Never thought Luke would be this long."

Morgan returned the smile of the blond, bearded Swede who insisted on calling her Missy. She found his Swedish accent mingled with Western twang quite pleasant. He was a bear of a man—six foot or so, with barreled chest, thick muscled arms, and broad shoulders that barely fit through a doorway—yet friendly, outgoing, and carefree.

"Thank you, Mr. Svensson," she called, raising her voice over the cacophony from inside. "But I'm fine. I'm sure Mr. Kincaid will arrive soon." She glanced at the sun as it set a notch lower. With each passing minute, the chill rose. At least her rising temper kept her blood bubbling.

"We won't be havin' any of that, now." He closed the door, muffling the voices and music, and strode to her side. "I told ya we go by first names here. We're like one happy family. Town's too small to do otherwise." His smile sent a twinkle to his eyes.

For one brief moment, Morgan thought of her family, the note she'd left on her bed. Were they distraught? She felt so unsure of herself in this ramshackle logging town, and she'd not seen much of it so far. Of course, there wasn't much to see. Just a vast wilderness—predominantly trees reaching halfway to the sky—far more remote than she'd expected. She felt no regret for her decision. *Yet.* Deep down she hoped she hadn't caused her parents, as uncaring and insensitive as they had been, to worry.

This town would be her new home, her new family. It had to be better than the life she'd endured till now. She eyed the four unpainted log buildings that made up the town proper: a general store, a good-sized saloon, a livery of sorts, and one community catchall serving as post office, bank, church, and anything else it was needed to be. Each building stood by itself. Handpainted signs over doors bore no fanciness: Carl Turner's General Store, Wet Your Whistle, Hank's Livery, Town's Building. She was a little too far away to read even the headlines on the many posters and announcements nailed to the outside of the latter. Set a few feet away from the row of buildings, a large bell hung from a wooden stand.

At the edge of town, ten or twelve tiny cabins, each on an acre or so of clearing, lined both sides of the wide road. Some boasted rough-sawn siding while others were constructed of logs, all weathered gray, with either stone or round metal chimneys. Hans had informed her Luke Kincaid's cabin was one of many nestled throughout the dark, tall-pined forest. Her new home.

This desolate community of hardworking loggers was a far cry from anything she'd envisioned. Had she made the biggest mistake of her life? She was too tired, hungry, cold, and annoyed to think it all out at the moment.

Hans squatted, took her chilled hands within his and rubbed them. "Ya can stay another half hour. Then, yur comin' inside. Ya upset about Rosie? Is that why ya won't come in?"

Morgan smiled at his misplaced concern. She'd not been the least bit insulted when he chose the robust, red-haired dance hall girl, Rosie O'Hara, over her. The two had taken one look at each other and that had been that.

"Not at all. I'm very sure the two of you were made for each other. And I mean that from the bottom of my heart." After knowing him only a few hours, she liked this man—as a friend. She'd felt no attraction to him, as a wife-to-be should. But Rosie O'Hara had. Stars had danced in the woman's eyes the minute she laid eyes on him. And his eyes had mirrored Rosie's.

What will I feel when I see Mr. Luke Kincaid?

Now why had she thought there would be any instant attraction? They were strangers, for heaven's sake. As long as they got along, that would be as good a start as any. She intended to be a good wife. Love, if she was lucky, might come over time. If not, she reminded herself, she'd need to be content with his friendship, a true and everlasting type of partnership.

Once again a fleeting thought—disheartening, to say the least—whisked through her mind: Would he find fault with the new arrangement? Well, she'd not think about that possibility right now. It was his fault for being late. She felt a wave of satisfaction at that reminder.

Though Hans scowled as if still concerned, Morgan wanted none of the gaiety of the matched couples inside. Her anxiety fed her restlessness. Her temper needed the cool air.

"*Ja*, ya can stay another half hour. Then ya come in. Ya hear? You'll need a good stiff drink by then, to warm ya."

"Thank you. I promise I'll come in then." A stiff drink would probably put her to sleep. She'd never had more than small sips of delicate wine. Were the other women used to spirits? Besides the ten from various states who claimed they'd been dance hall girls, there was Sarah, a middle-aged widow, and eight spinsters ranging in age from their early twenties to forty.

He reached into his coat pocket and withdrew a pair of leather gloves. "Put these on. Yur hands'll be so cold, by the time ya come in, ya won't be able to nurse yur own drink." His blue eyes danced with laughter, his smile warm, friendly, and very welcome.

She slid the large gloves on and was instantly toastier. "Thank you. They do help."

Unfolding from his haunches, he nodded and returned to the others without glancing back. The rickety door squeaked on its hinges as it closed on the boisterous jubilee from within. Pulling the woolen shawl tighter around her, she leaned her head back. And waited.

****

Rolling wheels and heavy plodding of hooves brought a half-asleep Morgan slowly awake. She pried her eyelids open.

"Whoa." The deep-timbered voice reached her on the evening breeze. Instantly alert, her eyes widened, her senses soared. She scanned across the wide ruts to focus on the tall man in a thin buckskin jacket and matching pants as he leaped down from his perch. He'd stopped his two-team flatbed in front of the livery across from the saloon.

Could this be Luke Kincaid? With his broad-brimmed hat and the sky now gloomy gray, she could make out none of his features, other than a short-trimmed beard. He was agile, though, she noted when he jumped to the ground with ease. Straight wide shoulders stretched his coat. He carried himself with a commanding air of self-confidence as he strode to the back of the buckboard. Tough, lean, and sinewy came to mind. How was she to recognize him?

The saloon door opened, and three couples, talking and laughing, walked out onto the road. He paused in rearranging items on the flatbed to wave, and they steered toward him. As they congregated around the wagon, their laughter ebbed as they greeted him.

Morgan leaned forward to hear them. Useless. She watched handshakes and nodding as the men apparently introduced the women. They all laughed before turning away from the newcomer to head toward the cabins, each man with an arm around his bride or bride-to-be.

The man in the street resumed shoving large crates forward in the wagon. She squinted to catch his every move. Surprisingly, her anger dissolved and apprehension jumped in. If he was Luke, he seemed amicable enough. But how amicable would he be about the switch? Again the saloon door squawked. Hans took two steps toward her before noticing the wagon.

"Luke." Hans' voice boomed through the crisp air. "Ya son of a gun, where the hell ya been? I need to talk to ya, quick-like." He lumbered toward the wagon.

So *this* was him. Excitement mingled with trepidation. Her courage shrank away as fast as her anger had. Oh, why hadn't she been able to meet him right off, before her nerves got the better of her? Dare she join them? Knowing she must look as bedraggled as she felt, she hesitated. Well, she'd made the choice to come here. She'd best make the most of it. And now.

She pushed herself up, halfway, only to sag back down. Her legs, her backside, even her arms had turned to tingling mush. She grimaced, clenched her teeth, took a deep breath, then pushed again, grunting as she stood on unsteady legs. Glancing down at her large bag, she thought better of trying to wrestle with it. She would, sure as the stars now dusting the sky, land on her nose if she tried to carry the cumbersome thing on such wobbly legs. He'd have to fetch her trunk anyway. Let the oaf carry both.

Forsaking the baggage, she removed Hans' gloves, laid them on her trunk, and gingerly started across the dirt road. Her legs weighed a ton. Lifting her dress to clear her feet, she cautiously watched her footing as she sidestepped the deep ruts. Halfway there, she stubbed her right toe on a raised clump.

"Oh!" Morgan flailed her arms and stiffened her left leg to bear her weight, and her foot drove into a mound of dirt as she fought for balance. The mound gave way as if made of fine sand.

Luke swung around at her frenzied cry. His eyebrows rose and his eyes widened at the spectacle. He'd not seen anything more comical in a helluva long time—a woman frantically thrashing her arms every which way come Sunday as if batting at a swarm of bees. In a flurry of ruffled petticoats and yards of brown cotton, her legs flew upward till she was bent at the waist, the toes of her high-laced shoes saluting the sky. For a second she seemed suspended in air, as if sitting on an invisible carpet hovering two feet above the ground. Or more like she had been propelled through the air by a cannonball's impact in the gut.

Either way, he mused, gravity finally won out. With a resounding thud she landed flat on her rump, knees bent wide under the full skirt, a stunned look upon her colorless face. Despite the woman's disaster and despite his usual manners—drilled into him by his loving mother—and better sense, Luke let loose a howl. Tears sprang to his eyes as he doubled over in a fit of chortles.

"Yur ass is showing, ya moron," Hans said with

a snarl.

Luke roared all the more, thinking it a wonder the lady's ass wasn't showing.

His expression cold and furious, Hans rushed toward the woman. Hans' rancor sobered Luke. Well, almost. They'd clowned in mock anger, but they'd never crossed words. He found it difficult to totally suppress his mirth, but he too dashed to the middle of the road.

"Missy," Hans said, his concerned voice far different from a moment ago. Kneeling at her side, he brushed from her face the strands of hair that had pulled loose from her now drooping upsweep.

Hans gripped her shoulders. "Don't try to move yet. Catch yur wind first." The woman took a deep breath, shivered, then exhaled long and hard.

Luke skirted them and retrieved her shawl from where it had flown. He turned, placed it over her shoulders, and stood silent behind her. Without acknowledging him, she wiggled her shoulders to adjust it.

Hans leaned on his haunches. "Can ya move?"

Clutching the shawl with both fists, she squirmed from side to side as if testing body parts. "It takes more than one clumsy fall to do harm to these tough bones."

Her laughter tinkled through the evening's chill like soft chimes. Luke had to give her credit for her resilience. "Only my pride's hurt, Hans. If you'd help me up, I'd appreciate it."

Hans assisted her till she found sure ground beneath her feet. Only then did she turn and look straight at Luke.

"Thank you for rescuing my shawl." Her voice held a bit of shyness, her dark brown eyes mirrored equal embarrassment. Though the sky had turned ashen, he noted her becoming blush. He'd first thought her quite plain in her drab brown dress and matching shamble of hair. But with her cheeks rosy, her eyes gleaming like polished mahogany, her mere presence drew him. Warm and welcoming. Luke felt something stir deep inside. Unsettling, to say the least.

Luke nodded. “You’re more than welcome, ma’am.” Her eyes seemed to ask a gamut of questions before she turned to face Hans. Her footing faltered as she tried to balance between hilled clumps and valleys of dirt. Luke reached out instinctively. He caught her by the shoulders before she went down again. He couldn’t hold back his chuckle. Was the woman clumsy, or did she just have difficulty walking on uneven furrows?

“Let’s get you off the road before you have all three of us wallowing in the dirt like pigs.”

He guided her to the wagon, one hand clasping hers, the other at the small of her back. Hans followed at her other side. Releasing her hand, he noted how small, how warm it had felt within his. Thin as a sapling, she barely reached his shoulders, yet her hand had clutched his with a vise-like grip as she trekked across the road. No wispy willow here, he thought with a smile, although most women would kill for a waist as small as hers.

Before he could introduce himself, Hans spoke. “Missy, I need to talk to Luke for a bit.”

She lifted her chin and met Luke’s gaze with unforeseen boldness. Was this the same woman who had appeared so shy, topsy-turvy awkward, and hesitant a minute ago?

“I know exactly what you have to tell him, Hans. So, please, speak freely…or I can, for that matter.” Her gaze remained fixed. Lord, how dark her eyes were, how they glistened under the abating light. Could it have been a glint of apprehension he’d just caught?

Puzzled, he glanced at Hans. “Well, tell me. It

must be important." Jesus! Another accident? It couldn't be. He'd just left the logging site. Yet sheer dread gripped his chest.

Hans obviously read his gut reaction, shook his head. "No one's hurt. Nothing like that."

"Thank God." He felt a flood of relief. "So? Shoot."

Hans squared his shoulders, shoved his hands into his pockets. Luke knew the usually confident man fretted over something. Hands in the pockets always told the story.

"We…we was matchin' the list when I spotted the apple of my eye." Hans glanced at Missy, cleared his throat. "I chose that apple for my wife, Luke. No matter she be paired with someone else. Couldn't help myself."

Luke nodded. He might be foreman, but it didn't mean he had a say in the love life of the men, or in the matching of pairs, if all agreed. Ah, the problem. "And was that apple equally interested in you?"

He caught Missy's broad smile, a smile so infectious he found himself grinning. He knew the answer before Hans replied. But had Hans picked this woman? She didn't appear his type.

"*Ja.* Just about attacked me." Hans grinned, his chest inflating like a contented rooster's.

Well, the almost-attacking woman couldn't be Missy. She seemed way too reserved for any attack. That left one problem. "That leaves a man to claim the woman you didn't."

"*Ja.*" Since meeting Hans four months ago, Luke had never seen him act so uneasy. Hans' hands flinched in his pockets. Damn. Trouble always erupted when women were around a camp.

It came to him in a flash. Missy remained. Yet that couldn't be. She didn't fit the description of the woman Hans had chosen on paper two months ago. Hell, he lacked too much sleep to play guessing games. “So, spit it out. What happened?”

Luke watched Missy lean against the wagon. Lean? It looked as if she wanted to burrow into the wood.

Hans pulled his hands out of his pockets, gestured with them in front of him. “I chose my bride, and Albert claimed Lila.” Lila. Ah yes, Hans had raved about her. “Tom chose Sarah instead of Roberta, and Peter wanted Roberta.” Was anything ever simple? After a long and exhausting day of catastrophes, plus this hopscotch of brides, a headache threatened.

“And now the last two don’t match, is that it?”

Hans studied his boots, drove his hands back into his pockets then glanced at Missy. “We don’t know if they’ll match. They’ve…just met.”

It took a split second for Hans’ words to register, to become crystal clear. No. Hans knew why Luke had picked Rosie. He wouldn’t intentionally turn the tables on him. But lust and love would, by damn. It made men commit worse crimes.

He swallowed the lump in his throat. “You chose Rosie.” His words almost gagged him. He dreaded to hear Hans’ confirmation. Hans nodded.

Acid churned in his stomach, and a sour taste spiraled up to his mouth. He’d purposely picked a voluptuous dance hall woman who’d have no problem finding another man after he’d finished here. One who most likely would go along with his scheme and the proposition he offered.

Jesus! He was in a world of shit.

Chapter Two

Leaning hard and heavy against the wagon as if it might add a supportive hand in her time of need, Morgan watched Luke Kincaid digest Hans' words.

I won't cower. I won't. If he doesn't want me, so be it. She'd been kicked enough before. One more boot to her ego wouldn't matter. She'd go on. It was her nature. At least she'd inherited a stalwart backbone. One good Prescott trait, she thought, as her vigor revitalized.

The thought of yet another rejection threatened to crush that instantaneous verve to ashes, swamping her with despair until its heavy emptiness nearly choked her. She didn't want to leave.

Good Lord above, where will I go? Back home with my tail between my legs? Oh, no. She'd go to battle, if necessary. No matter how sour it became, she would not go home. Besides, she lacked enough funds for a return passage, or to go anywhere, for that matter.

Gathering courage, she levered herself off the wagon's solid strength, squared her shoulders, and raised her chin. Oh, if she only knew some tricks of feminine charm to woo a man. She'd never paid attention to that nonsense before. Now she wished she had.

Her entire future lay in this man's hands. Though he wore a full beard, his face appeared pleasant enough. More than pleasant, to be truthful. He looked to be in his early to mid thirties, with just enough deep-tanned crow's feet to add to his handsomeness.

She pulled on her patience and waited while admiring his tawny hair—more brown, really, with streaks of gold—though the almost shoulder length could stand a good trim. She found his eyes quite appealing. Deep green, as verdant as the long needles gracing the tall spruce trees that encircled the town. Expressive eyes. She'd witnessed their twinkling when he joked or smiled. Her pulse had galloped then, and repeated itself now.

He turned. Their gazes met. No twinkling now, she noted, just a very wary but indulgent glint. Disappointment bludgeoned her harder than she'd anticipated. What had she expected?

She'd prepared herself for a loveless, possibly a passionless marriage. But since her brief, trying encounter so far with him, she'd unconsciously longed to see some approval, some…

Some what? Had she really believed he would look at her with stargazing passion? Maybe her mother had been right when she'd said she possessed a mind as useless as a cauliflower. Her chest tightened at knowing that, if he did agree to wed her, there might never be more than calm repose in his gaze. God help her, she'd have to accept that.

"Seems we're a pair, you and I, Missy…"

Startled at his response, she managed a strained whisper. "It's Morgan, Morgan Prescott." With renewed hope, she took three steps and held out a hand.

Noting how his smile failed to reach his eyes, a renewed pang of despair hit its mark. He'd expected the well-endowed Rosie, not a plain woman with fewer curves than a pencil. It's a wonder he hadn't hightailed it out of here already.

He clasped her offered hand. Somewhere along

the line he'd removed his gloves, and his large calloused palm felt warm and reassuring. He frowned. Well, maybe not all that reassuring.

"It's a pleasure to meet you, Miss Prescott. But I thought your name was Mi..."

Morgan laughed at his confusion, gratified to release the pent-up fear of total rejection she'd harbored. He might not be overjoyed about the swap, but he hadn't rebuffed her. For that she gave thanks, holding onto the possibility of an amicable relationship. *That* she could live with. She hoped.

"Hans insisted on calling me Missy."

Hans obviously took that as a cue to step in, and he slapped Luke on the back. Morgan regretted his move, since Luke disengaged his hand from hers.

"Look at her, Luke. Does she look like a Morgan? Morgan's a man's name, or a breed of horse, or the last name of some highfalutin' dame, ain't it? *Ja*, she looks more like a Missy."

Leave it to Hans to ease the touchy situation. He'd been wary while giving the account of the brides. He appeared much more relaxed now. She pasted on a smile, yet cringed inside at how close—how very exact, actually—he'd pegged her name. Oh, yes, her mother's maiden name held much prestige indeed, even if they'd had to use it for her rather than the son they'd awaited.

"I'll have to think that one over," Luke replied as he again scrutinized her. He looked almost... regretful? No, more like he held back some other emotion. She wished she could read his thoughts better. He masked them all too well. Yet she sensed he wanted to say more.

Instead, he shrugged his shoulders. "I think we should have a drink, celebrate with the others."

"*Ja*, yur on," Hans said.

Morgan nodded.

Luke cupped her elbow with his hand as he

accompanied her across the uneven road. He smelled of horses, leather and tobacco. Not at all unpleasant. She reveled in the feel of his warm, sure hand.

"Preacher's still inside," Hans said, keeping close by her other side. "Be here two more days. Rosie and I tied the knot, first thing."

Although Luke's hand tightened on her elbow, his stride never faltered. "I think my fiancée and I need a little more time to get to know each other before we do that. She may decide I'm not what she wants."

Morgan toyed with the idea of simply blurting out her satisfaction, thought better of it, and for once kept her trap shut. Either he truly questioned her opinion of him or he wasn't too sure about *her*. More likely the latter. She couldn't fault him for wanting to chat a while. The others had had that opportunity all afternoon. And she knew she fell far short of voluptuous Rosie. As Hans pushed the door open, she caught Luke's brief stormy glare at him, and Hans' hooded scowl. It appeared she still trod on very uneven ground.

After numerous greetings were exchanged, Luke ushered her to the far end of the long bar. "What would you like, Mis…Morgan?"

She smiled at the bartender. "Wine, please."

The barkeeper—jowls drooping like a bulldog, the entire crown of his head as shiny as a polished apple—howled, slapped his knee, and looked at her as if she'd asked for a pot of gold, plus the rainbow, to boot. Others at surrounding tables hooted along with him. She felt her cheeks flame. What had she said that was so funny? It took the bald moron several minutes to settle down to where he could utter any words.

"Whiskey, beer, and tequila—that's Mexican for 'burnin' rotgut'—are your choices. We ain't got no fancy stuff in these parts, little lady."

So much for making a good impression. She felt like a fool.

Luke whispered in her ear. “Beer’s rather bitter. Try whiskey and water. That should be more mild.”

Morgan basked in his understanding of her naive ignorance. She put her faith in his suggestion and ordered. She sniffed the gold liquid, amazingly found it somewhat appealing, and took a good-sized swallow to quell her nervousness and quench her parched throat...

She would have loved to wring his neck.

If she could breathe.

She gasped, coughed, gagged, and frantically fought for cool air. White-hot flames seared her throat, burned her stomach to a crisp. She expected to breathe smoke any second.

The room erupted in roaring mirth, the insolent barkeep’s laughter booming the loudest. Luke’s laugh echoed right along with the others. Had he been sincere, or had he played a mean joke? Either way, she’d definitely give anything to get her hands around that big, thick neck.

****

Morgan gripped the wooden seat on each side of her as the wagon jounced and listed over deep furrows in the rock-strewn road. The sky had turned black, with only dots of tiny stars helping the radiant moonbeams to light their way. She still contemplated choking Luke for what had happened in the saloon.

They rode in awkward silence, other than the occasional call of a lone bird perched high in the wide-fanning cedars and the intermittent hoot of an owl in the far-off distance. She wished she dared say something, but she sensed Luke’s thoughts dug deep, if his frown offered any indication. They could talk at the cabin.

The chill had increased. With one hand holding

onto the seat for dear life, she clutched her shawl around her more tightly with the other. The road suddenly narrowed, turning inky as they traveled under the umbrella of the lofty, close-growing pines. Had it not been for the lantern hooked to Luke's side of the wagon, it would now be pitch black and her bearings completely lost.

Since Luke obviously wasn't inclined to break the strained silence, Morgan inhaled the sweet fragrance of evergreens and allowed the strong aroma to stir her senses pleasantly until, finally, she had to blink twice in order to focus on what looked to be several acres of cleared land just ahead and to her right. The moon, a bright beacon in the sky, bathed the log cabin in shimmering silver.

"That's it up ahead." Luke spoke for the first time.

As they bumped along, details of the small but inviting dwelling materialized. Fat logs with mud jammed between them gave it a sturdiness. She couldn't see any smoke from the chimney on the far end of the roof, yet the perfume of a present or recent fire lingered in the air.

"It's very nice. Did you build it?" She relished the thought of sitting by a warm fire, enjoying its glow, its aroma. How peaceful it felt here.

He pulled the two horses to a halt just in front of the structure while she scanned the small barn and corral set off to one side, less than a hundred feet away.

He glanced her way, his face expressionless, before looping the reins around the metal hook on the kickboard. He hopped over the side of the wagon. "No, it belonged to the previous foreman. Hans and I built the barn and corral for the teams."

He grabbed the lantern, skirted the back of the wagon, and appeared at her side. Setting the lantern on the ground, he turned and looked up at her, reaching up with two hands. “Let’s get you inside where it’s warmer.”

She leaned over, expecting him to take her offered hand. Instead, he grabbed her just above her waist and effortlessly hoisted her down. His gloved hands felt powerful, sure, and she blushed at the close contact—chest-to-chest, thigh-to-thigh—before she felt the solid soil beneath her feet. There seemed no cause for embarrassment, she realized, as he abruptly turned to the back of the wagon and hefted her trunk as if it weighed no more than a feather.

Feeling awkward and useless, a bit flustered after their contact, she retrieved the lantern and hurried to open the front door. She marveled at how easily he strode through the entrance and deftly deposited her luggage in the corner.

It took him only minutes to reload the woodstove and get the dwindling coals to catch fire. “I’ll unhook the team and be back shortly. Make yourself comfortable.” He struck a match, lit an oil lamp on the kitchen table, and took the lantern from her hands. When he leveled his gaze upon her, as if sizing her up, she felt more out of place than ever.

“I’d appreciate you putting some coffee on. We have some talking to do when I’m done.” With that he left, closing the door behind him.

She felt desolate. He hadn’t smiled since they’d left the saloon. Heck, he’d not said more than a few words to her since meeting her, if truth were told. She’d caught him studying her at intervals, while telling the others of the mishap at the logging site. She’d felt uneasy at his glances, then. His limited comments since had simply added more anxiety. She did, however, appreciate his apology for not realizing he should’ve warned her about the throat-scalding whiskey.

Was he conjuring up a way to send her packing? No, her imagination simply ran riot, trying to get the best of her. Maybe he just required more time to accustom himself to the switch. He didn't seem to really dislike her. Didn't appear actually annoyed. "Perplexed" better described his mood. Yes, that could be it. And most likely because of the change in partners. But why so perplexed? It would be easier to deal with annoyance than silent brooding.

She leaned against the door, scanning the one-room cabin as her eyes acclimated to the lamp's honeyed glow. To her left the woodstove offered welcome warmth. She wished he'd left the doors open so she could view the fire's golden flames. It must serve as cookstove, too, for a kettle rested on its top. Cut wood lay stacked in the corner. A bed filled the far left corner, while a rusty lantern sat unlit on a small table at its side; shirts and a coat hung from wooden pegs along the wall. A large trunk banked the foot of the bed.

Though cramped for space, one stuffed chair, angled at ninety degrees to the stove, faced a threadbare divan. Both looked very inviting after her ride on hard cold wood. She smiled at the nail barrel that crudely served as a side table. The floor, no more than hard-packed earth, lay under a large rag rug that had surely seen better days.

To her right, two long shelves above a counter housed cups, plates, pans and utensils. On the worn-smooth wooden counter sat a metal wash tin, tin pitcher, and tall glass jars of what looked like flour and sugar. Three burlap sacks and four wooden barrels stood under the counter. A small scarred table and two chairs graced the middle of the so-called kitchen. The only window was to the right of the door. Shutters hung on each side of it.

What a far cry from New York.

Luke had assured her, since there wasn't any other place for her to spend the night—not with half the camp just becoming newlyweds and the other half unmarried men—that it wouldn't be thought improper for her to stay at his cabin, although they hadn't had the preacher tie the knot as yet. Now she wondered if this had been such a good idea.

How did one undress and dress with only one room and no partitions? Well, she'd deal with that dilemma when the time came. Right now she needed to find the coffee.

"How in heaven's name do you make coffee?" she mumbled as she pawed through containers. Why hadn't she learned a few basic skills before coming? No time, she reminded herself. Well, she'd better learn how to improvise, and fast.

It took only a few minutes to find coffee beans in one of the sacks. And, praise the saints above, there was water in the kettle. Did one simply dump the beans into the water? She stood deep in thought as the door opened. Good grief, she wouldn't have even known how to start the fire had it not had coals. She wouldn't have known to stir the coals, either.

Luke kicked the door shut with his heel, strode to the corner, and dumped an armful of firewood onto the pile. When he turned, he frowned at the bowl of beans she held. Ever so slightly, his lips curled upward. *Oh, my!* Her heart tripped.

"Guess I should've realized you wouldn't know where things were." He came to her side and took the dish from her. Again the scent of horse, tobacco, and the man himself invaded her senses. Pleasant and intriguing.

"There's coffee already ground. Why don't you go get warm by the fire. I'll have this done in a minute."

Oh, no. No way would she miss her first lesson in cooking. Even if it consisted of mere coffee. Besides, she found she liked being close to him. How strange. She'd never experienced such a feeling before. Not with any of her New York suitors.

"I'm quite comfortable. I'll just watch, if you

don't mind. I need to know where things are." She leaned against the counter, praying she appeared none too eager. Could he hear her strange inner thoughts, her rapid pulse?

He shrugged his shoulders. "Suit yourself."

He withdrew a metal canister and a tin coffee pot from the bottom shelf on the wall, then dipped the pot into a large crock of water, just to the right. She'd not noticed that crock before. Fascinated, she watched him count out six scoops of ground coffee into the pot. *How simple.* As he ambled over to the woodstove, she breathed a sigh of relief. *I can do this. Easy as pie. Is pie easy?*

Again feeling useless, and needing to show him her eagerness to do her share, she reached up, retrieved two tarnished mugs from the shelf, and set them on the counter.

"Mor…Miss Prescott, come sit down. While the coffee cooks, we need to talk."

Just the way he looked at her, all stern and serious, his voice all business and no pleasure, sent shivers up her neck.

Chapter Three

She took the chair; he chose the divan. When his eyes locked with hers, she wished he'd smile again. Call her Morgan. Yet she knew this "talk" would be far from pleasant.

He brushed his beard with a hand as he held her gaze. "I don't know where to start, to be honest."

She felt her face flame. So he'd now tell her he didn't want her. Oh, how right her father had been. One look, just one look at her, and this man had decided she wasn't up to snuff. Would this be the story of her life? How could it be so unfair? Did all men judge women by their looks, or how fat their purse? She hadn't realized how much she obviously lacked in womanly charm. Granted she fell short of being a rare beauty, but she hadn't thought herself that ill on the eyes, either. Obviously, he preferred well-endowed bosoms, the flamboyant Rosie type.

Her rancor escalated. If that's what appealed to this man, then she preferred he not want her. People possessed greater qualities than beauty or wealth. Yet despite her self-preservationist attitude she found her heart ached, her future appeared bleak.

Feigning acceptance she hardly felt, she masked her dismay and held his gaze.

"You don't have to say any more, Mr. Kincaid. It's quite obvious how you feel about me." She took a calming breath, damning her hands for shaking on her lap, her lip for quivering. "I'll leave first thing in the morning, if that's soon enough for you." She damned the tears as they clouded her vision, as well.

“Aw, shit.” His eyes rounded. “Ah, sorry.” He swiped his beard with what now seemed to be an agitated hand. “This isn’t personal. It has nothing to do with you.”

His words were ridiculously silly, to say the least. No, blatantly humiliating is what they were. And she meant to tell him exactly that. With a scornful smile, her voice rose. “I believe it has everything to do with me, sir. I…”

“No, it doesn’t.” She flinched at his harsh bellow, grew apprehensive at watching his scowl stretch to ten times what it had been on the way here. Dear God, was he a violent man?

She remained silent but alert in case she had to bolt. He leaned forward, rested his forearms on his long thighs. Only when he pulled his glare from her, lowering his gaze to his boots, did she dare draw in a long-needed breath, then exhaled slowly.

He sighed so loudly she could have sworn he’d grumbled. When he raised his head, his glower chilled her bones. “I intended to make up an excuse, but I see that’s not going to be good enough.”

Excuse? All hope of staying vanished, leaving her heart and ego crushed and empty. “You don’t have to make any excuse. But I must tell you, I’m without adequate funds to go anywhere.”

He stared at her, wide-eyed. That either annoyed the starch out of him or he undoubtedly lacked money to send her on her way. Now what would she do? Lord, but she wished she could read his thoughts. Most of the time, so far, he had hidden them enough to stymie her.

“I’m not free to marry anyone. I’m engaged.”

Nothing he could have said would have astounded her more. When the shock ebbed, her rage flared at his conniving lie. She was more angered than when he’d made her sit for hours.

“Really?” she said with all the calm demeanor

she could muster despite her roiling fury. "And if Rosie had been available, would you have told her the same thing, Mr. Kincaid?"

His brows arched, he sat up straighter.

"No, I didn't think so." Her anger escalated, but not half as much as the hurt slicing through her did. How dare this man treat her with such disrespect, such callousness, as to fabricate such a story! Did he think her no more than a simpleton?

He rose from the divan, hands clenched at his sides. His face skewered into a scowl to equal hers. "Now, listen here. I'm telling the truth. If Rosie had come home with me, I had planned on telling her...on explaining..."

He turned away, raised his arms so that his large palms pushed against the overhead beam. She could never reach it even if she jumped. When he banged his large fist against that beam, she flinched. She had never considered her groom might be a violent man. *Oh, dear God.*

"Hell." He wheeled around. His eyes bored into her. "I'll tell you the truth. But only if you promise not to tell a soul. Men's lives are at stake here."

If he wanted her undivided attention, he had it now. *What in the world?* She sighed in relief that he now appeared to have a handle on his temper. "The truth would be nice."

He sat back down on the divan, rubbed his fingers briskly across his bearded chin. "It isn't nice. And the only reason I'm confiding in you is so you don't think the worst of me, or of yourself."

Their gazes met, hers questioning, his seeking. And somehow she knew this big man would tell her the God's honest truth. She also sensed he wasn't a violent man but a man frustrated because he'd been backed into a corner. And he didn't like it. Not one bit.

"I'll not tell a soul. I swear."

Crossing his arms over his chest, his gaze never wavered, just clung to hers as if weighing her words.

"Years past, I did a variety of undercover jobs for the government, flushing out the bad guys, if you will. After that I settled in San Francisco, opened my own private investigation firm."

He relaxed against the back of the divan, brought his right leg over the other so that the calf rested on his knee. "Right now, all the lumber being cut here goes to the railroad. Ever since work started on the tracks in this part of the country, there's been nothing but fluke accidents, damaged shipments, lost supplies, and, to date, twenty deaths."

Morgan's breath caught, her mind whirling at such numbers. "Dear Lord."

Grim-faced, he nodded. "My sentiments exactly. When stockholders began looking into the too-frequent accidents, the mounting deaths, they found they didn't appear to be quite so accidental. Since I've an avid interest in the Union Pacific Railroad, I decided I'd be the perfect one to come here to see what was really happening. The government agreed."

"You mean someone's trying to sabotage the railroad?"

"You got it. We knew there were many who opposed the rail coming through. We just didn't realize how determined they were."

When her brows rose, he went on to explain. "Some resent depleting the forest, whether it's because of all the wood we're cutting for tracks or just the land that's cleared for the rail system. Some farmers feel they've rights to the land. Even the shipping line owners on the coast know they'll lose trade once the railway is completed." His lips thinned as he cleared his throat.

"Others are either just plain prejudiced against the Swedes, the Irish, and the Chinese and don't want them here, or they can't stand that foreigners work for a buck-fifty while they, themselves, could earn more. Hell, both lumbermen and rail workers had to take up guns against the Indians when they tore up miles of track to keep their land free from the iron steamers coming through."

"That's horrible."

His lips formed a tight smile. "Yes, it is, but it's a fact. And it's getting worse instead of better. Now foremen at the track sites and at the lumber camps have to keep a close eye out for all sorts of bizarre catastrophes. All a little too contrived to be believed accidental. That's why I'm here. To uncover who's behind the latest series of murders."

Morgan frowned. His story had merit, but..."This all sounds logical, but what does all this have to do with me?"

He did smile at that. A big, engaging smile. And Lordy, if her heart didn't do a somersault. How very handsome. She chided herself for being as shallow as the feeble-minded men she'd claimed to detest for only valuing a pretty face.

"Guess that's where I figured wrong. You see, several other foremen were hired to be on the lookout for troublemakers, but obviously they didn't play their parts well enough. They must've stood out like an eyesore. They were found out and taken out, one way or the other." Chills scurried up her spine.

He shrugged. "I figured if I appeared to be one of the men seeking a wife along with the rest, it would give me one more ace at being just a regular. I thought if I chose someone like Rosie, I could tell her the truth. When the investigation finished, she could go her own way. She'd be no worse off. Actually, I'd planned to pay her well for her part."

His chortle shook his shoulders. "I never counted on someone like you popping up in her place."

What a mess she'd gotten herself into. What a disaster for him. No wonder he'd been so frustrated by the switch. For a moment Morgan wondered if he would lend the needed money for her departure. Then a rejuvenated hope flashed in her head like a bright light, and she smiled.

She'd set out to become a wife. Maybe fate had intervened and it wasn't meant for her to tie the knot until the right person came along. That'd be better, wouldn't it? What harm would it do to add a bit of adventure and intrigue, for a short time only, before resuming her quest?

"Are you really engaged?"

"Yes."

"Does anyone here know who you really are?"

He hesitated. "Only Hans."

Ah, the look that had passed between them. Now it made sense, and to her relief it hadn't been because Luke had been miffed over losing Rosie as the love of his life but because Hans had put him in an awkward and precarious position. She smiled.

"Is there any reason I can't take Rosie's role?"

The minute she asked, she realized how outlandish her offer sounded. Rosie had been a saloon girl, had most likely offered favors to any man. Certainly this man had counted on more than just a mock wife in the deal. Her face grew exceedingly warm. On fire, in fact.

"I mean, I…I would be willing to, at least…"

He held up his palms as his roar of laughter bounced off the walls. He undoubtedly understood why her cheeks were throbbing. "Hold on a minute. I know exactly what you meant. No need for you to be so embarrassed."

Morgan swallowed the lump in her throat. Maybe it was easy for him to think she shouldn't be embarrassed. She felt differently. Way differently.

"As to you filling the part, I'd never ask someone

like you to do such a thing."

Well, of all the nerve! Her pride rammed into her toenails. "Someone like me?"

"Look, I didn't mean to belittle you." His voice lowered, his face turned serious. "I can see I didn't phrase that very well. I apologize. I meant I would never ask just any woman to share this cabin for a month or two. My fiancée may be bedridden, but I'd no intention of cheating on her, even with Rosie. I only wanted a cover. It wouldn't have hurt Rosie's reputation any if she spent time here. But someone like you—I mean, you're clearly not a...a dancehall girl—would have a very soiled reputation afterward. Hell, you wouldn't have any reputation left."

His explanation should have made her back down. Any sensible, proper woman would have. But some mischievous part of her failed to listen. The challenge of being part of this undercover scheme drew her like a colossal magnet.

"You really hadn't...hadn't planned on Rosie being more than a so-called cover?"

His eyes widened. He looked absolutely astounded. "Here, now. I don't know what you're thinking. Hell, I do know what you're thinking, but you can stop right there."

Morgan laughed at this big man's distress. She couldn't help it. He probably faced bears in the woods with more courage than what he showed now. And he definitely didn't hide his expressions well at this point. More than likely, he didn't usually swear as often as he was now, either.

"I believe you know exactly what I'm thinking, Mr. Kincaid. And you're absolutely correct."

"You'd be out of your mind to do this. I won't..."

"What's changed?" she interrupted, determined to convince him. "You still need that cover. I'm here and just about penniless. I'm willing to take the money you would've offered Rosie. When the time comes, I'll be on my way. As for my reputation, when I leave and settle elsewhere, no one needs to know I spent time here. How can you find fault with that?"

Oops, back came his scowl. He stared at her, long and hard, yet he seemed to be ruminating on her words. *Keep ruminating all you want,* she mused, almost giggling.

He could scowl all he wanted, too. Logically, she was his answer. He needed her. That, in itself, meant volumes to her. He couldn't marry her, but marriage to someone else, somewhere else, sometime later, could wait. This situation held far more importance to her right now.

"Deal, Mr. Kincaid?" She held out her hand.

Chapter Four

Luke gaped at her as she offered a handshake. A handshake to bind the most preposterous deal he'd ever heard. He could live in close quarters with someone like Rosie. It'd be ludicrous to share space with an obviously respectable woman. Namely, Morgan Prescott.

How did a man who'd been celibate for two years, since the night of his engagement, remain unaffected by a woman who…who…*Hell.*

Who had the darkest, most compelling brown eyes he'd ever seen. The most charming musical laughter he'd ever heard. *Damn.*

He discarded the crazy fascination by critically eyeing her thin figure. Way too slender for his liking. Her drab, conservative clothing alone nearly twisted his head the other direction.

Yet she was a woman. A woman who sat pleased as punch, offering to stay with him in this small cabin. If he guessed correctly, a well-bred woman. And she'd blushed at her blunder. That alone spelled innocence, or pretty close.

So why in God's name had she come to this God-forsaken wilderness seeking a husband? Why would she offer such a set-up? His mind spun with a gamut of possibilities, but he detested standing on unstable ground or floundering in the dark. He had neither time nor inclination to pursue her reasons. He had enough problems to deal with. He had no choice but to turn her down.

"Why did you come here, Miss Prescott?" Why

the hell did he seek answers? He should've just said "no deal."

But he knew why he'd asked. And it damn well didn't sit well. Those doe-like eyes, beseeching, almost sad even when she smiled. Or maybe her magnanimous offer to help him had touched him in ways he knew better than to allow.

She retracted her hand as if he'd bitten it. Her eyes turned so crestfallen he nearly voiced regret for asking. His remorse didn't last long.

She sat up straight, looking for all the world like a haughty shrew. Luke postponed checking the coffee so he could watch those expressive eyes darken with irritation. Fascinating.

"I have my reasons, Mr. Kincaid. Leave it at that."

Ah, hah! Now that the tables had turned the other direction, she didn't like it one bit. Well, two could confess their secrets as well as one.

"Not good enough, Miss Prescott. For all I know, you could be a plant. Sent here to make me fall on my as…nose, to relay information to the other side anytime you get the opportunity."

Her back stiffened to match the poker a few feet away. Her eyes turned jet black. *No soft mahogany there anymore*, he thought. Only hard coal, ready to ignite. And if he pegged her right, he'd soon witness her soft-spoken voice crescendo into a thunderous tirade. He waited for steam to roll out of her ears, for flames to shoot from her mouth.

"How dare you? How can you even think such a thing?"

He'd not had to wait but a few seconds. Luke fought hard to hold back his laughter. She ignited marvelously, gorgeously so, when riled. All spit and hellfire. Her pink cheeks literally glowed. Fiery shards shot from her deep brown eyes, lighting them up like polished chestnuts. So, she hid the tiger behind the pussycat, did she?

“Miss Prescott, may I remind you, I don’t know you at all. And now you refuse to tell me where you came from, or why. Would you, in my place, think otherwise?”

He’d stymied her for sure on that one. She appeared too stunned to speak. She scrutinized him intensely, chewing her bottom lip. He could almost hear her mind working.

She glanced down at her lap. “Oh, how right Father was,” she mumbled in no more than a whisper, deflating before his eyes. Had he not leaned closer, he wouldn’t have heard her words.

“Right about what?”

Her head jerked up. She looked shocked he’d caught her words.

“Nothing,” she spat, obviously annoyed and wanting to drop the subject. She clutched her slender hands together.

Luke found himself annoyed at being put off but, truthfully, more than a little intrigued.

“Again, not good enough, Miss Prescott. I spoke honestly, possibly more honestly than I should have, since I don’t know you from a hill of beans. I expect the same from you.”

Coffee spurted and streamed from the pot’s spout, sizzling and hissing as it sloshed onto the cast iron stove. Luke stood, grabbed a mitt from the wall, and lifted the overflowing vessel.

Damn coffee, he thought in disgust. He set it down on the metal trivet and eyed it accusingly. *You couldn’t have waited just a few more minutes, could you?*

She rose and went to the counter to retrieve the cups. How graceful her movements, how proudly she held herself. As she walked back she cast him a shy glance. “Is it still good?”

“I hope so.” Her question gave him pause.

She held up one cup for him to fill, and he poured, filtering out the grounds by way of a small strainer that had hung on the wall. She watched, then lifted her eyes to meet his. "I'll tell you. Mine's not a pretty story either, but you have every right to know."

She had spunk, this one. Undoubtedly she hadn't wanted to tell, but she now appeared willing to reciprocate. He found himself admiring her willingness to compromise. He dismissed her question regarding the coffee for the moment, but he wouldn't forget it.

They sat with their coffees after she'd added two spoons of sugar to hers. He regretted not having the milk she'd asked for. He'd make sure they had some for her use. Now why had he thought that? She wasn't staying.

"I don't know where to start, either," she said, settling back against the chair.

"Start with the reason that made you come here. And be honest."

Honesty seemed to be foremost to this big man, Morgan thought. She too valued it above all else. If nothing else, they shared that similarity. If they had that much at least between them, then maybe they could pull this caper off.

But she'd omit some information. Wanting, needing to be judged for her own self-worth, she found herself reluctant to let others know she'd been raised with a silver spoon in her mouth.

"I lived in New York," she said, purposely leaving it vague as to whether the state or the city, "and walked in on my fiancé and sister when they were...shall we say, at a very intimate moment."

Saying it point blank had been far easier than she'd anticipated. The rest, hopefully, would be even less painful. He took a swig of coffee, apparently not shocked by her words.

“I’m sorry.” His green eyes narrowed speculatively. Was he indeed sorry?

“Thank you, but don’t be. Now that I’ve had time to think about it, have said it out loud, I realize it’s the best thing that ever happened to me.” And she found she truly meant it. The realization lent hope to her future.

A small smirk curled his lips.

“Malcolm, my fiancé, was a stiff shirt, if you know what I mean.” He nodded, and she wished he had smiled again. She liked it when his eyes gleamed, his face softened.

“Actually, he was quite boring and dead-set in his ways. We would’ve never suited. He constantly reprimanded me. As if I were a child, or had mush for brains. If I didn’t behave exactly as he thought I should, he’d scold worse than my parents. And that’s saying a lot.”

He chuckled, and she grinned back. “It’s the truth.”

“I can’t believe your parents thought you were anything less than prim and proper, Miss Prescott. It’s hard to picture you doing anything they’d have to scold you about.”

She laughed at his misconception, while inside the hurtful memories of all those times she’d received verbal lashings—so many she’d lost count—tore at her heart.

“You’re very kind to say that, but believe me, they thought me the black sheep of the family in every way. I couldn’t seem to do anything to their liking. Not a day went by that they didn’t lose their patience with me. They even…”

She bit back her words, astonished at her prater. Of course, both her parents had often reprimanded her for chattering. But then she’d been stating her views, whether on matters financial, political or otherwise serious. Never had she gone on about her own woes or dilemmas. The ache in her chest grew, as it did every time she thought how her parents regarded her as a pea goose because of her bold vocalization. What in the world would this man think of her rattling on like a meathead?

Embarrassed, she swallowed and clasped both hands around her mug. She glanced his way. He remained silent, his darkened eyes encouraging her to continue while void of any emotions. She found his expression a boost to finish what she'd started.

"They blamed me for Malcolm…for him seeking out my sister."

"They what?" He looked incredulous—sounded it, too.

"They blamed me."

"What had you done?" he asked, his forehead creasing. So he could show more emotion than just an occasional smile. That's all she needed to hoist a response.

"It's more what I hadn't done. At least, according to them. My mother thought I spent more time with my nose in books, or paying attention to the business and political world that shouldn't concern me, or helping those in need, than what I offered to Malcolm. She said I'd disgraced them." She cringed at how her mother hadn't been able to accept her views.

"And your father?"

The tightening in her chest became a painful ache. He'd hurt her worse. She'd tried to be the apple of his eye, eager to impress him with her knowledge of numbers, acting the poised lady when he'd expected it. She'd failed miserably. His haunting words slammed back to pierce her wounded heart. She clenched her teeth to fight the pain, the anguish that twisted her stomach. Tears didn't erupt. She'd cried rivers since leaving New York. There weren't any left.

"He said I..." She glanced away from Luke's intense gaze, bent her knuckles tighter. "Let's leave that alone, shall we? Just believe he felt the same way."

She stole a peek upward, hoping to see him nod his agreement to leave well enough alone. His frown had increased.

"What I believe, Miss Prescott, is that you're trying to make a deal. If you have any hope of me remotely considering it, you'd better spill it all out. I'm not convinced yet."

What a jackass! Who does he think he is? She wasn't here to confess all her sins and lamentable past. Yet she needed to sway him. And damn, if he wasn't sitting in the king's throne at the moment. Well, so much for retaining any pride in this crazy scheme.

She took a needed deep breath. "He said he doubted if I could ever be woman enough to hold any man."

Humiliated beyond words, she nevertheless glared at him. She had to. Otherwise she'd totally come apart. How true her father's words rang. Remembering Luke's engagement necessitated his rejection helped to buffer her despair. A little. What if he hadn't been already affianced?

He remained silent, his expression again unreadable. At least he wasn't frowning or casting pitiful eyes her direction. The silence grew tortuous. He most likely thought they were right. She might as well concede she had lost any leverage she'd hoped to gain.

"So you decided to venture off on your own, leave all that in the past, and start anew?"

"Yes." Thank goodness she hadn't unpacked her bags.

Luke watched her squirm. When she'd repeated her father's words, his heart had literally lurched.

Her parents sounded like the most uncaring, uncompassionate people he'd ever heard of. As for her fiancé, he'd like to punch the bastard square in the nose. Then kick him in the ass.

She'd been sorely mistreated and misunderstood by her parents. Thank God they hadn't broken her lively spirit before this. It would've been a sin. She'd been hurt, no doubt devastated, by her sister and the two-timing fiancé.

He knew better than to even consider her staying. But for some illogical, insane reason he felt a powerful need to help. To protect her. To offer her some kind of refurbishing of her self-confidence, pride, and soul. He was crazy.

"You realize how close these quarters are? How little privacy you'll have most of the time? I want you to understand what you're getting yourself into."

She literally beamed. Her eyes sparkled, eager and childlike, radiant as stars within the gray duskiness of the cabin. Her smile radiated pure sunshine, offsetting the nerve-racking series of morose events at the log site. His breath caught at her natural beauty.

Before a few minutes ago, he'd thought her a plain Jane by all accounts, other than her sweet voice, pleasing laughter, and her bewitching eyes. How very wrong he'd been.

What have I done? In so many words he'd agreed to craziness. Now, he'd not only have to pursue vandals, watching his back every blasted minute, but he'd have to tread cautiously in his cabin, steel himself against her feminine charm. And he wasn't made of steel.

Regretfully, he'd have to rescind his hasty decision. He had no choice. She'd have to accept it. He cleared his throat…

"I see how small this cabin is, and I know exactly what I'm getting myself into, Mr. Kincaid," she said, her smile pleased and confident as she set her mug on the nail cask. "But I also know you're a very honorable man. You said if Rosie were here, you wouldn't be unfaithful to your fiancée. That alone speaks a thousand words as to your character. I'm far from being a tempting Rosie, so I'm quite confident we can deal with any touchy situation."

She giggled. Actually giggled as she gazed at him with those big, glistening dark eyes. Only then did he realize his mouth hung open at her words. *Sweet Jesus.* Here she thought him a paragon of virtue, and already he had second thoughts. Scary thoughts.

"And I want you to know how wonderful it feels to confide honestly and openly to someone." Again, she held out her hand.

His mouth felt stuffed with cotton. How could he possibly turn this little lady down now that she felt so good about herself? She'd be devastated. Her spirit would be stripped away and crushed. And that would happen if he added to the cruel blows she'd already suffered.

Resigned to managing the best he could with his irrational blunder, he vowed to remain immune to her innocent allure. Maybe in a few days she'd see how outrageous, how ill-advised, this setup was and leave.

Luke extended his hand. When they clasped palms, heat radiated all the way up his arm.

Her smile widened, her eyes glimmered as she shook his hand enthusiastically.

Damn! She'd decide to leave tomorrow, if he was lucky. This insane situation would be a helluva lot more difficult than flushing out the bad guys, if she were to stay.

Yep, he was in a world of deep shit. Deeper than what he'd originally thought.

Chapter Five

Ribbons of sunlight, bright and invigorating, streamed through the window, bathing the entire room in rich gold. Their warmth penetrated Morgan's cheeks as she lay cozy in bed, surveying the cabin. They encouraged a zest to hop out of bed and start her first real day in her new surroundings. The aroma of fresh coffee, warm and soothing, swirled through the cabin.

She shot a glance toward the divan where Luke had spent the night. The blanket lay neatly folded on top of his pillow at the far end of the make-do bed.

Anxious to be up and dressed before he returned, she sprang from the bed. Or had he already gone to the logging site? No sooner had her bare feet hit the hard dirt than she heard a heavy thud outside. Disregarding the chilliness of the smooth earth, she grabbed the ragged quilt to cover her cotton nightgown and strained to listen.

Thud! Crack! Thud! Crack!

Rooted to the spot, she tried to figure out what the strange noise could be. Without further thought to her state of dress, she dropped the quilt and ran to the window to peer out.

There was Luke, bending over to retrieve a hunk of wood he'd just split with an ax. His discarded coat lay on a stump not five feet away, so he only wore a plaid flannel shirt tucked into his pants. The buckskins clung to his long, muscular thighs, pulling taut over his backside as he reached.

She gulped down the onslaught of saliva, felt her

cheeks heat. She'd never paid attention to that part of the male anatomy before. But she did now. And found his very appealing. So appealing her blood rushed like a flood-swollen stream, her pulse bounding like a runaway horse.

He leaned more to the right, stretching farther to grab another hunk of wood. The well-tanned animal hide strained across his buttocks.

"Oh, my." Her heart drummed. Thank goodness he straightened to pitch the two pieces onto a stack of wood a few feet away. But would her heart ever return to an even beat?

She closed her eyes, took a deep breath, and reminded herself he was engaged. An engaged man she'd be sharing this teeny cabin with for heaven only knew how long. She had no right to ogle another woman's man. She'd best focus on the coffee.

Morgan turned from the window, resolving to view him only as a friend—hopefully they'd become good friends—who needed her help. Only her help. He'd been good enough to go along with her plan, so she'd do her best to fulfill that role, then get on with her life. What that would entail remained to be seen. But for now, she'd concentrate on the duty at hand.

As she grabbed a cup and went to the coffee, she laughed at how silly her thoughts had been moments ago. She'd thought she was smitten with Malcolm, but she'd never felt the stirring experienced when gazing upon Luke Kincaid's behind. Heaven above, she'd never felt her blood pumping or her heart pounding even when Malcolm kissed her.

She wrinkled her nose as she remembered Malcolm's lips on hers. Firm and dry, dutiful and unmoving. The few light pecks he'd stolen had left her wanting. Empty. She hadn't questioned their lack of luster before. But by golly she did now. Maybe she did need a man more than she thought. In the future. For now, she'd have to remember every minute of the day that Luke was already spoken for. Very much unavailable.

Maybe she could learn why men like Luke acted the way they did. She'd have plenty of time to study his habits, see what pleased him, annoyed him. She hardly knew him, yet found herself already respecting his wisdom, determination, and purpose. Definitely his physique.

To her amazement, she realized she'd simply and docilely set her cap for men her family had approved. The so-called proper ones. She'd never analyzed what type she desired to share her entire life with. Oh, no, she'd only considered those who were socially correct, who could support her the way her family thought she should be supported.

Sipping her coffee, she took a quick look out the window. As Luke grabbed his coat, she found contentment settle within her. Yes, she'd study him, and the other men too, for that matter. And when her time here ended, with any luck she'd know what she wanted out of life and the type of man who would fill her dreams. Yet as Luke ambled toward the cabin, she questioned why her blood raced, why her heart despaired so at knowing he couldn't be the one to fill those dreams.

"So, the sleepyhead's up." Luke's wide smile matched the sunny rays. She decided then and there she wanted a man who could smile easily. A smile that would thrill her as his did.

"Good morning." Morgan set her cup down and pulled her quilt more tightly around her. "Would you like a cup of coffee?"

She watched the play of muscled biceps, the flexing of cords under the back of his shirt, as he hung his coat on the peg by the door. She swallowed, wondering how long she could share this confining cabin and not become totally undone.

"I'll get it." He headed for the kitchen counter.

"No need for you to wait on me. I've done for myself for a long time. No sense in changing now."

"Oh, it's no bother." She took a step toward him, shifting her hold on the dragging quilt. "After all, you supply the firewood. The least I can do is get you a cup of coffee."

She took another step, then stopped to catch the slipping coverlet. He skidded to a halt, peering at her as if he'd just noticed her attire, or lack of it. He gaped as she shifted from one foot to the other while gathering up the cumbersome material. *My, how he can frown.*

"I...ah...obviously came in too soon." He pivoted on the balls of his feet, quite agilely for a man his size, and strode to the door. He grabbed his coat and flung the door open.

"Let me know when you're dressed," he said without turning. No sooner had the door slammed shut than Morgan burst out laughing. For the second time since meeting this bear of a man, she'd witnessed his awkward unsettling. This soon-to-be mock marriage could easily become a comedy.

They didn't know each other well enough to be friends as yet, but she appreciated his respect and courtesy. He did get rattled easily, though. How in heaven's name did he expect to capture the bad guys when he couldn't mask his uneasiness? He'd have to work on that one. Otherwise he'd be found out in an instant. She'd have to either bring that flaw to his attention or come up with a way for him to hide his expressions. At least at certain times.

As quickly as she could she sponge-bathed before donning a blue skirt and white high-collared, long-sleeved blouse. She brushed her hair and pulled it back with a dark blue ribbon, letting it hang down her back. She longed for a mirror. *This isn't New York,* she thought thankfully. What could she expect in this wilderness? New challenges, untold adventures, that's what. She had a decent roof over her head. The rest would unfold as it would.

And poor Luke. He'd not had his coffee, after laboring out in the chilled morning. Determined to avoid making the man regret his decision, to allow him to come and go without any awkwardness, she scurried to open the door.

He leaned against the woodpile, surveying the dense woods beyond the clearing, his back toward her. Smoke curled upward in thin curls as he exhaled from his pipe. His coat collar, turned up against the crisp morning air, parted his lengthy hair unevenly. The sun gleamed off the disheveled mane so the lighter strands glistened like gold silk threads among nut-brown satin. Would his hair feel as soft as it looked? Her fingers curled in reflex. She shook her head to arrest her disturbing, unwanted reaction. God in heaven, today was only Day One.

With a sigh and a frown at her ridiculousness, she called, "I'll get your coffee."

He turned and nodded, his expression bland. She watched him raise his foot, tap his pipe against his boot, then crush tobacco into the lightly dewed ground with his heel. He scuffed the dirt back and forth several times with the toe of his boot before he stomped the area again.

A forest fire in woods this congested and lofty would be a nightmarish disaster, one she could hardly fathom. His meticulous caution added another plus to the man.

Did the man only possess traits she found appealing? He must have a flaw somewhere, other than his occasional uneasy expression. And that would be a flaw primarily where the culprits were concerned. She'd have to find another. And when she did, she'd have to dwell on it. Otherwise, this situation would be more than arduous. It would be impossible.

Pulling her eyes away from the man who in less than twenty-four hours had turned her thoughts to chaos, she left the door open and forced her feet back through the cabin to retrieve another mug from the cupboard.

Luke entered, hung his coat, then pulled out a piece of thin rawhide from his pocket. He gathered his hair back and tied the thong around it. Since his hair fell just shy of shoulder length, the queue equaled a mere inch or so. His pulled-back hair emphasized the ruggedness of his cheekbones, the square chin. Handsome, indeed. Her pulse tripped and hummed. Oh, she trod on precarious ground. *Remember, you're only his employee.*

With hands a bit shaky, she poured his coffee and walked to his side on all-too-rubbery legs. It wasn't going to be easy, this remaining a simple business partner.

"Thanks." He accepted the tin mug and took a sip while his eyes scanned her attire. His brows rose ever so slightly as his scrutiny lingered on her hair. His smile sent instant heat across her cheeks. Could that be approval she saw, or mere revelation at how her hair hung almost to her waist? Maybe his expressions weren't so easy to read after all.

"I'll try to remember to give you time to dress so we don't have another awkward scene. It'll take some getting used to, but I'm sure we can manage."

"It was my fault. I should've dressed as soon as I got up." *Instead of watching you like a drooling female Peeping Tom.* She hoped she sounded less rattled by his nearness than she felt. Indeed, situations like this needed to be avoided. "There's no way you could have known if I had dressed, or even had awakened." His smile widened. Her cheeks felt like glowing coals.

"I'll knock and call out from now on." He swigged his coffee.

She refused to make him feel uncomfortable in his own home or possibly regret he'd allowed her to stay.

"Oh, no, please. You shouldn't have to knock at your own door. Just simply wake me when you get up. I can dres..." And what? Dress in front of him? Her eyes rounded at the vision.

His laughter, deep and robust, filled the small confine. His appeal grew tenfold, if that were possible. He obviously had formed the same ridiculous picture. *Fool. Stupid solution.*

His smile lingered as he set his coffee down on the kitchen table, pulled out a ladderback chair, and sat. "You're right," he said, to her amazement. "We need some safe ground rules here. I've chores every morning in the barn before breakfast, so I'll make you a deal."

He paused as if waiting for her answer. She nodded for him to continue, pulled out the other chair, and joined him. She self-consciously fingered her mug.

"If you hear me up, keep your back turned or your eyes shut to allow me privacy till I've washed and dressed. I'll put the coffee on, then wake you. It takes me half an hour to tend the animals, so you'll have plenty of time to do whatever you have to do before I come back. If you'll start breakfast, I'll help when I come in. I'd also appreciate it if you'd help me fix a lunch to take with me. I usually leave right after breakfast and return just before supper."

Breakfast? Lunch? Supper? Oh, heavens above.

"Certainly. That sounds fine." She smiled while the stuffing poured right out of her. Could she handle cooking? She felt positive she could do the cleaning, and the gardening. How hard could that be? But the cooking? She'd have to try. They were in this fifty-fifty.

"Good. You probably saw the bucket of lime in

the privy last night. I usually add a scoop every few days, so if you notice it getting rank, just dump some down."

Her cheeks heated till she thought she'd choke on the sip of coffee she'd just taken. Nothing would be sacred between them. How casual he sounded when talking about such personal, private matters. Dear Lord, awkwardness surely would plague her like a tight glove.

No, she'd not act foolish and naive. This was a wilderness cabin. Accommodations crude. And they were in this together. Of course he'd expect her to do anything required to make it run efficiently. She could pour lime from a scoop as well as the next. And be proud of it, by God. No way would she let him know she'd led a pampered life.

This venture fell way short from the glamour she'd envisioned. Yet it still held appeal. Even with the privy and its lime, the cooking dilemma, the awkwardness of sharing close quarters.

"What do you like to eat? Give me some ideas."

He outlined his likes and dislikes without flourish. For breakfast he preferred something simple. Oatmeal, bread with jam, coffee, and a slab of bacon or ham, even beef if they had it.

He thought that simple?

"If we're lucky, we might have enough eggs to have them occasionally for breakfast, but I try to save them for supper. Now that you're here, we'll put aside a few for baking. I tried baking and gave it up quick. I tried to rush it too much."

Eggs for supper? She'd never heard the likes. Eggs were for breakfast. At least in New York. For sure, eggs would be an easy meal. She marveled at finding out you put eggs in baked goods. Could you beat that? Naturally he'd assume she knew.

His lunch, he went on, would consist of cheese, bread, a strip of dried beef, an apple or canned fruit, and a canteen of water. Now that she could handle.

Supper, other than the easy eggs, would be her downfall. Most of the time he wanted meat: pork, chicken if they had it, but mostly beef. He liked steak quick-fired to medium rare, or falling apart if a roast. Beans, he informed her, could satisfy him for a good hearty meal as long as thick slices of bread accompanied it. She prayed beans were as easy as they sounded. The bread or cornmeal? *Oh, Lord!* At least he'd not expect the fancier dishes servants set before her parents. *Thank God for small wonders.*

"We get carrots, potatoes, squash, and a few other vegetables every two weeks. Eggs and meat, too. Most things come by ship to Seattle and then are hauled to surrounding areas. We also rely on local farmers. Everything goes like wildfire. First come, first rights. I'll show you the storage pit that keeps food fresh. Put anything you need on my bill at Carl Turner's store. If you're going in for a big order, let me know that morning, and I'll get it before coming back that evening." He leaned back and finished his coffee in one long swallow.

"Last year, a few of the men started small gardens, but they didn't have much time to plant or tend them. Of course, now that most have wives, the women will take over that chore."

Now that she'd like. That she could do. Oh, yes, and flowers, too.

He wiggled his eyebrows. "I'll enjoy having decent bread. I'm the first to admit I'm no bread maker. Rather than chew my leather, I bought bread from Monk if he had any left. That man can sure bake bread."

Morgan swallowed the dry lump in her throat. Luke's leather had most likely been better chewing than any she would bake. What ingredients went into making bread? *Oh, dear.*

"And it's been awhile since any of us have had

cake, pies, or cookies." He grinned like a little boy anxiously awaiting a savory confection. "You can be sure most of the men will have their wives baking from sunup till sundown. Since I don't bake, I haven't kept much milk around, but we will from now on." Did he hint he'd like the same? *Oh, boy.* He'd have a long wait, unless she came up with a quick, easy miracle. Good grief, she didn't even own a cookbook. Maybe one of the other women would lend her one. At least until she knew what was what.

Though the whole ordeal sounded scary, her mind swirled with growing anticipation. Her first priority, her first full day in camp, would be to procure a cookbook.

"Who's Monk? I don't remember meeting him." She hoped to pull the conversation away from being tripped up on her expertise. Tripped up? She had no expertise.

He grinned again as he levered himself from the table. "You'll meet him eventually. He lives at the river's edge. If you think this cabin's small, his is no bigger than this kitchen. But he bakes bread that melts on your tongue. I swear he must bake all night. He always has eight to ten loaves every day, yet never misses putting in a twelve- to fifteen-hour day at work. Guess you could say he's a loner. He doesn't like crowds. Just keeps to himself, mostly."

"He sounds like a monk. Is that how he got his name?"

He laughed and strode to the counter. "No, he's one of the monkeys. The best there is."

He reached for a jar of oats on the counter and pulled down a pan from the cupboard.

"Monkeys?" She rose so she could study what he'd do with the oats. *Lesson number two.*

He poured water, maybe two cupfuls, into the pan from the pitcher, took a pinch of what she assumed to be salt from a small crock and dropped it into the water. After dumping about two-thirds of a cup of oats into the water, he carried the pan to the stove.

Ah-hah, she could do this. She felt a burst of enthusiasm just knowing she might be able to handle some things he expected of her. Oh, how good it felt.

****

Two hours after Luke left in the wagon, Morgan was eagerly anticipating a venture to the makeshift town. She'd swept the floor and made sure every wood chip had been flung out the door. She'd hauled pails of water from the large wooden barrel outside, heated it, and washed and dried the dishes. She'd only come away with one small burn on her right index finger when that digit had snuck past the potholder. It smarted, but she was more proud of her accomplishments than she'd been in a long time. She'd even walked back to the pond Luke had showed her this morning, no more than one hundred and fifty feet behind the cabin. Loons glided across the calm water during both visits. She'd never seen loons and found them fascinating. Luke said he'd tell her more about them later. She looked forward to it.

Giving one more inspection to her new home, she felt pleased. Her bed looked tidy, though she scowled at the quilt's fraying edges. Maybe tonight she'd try to mend the poor thing. "Try" seemed a mighty big word. But she'd scrubbed the counter till it gleamed, loaded the woodstove, and filled the kettles plus a few large glass jugs with water. And, oh, yes, she'd even dumped lime down the offensive privy hole. Now for supper.

Grabbing her woolen shawl, she headed out to search for the bible that would prevent Luke from starving to death.

Chapter Six

Morgan stumbled over yet another deep rut. Her wide, two-inch heels sank into the pine-carpeted mush, but she caught herself with one hand against a tree before she lost her footing. Again. She wasn't about to land on her backside like last night.

Pulling her feet out of the muck, she found sure footing and once again started down the skewed wagon path. She gazed at the lofty columns that surrounded her.

"How beautiful," she whispered as she peered at beams of sunlight just barely threading through the towering giants. In New York, she'd loved to fuss with planting flowers, to see their beauty surround the grounds around her home. She'd enjoyed watching maples and oaks bud in the spring until their rich foliage formed magnificent green plumes. And marveled as they shifted their dress to red, gold, orange, brilliant and fiery, in autumn.

But here stood sheer wonder. Walls and towers of sky-reaching glory. As green as green could be. Varying shades of brown bark, ranging from thin and smooth as paper to thick and craggy as rock, contrasted with the sweeping and outstretched arms of emerald. Pungent pine vied with the sweetness of cedar, filling the air with aromatic freshness, clean and invigorating. She breathed in the welcome headiness.

By the time Morgan stepped past the last spiraling firs and glanced at the line of cabins, her heels burned and her ankles screamed. No doubt she had ten blisters—on each foot—from walking in ridiculous shoes on the uneven, mushy road.

Stifling back a whimper as her raw flesh stung with every footstep, she wondered which cabin she should try first. *The nearest sounds good.* No sense going any farther than necessary.

She knocked lightly on the first door. Clasping the front of her shawl with one hand so it wouldn't fall off, she brushed her skirt with the other to rid it of the pine needles and burrs accumulated along the way. The weight of her dampened hem pulled heavily at her waist, and she vowed she would take up the hem by two or maybe three inches on everything she owned, if walking to town became an everyday ritual.

She hadn't realized the wagon path would be so soggy. Undoubtedly the night's dew had been heavy, and though the morning sun blazed bright now, the dense forest shielded the road from its drying rays.

Morgan knocked once more. "Is anyone home?"

Though her feet felt rubbed raw and her skirt hem was a dampened mess, she smiled in appreciation of the glorified nature she'd witnessed. Things hadn't gone as planned, but the thrill at seeing such rugged magnificence was reward. At least for now. Her adventure held potential.

No one answered. Disheartened, she lifted her skirt and trudged to the next one down the line, each step more painful than the one before. At the second door, she knocked louder.

"Just a minute," came a voice. Morgan sighed in relief. To sit down, to remove her shoes, would be heaven. She glanced down at the mud and pine needles rimming her footwear. Quickly she wiped the sides against a pile of rocks off to the side.

She tried to connect the voice she'd just heard with the many faces she'd met. Out of the eight widows and ten dance hall ladies, she couldn't place the voice. She'd talked to each one of them on the way here, but through the door and with the voice raised, she had no idea who she might face. It didn't matter. Just a chair would be welcome.

The door swung open, and Morgan smiled at Sarah Parsons. No, she corrected, she was now Sarah…Hellmann. She'd married Tom Hellmann. Oh, thank goodness. Sarah had been one of the widows, about forty-five, maybe a bit more. Morgan prayed she owned a cookbook.

"Why, Morgan. What a pleasant surprise. Please come in, honey." Sarah stepped back, opening the door wider, her smile as pleasant as the sweet apple scent within the cabin.

"I hope I'm not intruding, Sarah. If I am, I can go to the next cabin." But she took one step in, scanning the room for Tom. Lord, here they were newlyweds, and she stood on their doorstep first thing after the wedding night. Why hadn't she thought of that sooner?

"Heavens, no. You come right in and make yourself at home." Sarah took her arm and led her in before closing the door. "It's so good to see you. I was hopin' to see some of you today. We were all so tired from our trip, and with all the excitement of so many weddings, I didn't know how long it would be before any of us women could get together."

Sarah wiped her flour-covered hands on her apron. "You just sit down at the table and I'll get us some tea. How's that sound?"

"I would love some, thank you." She noticed the three mounds of dough on the floured counter. "Are you sure I'm not interrupting?"

Lifting the kettle to fill two cups, Sarah laughed "I'm just bakin'. Figured I'd bake up a storm for Tom. Wouldn't want him to think he married me for just my looks, now, would I?"

As her smile widened, her eyes twinkled. Her

brown hair, pulled back in a tight bun, matched her eyes. She was slightly plump but pleasant looking, with a gentle smile that drew one to her instantly. Having married a farmer against her well-to-do parents' wishes, they'd disowned her. She'd had no one to turn to after her husband's fatal heart attack.

Morgan had immediately taken to Sarah, had talked to her numerous times on the trip, and had enjoyed her openness and friendship. She couldn't remember Sarah looking as youthful or so very happy on that trip as she did right now.

A warm contentment filled Morgan at seeing Sarah so cheerful. Yet her heart felt empty and lonely at her own situation. Well, she'd made her own bed, now she'd have to lie in it.

"Oh, I think he knows exactly what he got. He's very lucky. I hope he realizes it."

Sarah seemed to glow at that remark. "I'm the lucky one, Morgan." Her voice turned serious, soft. "I never thought I'd find another man as good and decent as my Jed. But just bein' with Tom for one night, I thank God I dared come here."

"You were pretty scared on the way out." Morgan laughed.

"Oh, don't you know it." Sarah arranged a small pottery pitcher, matching sugar bowl, and the steeped teas on a wooden tray and carried them to the table. "I'm sure glad I brought my household things with me. Tom didn't have much here to make it homey." She sat down across from Morgan and beamed as she handed Morgan her cup and a spoon.

"But I feel blessed I ended up with Tom. Why with so much commotion when everyone started changin' partners, I thought I'd just as soon run back the way I came."

"I'm so happy for the two of you. You deserve a good man."

"How about you? Are you happy? We left so

quickly after your…ah…"

"Luke, Luke Kincaid," Morgan supplied. *But he's not mine.*

"That's right, I'm sorry I forgot." She took the sugar bowl Morgan handed her and stirred a spoonful of sugar into her tea. "We left so quick after you came in that I couldn't remember. Everything seemed like a blur by then. Right from the first I sensed my good fortune with Tom, but I still felt so…uneasy, if you know what I mean. I'd just met him, and we were goin' off to his cabin as husband and wife." She laughed shyly as she set the cream down. She blushed.

"I can't begin to tell you how sweet and understanding he is. He may look like a big lout, but he's as patient and gentle as a lamb with me."

Morgan sipped her tea, again feeling pure happiness for her friend while swallowing her own woes. Tom's height and shoulders seemed just shy of Luke's, if she remembered correctly. The sandy-blond man wasn't terribly handsome, but he was far from ugly.

Why couldn't she have found the perfect match? Even less than perfect? She'd been willing to create a happy marriage, be a good wife, work side by side for better or worse, settling for a strong friendship, a partnership rather than any devotional love. She'd failed to gain either.

"And Lord above, can that man kiss." Sarah closed her eyes, and dreaminess spread across her face. Surprised at Sarah's outspokenness, Morgan's face heated.

Sarah opened her eyes and grinned. "Well, let's just say he can do a lot more than just kiss well. It must be the good, clean air here that makes these men so strappin' fine, I tell you."

Morgan's eyes widened at Sarah's candor, and she nearly choked on the tea. Her cup clunked against the table as she set it down. Sarah roared with laughter.

"I'm sorry. I've embarrassed you. I shouldn't have said that. You're a good deal younger than I, and I've overlooked the fact that you were never married before. Please forgive my runaway mouth." She appeared to be more embarrassed now than Morgan actually felt.

"It's all right, really. If that part of your marriage is that good too, you're twice blessed."

"Oh, and don't I know it. Jed, God rest his soul, was a hard-workin' man, a good provider, and a sweet, lovin' husband. But I never felt…Oh, here I go again." She put her hands to her rosy cheeks. "My mouth seems to run faster than a river today."

Morgan laughed. "I believe you're happy and very pleased. That's all that counts."

Sarah sipped her tea, then leaned toward her. "You never did answer me if you're happy. Guess I got to rattlin' on so, I never gave you chance. What's your Luke like? He's one of the most handsome, rugged men I've ever seen, and the men speak very highly of him."

Morgan forced back the truth of her relationship with a meager smile. "He's very nice. He's hard-working, from what I've gathered so far. We haven't really got to know each other as well as the others did. Last night we were both so tired we didn't talk much, and then he went off to the logging camp first thing this morning."

"Did you marry?" Sarah seemed to watch her curiously, as if she sensed her evasiveness.

"Ah, no. Maybe tomorrow. We agreed we needed a little time to make sure we can tolerate each other, since he got there so late." Boy, if that didn't sound like a lame excuse. "I'm sure we'll get a chance to talk more tonight."

Sarah said nothing for a few seconds. Morgan

grew uneasy under her scrutiny.

"Honey, you don't have to be coy with me. I'm your friend. I know you've never been married. Are you a virgin?"

Her face felt scorched. Sarah was old enough to be her mother, but Morgan had never had any kind of discussion, most assuredly not this kind, with her mother. Maybe she should have.

"Yes."

Sarah smiled and took Morgan's hands within hers. "I'm forty-eight years old, old enough to be your mother. I know you said you left home to get away from your parents, but I'll say this like a mother." Her eyes softened and met Morgan's directly.

"You have every right to get to know Luke before you make a commitment. Don't let any of the others tell you differently, or try to rush you. If he's not someone you can respect, stick by through thick and thin, and let him enter your bed willingly, then don't settle for any less."

Morgan sat silent, absorbing what Sarah said. She searched her friend's face, wondered where these sincere words really stemmed from. She didn't have long to wonder.

"I'll tell you a secret I haven't told many. My parents tried to force me to marry a lawyer. Raleigh Dunbar was his name. I give thanks every day since that I stood up to them. I could neither respect him for his holier-than-thou attitude, nor for the condescendin' way he treated me. But Lord I tried, wantin' to please my parents at first. So I allowed him a few stolen kisses, thinkin' maybe a spark would ignite and I'd find myself attracted to him despite his pious attitude. I cringe every time I think of his kisses. Sloppy, wet, clumsy. No spark, no thrill. Nothing, except maybe repulsion." She shook her head.

"At first I thought there might be something

wrong with me. Maybe I didn't do it right, maybe I expected more from a man's kiss. I'd heard many a woman say they did their duty to their man and that was that. They didn't seem to relish what went on at night any more than they liked doin' the wash. But somehow I knew there might be more with the right person. I'd sensed it from seein' it in the eyes of so many others." She sat back, grinned, and hugged herself.

"Oh, and did I find out I had it right. Because Jed came along, in his dirty old work clothes, his hair windblown, dirt under his nails, carefree and fancy free. But he was a hardworking man, loved the outdoors, and cherished people as if he'd been put on the earth to help each and every one." Her eyes turned dreamy, actually glistened.

"I first saw him standin' in the store buyin' candy and a blue ribbon. As I listened to his conversation with Mr. Riley, I found out they were for Calista, his crippled sister of twelve. I eavesdropped more and learned that his money didn't come none too easy, from what Mr. Riley implied. I think I gave my heart to him that very instant, and there weren't no turnin' back. I never wanted to. I cherished every day for twenty years. We never had any children, but we raised his siblings after his parents died, and we had a good, happy life together."

Morgan had to blink back tears of the touching young love story. She'd been born with a romantic heart, and Sarah's words reached that, deep down inside.

"After grievin' for years, I've found another I feel just as close to. If it's possible to fall in love in one instant, then I've done it twice and thank my lucky stars. I've no regrets, I tell ya."

She again clasped Morgan's hands. "Always listen to your heart, honey. It'll guide you best. If

Luke's the one, you'll know. Your heart'll flutter, your blood'll run hot, and you'll want to lay down your very life for him if need be. That's what it's all about. If not, don't settle for less. Believe me, I've seen too many unhappy women—unhappy men, too. They turn bitter and cold without love. Don't sell yourself short. Take all the time in the world before you step."

Morgan trapped the woman's words of wisdom within her bosom. She'd store this talk away like a treasure. Luke Kincaid set her heart to fluttering, heated her blood. But could it be only lust she felt? She didn't know him well enough to lay down her life. *What in heaven's name are you thinking? He's already taken.*

But surely another man could make her pulse run wild. It had to be another. Guilt weighed heavily on Morgan's mind as she withheld the truth of her situation and why Luke had come here. Yet she couldn't confide in Sarah. That would break her solemn vow to Luke. It wouldn't be fair to him, and it could spell disaster for him and the others if it ever leaked out.

"That was beautiful, Sarah. And I'll always remember it and heed your advice."

"That's all I ask, honey. You deserve a life as good as I have. It'll come. Do you feel any attraction to your Luke?"

Honesty flared easily this time. "Yes. I get all tied up in knots when he's near me, and my heart pounds like horses racing across a field." She pictured him leaning over, long muscular legs straining, buttocks pulling buckskins tight. She swallowed.

Sarah's chuckle filled the room before she took a big gulp of tea. "Oh, we'll be havin' us another weddin' sure as anythin'."

Sarah hopped up from the table and scurried to

the stove, leaving Morgan with a bitter taste in her mouth. Morgan watched Sarah grab two thick potholders, open the oven door, remove two apple pies, and set them on cast iron trivets on the counter. The pies had smelled good while baking. Now the fragrance of cinnamon and sugared apples laced with heavenly scents of cooked dough assailed Morgan's nose till her mouth watered and her belly grumbled.

"Land's sake, I got so engrossed in talkin' I almost over-baked these."

"They smell wonderful."

"They do at that, don't they?" She beamed, laying the potholders down. "I was so happy Tom had just about everythin' I needed. But I had to get cinnamon from Carl Turner's store first thing this mornin'. Carl doesn't stock much spices, but he said he'll order anything for any of us."

Morgan remembered why she'd come. "Speaking of things to cook and bake, do you by chance have a cookbook, or even some recipes I could borrow?"

"Land's sake, do I. A real good book my grandma passed down years back. It's got more recipes written down over the years than you can shake a leg at. What you figurin' on makin'?"

"Food."

Sarah appeared stunned for an instant before her loud guffaws filled the room. "Food. Just food? Any food?"

Her guffaws settled down to light chuckles as she wiped her eyes with the end of her apron. "I'm sorry. I didn't mean to laugh. It just struck me so funny." She dabbed her eyes again.

Morgan found herself laughing along with her at the absurdity. "Sarah, I've never cooked anything in my life. I've stirred simmering pots and dished out helpings to the needy at the mission back home. A few times I had to add water, salt, or pepper to whatever, even added a few diced vegetables. But that's all."

"You've never made anythin' from scratch?"

"From scratch?"

Sarah shook her head, her eyes full of wonder. "From the start."

Morgan shook her head.

"Honey, we've got our work cut out for us if you're goin' to draw your Luke in through his stomach. Let's get to work."

After Morgan removed her shoes and thin cotton stockings, groaning all the while, Sarah applied salve to the broken blisters. It worked wonders. Then they got down to business.

For the next few hours Morgan peeled, chopped, sliced, and diced vegetables and meat until she saw double. She added spices, herbs, and the right amount of water to the cast iron pot and carried it to the stove. Morgan sighed as she stretched her back, thinking her work finally done.

But relentless Sarah had a few more things to teach. She was hell bent on Morgan satisfying Luke Kincaid's appetite, come hell or high water.

Next came the recipes. Morgan wrote out so many her fingers cramped, threatening to fall off, digit by digit. Sarah kept her to the more simple ones, the ones with the fewest or the easiest to find ingredients. Meanwhile, Sarah jotted down some of the basics for starters: how to cook a roast, techniques to dry beef and to salt pork, how to mash potatoes, the frying of an egg and bacon, and the do's and don'ts of making butter and skimming cream.

Once the three loaves of bread had risen, Sarah instructed her how to prepare the pans, set the dough in, and coat their tops with a light brushing of melted butter. Morgan had never realized how much work and time it took from preparation to the finished edible product.

As Morgan placed the three loaves in the oven, she felt like she could drop to the floor and sleep for hours. Dear Lord above, she felt exhausted, yet the bread hadn't baked, the soup had barely started to boil, and Sarah, the maniac cook, the abuser of cooking students, sat drinking her tea and smiling like a contented cat.

If Sarah hadn't helped her so much, had the patience of a saint the entire day, Morgan would have growled at her. She plopped into a chair and stretched her neck.

"I think you deserve another cup of tea. Or would you prefer coffee, honey?"

"I think I deserve something stronger. Got any whiskey?"

They laughed, they hugged, and they inhaled the aromas of simmering soup, baking bread, and succulent cooling pies. And they drank coffee sweetened with a bit of sugar, topped with a hefty plop of cream...and laced with a very generous amount of whiskey.

It'd been a good day, Morgan thought as she sipped her delectable drink and watched the sun descend farther in the clear sky. Now she had to gather her recipes and notes, hike home, and cook supper. All she wanted to do was sleep.

"I better go before the sun goes completely down. It'll take me awhile to decide what to make for supper and get started. Luke said he'd be home by seven or seven-thirty."

"Well, now, Luke came by for Tom with some of the others. They all rode together in the wagon. Tom said that's the way they do it most times. So you can just wait here for your man."

Morgan wanted desperately to correct Sarah as to *her man*, but again bit her tongue. Thank heavens she wouldn't have to walk that distance with raw ankles.

"But I'll have to get sup..."

"You have supper, honey," Sarah smiled. "Did you think I'd have you do all that work and not share the rewards? You'll have soup, bread, and pie tonight and be proud of it. I'll give you butter, too, until us women can get some made. Tom buys it from some man named Monk."

Morgan relaxed back in her chair. "Luke told me about Monk. He said he loves to bake. He must have a number of talents."

The two indulged in one more whiskey-laced coffee and were buzzing like glassy-eyed bees, laughing as they shared stories, by the time the wagon rumbled to the door. Sarah called out to Luke to let him know Morgan waited inside.

Tom and Luke halted just inside the doorway and simply gaped at the two. Morgan noted how each of them shrugged their shoulders and eyed each other while she and Sarah hummed as they quickly divided and packed up food.

Morgan had to bite back a smile at seeing the bewildered men. They appeared perplexed that Sarah and she were excessively jovial for having cooked up enough to feed several families.

But Morgan felt proud as punch. Nothing could put a damper on her mood. She'd had her first lesson in cooking.

Chapter Seven

Luke had tended the animals in the barn and reloaded the woodstove till the flames licked at the stack of logs by the time Morgan had set the table, laid out the food, and begun slicing thick pieces of bread at the table.

They'd not said more than a few comments about the evening's chilliness as they made their way home. How short that distance seemed when one rode instead of hiking in wobbly shoes. Could he be miffed that she hadn't been more talkative, willing to hear about his day?

Thinking to correct her error, she asked, "How did your day go? I hope nothing unusual happened."

He gave her a wry look as he ambled to the basin at the counter to wash his hands. Was he in a foul mood, or what? No, he'd worn a bit of a smirk. Her hands trembled as she ladled the soup into two chipped pottery bowls, all the time glancing sideways at him as he wiped his hands on the towel. When he came to the table, she wished she could read his thoughts.

He pulled back his chair and sat. "Nothing horrendous, for a change. A few cuts and scratches, and Peter twisted his foot hauling some brush, but nothing we couldn't handle."

Sighing with relief just to have him speak a sentence, Morgan poured the coffee and sat. "Will Peter's foot be all right?"

"He'll be back on the job tomorrow, no worse for the wear."

Morgan noticed how large his hands were as he spread a slab of golden butter on the warm bread. Nice hands, strong, with long thick fingers, callused from hard work, nails snipped short. Her pulse quickened at wondering how gentle those hands could be.

Oh, for shame. Here she sat fantasizing about another woman's fiancé. A man who openly offered friendship and a job. She should be thankful he'd gone along with her idea, not eyeing him like some scrumptious dessert. She'd best be satisfied with a piece of apple pie to satisfy her sweet tooth.

"This soup's delicious. At least I'm blessed with good cooking while you're here, thank God. I've a hearty appetite, so your cooking won't go to waste, believe me."

Though his compliment boosted her vacillating ego, she felt obligated to tell the truth of the matter. "Sarah might have said I made the soup, but I merely put it together. She instructed me the entire time. I wouldn't have known what to put in or how much, if she hadn't. And she made the pies and bread. I only baked the loaves once they had risen."

He took a sip of coffee, smiled. That smile tripped her heart. "Nonetheless, it's still great."

Morgan laughed. "I hope you say that tomorrow when I cook by myself." Yet she felt a tremendous sense of accomplishment for today's tiring but rewarding efforts. So tiring, she found herself half-heartedly picking at her food and yawning.

"You better stay away from laced coffee tomorrow, if you're going to stay awake long enough to cook." He chuckled at her stricken face as he filled his bowl again.

If she thought her cheeks might have pinkened at his compliment, now they blazed at his embarrassing barb. "It tasted so good. I can't believe how relaxed it made me."

"Relaxed?" He guffawed. "You damn near slept all the way home."

She felt that fire streak all the way down to her neck. "I'm so sorry. I…I didn't realize—"

"Don't apologize." He smeared butter across another slice of bread. "I needed some quiet time anyway. After the busy day, I guess I was envious I couldn't sleep along with you."

"I'm not used to liquor. The first one tasted good, and the second one tasted even better."

He smiled. "You deserved it. You had a long day yesterday, found out you're without a husband, and put in another long day today. I, ah, take it you haven't cook much before?"

She swallowed a spoonful of soup. "Uh…not much." Oh, she'd surely go to hell for stretching that truth. Her "not much" consisted of this afternoon's introduction.

"I'm sure you'll do fine. Like I said before, put anything you might need on my tab at the store. And I don't mind helping with things you're not familiar with."

"Thank you, I appreciate that." She'd probably need his help a lot more than he thought. But she had to try on her own first. And he looked skeptical enough already. No sense in scaring the man half to death, having him think she might starve him. Worse yet, poison him.

He pushed his bowl to the side, lifted the coffee pot from the trivet, and refilled their mugs. "How about some of that pie? Sure smells good."

And it did. Still warm from the oven and wrapped in a towel to keep it that way, the cinnamon-apple bouquet sweetened the dimly lit room. After she cut two pieces, a generous portion for him, hers a bit smaller, they moaned their contentment as they savored its perfection.

"My stomach's so full I'll sleep like a baby," Luke

said, carrying dishes to the counter.

"You go sit by the fire. I'll have these dishes done in no time." Then bed. Heaven.

"Sure you don't want some help?"

He sounded as if he'd expected to help. Yet she recognized the hopeful glint in his eyes that said he'd be none too pleased to go relax. Lord, she could drown in that deep jade if she let herself. If she had the right to. She admonished herself for even thinking such a thing.

"I'm sure." She laughed and gave him in a light shove toward the living room area. "Now git."

He laughed good-naturedly as he moseyed over to the stove, opened the doors, and squatted down to stir the wood with a poker. How relaxed he seemed in this crude little cabin.

As he plopped down on the divan she felt her heart flutter, her insides warm. How broad his shoulders were, how long his legs were as he stretched them straight out. All raw strength, tendered with a gentleness of caring. Would he be as tender when he loved a woman? *Oh, Morgan, get your senses, girl.*

Flustered, she vigorously wiped a bowl dry, trying to concentrate on the flames as they curled smoothly around the glowing logs. As she watched the golden fingers fan and stroke the wood she thought of his long fingers. Would they ignite a woman's skin as he caressed…

Her hands stilled, clutching the bowl and towel against her pounding chest. *Dear God in heaven.* How sinful to covet another's fiancé. Her lust, and that's all it must be, she surmised, was misplaced, unwanted, and frustrating, to say the least.

Spinning around to face the metal basin, she directed her thoughts to doing the chores expected of her, and only that.

But how different, how fulfilling it could have

been to have Luke Kincaid as her spouse. Now, with the golden glow from the opened stove, the succulent aroma of soup, bread, and pie still lingering, she longed for a quiet evening of two people, two married people, snuggled up close on the divan, sharing their thoughts, planning a future together.

Wiping the last dish, she battled her fanciful notions and decided she'd better go to bed rather than torment her empty heart. She'd conceded she could settle for a marriage based on friendship, a partnership if nothing else. Now, though Luke could not fulfill even that much of her dream, she found she craved more in a relationship. She wanted love, a true caring, through-thick-and-thin, till-death-do-them-part type of alliance. And she realized with a sickening despair she could have easily fallen in love with someone like Luke Kincaid. God help her, if he weren't already spoken for, she'd be trying her damnedest to make him reciprocate her feelings. How ironic to realize how desperately she longed for love, only to be faced with such an impossibility. All Sarah's talk had put cobwebs in her head. Silly daydreams she had no business thinking about.

Biting back the sheer heaviness of woe, she wiped her hands and carried the basin to the door. No sooner had she fumbled for the latch than Luke appeared at her side.

"Here, let me get that. You look dead on your feet."

Oh, if he only knew her bent shoulders and wearied eyes were not due solely to fatigue but to heartache, strong and aching. It pierced her very soul. How could she ever remain here long enough for him to see his job through? How could she ever keep her feelings hidden, her heart in one piece? She already cared way too much for this big, strapping man.

"Thank you." As he unburdened her of the

cumbersome metal pan, she opened the door, stepped back, and watched him stride outside to dump the soapy water onto the starlit ground.

How very courteous, how helpful and considerate he was. Did his fiancée appreciate what she had? She certainly hoped so. A man as good as Luke deserved the best.

With a heavy heart, albeit honest admission, Morgan acknowledged she fell short of being worthy of such a man. She lacked most skills a man sought in a wife, she lied by omission of her ineptness, and she'd come to this wilderness for her own selfish reasons. To add to her transgressions, she coveted another woman's fiancé. Would she find a man as good as Luke Kincaid? Did she even deserve such a gift?

When Luke re-entered the cabin, she fought to clear her troubled mind. Berating her rapid pulse, she watched him close the door and return the basin to the counter.

"It's getting mighty chilly out there," Luke said, rubbing his forearms with his large hands as he went to stand in front of the open stove. "I'll be happy when the weather breaks and the evenings start warmin' a bit."

"When is the last frost here?" Morgan drew up next to him to enjoy the heat pouring out through the screen.

His eyes sparkled, looking hopeful and eager. "We're past frost, but the nights don't know it yet. Another week and we should see sure signs of spring. By the way, when the weather gets warm, you can open that piece of wood latched to the wall and let the west wind blow through. There's a screen under it."

She'd noticed the small rectangle board above the bed but had forgotten to ask its purpose. She failed to hold back a yawn. "I love spring. I always get so excited to plant flowers and watch them grow."

Luke's brows arched. "So, the lady wants flowers, does she? Well, you can plant all the flowers you like as long as you put in some vegetables, too. How's that for a deal?"

Another yawn escaped. "Sounds...wonderful."

Luke laughed and turned her by her shoulders to face the bed. "Go to bed before you fall asleep standing here. You can dream about pretty flowers and tasty vegetables. But without sleep you'll never make it through tomorrow."

She moseyed to the bed, turned down the quilt. "Right. Could sleep for a week."

Luke almost laughed out loud at her trance-like fatigue. At least she'd been honest when she admitted she hadn't cooked much before, and he appreciated that honesty. But he knew without a doubt she'd left out some very important aspects of her life. She avoided talking or relating any more than she had to when it came to where she hailed from or what kind of life she'd led. Most likely she thought she did it well. And why did she feel she had to hide the facts?

But he knew way more than she'd allowed herself to say. Her speech alone spoke volumes. A very good upbringing—better than very good, if he read things right. He'd noted her gentle movements as she plumped the pillows, though she was obviously dazed by fatigue. Even the way she walked and held herself indicated years of proper direction and training. Morgan Prescott didn't herald from some poor farm in mid-New York, that's for sure.

Realizing that fact, he'd purposefully avoided informing her of his wealthy status, assuming she just might clam up or shy away from him more. He'd keep that tidbit a secret for as long as necessary. She apparently wanted to hide her upbringing. He itched to know more about her. But the only way he might accomplish that is if he kept his truths hidden as well.

Exhaustion showed in her face as Morgan automatically started unbuttoning her blouse at the bedside without any thought of him standing in the lamps' glow. He hid a laugh.

"Gather your nightdress, and I'll blow out the lamps," he said, closing the stove's doors.

Her hand froze on the third button as if her state of undress just dawned on her. Poor thing, eyes rounded, speechless, she wearily gathered her nightgown. A protectiveness lambasted him, strong and possessive. Here stood a woman, more girl actually, if one considered life's experiences, alone and trying to make her way in the world with no idea how tough it might be.

She needed someone to protect her. He found himself more than willing to fill those shoes for the present. But what would she do after they parted? It bothered him to think of her fumbling along life's trying trails at that point.

Well, he wouldn't worry about that dilemma until they had to face it. He'd make sure she had a secure place when the time came. He'd be her big brother and insure her safety.

Brother? He almost laughed. Wrong. She aroused feelings in him he had no right to feel. He'd thought all day about her pleasant smile, her strong determination to make a life for herself. He'd been eager to see that smile, to witness the sparkle in those big dark eyes upon returning home. Damn! He had no business being anxious for any of it.

Guilt burdened his heart as he thought of his fiancée. Sweet Lucy. With her debilitating illness, her own pleasant smile. At least it'd once been full of happiness, her eyes so full of sparkle just like Morgan's, except those eyes were deep blue. She'd once laughed just like Morgan. So long ago, so very long ago.

His chest twisted with remorse at knowing Lucy lay at home suffering, totally frustrated at becoming an invalid. Yes, guilt hung enormously weighty, and he regretted the attraction he felt toward his housemate. His employee, he corrected himself. He scoffed at the word. What in the hell had he been thinking when he agreed to this bizarre set-up? Crazy is as crazy does.

Well, if he found Morgan at all appealing—and he did to a certain extent, no denying it—it was his own damn fault. He'd have to grin and bear it. He and Lucy had agreed to stay together so he could see to her care. They were, after all, best of friends. Should've remained that way, he thought, instead of trying to make more out of it with a future marriage. But they'd agreed to stick it out. Come good or come bad, they'd agreed, mutually. He wouldn't let her down for all the pretty faces and bright smiles in the world. No matter how tempting. He owed her that much. He wouldn't, couldn't forget it.

With that resolved in his mind, he blew out the lamps, shucked down to his drawers, and settled onto the divan. It'd be a long haul, this nasty business of flushing out the bad guys. A very long, agonizing haul, if he pegged it right. And an even harder time of it since Morgan Prescott had walked into his life.

He stared at the ceiling, now pitch black. Sleep eluded him. Lucy was more like a sister. Morgan…well, Morgan was…

Oh, God.

Chapter Eight

Broad shafts of sunlight pushed their way past the towering peaks of hemlock, cedar, and fir painting the air with a diamond-dust glimmer. Its beauty called Morgan like a bright beacon. Yet she nipped her excitement, shut the door, and faithfully endured the morning chores first.

Once the cabin gleamed spic and span, she sprinkled a few dried herbs over the chunk of beef, added a cup of water to the cast iron pot, and set it atop the stove over a slow fire.

"Amazing," she laughed, sliding the cover off the cold storage. It consisted of a three-foot square hole covered with a heavy metal plate. Yet it preserved wrapped vegetables, fruits and meats—according to Luke fairly efficiently—right smack beneath the kitchen counter.

She'd been naïve to think it would be outside, where animals could pick up the scent. But, by golly, she'd learn. She welcomed learning, and being here seemed more right each minute. This primitive camp opened up a whole new world. She loved it.

Anxious to be outside, to purchase seeds, she peeled and cut potatoes, carrots, and squash like there'd be no tomorrow, then set them in a bowl of water until time to add them to the pot. There'd be enough bread and pie from last night, so she wouldn't have to waste such a brilliant day on baking. *Thank goodness for small wonders.*

Having donned flat shoes this time, she set out to cover the ground to Mr. Turner's store in record time.

****

Morgan knelt as she used a hand spade to till an area extending two feet out from the cabin. She removed her new work gloves. Lovingly, she sifted the warm dirt through her fingers and savored how good it felt to dig, to feel the grains of God's good earth. A gentle breeze carried the scent of pine her way: clean, almost pungent, yet heady and pleasant. "This is what it's all about. I love it. I love it. I love it."

Leaning back on her heels, she proudly inspected the two beds she'd turned, a good six inches deep. They stretched from each side of the door to each corner of the cabin.

Now she'd mix in humus and manure she'd hauled back in Mr. Turner's borrowed wheel barrel. Pushing that wobbly thing had been the hard part. That and turning the soil, which hadn't yielded as easily as the sandier earth back home. Yet she smiled in satisfaction at her labor of love.

She swiped rivulets of perspiration from her cheeks and forehead with her forearm, pushed back the loose tendrils from around her face. Only then did she notice the darkened circles on her dress under her arms, felt the fabric stick to her heated back. What a mess she was.

She looked up at the waning sunlight. "Oh, my, Luke'll be home in a couple of hours."

She'd not yet put the vegetables on, she realized. Yet, she'd rather mix in the manure and humus. Ah, but once she added them and set the table, there'd be no reason not to return. She'd only need a few minutes to wash and don a clean dress before Luke arrived. Standing up, she brushed off the accumulation of dirt and eyed the numerous pouches of seeds.

"I'll be back," she said as she dashed inside.

After washing her hands, she dumped the vegetables and a bit of water into the pot, then added two logs to the fire. She grinned, confident everything would be done in time.

She made short work of setting the table. On the way back from town she'd snapped off several thin branches of a bush bearing tiny orange berries and had placed them in a glass of water. She had no idea what they were, but they'd caught her eye. Now, she arranged them into a bouquet, just so, and set it in the middle of the table. The cabin might be crude, but she smiled in satisfaction at the hominess the small colorful cluster brought to the room.

Oh, yes, she'd still have time to sow seeds. So they could soak up the coming days of sunshine and rain, could be nourished by the fertility she'd created. Out the door she flew.

After she shoveled manure and humus into piles over the beds, she again knelt on her knees and worked them into the soil with her hands. "Now the fun part."

Morgan laid out the ten packets of seeds in front of her on the ground to decide which seeds would go where. She had to study them only a moment. Her mind's eye saw it clearly.

To the door's left, colorful asters would stand tall and hug the cabin while banked by clustering marigolds in varying bright shades of gold. Dainty pansies would flit in the breeze, adding a sweet charm in front. She set the packets in place, glanced to the right.

Daisies, stark and white, would frolic in back, supported by splashes of radiant zinnias. Petunias, pink and deep purple, would kiss the ground, forming a border.

The other four packets would wait a day or two. She'd cluster them throughout the yard. Then start the vegetables. Determined to finish, she began strewing seeds, handling them like precious gems. To her, she realized, they were every bit as precious. Who would have thought so many varieties of seed would be available out in this wilderness.

Dusk snuck up, covering the land with a thin gray veil, turning the air a bit chilly. Heated by her endeavor, her eyes and mind affixed to her work, she'd not noticed the subtle changes until she heard the plod of workhorses, the rumbling of heavy wheels.

She gasped as the wagon broke through the trees and rolled across the clearing.

"Whoa, there!" Luke commanded. The wagon churned to a stop. Still on her knees, she glanced over her shoulder, and saw his eyebrows raise, a lazy smile curl his lips. She peered down at her disheveled attire and sat back on her legs, dismayed she'd let time fly by.

She watched him jump down and begin to unfasten the riggings. "I didn't realize it was so late," she said, removing her gloves to brush herself off, hoping to make herself somewhat presentable.

His chuckle mingled with the jingling of the lines. "See you found the shovel. You about finished there?"

Morgan detected no disgust at her shabbiness. She relaxed at his continued smile, giving thanks for small favors. This close to dinnertime with her looking as she did, her parents would have had apoplexy. Well, what did she expect? As his employee, she shouldn't be out to impress him, and he most likely could care less what she looked like.

She glanced at the remaining packet. "Yes. I'm on my last packet of seeds for today."

He stepped back leading the two horses toward the barn by the reins. "Then you might as well finish. I'll be awhile getting these two settled in and the rest fed."

With that said, he turned and led the animals away.

Morgan eagerly replaced her gloves, ripped open the petunia packet, and sprinkled the seeds over the trough she'd made, then brushed the soil over her babies and packed it down lightly. She could water them after supper.

Placing the tools, gloves and packets in the wheel barrel, she then brushed off her dress as best she could, only to smudge the soiled areas more. She made a beeline for the cabin.

The minute she opened the door, pungent fumes of charred meat stung her eyes, and her nose curled in rebellion. At least no smoke filled the room, thank the good Lord, but their supper definitely lacked any delectable aroma. Stunk to high heavens, in fact.

Leaving the door open so she could breathe, she scurried across the room, grabbed a potholder and lifted the lid. She knew what she'd find; she only needed to see the evidence with her own eyes. She wished she hadn't.

A poof of contained smoke, strong and stinging to her eyes and nostrils, billowed upward. She had to look away long enough for her eyes to somewhat stop watering before she could turn back to view the pot's contents. Ruined. Entirely ruined.

One shriveled, incinerated black piece of what resembled a hunk of coal sat under the bed of dried and wrinkled vegetables. Of course, if she hadn't known they were vegetables, she would never have been able to guess what they were.

Tears of despair mixed with smarting ones. Foolishly zealous, she'd added more wood. Utterly stupid, she'd not periodically checked the food. As she stared at the cremated supper, rage at her ineptness boiled within her. It helped daunt her tears. It'd been her own damn fault.

"What the hell..."

Morgan spun around at Luke's bark. He stood in the doorway, his hand cupped over his nose, his glassy eyes squinting. "Good God, woman, tell me that's not our supper." His bellows resounded through the caustic air. They lashed her pride as much as the foul odor knifed her eyes.

"We *have* no supper." She held his gaze, humiliation nearly choking her, the pleasure of her outside accomplishments vanishing. Lord, would she ever do anything right?

Had he ever seen such self-rejection? If so, it sure as hell had never hit him with such intensity.

He watched her lips quiver, her eyes tear, her shoulders slump till he thought she might keel over. His stunned outrage vanished on the cool evening's breeze crowding the door. In its place rose the urge to embrace and console her. It rushed him with an overwhelming potent force. He took a step toward her…

Stopped. His better sense demanded he verbally comfort her. It'd do neither of them any good if he were to touch her. He'd not be able to sleep for a week.

"Maybe we can salvage some of it." He crossed the room, positive there'd be little hope.

"I think we better have those eggs. *If* I can cook *them*." Her whispered words smacked of bitter self-reproach.

Luke leaned over and peered into the scorch-encrusted pot. Definitely no saving the offensive mess. His nose rebelled and his eyes watered. A chuckle nearly escaped.

"Eggs'll be fine." With a potholder, he grabbed the handle of the pot and strode out the door.

Returning to the cabin, he opted to leave the door open, raised the window, then unlatched the wood panel from the back opening. His gaze fell directly on Morgan. She sat on the divan, her shoulders slumped, her chin hanging low.

"If you help me get out the ham and eggs, I promise you a meal that'll stick to your ribs."

She raised her head, met his gaze. No tears flowed; he saw only raw hurt and anger. His chest tightened, realizing how hard she held herself in check. She wasn't the fragile thing he'd first pegged her. He came to her side, extending a hand. "Come on. With the two of us, we'll be eating in no time." Flashing her a grin, he hoped it would encourage her to push her mistake aside.

"I hope it doesn't stick to my ribs as well as that roast stuck to the pot." A shy smile tipped the corners of her mouth.

That-a-girl. "Let's hope it doesn't stick that well." They laughed together as she took his hand, stood, and let him lead her to the storage area.

****

The eggs, turned over once, thick slabs of ham fried golden brown, and sliced bread warmed by the stove had been remarkably tasty. Quite satisfying and filling, and her redeeming salvation, Morgan thought as she inhaled the once-again-fresh air within the cabin. She actually relaxed as they finished their pie and Luke related the happenings at the lumber site.

Swallowing her last bite, she leaned back and watched Luke devour the huge piece he'd had her serve him. What a patient, considerate man. "Thank you."

Luke paused with his fork midair. His brows rose. "For what?" He took his final bite and chewed as if truly oblivious.

She marveled at how he'd restrained his annoyance. "For not saying I'm stupid, for helping me fix another meal, and for making me cook it so I'd gain some confidence back."

His grin came quick and wide. Her heart

thudded just watching his eyes glisten.

"I did all that, did I?" He put down his fork, wiped his mouth on his napkin. How long his fingers were, how big his hands. Hands so strong and capable. Seemed she always noticed them.

"Yes, you did. And I thank you."

He shrugged as if nothing out of the ordinary had happened. "You weren't stupid. Stupid is when someone won't try. And if they don't try, they never learn. We learn by our mistakes. And you're a quick learner. You won't let that happen again."

His confidence in her sent a warm glow spiraling through her. Where had this rugged man gained his wisdom and compassion? It was humbling.

Embarrassed and more than furious with herself at how she reacted to his praise and steady gaze, she gathered dishes from the table and strode to the counter.

"What's the best way to scour the pot?" Lord, she hated to ask such a stupid—no, not stupid, maybe naïve—question. But she had no idea how to remove the thick black grime. Would he now realize the full scope of her ineptitude at so many things he'd banked on her knowing? She caught his grin out of the corner of her eye as she fetched the kettle of water from the stove.

"I'll dump the food out back, then just soak it in hot soapy water. By morning you should be able to get most of it off with a spoon or knife," he said, carrying the last utensils over. "A wire brush might help. I'll get it from the barn. When the pot's clean, fill it with lard and let it simmer on the stove for several hours. After it cools, dump the lard out, wipe it out with a rag, and coat the outside with the lard, too. That'll cure the cast iron and prevent it from rusting."

Rinsing the cleaned plates, she sighed in relief

that he hadn't glared at her incredulously. And, praise the saints above, he hadn't laughed outright.

She wondered just how long it would take to scrape the pot. Most likely all day. She deserved every minute of the tedious labor, she thought in despair. After all, if he could overlook her stupidity, and that's what it definitely had been, then she could do the necessary rectifying.

"Well, at least you had no trouble today at the site, right?" she asked, directing their conversation in other directions as she dried the last plate.

"Not really," he answered, banking the fire to ward off the now chilling night.

Could it be her imagination, or had he been evasive? "Not really?"

"Don't worry about it. You have enough here to think about." He came up behind her just as she stretched up on tiptoes to put the plates she'd dried onto the shelf overhead.

He reached over her head and took the two plates from her fingers. As he slid the dishes onto the shelf, Morgan experienced a curl of heat from where his fingers had skimmed hers. It traveled up her arms. This closeness was all too intimate for her to think straight.

"I'll get the pot." He went outside. She wrapped the remaining bread while she waited for his return. He'd definitely hedged on answering her. She should feel touched by his effort to prevent her worry. Instead, she bristled at his reluctance to share what had happened. They were in this fifty-fifty. That meant she should share the good with the bad. She had a right to know what they were up against. What to expect. Did he think her too faint-hearted to hear of mishaps? Desire to console him if he needed consoling seemed as natural as saying good morning. She'd prefer the luxury of offering some input if she could.

"It smells a little better," he said as he carried the still-offensive vessel to her side. "Doesn't look much better, though." He laughed, handing it to her. "Be happy there wasn't any real smoke, otherwise someone might have rung the bell."

"The bell? You mean the big bell in town? I'd meant to you ask you about it. "

"I should've told you before. It's used in case of a fire. Everyone within hearing distance will come running. Fires are our biggest threat. The wide clearings around each cabin and in town hopefully will prevent any fire from reaching the forests. If you hear it ringing, stop what you're doing and follow the smoke, or the smell, and then see what you can do to help."

"I will," she said, thankful the bell hadn't been rung. Her nose crinkled as she got a good whiff of the smelly pot. Almost hating to touch it, she accepted it and placed it in the empty basin. He lifted the other basin of hot soapy water and poured it for her.

"Just let it be for tonight. Tomorrow you can try to save it." Again his lips curled.

How devastatingly handsome he was when he smiled like that. Yet remembering his evasiveness of minutes ago cleared her dreamy mind.

"What happened today?" She wiped her hands on the towel, then handed it to him.

"I told you—"

"Don't try to protect me, Luke Kincaid," she said, folding her arms across her chest, her senses offended. "I may lack many skills I should have, but I do have a brain. And right now it's furious. I'm not a little girl you have to keep in the dark so I won't become alarmed."

She stared him down. Well, up, if truth be told.

He shrugged. "I just don't want you fretting about something you have no control over."

"No...Oh!" Her hands went to her hips. "I have a right to know. We're partners. That was the deal. We agreed to be honest, up front. That includes what happens out there."

He leaned against the counter, grinning, his eyes glinting humor. Looking all too blasted handsome by far, she thought, incensed by his obvious amusement.

The ass.

"You're very pretty when you get all riled. Did anyone ever tell you that?"

She clamped her mouth shut, halting her heated retort. She felt rattled by his nearness, his unexpected compliment. She wasn't sure how to respond to such praise. That'd been a rarity for her in her past.

"I..." Lord, words completely left her.

"I planned to go out and have a smoke," he said, thankfully saving her from more embarrassment. "But I'll tell you what you want to hear, first. Let's sit," he suggested as he put his palm against her back and motioned her toward the living room with a gentle nudge.

With her mind still tilted off center, especially now, with his gentle touch thrumming through her, she did his bidding. Once seated on the soft chair, she found her voice.

"You don't have to go outside to smoke, Luke. I find no offense in pipes. I'm sure you smoked in here before I came, and I apologize for you feeling as if you have to go out. Please go ahead. I really don't mind."

"You sure?"

"Very. Now, what happened?"

"Hank Jefferys, he's one of the chuters, had an accident when one of the chutes collapsed." He took several quick puffs inward on the highly polished tortoiseshell pipe as he held the match to the tobacco. She watched the bowl's contents glow, the smoke spiraling upward from his lips. A pleasing smell, sweet yet pungent, filled the air. He leaned back against the divan, holding the pipe an inch from his lips. How pleasant to watch a man enjoy such a simple pleasure.

When she frowned, he must have recognized her puzzlement over his statement. "If we down trees close enough to the river, we use oxen to drag them along what we call a skid road and push them into the water. Higher up and farther away, we use a high wire and chains to lift the logs up and onto a chute that sails them over the high banks and plunges them into the river. A chuter's one who loads the logs onto the chute."

When she nodded understanding, he continued. "The chute Hank was using separated at one of the connections. Logs went flying everywhere like they were matchsticks dumped from a box. Not just little logs, Morgan, but trunks four to five feet in diameter and two to three times their girth in length." He ran agitated fingers through his hair and took a quick puff on his pipe.

"Hank tried to jump out of the way, but two fell on him. They pinned him under their weight." His jaw squared and his cheekbones flexed as his eyes turned as dark as the angered sea she'd watched on the way to Seattle. "It's my job to see something like this doesn't happen."

She gasped, sitting up straighter in the chair as she pictured the scene of such huge columns of wood landing on a person. She cringed at hearing Luke's last words. Those few words spoke blatantly of his dejection, his guilt, and self-reproach. Whether the accident had been instigated by the mischief-makers or simply a fault of his own men, it obviously weighed mighty heavy on his conscience. He wasn't one to take his responsibilities lightly, she reasoned, knowing how conscientious he was in every aspect of his life. And right now his eyes bore witness to the sorrow, regret, and self-aimed anger he experienced.

"I'm so sorry, Luke. How bad is he?" She held her breath after asking. The man's injuries were sure to be severe. She felt a potent need to take Luke's hands in hers, offer him comfort in his time of such troubled thoughts. He'd most likely not welcome any pity. She doubted she could bear the intimacy of holding his strong hands within hers, though. No matter how much she wanted to.

As if foreign to him, he fingered the pipe bowl between two fingers, and stared at it. After a moment, he raised his troubled gaze back to her. "He's pretty busted up. Both thighs were crushed and most of his ribs. It was hard to tell if he had any internal bleeding in his belly or anywhere else." His eyes brightened a fraction. "At least he was conscious. In a lot of pain, but he didn't seem to have any back injury or feel like his gut had been torn inside."

"Where is he now? There's no doctor here, is there?"

"No, no doctor close by," he said through tight lips. "I sent a man by horseback to where Dr. Loomis lives, this side of Seattle. He'll find him before the wagon gets there."

Dear God, could a man last that long, being so hurt and having to travel rough terrain? She kept her concern silent rather than voice it aloud and cause him further distress.

"We patched him the best we could, gave him enough laudanum to knock him out. Three went with him, and two of them are pretty good at patching things up till Loomis takes over."

"But it was an accident, wasn't it?" she asked, hoping she'd hear his confirmation. "Surely the mischief-makers couldn't have had anything to do with such a thing."

She watched those eyes turn to heated jade, almost feral. He'd seemed so easygoing, more than accepting and understanding when she botched things up. She'd never thought to see this side of him and was thankful his wrath aimed elsewhere.

His fingers tightened around the pipe, his lips thinned, his eyes narrowed as he fixed her with a heated glare. She knew what his answer would be before he stated it.

"It was no accident, Morgan. Whoever did this isn't inexperienced at sabotage. And that's putting it mildly. They're vicious, merciless criminals, out to maim or kill anyone in their way. We make it a point to carefully check every piece of equipment every day to avoid something like this. Two of the men checked that chute before we left last night, knowing we'd use it today. Hell, even Hank, in so much pain, swore he'd checked it before leaving last night. I believe all of them. None of them would overlook our hard and fast rule. No way could that chute come apart without some tampering to the bolts and metal straps. I'll check tomorrow."

Silent, he held her gaze. Her mind scrambled for words to console him, to devise a plan to see this couldn't happen again, and realized how futile her efforts were. How could she be of any help? Yet she had to let him know she'd be there for him if he needed her.

"If I can ever help some way, I'll be more than glad to do it. And I'll pray with all my heart Hank recovers readily. I volunteered at the hospital occasionally, so I have some skill at caring for minor injuries if you ever need me."

For the first time since he'd disclosed what happened, he smiled. "You probably wouldn't have been able to do more, but thanks for your offer. And I'd appreciate any prayers for Hank. He'll need them. It's good to know you're willing to give some quick medical help. Thanks again. "

She smiled tentatively. "I've never seen logging. I feel so ignorant when you talk about monkeys and chuters and high wires. I never realized so much went into it. Or how dangerous it could be, even without someone trying to sabotage your efforts. It's really quite fascinating."

The glow of his smile warmed her clear across the room. "You're welcome to go with me to the site any day you like. As long as you stay where I tell you to stay so you won't get hurt."

"Do you mean it?" A thrill ran through her. There'd been only a handful of people in her life who'd shown any sincere regard for her desire to expand her knowledge. Most people had scoffed at her, a woman, for being even slightly interested in such things.

"I'd not offer if I wasn't serious. You name the day, and I'll take you." He turned his pipe upside down over the metal bowl that served as an ashtray and tapped out the tobacco. "It'll be a long day, most likely boring at times. But I'll try to stay close by and explain things as they happen so you can understand why we do things the way we do."

He seemed pleased she wanted to join him. His kindness shot to the deepest recess of her heart, while her pulse beat in anticipation, her excitement difficult to contain.

"I'd love to go. I can plant vegetables any day. Is one day better than another?"

When he shrugged his broad shoulders, she had to once again remind herself they were friends, to remember that for her own good.

"How's the day after tomorrow sound?"

"That would be perfect," she quickly answered, eager to see just what the loggers did.

His brow furrowed. Before she could comment,

he spoke.

"The preacher's only here for three more days. Not that it's any concern to anyone in this camp, but I think it's time I made a decent woman out of you." He leaned forward, rested his thick forearms across his thighs. "I'd planned to suggest we get married tomorrow night after supper, but out of respect for Hank, it might be better to wait a day. After we get back from the site, we could eat tomorrow's leftovers, then go straight to the saloon. What do you think?"

She grew uneasy, confused as he studied her with an enigmatic gaze. She bit her lip until it throbbed like her pulse. She knew it had to be done. But how…

"You're…engaged. I know we have to pretend we're married, but how can you actually stand before a minister…say vows that aren't…that aren't…"

He reached over, took her hands within his, squeezed gently. How large, how warm his felt. Again a sick kind of yearning assaulted her. If it could only be real. She chided herself for coveting another's fiancé. But covet him she did.

Certainly it could be no more than appreciation and a strong attraction she felt. After all, he'd allowed her to stay, had given her a means to earn money she'd need when she left. He'd been good-natured and tolerant of her ignorance.

And as far as his way-too-handsome face and magnificent physique setting her heart to hammering… Well, any single woman who shared such close quarters with him would feel an attraction. What really bothered her, she honestly admitted, was how her feelings for him grew every day. Knowing how easily she could allow herself to feel more, she closed her eyes and willed her useless thoughts away. That wasn't easy.

"I can say the vows because my name isn't Luke Kincaid. They'll be meaningless."

His confession should have shocked her, made her feel a hundred times better. Instead, her guilt and selfish yearnings seared deeper. She knew so little of him, didn't even know his true name, yet fantasized him being hers. She'd looked forward to her wedding day. She'd convinced herself that day would start a bright new future, hoping she and her husband would eventually feel some bond. Now that day would be no more than meaningless words said to someone she'd never have any future with. What a mockery.

"Your name isn't Luke?" Would it be easier to think of him as Luke, a fantasy man who only existed in her dreams? Would it lessen the ache from longing, the loneliness that threatened to destroy her composure? Could she separate the two, only feel drawn to the fictitious Luke?

"My name is Luke, but my last isn't Kincaid."

Distrusting her voice, she could only nod. No, no matter what other name he might have said, it would have made no difference. Swallowing down a lump, she cleared her throat.

"Two days would be fine." She forced a plaintive smile. It'd make no difference. He wasn't hers. Never would be.

There'd be no wedding night, no bright future with this man. All she could do was play her part for now. And when they walked their separate ways, she'd lose more than a friend and employer. She'd leave behind memories. No, she'd leave behind far more than treasured memories. If she wasn't careful, wise to the extreme, she just might leave part, if not all, of her heart as well.

Chapter Nine

The next morning Morgan found her excitement and frustration colliding to send her into a whirlwind of restless energy. Her adrenaline surged as she anticipated tomorrow's venture to the logging site—her feet light, her steps swift, her hands unable to go slower than a mile a minute.

She also realized her elation stemmed from Luke welcoming her company, his offering this outing because he appreciated her earnest zest to learn.

At the same time, mixed feelings regarding the wedding skyrocketed her anxiety, driving her to clean more thoroughly than she ever thought possible, in order to block out the event.

Determined to maintain her sanity, to avoid stewing about the mock marriage and focus on the thrilling aspect of seeing the men work tomorrow, she scrubbed everything that could possibly be scrubbed, harder than necessary. Corners that had never seen the light of day gleamed. She even dragged the rag rug outside—no easy feat to lug it outside and heft the cumbersome thing over two sawhorses she'd confiscated from the barn—and pounded the living daylights out of it with the broom, then grabbed the shovel and let it have it.

Sweat streamed down her temples and dripped off her nose as she hauled the hefty load back inside. Once it lay flat on the floor, she swiped her face with a towel, stretched her aching back, then plopped down on the divan that yet had to be moved back in place. With legs sprawled out in the most unladylike fashion, she took several deep breaths.

Total exhaustion, swift and draining, set in once she relaxed. She glowered, first at the stand, then at the chair she'd shoved into the kitchen, wishing each piece had wheels.

"No wonder mother has maids and servants."

Yet, as she eyed the spic-and-span interior, now absent of cobwebs and the smell of ancient dust, she smiled with pride. And damned if her fatiguing efforts didn't feel good.

With a jolt of invigoration, she pushed herself up, before lethargy returned, and began arranging the furniture. She positioned the couch to face the stove, angled the threadbare chair kitty-corner to its right, and set the nail-keg table between them.

For the fourth time in two hours she checked the stew in the kettle. No burning today, she vowed as she stirred the simmering contents. Sarah had brought biscuits and part of a chocolate cake with white frosting, earlier. Now Morgan felt even more grateful for the welcome addition. Maybe in a few days she'd hazard to bake. Until her courage returned to tackle such a feat, Luke would have to be content with Sarah's generous bounty.

****

By the time she heard the wagon, Morgan had the table set, her bath finished, and herself dressed in a clean shirtwaist and skirt. As she waited for him to tend the horses, she arranged the two sprays of feathery pine branches she'd picked only a few minutes ago, one on the table, the other on the stand in the living room. They at least added a bit of color and pleasant scent to the tidy cabin, she mused as she inhaled their fresh, clean fragrance.

Would he notice how much she'd cleaned, the pains she'd taken in making the stew? Would it matter to him that she'd poured her heart and soul into trying to do things right? Would it be to his liking that she'd rearranged the furniture, turned the rug, and added silly pines throughout? Oh, Lord, she was in a tizzy. Maybe she should've left well enough alone.

By the time Luke entered, she'd worked herself into another sweat. Dreading what might come if he took offense to her meddling where it wasn't wanted, she stirred the stew with so much force she nearly sent it spilling over the rim.

He hesitated in the doorway. He eyed the furniture, the rug, surveying the entire interior with a slow sweep of his head. Her heart nearly leaped out of her chest at his broad smile.

"You've certainly been the busy beaver today."

"I hope you like it." What a totally dumb thing to say.

"Believe me, I more than like it."

He stepped in farther, closed the door, and removed his jacket. When he turned and hung it on the hook to his left, she heard him chuckle.

"Good God, even the corner behind the wood pile is spotless. Poor spiders. They won't know where to nest anymore." He turned and grinned. "You know some people purposely keep a few spider webs on a log pile. They believe the webs help clot blood on a wound."

Her face heated, though his words pleased her immensely. She fairly beamed. "Supper's ready anytime you like. And no, I didn't know. I'll keep a few webs, but only a few."

"Smells great," he said, his brows drawing downward with a frown as he peered at the rug. She watched as he leaned over and scrutinized it more closely.

What on earth? Had he seen a spider running for cover? She'd thought she had rid the place of them. At least temporarily. Setting the wooden spoon across the pot's rim, she leaned forward, eager to see what his attention centered on.

"What is it?" she asked unable to see anything out of the ordinary.

"This can't be the same rug. When I left it was gray, maybe a few dull colors in it."

He cocked his head and their gazes met. When his eyes twinkled, a warm glow of satisfaction rippled through her. Pride nearly seeped from her pores.

"I dragged it outside and just about beat it to shreds." It had been a long time, a very long time, other than at the mission, since she'd felt the overwhelming tide of pride in something she'd accomplished. He certainly boosted her so-often battered self-esteem.

"It did wonders. Must have been some kind of day, for you to haul that bugger out and back. But it's sure a lot easier to breathe in here now. And supper sure smells good."

Feeling a bit self-conscious at his praise, and more rattled to feel the scudding of her heart as she stared into his warm eyes, she pulled her gaze away. She had to avoid times like this. Yet she only wanted to gaze into those dark green depths. *Lord, forgive my sin.*

"It's only beef stew. I'll dish it up if you're ready." By golly, it did smell good.

"That'll be fine. Just let me wash my face and hands."

While Luke cleaned up at the kitchen dishpan, Morgan took the stew pot to the table, set it on the trivet, and ladled hefty portions into bowls. As she carried the warmed biscuits over, her stomach growled with immense appetite. She wanted to devour the entire pot.

If she hadn't been so famished, and if Luke hadn't suggested adding quite a bit more pepper and salt, she would have curled up her nose at the bland flavor.

"It's okay for the cook to sample beforehand. I remember my mother always did." He laughed. "I think, from the little she ate at the table, she'd done a little more than just taste."

She stared at him, flabbergasted at such a suggestion. She'd never heard of such a thing. Why, her mother would be utterly appalled—she'd die of apoplexy!—if she ever thought she might gain germs of one of the cooks if they were to indulge in such habits. The picture her mind conjured up of her mother in a collapsing vapor made her smile.

"What's so funny?" he asked, wiping his mouth on his napkin.

"I…I guess I never thought about tasting it as it cooked."

"You don't have hoof-and-mouth, do you?" he asked, shuddering and flinching his shoulders. His grin belied his concern.

Despite her drooping confidence of minutes ago at having prepared such a tasteless meal, she burst out laughing. He certainly did boost her ego.

"No, I don't have hoof-and-mouth." She sent him a glare.

He exhaled an exaggerated sigh. "Well, thank God for that. So, no problem. Just taste what you're cooking and flavor it."

His expression grew serious. His brow furrowed as he rubbed his chin between his thumb and forefinger. "On second thought, you'd better wash the spoon off each time after sampling, before you put it back in. You might have consumption, or the plague, for that matter."

She had just dabbed the corners of mouth with her napkin. Before she realized what she'd done, she threw her napkin across the table. It hit him square in the face.

His laughter filled the room as he grabbed the cloth. Her mirth joined his.

She began gathering the dishes. "You're terrible, you know."

"I've been called worse. Is that the best you can do?"

His clowning tickled a spot, deep inside, she'd long ago suppressed. She'd almost forgotten what it could be like to laugh out loud instead of hiding behind a demure smile. How long had it been since she'd let down her guard? A long, long time ago, when alone.

When she'd sneak outside while others abided the afternoon naptime. Oh, yes, she'd laughed as she frolicked in the tall grass behind the school's dormitory. Running with the wind as she chased fluttering butterflies, pretending to be a light-footed fairy as she danced carefully over the wildflowers, darting after squirrels and rabbits scurrying back to their hidden homes…

So very long ago.

She banished her reflections as Luke pushed back his chair and rose from the table.

"Can't think of anything else to call me?" He smirked as he stacked his dishes and took them to the counter.

"None that should fall from my lips." With a grin of her own, she carried the kettle of water from the stove and poured a good amount into the basin.

"Chicken."

He stood behind her. She felt the heat from his body. Her blood turned fevered. How much longer could she hide her attraction? Knowing it would complicate their situation, force him to send her packing if he ever sensed her misplaced desire, she firmly buried her crazy yearnings.

"I'm simply smart enough to hold my tongue before I bury myself." She added soap and cool water from the pitcher.

His laughter floated around her, seeped into every pore. Dear God. How long would it be before he read it in her eyes? She'd have to avoid locking her gaze with his from now on.

"Yep, one mighty smart lady, indeed."

His words zoomed through her as if he'd stroked her skin with a feathery touch. Her knees weakened, her senses turned dizzy with want. She fought the headiness as her body shook from the sheer effort it took. *Dear God, Dear God, Dear God!*

"Need some help?" His breath fanned her nape, his male scent surrounding her, invading her senses. She swayed and nearly dropped the plate she fought to rinse.

"Ah, no." She swallowed, willed her hands to stop shaking. "Go sit down and enjoy your pipe. You worked a lot harder than I did today. I'll have these done in no time." Lord, but she could babble when her nerves were so strung out. Did he sense her nervousness, hear it in her voice? She had to stop allowing his nearness to rattle her so.

"If you're sure. I'm more than willing to help."

As soon as he stepped back—to a much safer distance—she gathered her wits, turned her head far enough to acknowledge him, yet not far enough to meet his gaze, and grinned. "I'm sure. Now go before I throw the dishrag at you. It won't be as easy to pull off your face as a napkin."

He chuckled. "Guess I better leave well enough alone."

"Smart man."

Luke retreated, sat on the divan, and struck a wooden match on his boot heel. Steadying the flame above the bowl, he took several long drags till the tobacco caught sufficiently. The satisfying sweetness of cherry blend touched his tongue, its fragrant aroma filling his nostrils.

He relaxed against the worn cushions, propped his boots up on the crude table, and smiled. And realized he did so not solely from the pleasure of relaxing and smoking the pipe but because of their easy banter after dinner.

More to the point, it pleased him to see Morgan's carefree nature spring to life. He'd enjoyed her joking, seeing her cautious inhibitions regarding cooking lift from her shoulders. Had she been censured for every move she made, before? It sure seemed that way. What kind of a life had she led? Not a pleasant one, if he figured right. Oh, yeah, he felt more than gratified she could discard those reserved mannerisms and be at ease around him.

But the more she did so, the more he witnessed her cheery side—the one that bubbled with excitement and enthusiasm, the one that put the bright sparkle in those eyes and a sunny smile on that sweet face—the more he felt threatened.

How long would it be before he found himself in a world of big trouble? She needed to leave sometime soon. Until then, he'd have to give her a wide berth. It'd be the only way this situation could work. The only way he could combat unwanted feelings that surreptitiously crept up on him, the desire that tormented him every time he looked at her, thought about her.

God have mercy on both them if he were ever tempted to act on his emotions. Oh, yeah, he would keep a good distance away. But would it be enough?

Chapter Ten

Though Morgan had slept like a baby through the night, her enthusiasm for the day to begin bubbled just beneath her subconscious. She awoke, wide-eyed and raring to go. But hearing Luke's footsteps tap against the packed dirt, she contained her eagerness to leap out of bed. Honoring their agreement of privacy, she kept her back to him.

Excitement jittered inside her. It became a chore to simply stare at the wall. She heard water being poured, a few splashes, the rustling of a towel. It took all her will power not to roll over, to steal a smidgeon of a peek at him while he performed his morning ritual. Temptation grew. Shook her with its force until she had to squeeze the quilt in both fists to resist.

Her mind's eye envisioned him leaning over the basin, his shoulders broad, his back unclothed and tapering down to the trim waist, snug buckskins hugging that appealing backside, molding long, muscular legs. His large hands splaying over his face as he briskly lathered his bearded face, then splashing water over it to rinse. Droplets of water clinging to his tanned cheeks, glistening on his bare chest and arms in the soft glow of the oil lamps while the fading night still painted the windows black…

Her throat went dry; her mouth salivated. The sudden urge to run her fingers through his beard and over his wet skin gripped her with a jolting force. Would his beard feel soft as raw cotton or bristly like straw? Would his skin be as smooth as a baby's bottom or like textured leather? A warmth eddied a path through her limbs, inciting a thrilling headiness, and settled at the junction of her thighs. She squirmed from the ache of it.

Good heavens above, perspiration coated her skin. She closed her eyes, shocked at her musings, appalled at the way her mind wandered, how easily her body reacted over such silly fantasies. Over him. Him, who was as unavailable as the man in the moon.

She definitely needed this outing. A means to focus her attention on the logging site in order to keep her head on straight. Otherwise she…she didn't have the foggiest notion which way her mind would go. Or what her silly heart might decide to long for.

Had her heart become involved? No, she insisted. Yet she knew she teetered on an untenable edge. Dear God, don't let it be. Her crazy notion had to be simple longing. The desire to have her own man, a home she'd call her own. Certainly, that's all it was. Funny, she mused, she'd always known someday she would marry, had looked forward to it, eventually, as most women did, but had never realized how much she longed for it.

"Wake up, sleepyhead. Time's flying by while you lie like a slug-a-bug. Up and at 'em."

His words stilled her jumbled mind. Feigning a yawn, she snuggled further under the quilt as if he'd truly awakened her. Good Lord above, if he only knew how her pulse had pitter-pattered at hearing him simply wash, the fantasies she'd conjured up. Oh, for shame, for shame.

"Come on. Clear that sand from your eyes. I'm going out to the barn to do chores and hook up the team. You'll need to be ready, breakfast on the table and lunches packed, by the time I get back, if you're going with me."

She rolled over, watched him pull his jacket from the hook, and stretch into it. Like every morning, merely seeing his bright smile, his sinewy physique, stirred her awareness, rattled her senses. Caused her wistful daydreams to leap non-sensibly.

Concentrate on what the day will bring.

With her voice almost a croak she said, "I'll be ready."

He nodded before closing the door. She shook her head to clear her thoughts. Determined to focus on anything other than the handsome man who set her heart to racing and her mind reeling in turmoil, she scurried out of bed.

****

Morgan's inquisitive eyes grew round as they pulled closer to the men already busy at setting their equipment in place to start the day. She'd fidgeted in anticipation ever since she mounted the wagon, had been running her mouth non-stop the whole way, squirming ever since they stopped to pick up Tom Hellmann, then Monk. All three men had politely and eagerly answered her questions, explaining various aspects of logging.

As Luke swooped her down off the seat, his powerful hands at her waist, she felt a thrill spiral through her from her head to her toes. Flustered by his innocent touch and the close proximity of their bodies as her feet touched the ground, she took a deep breath and quickly stepped back to calm her racing pulse. His eyes held a faint glint of humor. Had he felt her shiver? Hopefully he'd attribute it to her excitement. With great effort, she pulled her gaze away from his.

She spotted a man starting to shin up a wide tree. Fascinated, relieved to focus on something besides the man at her side, she turned fully toward the sight to watch.

The man wore spurs on his leather boots. An ax and saw dangled from his waist, while a thick rope belted him to the tree. He dug the spurs into the bark, flicked the rope upward, and climbed. Dug in, flicked the rope, climbed. Over and over he repeated the process, setting a rhythm until he reached the first parting limbs, almost halfway up.

Craning her neck, she followed his progress. He pressed the spurs in harder, leaned back a bit more, then pulled out his ax. With swift, effective whacks he chopped off the nearest limb and tackled the next within arm's reach. Harmlessly, they sailed down like great green ostrich feathers magnetized by the earth. As they pummeled the needle-covered ground, crisp snaps and sharp cracks rent the air. Then, only silence remained, the thick blanket of needles sending forth the scent of pine, fresh and robust, until the air filled with the intoxicating perfume.

Only then did she realize not a soul stood anywhere near the area. They knew to stay clear. "That's Stew Hawlings," Luke said at her side. "He's what's called a high climber. The bark's soft enough so he can bite those spurs in all the way to the top."

"He goes to the very top?" She turned her gaze to Luke. "But it's so high."

He grinned and nodded, then glanced upward. "That tree's about the average size we take down, but he's gone up ones that would make that look like a seedling."

Silently they watched as several more limbs sailed down, one splintering as it collided with the hard earth, the others thudding into the thick layer of pine needles. Though engrossed in Stew's toil, she still found herself sneaking a side glance at Luke's neck as it stretched back, intrigued by its thickness, how much the taut cords resembled rope.

"Actually," he said as he turned his head toward her, "he'll stop maybe ten to fifteen, sometimes twenty feet from the very top. I need to give some orders along the line, check out a few things before they start. If you promise not to go any closer, you can stay here and watch. Those limbs pretty much fall straight down, but one can always catch a slight wind. He'll be cutting the top shortly, and that's something I think you'll want to see. As soon as I'm done, I'll be back to take you around."

"I'd like to watch for a little longer. I'll stay right here until you get back. You needn't hurry on my account."

He smiled knowingly. "I'm glad you think it's so interesting. And I'm glad you came."

"Me, too." She returned his smile, wondering if spending the day at his side might prove total insanity—trouble waiting to happen, if mere glances his way could heat her blood so easily.

"Make sure you don't get any closer. I won't be long."

She watched his long-legged strides as he approached the others, a good hundred yards to her right. He seemed so confident, so in charge. She marveled at how easily he'd adapted to his role, a role foreign to him before coming here. She'd witnessed the friendly greetings from the group as they'd pulled to a stop, had recognized the respect in the many eyes directed his way. Her admiration for him had heightened considerably at knowing so many welcomed his expertise and authority. That's all she needed, she thought, sighing in despair. Just add another trait to his irresistible charm. Lord, she'd be doomed if she didn't straighten up and think logically.

As another limb crashed into a heap at the base of the tall column, her gaze swung back to the high climber. Better to focus on him than to mull over her foolish attraction to the boss. Stew had already ascended another twenty feet, climbing higher to reach the next fanning limb.

Morgan stood transfixed, observing limb after limb being axed or sawed. When he reached about twenty feet from the top, he leaned back against the rope and scanned the area left to right as if surveying the ends of the earth.

Only when someone touched her shoulder, and she turned her head to see it was Luke, did she realize she'd laughed out loud.

"He must be checking the wind, or how far up to go." She laughed again. "But I swear he looks as if he's just looking around like he hasn't a care in the world."

Luke chuckled, lightly squeezed her shoulder. How nice his palm felt, warm and so strong. Uh, oh. That silly little flutter that shouldn't be there stirred again in her chest.

"Yeah. That's exactly what's he's doing. Just looking around." He removed his hand and shook his head as if perturbed by Stew's action, yet his eyes twinkled with humor.

"The man's the best at what he does. But every time he reaches the mark where he'll top the tree—that's where he saws the top off," he explained. "He takes his damn good old time and enjoys the scenery."

She giggled at the mock annoyance in his voice. He chuckled along with her.

"You mean he really is just taking in the sights?"

"That's precisely what I mean. The company pays him top dollar by the hour, and he has the bold arrogance, the irritating audacity, to sit up there and daydream."

Oh, how hard he tried to sound exasperated, but the sparkle in his eyes told her another story. She laughed harder.

When Luke's brow creased, she basked in the

play of emotions on his face. The company might find it most annoying to know Stew deliberately wasted their money, but Luke didn't find it half as provoking. More humorous, if she read him correctly.

"I would think you could put a stop to it, since you're his boss." She really did try to go along with his feigned indignation as she took a step back to lean a shoulder against a thin tree. She needed to add a bit of distance between them. His scent, clean and manly, was just as intoxicating as the strong pine. More heady, actually, when mixed with his nearness.

"Sh…yeah, well, I may be boss," he said, shoving his hands in his pockets, "but you see how much clout I have when he's up there a hundred and eighty feet above me."

He offered her a sudden, arresting smile. One she found irresistibly devastating, way too sensuous for her to breathe normally. It weakened her knees until they just about folded beneath her. And as their gazes met, locked for one long moment, she could have sworn the rest of the world had suddenly vanished. Unwillingly, she felt something flare inside, something she dare not analyze. Something she knew she had to fight.

Shifting her attention to safer ground, she gazed up at Stew as he waved to the crew below. They too, she noted, stood out of harm's way, yet close enough to observe the coming spectacle while they began their own work. After the men returned his wave, Stew started topping the tree. The blade's hum echoed through the dense forest, all the way down to them.

Her excitement mounted as she waited for the finale. After several strokes, Stew paused, reached in his pocket, and retrieved a small object. He then glided the object along the cutting edge of the saw. Puzzled, she scowled, yet became more than eager to understand firsthand.

"What's he doing?" she asked, her gaze glued on Stew.

Luke took a step closer to her. She should have known better than to turn her head in his direction. How very handsome, this bearded man. Tall, all muscle, no classical refinement here, just rugged and sturdy. And all very appealing, disturbingly so.

"He's started the undercut," Luke explained, his gaze directed to the logger, "just like we do on the ground. It's a slanted cut so we can form a wedge. He's oiling the saw with kerosene from that little bottle, so the saw will glide easier, bite better. Once he's halfway through, he'll chop out a wedge with his ax. Keep watching."

She nodded, compelling her gaze upward. Stew repeated the process—saw, oil, saw, oil, till he must have been satisfied with the progress. Pocketing the bottle, he refastened his saw to his waist and started chipping away with his ax.

"He'll start sawing the back now," Luke explained as Stew holstered the ax before positioning the saw on the far side of the trunk. "That cut will open. This is the touchy part. Where skill and experience count one hundred percent."

As their gaze remained glued to the laboring man high above, Luke continued. "A high climber has to loosen his spurs exactly at the critical moment. He's got to be ready to move down and fast. If the tree splits, it can literally crush a man to death."

Morgan's throat went dry, her eyes widened in anticipation of success, in fear that Stew might fail to move quickly enough.

The top section swayed toward Stew. Her breath caught. As he sawed faster, perspiration broke out across her forehead. She wondered how much sweat poured down his. In one fluid, agile move, Stew swung to the backside of the tree. Morgan held her breath. His "Timber!" rang through the forest like an echoing foghorn. He sawed like there was no tomorrow.

Morgan trembled as her eyes took it all in. The rearing back of the trunk, the top breaking loose to sail through the air, soaring to the ground. Disregarding the top's crash to earth, her attention riveted on Stew as he clung to the tree. She swallowed back the lump in her throat as the tree snapped back from the thrust like a gigantic, quivering bowstring, then pitched forward. It arced the sky while the daredevil rode out the dangerous turbulence.

Stew's gleeful whoop bellowed across the land as the stately column bucked back and forth. Birds squawked in protest, scattering across the blue sky as they vacated their hidden domains within the surrounding pines. Only then, with Stew's loud yee-haw, did Morgan realize the man up there on top of nature's tall ladder was thoroughly enjoying his wild ride as much as—maybe more than—a child on a brand-new pony.

"Damn fool," Luke grumbled, yet his chortles joined forces with the fading blare. Oh, how she loved that rich, deep mirth. The tree slowed its swaying, then came to a standstill.

The men closest to them cheered, waving approval as Stew started sashaying back down to earth. While he shinned his rope-clinging descent, men scurried to the base of the defoliated trunk like ants working their hill. Fascinated, she watched three gather limbs and haul them farther away. Two others carried one huge saw to the tree's base.

Luke grasped her hand within his. "Come on, I'll show you what else is going on while they start their cuts. It'll take awhile before anything else interesting happens here."

Warmth brooked through her at his touch. She knew she should avoid such contact. It only stirred her blood more for what she had to forego. Despite her good sense, she allowed him to lead her away as she simply enjoyed their handholding.

Giving one last look over her shoulder at the enormous straight saw on the ground, the men busy at using axes to notch out what looked to be rectangles in the trunk, she scowled, reluctant to leave yet another eye-opening finale.

"Don't worry, I'll bring you back before it topples," he grinned at her obvious hesitation.

Only then, when she turned back to Luke, following at his side, did she notice ten or so others gathered across the clearing. The land curved gradually upward till land seemed to meet sky. Blue sky, bright and clear, offered a perfect day for the crews to accomplish what had to be done. She'd been so engrossed in Stew's spectacular ascent that she'd been oblivious to others working as diligently. *Amazing.*

With her interest piqued, her attention shifted to the team of four oxen straining, their mighty hooves burrowing deeply into the trampled soil. They hauled a tree, one she estimated must measure maybe thirty feet long and four to five feet wide, up the steady incline to where most of the men stood on the bank's crest.

Though anxious to see another aspect of lumbering, Morgan asked, "Why were the men axing out holes in that tree?"

Luke slowed his walk, his hand gently gloving hers. "They notch out rectangles just big enough to insert flat slabs to stand on. Like a ladder. They'll repeat it until they reach ten to twelve feet off the ground. Two men will saw a slant through half of the tree. It's easier cutting up higher, away from the base's fan. Plus we'll end up with a much straighter log. We saw closer to the ground if the tree's diameter is smaller. After the first cut, they'll saw out a wedge like Stew did with his ax. We'll go back to see the last part. I promised, remember? You'll see it fall."

Content for now with his explanation, Morgan stored that knowledge as they started up the slope. She could see the oxen's hides ripple with sheer effort, their legs toiling for all they were worth. The huge tree, fastened to the beasts by ropes, scuffled along the ground. Dismayed by the sight of the laboring animals, she pressed her lips together. She knew these were work animals, yet her heart ached to see such a grueling struggle.

Luke drew to a stop within ten feet of the pull. From this closer distance, Morgan noted how debarked logs, four abreast, had been buried into the path the tree rode on. They were just visible, just enough out of the earth that the tree would skid along more easily, she assumed. The oxen's hooves, because of the wide yoke between them, were able to dig into the ground adjacent to the buried logs. Their struggle still seemed brutally cruel.

"Those poor animals," she whispered before she realized she'd said it aloud. Would Luke take offense? Her gaze flew to his.

His smile, the softening of his eyes spoke his understanding. Her heart hammered.

"At first they strain a bit to get the tree in motion, but keep watching. After a minute or two, you'll see how the momentum becomes smoother so they can haul easily. Besides, God gave those big guys muscles and endurance you and I can't even imagine. They don't get hurt, or become sore. And believe me, they're just as content doing this as they are munching on their feed. The men assigned to their care make sure they're treated well after a long hard day. The same goes for the horses and mules."

Relieved by his explanation, and seeing the oxen struggle less as their burden now glided along more smoothly, she nodded.

When the oxen had gained the bank's edge, two men grabbed the yoke, halting their progress. Two others untied the tree. Once the animals were freed, they were led back down the way they'd come, apparently to repeat the process.

Luke took Morgan's hand again. "Come on, let's go to where you'll have a bird's eye view." Hand in hand, they scurried up the slope while four men positioned themselves along the prone tree.

Reaching the top, ten feet to the left of the men, Luke's hand tightened on hers. "This is close enough."

"The little lady wants to watch, huh, Buck?" one of the bearded men asked as he set a peculiar-looking tool onto the tree. *Buck?*

"Guess so, Martin," Luke smiled. "We'll keep out of your way. You go ahead and get that sucker down there."

"Take but a minute," Martin offered with a broad grin. The other three smiled, nodded their hello. Morgan eagerly returned their greeting.

She watched the three dig similar tools into the tree before she turned her gaze to the far side of the bank. Her breath caught at the sight.

The land dropped away at an almost straight decline, leaving them standing on a perch maybe five hundred feet above a gently flowing river where logs bobbled and bumped against each other, blanketing most of the glistening waterway. Downriver, a manmade dam allowed water to spill through while confining the logs.

A wide wooden chute, with supports every ten or so feet under it, ran down the length of land, almost from where the four men turned the new-cut log to the edge where the chute plunged into the clear azure stream. A hawk glided high overhead, as if inspecting the nestled, water-soaked logs for prey. Four men walked on the river's edge, two on each side, long poles in their hands as their muffled calls to each other rose upward. The air stirred with a mild breeze, ruffling the loose hairs at Morgan's temples, tousling the low verdant foliage, sun-kissed and thriving, along the wide riverbank. It carried a clean pine scent, the freshness of flowing water.

"It's so beautiful here." She turned to look at Luke.

"Yes, it is." His eyes gleamed in the bright sunlight, his smile just as sunny. Their gazes locked. Did he know how rapidly her pulse beat? Did he feel any stirring at all? She doubted it. Damning her silly imagination, she told herself to be grateful he obviously had better control of his senses than she did. Because if he didn't, they'd be in a world of deep trouble.

He let go of her hand and turned his attention to the men. She followed suit, knowing it best to center on the events, thankful he thought nothing of their handholding, of their everyday nearness. Yet she thought of the night ahead. Their wedding.

She reminded herself it did no good to dwell on what might have been had the situation between them been different. And called herself the biggest, dumbest fool in Washington.

Thankfully, her spirits lifted as the men, having turned the log ninety degrees with the spear-like tools, began tipping its end downward till it rested on the chute.

"Those hooks they're using are called peaveys," Luke explained. "Years back, loggers used swing dogs to move the logs around, but they were dangerous, and the work was no less than back-breaking. Some guy called Peavey, from Maine, came up with this idea. As you can see, it's no more than a long ash handle, an iron collar, and a curved spike-hook that swings back and bites into the log. The hook and collar move up and down but not sideways, allowing the users to have complete control in maneuvering a big log. I don't believe anyone uses the old swing dogs anymore. Peaveys are a major breakthrough for all loggers."

While Luke stood engrossed in the men's efforts, Morgan stole a quick glance his way. His voice had been full of pride. His face mirrored keen interest, concern for the men's welfare, and appreciation of a job well done. His features spoke of such strength of character she found her throat went dry.

She might be unable to claim this man at her side as a true husband, would never know him as a lover, but she'd always have a glowing admiration for him for what he believed in, for his genuine concern for others. Everyone she'd met obviously liked and duly respected him, especially as a competent, fair boss. That, in her book, spelled integrity with a capital I.

How easy it would be to give her heart to such a brilliant, caring man. Was that already happening? Dear God! She shivered despite the day's heat. What a frightening notion. She buried her silly daydreams, the scary possibility, and zeroed in on the men. They'd repositioned the peaveys and, on the count of three, heaved in unison. The log scudded a few inches till it teetered, nose facing the river, its end poked skyward. Watching carefully, she smiled as one of the men reached down and poured what looked like thin grease down the chute. On another count of three, the men again heaved in unison.

The tree inched forward; they released their hooks. It started moving, picking up speed quickly. Morgan's breath caught. Down, down it sped. Faster and faster it flew.

The hurling missile plunged into the river as if a

cannonball had been blasted. Water shot up in all directions, its whoosh thundering up the hillside. A glistening crystal fan sprayed the warm air, arcing skyward in a shimmering ray of colors. Just as suddenly, it descended like a dropped curtain.

The men beside her bellowed approval. Below, men gleefully jumped up and down, their own shouts lost in the distance, no more than drowned muffles.

"Did you time it, Martin?" Luke called above the cacophony, his laughter joining the hoopla.

"Twenty seconds flat again, Buck."

"Got to beat that, or the other camps'll show you up." Luke grinned as he winked at her.

"Next time we'll have her a-flyin' and a-singin'," Martin yelled back as he swiped his forearm across his forehead. His lips were pressed thin as if disgusted with the slow time. And here she'd thought the log had moved like lightning.

Luke nodded. "You do that. And make it count next time."

Martin saluted, picked up his peavey, and checked its hook.

"It's a well-known contest, to be the fastest chuter," Luke explained. "Every camp for miles around keeps a record of their times, so they can brag."

"Why do they call you Buck?"

He grinned sheepishly. "A woods boss is called a bull buck. They just like to get my goat." Was she supposed to understand? Luke took her hand. "Come on," he started leading her down the steep slope toward the river, "you'll love this part."

She hesitated a moment, unsure she wanted to follow him down the drastic decline, then clutched his hand in a death grip and dug in her heels with every step. When her footing slipped over a smooth rock, he righted her.

He dipped his head to the right. "We'll just go as

far as that big rock."

She eyed the large boulder. "Thank goodness." Mimicking his sideways steps, she felt her knees shake with each precarious inch she took, her palms sweating. Yet she knew Luke would be there, instantly providing assistance, if she were to falter.

They reached the flat-topped stone. "Sit here, and you'll see why Monk earned his name."

With knees wobbly, her palm clammy within his, she managed to get around the front of the rock and set herself down. She didn't release his hand or glance toward the river until she felt secure on her perch.

Then her eyes widened.

From this distance, she would not have recognized Monk. He gamboled across the wide expanse of bobbing logs as if he were high stepping to a lively tune on a dance floor. With both hands he gripped a long pole horizontally, cocking it one way and then the other for balance, his steps sure and fast, light and bouncy.

"See that jammed log?"

"Yes." It was, she realized, the one that had failed to break the twenty-second mark. Now it floated halfway across the river, angled and half roosted over another.

"He'll break it loose so it aligns with the others. If that one's left like it is, the next few coming down will likely pile up to make it worse. If that happens, they'll put way too much pressure on the dam. Or, when we blow the dam to release the load downstream, the jam can go crazy. Then all hell would break loose."

Appreciative of his explanation, she nodded, too thoroughly engrossed in Monk's skip-dance journey across the logs to turn Luke's way. Besides, it was best to avoid glancing his way. No sense in starting her treacherous musings all over again.

Monk balanced beside the disorderly newcomer and used his long pole much like a lance. He pushed and prodded, without any luck. Without hesitation, he hopped onto the half of the mischievous log that floated in the water. And, heaven behold, she thought in wonder, he began a tap dance to equal the best.

Was there music down there? His feet skipped, shuffled, tapped, all in rhythm to some tune in his mind. And as he did, the log started spinning to match the tempo of his feet.

Its revolving made her dizzy, until she had to blink to keep focus. In a move as graceful as any ballerina's, Monk leaped to the next log. Using the pole, he pushed the spinning log with all his might. The log barreled off its prey and splashed into the water, dousing Monk with a blast. It bobbed free, straightened out, and bumped the others. In perfect alignment.

The men along the riverbanks whooped at Monk's success. With his own howl he danced back across the moving walkway.

How much like young children these big lumbermen were, she thought in amazement, her laughter bubbling forth. Clowns, was more like it. But they were men, hardworking, with a mutual cause, and obviously true friends. Friends who watched out for each other, shared the good and bad, swore and sweated together, and who could laugh and banter with or at each other. The beauty of such a close-knit group touched her deep down inside. And their leader? Why, he'd already captured her heart.

Had he captured it? Dear, merciful Lord! How, why had she let this happen? She'd better reroute her emotions, and fast, if that were true. But how could she change how she felt? The solution remained far from any answer she could conjure up at present. Yet she vowed, then and there, she'd search for one.

She had to.

There could be no other recourse.

Chapter Eleven

Luke's breath hitched as he canvassed Morgan's engrossed fascination with Monk's antics. Her face spoke a thousand words. He marveled at her wide-eyed wonder, so intent and vital, so very natural and innocent. She thrived on viewing new happenings, anything different that offered insight, or greater knowledge. Her eagerness to absorb it all was like a recurring thirst, never quite satisfied, always ready to be quenched yet again and again. So much like an enthusiastic child.

He'd noted her deep-hearted concern when Monk fought for balance. Remembered the same expression when she'd watched others toil at their perilous tasks. Hell, she'd been equally distressed over the oxen. Morgan Prescott closeted her past, most of it, at least, but she had a heart as wide as the valley below.

Hearing her hearty laugh, observing her bright smile as Monk did his little dance at success, he felt a longing deep in his chest, constrictively painful, gratifyingly buoyant. It damn well wasn't how he should be feeling. What was happening to him, for Christ's sake? He'd offered to be her employer, her protector while she assisted him in his scam. He wanted to be, should be, a mere friend.

She might possess the eagerness of a zealous child, but as his gaze roamed her shapely curves, as he inhaled her clean, womanly scent, he had to admit she was all woman, through and through. A vivacious woman with a heart as warm and compassionate as a caring mother, plus an infectious zest for life that made him want to sit up and grab at life's pleasures along with her.

Regrettably, she'd whittled her way into his life far more than merely being a friend. More often than not, she occupied his mind and coerced a yearning in his heart too potent, too deep-seated, more than he could ever allow. Somehow, he'd have to keep their relationship at the level it should be. How he would do that posed the problem. Neither one of them could afford otherwise.

He'd think of Lucy more often, he concluded. Yet every day he did think of her in some way. Obviously that wasn't enough. From now on he would dwell on her, day in and night out. It'd be the only way to fight what could spell disaster.

"He's extraordinary!" Morgan laughed, clapping her hands in a round of applause along with the others.

Reluctantly, Luke glanced down toward Monk just as the man sprang off the logs to find sure footing along the bank below.

"That he is. The others down there are good, but Monk is the best I've ever seen." He watched Monk wipe the sweat from his brow with his forearm, then head, as usual, toward the wagon where a cup of coffee would wet his whistle after such a feat.

"He makes it look so easy," she said, swiping at a strand of hair that had pulled loose and now floated across her cheek with the gentle breeze. "As if it's all fun and games and no work or danger at all."

He watched her tuck the wayward lock behind her ear, noted how the sun's rays kissed the rich brown strands till various shades of fiery copper shimmered and mellow gold gleamed. His fingers itched to thread through each and every strand, to feel their silkiness, the soft curls. The thought jolted him.

He'd just resigned himself to making sure he kept their relationship platonic. What the hell was he thinking? Why the devil did he torment himself with crazy daydreams?

"Believe me," he said, unable to pull his eyes from her glorious thick mane, her bright-eyed face, "most of the men here do enjoy their work. Half the time, I swear, I don't think they look at it as a job."

Her smile widened. His heart lurched, his pulse quickened. He wiped his sweaty palms down his thighs.

"That's so wonderful. It certainly must make your job much easier, more enjoyable."

He swallowed. "Yeah. Yeah, it does."

With a great need to distance himself from her, to halt his alarming yearnings, he knew he'd better get her back to watch the toppling. Then he could immerse his energies elsewhere. He inhaled deeply and held out his hand to assist her over the rise.

When her small hand joined his, he sucked in a breath. Shit, he didn't want to feel such heated stirrings at her mere touch. But feel them he did. He gritted his teeth, prayed his sweaty hand didn't give him away, and led the way back.

None too slowly.

****

"You'll be out of harm's way if you sit on this stump." Luke stopped a good distance from where the men labored like crazy. With a man on each end pushing and pulling, the saw's blade filled the forest with a resonant, rhythmic hum.

She perched on a low stump, eager to view the next phase, dismayed to know Luke would abandon her at any moment. How ridiculous to feel the latter. After all, he'd been nice enough to bring her. He had a job to do. And he belonged to someone else.

With Luke's hasty departure, Morgan pushed

the fruitless fantasies from her mind and set an intent eye on the men felling the massive tree. And indeed, what a show they put on, she thought, as her adrenaline surged. Her fascination extended throughout sawing the tall column in half once it lay on the ground and the oxen hauling their burden up the bank. When the men coaxed her, assuring her safety, she eagerly accompanied them to observe as the two sections zoomed down the chute.

She hadn't realized several hours had passed until Luke came to her side and pronounced shutdown. It had been one wonderful day.

****

So now, in the eyes of all in the camp, we are married. Dear God above. Morgan felt like a blaspheming heathen. After a meager reheated supper and a hasty jaunt to the saloon, she, by all accounts, was Mrs. Luke Kincaid. The name tasted bitter on her silent tongue. It made this whole business she'd ventured into seem more heart-wrenching.

Accepting well wishes and jarring bear hugs from Rosie, Hans, and then everyone else present, she plastered on a smile of false contentment. And, all the while, she prayed Sarah's feelings wouldn't be hurt when she found out Morgan had chosen Rosie to stand up for her.

She'd had no choice, really, and had literally begged Rosie to do the honors since Luke had chosen Hans to be his best man. No way could she have fooled Sarah's keen instincts and perceptive eye during the ceremony. She would simply explain it had been a spur-of-the-moment decision upon finding the minister planning to leave within a day or two. Yes, she'd done the right thing. Yet the lie still didn't sit right.

But she would try her best to please Luke, to aid him all she could, and see to his needs as far as keeping a well-run household. Yes, she'd do her part while trying to bury her lie and her wistful reveries until she no longer could think about them.

****

"My God, woman, couldn't you smell it?"

Smoke billowed out the cabin door as soon as Luke flung it wide open, its hinges protesting. He ducked and stepped back and sideways as the cool breeze drew offensive black clouds outward in a rush, sending them spiraling upward in belching poufs. Hands on his hips, he stared at the rising haze as it poured skyward, filling the air with an acrid odor.

Standing behind him, Morgan shuddered at his bellow and cringed, watching helplessly as the thick curls of smoke rose above the roof to hang in the air like thick, heavy fog.

There'd be no bread tonight.

They'd be lucky if they were able to eat anything else within the cabin for the next week. How had this happened? She'd been so careful. At least she'd thought so. Diligently she had read and reread the instructions, kneaded until her wrists ached, allowed ample time for the second rise, checked the stove for the correct temperature as Sarah had advised.

Despite feeling disgusted and humiliated that she'd made another big error in front of Luke, she fought to remain undaunted and keep down the tears threatening to weaken her mettle. She'd cowered, hung her head, and accepted severe reprimands in the past. With her decision to come to Washington she'd made a pact with herself. She'd own up to her inept blunders when need be, but she'd be damned if she'd meekly be put down again. It certainly seemed harder to do so than she'd thought, but by God she would not cower as before.

"Apparently I did something wrong." She wrung

her hands back and forth, yet held her chin up, met his gaze straight on, though her eyes burned and watered from the foul smell.

"Apparently? I'd say..." He burst out laughing.

So much for not allowing herself to feel stupid. Her temper got the best of her. "What the hell's so funny, Luke Kincaid? This isn't a laughing matter."

She rammed a tightened fist against each hip, glaring at him so he'd feel as rotten as she did. The imbecile.

"I'd say the whole thing better be a laughing matter for now. When you're scrubbing smoke from everything in there, you won't feel like laughing. Do you know you swore?"

She fumed at his none-too-funny joke. It was far from any laughing matter to be the brunt of his hilarity.

"What the hell are you coo...*were* you cooking in there?"

Oh, how she'd love to wipe that smirk off his face. He held laughter back now, just barely. Yes, "imbecile" described him perfectly. And if she wanted to swear, by God she would.

"I was baking bread, Mr. Smarty Pants. And I followed everything I had written down. To a tee." Lord, but she felt deflated, she thought, letting her shoulders slump in defeat.

"Bread?" He glanced at the door, a smirk still playing along his lips. The smoke continued to accumulate within the confines of the cabin and then pour out the door. The air became heavier, more pungent. Her nose wrinkled, her eyes stung.

She watched him amble to the doorway, crouch over, lowering his head below the low-lying clouds and peek inside. He turned his head her direction.

"Where's the potholders?"

"On the hooks."

"I'm going in to bring the loaves out. How

many?"

"Five...but you shouldn't have to do it. It's my fault."

He hesitated as if he considered she might be right. "I'll get them." He took a red handkerchief from his pocket, folded it into a triangle to cover his nose and mouth, and tied it behind his head. In he went.

Once he'd brought all five tins outside to sit on the ground and scraped out charred dough that had oozed all over the oven, the air in the cabin started to clear. He eagerly accepted the glass of water Morgan offered. Plopping down on a stump, he wiped his sweaty forehead and tearing eyes with his handkerchief and then took large gulps to quench his parched throat.

He glanced at the charred mess she'd removed from the blackened and encrusted pans. Damn. Only moments ago she'd sounded so pleased at baking bread. "I'd say your bread rose more than enough."

He watched her scowl at the dark scrapings he'd chiseled from the oven's shelves before bringing them outside on a board. "I'd say your conclusion is right. I'm just not sure why. Will someone be ringing the bell?"

"Wasn't quite enough smoke for anyone to see." He chuckled. "And I'm sure Sarah will know what happened." Now that the worst had been put to rest, he regretted the flare of his temper, wishing he could make her feel better. He hated it when she looked so crestfallen.

"I certainly hope so. Otherwise, I don't believe I'll ever try baking again."

His brow rose in surprise as he ladled water into his glass. "Never figured you for a quitter."

Her glower grew fierce as she eyed the cremated debris. "I'd not call it quitting to know when one is better off not attempting the impossible. I'd call it good sense." Her lips curled upward a fraction.

That a girl. He'd hoped for that response. He felt himself relax. She'd feel better soon and get her confidence back.

He laughed, nearly gagging on the mouthful of water he'd just taken. "I remember a very wise saying: 'If at first you don't succeed, try, try again.'"

Her smile broadened, her dark eyes took on the twinkles he found so bewitching. His heart flitted. "It's your cabin. If you don't value it any more than that, I'll certainly try again."

They were both smiling when their gazes locked.

Luke swallowed the lump in his throat and knew it had nothing to do with the smoke. His pulse quickened. He felt that potent urge once again to enfold her within his arms, to reassure her everything would be better next time. To wipe away all her feelings of inadequacy. To soothe her ruffled feathers.

He nearly reached for her but came to his senses, thank God. *You're walking on forbidden ground here,* he reminded himself. Walking too fine a line for either of them.

With sheer will power, he dragged his gaze from hers. "It's you who'll have to clean up the mess. I don't mind another attempt, as long as you clean up after." He forced a grin, gulped down another long draught of water to relieve his tight throat. It didn't begin to placate the heated turmoil within.

He again questioned her past. Obviously she'd not had much training in cooking or baking. He remembered her so-called eagerness to watch him fix coffee and prepare the oatmeal. She'd stated she needed to know where things were. Had she been observing him even then to see how to do those simple tasks? This woman didn't hail from a run-of-the-mill family. He'd be more observant from now on and see what the future told.

Chapter Twelve

Spending the next afternoon at Sarah's was exactly what Morgan needed to boost her blue spirit. Just being in the zealous woman's presence and watching her buzz to and fro as she merrily flitted throughout her kitchen would boost the heaviest of hearts. After drying the large pottery bowl, Morgan reached up to put it into the overhead cupboard. She felt the skittish apprehension at attempting to bake bread again lessen a few degrees. Felt her first true smile of the day.

"I'm sure that's what happened," Sarah said, testing the two chocolate cakes cooling on racks with the back of her hand. She nodded as if satisfied. "It couldn't be anything else, dear."

Morgan watched Sarah hold over one layer a sparkling glass plate that seemed out of place in the crude cabin, then slip her thumbs under the cooling rack. Before Morgan could blink an eye, Sarah had the rack, cake, and plate inverted. Lo and behold, the cake rested perfectly in the middle of the glorious platter.

Amazed at the impressive maneuver, Morgan wondered if she'd ever match such a feat. Instead of the smooth flowing expertise, she'd most likely end up with one very smashed, totally ruined cake upon the dirt floor. It'd be some time before she'd try that same trick, she conceded. She'd get the cake off the rack one way or the other, but not by flipping—not for a while, anyway.

"I could swear the water was only lukewarm."

She stacked the cleaned cake pans on top of each other and bent to put them below the counter where Sarah said they belonged.

"Yes, but yeast can be very persnickety. Just a few degrees too warm can cause it to go wild." Sitting at the table, Sarah paused in stirring the chocolate butter icing, dabbed her finger in and tasted. Her eyes lit with pleasure. "Mmm! That's the best frosting this side of the Mississippi, if I do say so myself." She set the bowl down, lifted a bread knife, and began frosting the top of one round layer. "My grandma once told me to sprinkle a few drops on my inner wrist, like testing milk for a baby. If it feels warm and toasty, then it's just a mite too hot."

She licked frosting off her thumb, then set the second layer atop the first. Morgan smiled, remembering how Luke said most good cooks sample their creations. Sarah was no exception.

"Been so long since I've been baking, I plum forgot her little tip. I'm sorry I didn't think to mention it to you."

Every step in baking the cake and making the frosting had been surveyed by Morgan's eagle eye. Baking a cake seemed far less tedious than the blasted bread. She'd attempt one, and soon. For sure Luke would like a cake. Though her courage to try bread once more had been fortified, she'd definitely prefer to make a cake first. Way before she tackled bread again.

****

The churning and clatter of wooden wheels mixed with the heavy plodding of horses heralded Luke's arrival at Sarah's cabin. Morgan glanced out the front window, surprised at her eagerness to see him. This excitement, this anticipation she felt each time she knew he drew near had to stop. Yet her heart beat faster and her happiness bubbled forth.

She had to squint through the panes now that

dusk had set in. The tall forest rose behind the wagon, resembling a huge black mountain, while the setting sun glinted over the wagon in a silver veil. Her eyes feasted on the strong, tall man up on the high seat as he laughed and said his farewell to Tom. Her pulse scurried, her cheeks heated.

Sarah opened the door. “Luke, hold on. Morgan’s just gathering her things. She’ll be right out.”

Morgan chided herself for her non-sensible reaction as she grabbed her shawl and Sarah’s basket.

“Thank you so much for the two pieces of cake, Sarah. Luke will drool when he sees them.”

“Land sakes, dear, it’s the least I can do. Got to keep that man happy while you learn.” Her smile, as always, was genuine, her eyes filled with warmth. “And you will, you know. You’ve already come a long ways. You just need more practice.”

Morgan laughed and hugged her friend, basket and all. “How can I not succeed, with you rooting for me and leading the way step by step?” Though Sarah had said she understood completely, Morgan still regretted she’d chosen Rosie to stand up for her.

Sarah returned the hug, her grip energetic and almost crushing before she stepped back. “You better believe it. So you just set your mind to it, young lady, and you’ll be a superb cook in no time. And you try that spice cake tomorrow. You’ve got everything you need, so go to it.”

****

The next morning, as soon as Luke left, Morgan set the basket on the table, anxious to create a cake. If she accomplished nothing else today, so be it. She’d take it slow. Withdrawing each item, she cautiously read instructions, measured precisely.

All last evening she’d been eager for her next essay at baking. Especially after watching how Luke had gobbled down Sarah’s chocolate cake. His eyes had turned a deep jade, twinkling with pure pleasure as he licked the last crumbs and frosting from his lips with a sigh. Her pulse had quickened at seeing his tongue skim his lips. Good Lord, even now, with just the memory of that sensuous act, she felt all hot and bothered.

Shaking her head at her wayward reaction, she forced her mind to the task ahead. Better to concentrate on her project than to let her heart feed such thoughts. She threw herself into baking the best damn cake this side of the Mississippi.

****

"The meal was delicious, Morgan. You outdid yourself."

Morgan beamed at Luke's compliment. It had been a simple dinner. Fried slabs of ham, boiled squash and potatoes, bread and butter that Luke had bought from Monk. Nonetheless, she found herself proud that all had gone so well.

Now for the final test, she thought with trepidation. The cake certainly looked delectable. Smelled so, too, if she said so herself. With hands a bit shaky, she carted the last dishes to the counter, picked up her creation, and brought it to the table.

"You want more coffee?" Luke asked, lifting the pot from the trivet.

"Yes, please."

She sliced two pieces of cake and placed them on plates while Luke filled both cups. She had caught his grin of approval when he spotted the cake as he entered the cabin. She'd laughed silently. He most likely had been amazed the cabin didn't reek of smoke again and was shocked to find she'd actually baked without some catastrophe.

From beneath lowered lashes, Morgan peered his way as he took his first bite of cake. She didn't realize she had held her breath until his smile crinkled the lines around his eyes. Her breath left her lungs with a whoosh.

"Woman, you might find bread-making an ordeal, but your cake is perfection. You can bake me any kind, any time your heart desires."

His words sent such contentment, such self-satisfaction spiraling through her she had to blink back joyful tears. Elation nearly clogged her throat. All morning she had sweated through the entire process. All afternoon she had fretted it wouldn't be as good as she hoped.

And all the while she had thought her anxiety stemmed from simply needing to do something this new and strange, to master what she thought of as a big step. Now she realized she wanted to please Luke just as much as she wanted to satisfy herself. Maybe even more so.

Of course she would want to please her friend and partner. No, there was more. Oh, the shame of it. Guilt poured over her at harboring such a sinful longing. She knew, no matter how much she tried to pretend otherwise, her feelings ran much deeper. Deeper with each passing day.

Determined to set her thinking straight, to ignore the constant pull of her tender heartstrings, she lifted a piece of cake to her mouth.

Tangy cinnamon and succulent nutmeg tickled her tongue, pleasantly teased her nose, while she savored the sweetness of both cake and creamy frosting. With soothing delight, she closed her eyes and let the deliciousness melt within her mouth.

"I take it you agree," he laughed, bringing her eyes open.

She watched him take another large bite, hold it and swirl it around in his mouth, as if reluctant to swallow it down and lose its flavor.

He finally swallowed. "Mmm, my God, that's good. I might be stuffed right now, but I think I might have to have another piece after a while."

His eyes took on that deep shade of jade, twinkling and gleaming as if dusted by a thousand stars. The magnetism of his smile brought about one of her own, while her heart hammered within her chest. If only his eyes would darken like that when he looked at her. She gripped the fork tighter.

"I'm glad it turned out so well. You don't know how much I worried about it all day." She prayed he couldn't read her mind.

"Like I said before, you can bake me a cake any time you like." His smile broadened. "You'll have to take Sarah and Tom some. She'll be as pleased as you are at your success."

"What a wonderful idea. For a change, I can take them something. I'll do it tomorrow, first thing." Of course, she silently mused, that's after I bake another kind for you.

Their eyes met and, for one breathless minute, she found it difficult to breathe. For the briefest moment, there seemed to be a spark of some indefinable emotion in his eyes. She averted her gaze, unsettled by the tide of emotions stirring inside. Staring at those intriguing eyes, that wide, full mouth, his broad shoulders, could get a woman in trouble. She knew so little about him, really. Talking would surely bring her to her senses.

She pushed away from the table and gathered the empty plates and forks so she could busy her hands and cease her useless thoughts. The cups full of coffee she left, intending to finish hers after she calmed down by doing the dishes.

"Do you like cakes better than pies?" How utterly dumb and feminine. Why couldn't she have asked something else?

He leaned back against the chair slats, held up a match to his pipe and took a long drag to catch the flame as she brought the kettle to the kitchen.

"I like just about every kind of food, as you

probably realize, but yes, I prefer cakes to pies."

She nodded, feeling restless, pondering how to quash the unsettling that she always felt when her heart screamed she wanted more from this man than he could offer. He had a fiancée, after all. She scrubbed the plate harder.

Had he ever even mentioned her name? Maybe if she could view her more vividly she could negate these crazy cravings.

"You know, I don't know much about you," she said, making quick work of the dishes and pans. While she wiped them dry, she sniffed the air, pleased with the fragrance of his tobacco as he puffed small billows into the air.

His brows arched and she noticed the inherent strength in his face, how the lamp's glow glinted off the lighter strands of hair, turning them a deep gold against the rich chestnut.

"What's there to know?" His grin flashed, dazzling against his bearded face.

Lord, just the briefest grin had her pulse darting. Turning back to the cupboards, she replaced the dishes where they belonged, then wiped her hands dry. She wondered if she would be prying if she were to ask about his intended. It would be safe ground. Safer and more sensible, by a long shot.

Casually as she could, she asked, "What's your fiancée's name?"

She sat down and lifted her cup to take a sip. His expression stilled, grew somber. He quickly tried to mask his reaction with a bland smile, but not quick enough that she hadn't noticed. She'd recognized the unspoken pain, alive and glowing in his eyes for that split second.

As clear as a bell, she recalled him saying she'd been ill. Stirring uneasily in the chair, she chastised herself for asking about something that obviously distressed him. She shuddered inwardly at the thought of causing him sorrow.

"Her name's Lucilla, but she goes by Lucy." His face reflected his tension.

Contrite, Morgan placed her hand on his. Felt its warmth, the rougher skin against her softness. The unruly flutter of her heart only accentuated the annoyance she felt with herself. To her dismay, her voice broke. "I'm sorry, Luke."

His luminous eyes widened. "What are you sorry for?"

She forced herself to settle down as she withdrew her hand. *This is not the time to let your emotions rule.* She almost laughed at the absurdity. She'd never be able to let her emotions show to him. At least not the passion she felt toward him.

"I'm sorry I asked about your fiancée and dredged up reminders of her illness."

His eyes softened and he seemed to relax. "You didn't. No more than every day holds."

"Well, I won't ask again. I am sorry."

His smile brightened, his eyes warm and contemplative. "No reason to be. She's been sick for a long time. I'm pretty used to it, but at times, times like now, when I've left her care totally to others, I feel like I'm letting her down."

She felt his need to be reassured as if it were a tangible force, groping and prodding her to provide it. Yet without knowing the full details she felt at a loss to give any reinforcement. She had thought gaining a name and possibly a bit of information regarding his intended would bring reality closer, stop her willful longing. Did she possess enough fortitude to discuss Lucy in more detail? Instead of curbing her attraction toward him, more information might just break her heart in two.

He squirmed in the chair, his fingers, tapered and strong, playing with the cup's handle as if anxious to talk more. Despite her dread, she felt compelled to offer him the release he might need. After all, she had started this damn discussion. Now she'd have to bear it. Full measure.

"I'm sure you must have left her in capable hands." Morgan took a sip of her coffee. It had now cooled considerably, but at least it helped quench the dryness.

He, too, took a hefty gulp of the brew. Setting the cup down, he frowned as his eyes met hers. "I hope you're right. I've had several different people care for her. They don't stay very long. I only recently hired Mrs. Aueteby. She seemed capable, but I never know."

"What does...she suffer from?" She found it too difficult to say her actual name just yet. Would she ever be able to say it aloud without feeling such an agonizing maelstrom? Merely thinking of her as...as...Lucy signified her as a real person. An ailing woman, but the one who had captured Luke's heart, who now stole his attention. The thought pierced her tender chest as if a sharp knife had been thrust into it.

She watched as he leaned back in the chair and drew on his pipe again. As he exhaled, a cloud of sweet smoke rose overhead.

"She has amyotrophic lateral sclerosis," he replied, his voice resigned.

"Ama..."

His eyes glimmered with humor. "Amyo... trophic lateral scler...osis." When her brows drew together, he continued. "It's a degenerative disease that affects the spinal cord. At first, when she would lose the strength in her legs and fall, the doctor said she was much too young to have it. But after the symptoms worsened, he concluded he'd been right. I took her to the best specialists in the country, to see if another could help some way. But they all agreed it would progress, worsen day by day. Since it's only been discovered recently, there's no cure." His words faded as if his throat had clogged.

"How old is Lucy?" She forced herself to call her by name. It was the least she could do while he sat there remembering, suffering, agonizing over his love.

"She's now twenty-eight. Twenty-six when we became engaged." His square jaw, though hidden beneath the beard, tensed visibly, and the fingers of his right hand clenched the pipe bowl till she thought it might splinter.

"How long has she been ill?"

He glanced across the room as if it tormented him to continue. Should she forget this discussion? Maybe this wasn't what he needed. She wished she had kept her big mouth shut.

"Since about a week after the engagement." His mouth twisted wryly before he brought the pipe to his lips.

Dear God, a week of engagement bliss, and then disaster. Her heart ached so mightily she had to fight back the urge to wrap her arms around him, to comfort him. Surprisingly, she also experienced overwhelming despair for Lucy. How strange, she thought, to feel something that strong about a woman she neither knew nor had wanted to know. A woman who, by all accounts, would have every right to despise Morgan for coveting her fiancé.

"That's so unfair." Her eyes brimmed with sincere moisture she could no longer suppress. Frustrated by a conglomeration of feelings, she threaded her hands together on her lap to stop their trembling.

"Life's full of surprises, Morgan. Whether they're fair or not, we learn to live with them." His voice sounded gruff and bitter. Could she blame him?

"Yes, but to be denied a happy marriage, an

engagement of more than a short week…it's too…" She bit her lower lip to curtail threatening tears. She'd believed her life to be so unhappy. How insignificant her troubles seemed, now that she'd heard of Lucy's devastation.

"Is she able to walk at all?" she asked, needing facts so she could gather her composure.

He held her gaze, his flat, vacant eyes prolonging the moment. "No, she became bedridden within several months after her legs started weakening. She has some use of her arms or hands, but they tire easily. Even her speech is down to a whisper. Most of the time she only nods, to save her energy. When I left, it was becoming a chore for her to eat or take liquids. Eventually she'll lose what arm and hand movement she has, and speech—she won't be able even to whisper. I've tried to spend as much time with her as I can, and when I'm not there I've had staff looking after her. I write to her about once a week, during lunch. I had a hard time making the decision to leave for this long, but she encouraged me to do it."

His words took her breath away. Poor, poor Lucy. Unable to block out the pathetic picture of a twenty-eight-year-old woman in such dire straits, most likely a beauty and sweetness personified since he'd chosen her for his fianceé, she allowed the tears free rein.

"I'm so sorry, Luke…truly sorry. These past two years must have very hard on both of you. All your plans destroyed, all your hopes for a family… You…must love her very much."

As she swiped the wetness from her cheeks with trembling fingers, guilt rose up like an iron weight. How could she have ever let herself fantasize about Luke the way she had? It had been sinful enough before, but now regret, raw and painful as any brutal wound, twisted and burned in her gut. She deserved every torture her conscience could conjure up. More, actually.

His expression turned taut, derisive. His gaze lowered as did his voice. "Yes, I love Lucy very much. Always have, ever since we were youngsters running through the fields to see who could catch a frog first at the pond."

His declaration gut-punched her, staggered her mind till it spun like a top. What had she expected? She should be happy he had been there for her through this trying time. And truly she was. Yet, at the same time, knife-piercing torment thrust deep within her heart, leaving her totally disheartened. Maybe she had a simple mind, a closed-eyed naivety. If so, she needed to be wiser, to toughen up.

Lifting her chin, she struggled for self-control. "She's very lucky to have you."

He stiffened as though she'd struck him. When he spoke, his tongue turned heavy with sarcasm. "She isn't anything of the sort."

She gasped at his vehement response. "How can you say that?"

He sighed, deep and long, and hunched over till his arms rested on his thighs. He'd rolled back his sleeves, and she watched the sinew of his forearms grow taut and flex, his hands fist tightly. She could almost feel his inner battle to temper his simmering anger. When he raised his head, unspoken pain reared alive and glowing in his eyes, cold as green ice.

"We were too close, too good friends, that's why. More like brother and sister. Unfortunately, we didn't realize what a detriment that would be until the night we became engaged." He pulled his gaze from her, leaving her frowning in question.

She had to mentally repeat what he might have inferred. Had they become lovers? Her heart took a tumble, air swooshed from her lungs. Heavenly days.

She could only stare, wordlessly.

The silence lengthened between them, making her uncomfortable. What could she possibly say at this point? He saved her from further dilemma when he cleared his throat.

"Believe me when I say I love Lucy with all my heart. I'd give my life for hers if it would do any good. Her parents died when their house burned down while she was visiting her ailing aunt back east. Her aunt died during Lucy's stay. Lucy was left penniless and alone. We were such good friends I proposed marriage, thinking it would be a good, logical match."

He leaned back, set the unlit pipe on the table, and then ran a hand across his beard. His sigh nearly tore her heart in two. He looked her straight in the eye. The urge to squirm became paramount, yet she sat still so he might unburden his frustrations.

"Without going into detail, the night I proposed, we drank wine, too much wine, and got more than a bit carried away. I didn't take her innocence, but it left us both feeling more than awkward, more than disappointed. We both realized our feelings for one another lacked the kind of passion one hopes for in a marriage. Yet we agreed to give it time, to make our future marriage work in all other ways. We hoped eventually we would find that special spark."

Morgan's eyes widened.

His lips curled slightly, obviously reading her surprise at his bluntness.

She managed a shy smile but, sinner that she'd become, felt enormous relief.

"By the end of that week, her health had deteriorated. Our engagement became a relationship of near invalid and caregiver. Don't get me wrong. I still love her dearly. Always will. But like a sister. I've tried to provide the best care and comfort for her. And, hopefully, some happiness. As happy as she can be under such dire circumstances. But unfortunately she wasn't lucky to have me as her fiancé. She'll never know the true meaning of…"

A passionate love, she silently finished for him.

"A lover," he whispered dejectedly.

And neither will I, as long as you're her fiancé. Tears of anguish for this man, and for Lucy, clogged her throat. She had to swallow down the lump before exhaling. Yet her eyes remained dry. They might have lacked that spark he'd spoken of, but the love he and Lucy shared was far too precious, too far beyond most people's good fortune, to shed tears of sadness.

"Like I said, she's a very lucky lady. Without your tender love and consistent caring, I'm sure she would have had a much harder time throughout her illness. You should be overjoyed you were the one she accepted. Had it been anyone else, she might not have had the means to hire good help, or the understanding of such a patient and attentive fiancé or husband. It sounds to me as if you've been her security by always being there for her—in body or mind, her very best friend, and her reason to go on living. Be thankful you've given her such a very precious gift. Many people never experience such a relationship as you two have shared."

He frowned, his eyes level under drawn brows. His gaze met hers, and for one instant a smidgen of a smile found its way through the mask of uncertainty. She watched several expressions streak across his face—doubt and wistfulness, pain and fulfillment—then a wide grin overtook his features.

He chuckled. "For someone who's been so vilified in the past, has so many travails at cooking, and has your streak of stubbornness, you possess the most uncanny compassion and wisdom I've ever had the pleasure of encountering. Thank you."

Easily, Morgan returned his broad smile, feeling a warm glow flow through her while she gloried briefly in the shared moment. Putting her own feelings aside, her heart sang with delight at hearing he recognized and accepted what he had bestowed upon his fiancée. How blissfully happy, fully alive, she felt at his praise.

Praise? He had called her stubborn.

She sat up straighter, lifted her chin and placed hands to hips. “I’m never stubborn.”

Luke whooped with laughter at her comeback. He had calculated mere seconds for his words to register. She’d not disappointed him. He watched those dark eyes ignite with amber sparks, as if yellow diamonds glimmered on a soft bed of sable. Unfortunately, not only did he appreciate such loveliness, but his libido caught flame, as well. Too damn easily, by far. Oh, yeah, some tower of security for Lucy, all right.

“Yes, stubborn.” He chuckled to hide his tumultuous reaction. He felt frustrated, disgusted. “Once you make your mind up to do something, nothing stands in your way. You set out for God’s country thinking you had no other choice, didn’t you? And when I intended to send you back, you stood your ground, convincing me to let you stay. I’d say that’s stubborn.”

She wrinkled her nose, eying him with irritation, yet her lips twitched. “Is that so bad?”

When their gazes locked, he found it incredibly difficult to think past his raging yearnings.

“No, not at all,” he forced past his dry throat, unable to pull his eyes away, almost drowning in those dark chestnut pools and wondering if that wasn’t what he truly wanted. A gamut of conflicting emotions rushed his senses; he was swimming through a haze of feelings and desires too complex to decipher. Unbidden hunger, raw and swift, rose up like a demon from hell, made him long to reach out, to touch that petal-soft skin, to kiss those delectable lips till they reddened, to assault her senses until they matched his…

Girding himself with resolve, he pushed up from the table. He needed to separate himself from this woman before he overlooked the fact he had an ailing fiancée back home. Cool air and a safe distance would certainly help. At least he hoped it would.

He moved to the door. "I need to check the animals before turning in. They had a long day." Grabbing his jacket off the peg, he was none too happy with himself when he saw the sudden astounded widening of her eyes. What must she think of his jack-in-the-box reaction? Most likely she thought him a mixed-up fool.

Ten kinds of a fool, he chided, closing the door. A fool for losing himself in her eyes even for a moment; for allowing his libido to rise as it had; for his reckless musings every time he thought about her; for forgetting her innocence, her dependence upon him. A selfish fool for betraying sweet Lucy—though only mentally—who lay fighting for her life.

He stormed across the darkened yard, hammering the new blades of grass with his heavy steps. He needed to focus on the problems he'd been sent here to rectify. He'd avoided telling Morgan of the trouble at the camp today, of their equipment being half destroyed. Maybe he should have told her, concentrated on the issue at hand instead of dreaming pipe dreams.

The whole damn world seemed suddenly dark and dreary. No matter how he looked at it.

Chapter Thirteen

Oh, but some days were filled with euphoria, Morgan thought with satisfaction. Humming a merry tune, she pinned the last shirt of Luke's to the clothesline he'd strung before leaving this morning.

Sunshine, warm and vibrant, tweaked through the overhead foliage, kissing her skin as if she were languishing in a muscle-relaxing steam bath. The fresh, cool breeze laced with the scent of crisp pine assaulted her, while the summer's brightness filled her with soaring enthusiasm.

Watching the clothes frolic in the light breeze, she nodded in pleasure at her productive day. She'd weeded her vegetable garden, small but heralding enough summer and winter squash, cabbage, lettuce, tomatoes, onions, and potatoes to supply them well. She'd hand-tilled around the flowerbeds, picked a glorious bouquet of fragrant blooms to grace their table, and finished the large wash load. Now she had only to pare the sweet potatoes and turnips she'd purchased at the store yesterday and start those simmering with ham hocks before folding the clothes that soon would be dry. If any needed ironing, she would have that done, too, before Luke returned.

Oh, yes, she marveled, a day to feel gratified to be alive and well. Her feet danced up the two steps of the cabin, her eagerness to take on the world inspiring her to hum louder.

****

"Oh, my dear God!" Morgan stared at the

scorched imprint on the sleeve of Luke's blue denim shirt as she raised the iron.

I am witless! She'd only left the heavy thing sitting a few seconds on the stretched-out fabric while she rushed to the window to see Luke's arrival. Knowing it nonsense to let her heart take flight every time she heard the creak of wagon wheels, she'd been nonetheless drawn to catch a quick glimpse of him before he housed the animals.

"Heavenly days, what will he say?" She cringed. How could such a wonderful day turn sour in the space of a few seconds? *A few irresponsible seconds,* she scolded. Glaring at the ruined shirt, she toyed with the idea of hiding it. Yet her conscience pulled too strong. Taking a deep breath, she set the iron on the trivet, laid the shirt over a chair, and with fumbling hands folded the towel she used to protect the counter. She busied herself by putting her clothing away, all the while bracing herself for his reaction when he saw the evidence of her recklessness in clear view.

Luke grinned as he came through the door, his wide-brimmed hat in his hand. "Garden looks good. Real good. Even your flower beds." He hung his hat on a peg, then wiped his forehead with his forearm as he watched her place his stack of clothes on the divan.

"Been mighty busy, I see." When he raised his nose and inhaled deeply, his eyes glowed his approval. "Mighty busy."

She really did try to smile, but knowing his appreciation would pale... Ha, it would vanish...in light of her gaffe. She trembled, instead.

"Hey, you all right?" He took a step toward her, frowning, his eyes full of concern.

His regard nearly undid her. Yet she kept her chin up in determination to confess.

"It was a wonderful day until a few minutes

ago." This was harder than she'd thought. She lowered her chin a notch.

Without hesitation, his long strides brought him within inches of her. He placed a hand on her right shoulder and lifted her chin with his other.

"Can't be that bad. Everything looks great—smells great, too." Whether from his coaxing smile or the warmth of his hand on her shoulder, or maybe the gentleness of his thumb and index finger on her chin, she wasn't sure, but she shuddered.

Dear God above, she hated to tell him she'd done something else wrong. "I scorched your shirt."

He did hesitate at that. Only for a moment, but she saw the light dim in his eyes.

He exhaled, nodded. She wished he would smile.

"I think I can live with a little scorch." His lips thankfully curled a fraction.

She dreaded to see his smile leave again. "It's not a little scorch." Oops, that frown reappeared. Her despair increased at knowing that his mere frown would turn glowering.

He turned his head to scan the room. Her own eyes darted to the shirt, her breath abandoning her as if she'd had the wind knocked out of her.

"Holy sh…"

Her gaze arrowed up to see his expression. She wished she hadn't looked. He closed his eyes, reopened them. Simply stared. Actually, he glared at the ruination she'd caused.

She compressed her lips, prepared for his bellow. His one hand tightened on her shoulder, his fingers curled beneath her chin. She quivered. Any pluck she'd had evaporated into thin air.

As quickly as his fingers had tightened, they fell away when he stepped back. She knew she should be thankful he hadn't squeezed the life out of her. Instead, a twinge of disappointment assailed her at the loss of his touch.

"I'm sorry, Luke. I'll buy you a new one with the money I earn. I..."

"Forget it. I have plenty of others. I can always buy new. It's not the end of the world." His smile felt heaven-sent. "But I swear, woman, you must have a penchant for burning anything in your way." Though his barb stung deep, his laughter made her relax.

About to offer another earnest apology, she nearly jumped out of her skin as his head snapped toward the folded pile on the divan. If she'd thought his previous glare fiery before, she'd been mistaken. His present glower would surely ignite the clothes.

He paled considerably, his eyes wide, his stance stiffening. "Please tell me you didn't wash my buckskins."

She'd been almost over-eager to inform him how she'd scrubbed them in the hottest soapy water her hands could stand till they were actually squeaky clean. Now, acutely aware of his distress, reading his sheer horror, she judged it much better not to share that piece of news.

"You did, didn't you? Those are my buckskins—neatly folded, well washed, and dried."

Maybe she should simply jump down the privy with that lime she'd dumped in earlier. What had she done so wrong? You had to wash clothes with soap and water. Even she knew that. Surely he couldn't continue to wear them with so much dust and dirt caked on them.

She knew he would never hit her. He wasn't the type to strike a woman. Yet she took a step back and sighed in relief to add a smidgen of space between them before he could whiplash her with his tongue. When her hands began their quiver, she gripped the folds of her skirt tightly.

"Yes, I wa—"

"Holy H. Christ!" For sure, his thunderous roar blew dust from the hard-packed dirt under her feet.

She saw his back, arms, and legs all stiffen until he resembled one of those towering trees he instructed to be cut down. He appeared breathless, his cheeks flushed to deep red.

She dared not breathe. Lord, she was too frightened, too confused, to even quiver.

He inhaled deeply, his face returning to a more normal flesh tone. His fists remained tightly clenched at his sides. How large those fists were. Thank goodness he could control his temper. She also figured it a good bet there must be another means of washing certain clothing. They'd certainly been soft as fleece, rich in color. This business of clean buckskins stymied her.

She watched, wide-eyed, as he stormed across the room, yanked the pants and tunic from the middle of the pile, and held them up for inspection. Her puzzlement soon came to rest.

She'd been so busy gathering the clothes, so intent on folding them neatly, she had failed to give them more than a glance to assure they were spanking clean. But now she saw…

Oh, heavenly days! They would much better fit a child of ten. A very slender, short one.

She gulped, the lump in her throat as big and round as the winter squash she'd pared.

Luke held up his favorite garments. He'd had this set of buckskins for too long to remember. Had loved their feel, the precise way they fit, the easy maneuverability they offered.

How could she have washed them? Anyone with one iota of common sense would know not to wash buckskins. Especially not in the hot water she had obviously used. His mind sizzled. Not only because of the damn buckskins, but it just added to his day of stress at the logging site, as well as trying to concentrate on Lucy rather than Morgan. The headache he'd had all day increased, pounding at the base of his skull and creeping around to both temples until they throbbed.

Only when his fists crushed the fabric he held out at arm's length did he realize how complete the silence had become. Had she fled?

Clamping a rein on his near-to-explosion temper, he glanced over his shoulder.

She stood rigid as a fence post. Wide eyes, dark as night, stared back at him from a face as pale as death. Panic-stricken, frozen to the spot. As if she expected him to beat her. He winced, realizing how truly frightened she was. Of him. As disgust soured his entire insides, the volatile fuse that had threatened to explode lost its spark. In that rapid cooling off, he realized Morgan, from back east—somewhere in New York—had no clue how to care for buckskins.

Clutching the garments to his chest, he sighed. His favorite tunic and pants might be ruined, but they could easily be replaced. He could well afford twenty more. The chasm he'd created between himself and Morgan might never be healed.

"If you've a mind to don a set of buckskins, these might fit." He held them out toward her, offering them as a peace offering. Dare she take them? Or had he frightened her so badly she'd give him a wide berth from now on? The thought pierced like a razor-sharp lance.

Her eyes remained round, wary as an innocent doe staring down the barrel of a rifle. He felt the nauseating plummet of despair, a wretchedness that twisted his gut.

He saw a light flicker within the brown pools, a glint of those amber sparkles he so loved to see. He watched, praying for forgiveness as a shudder shook her shoulders. Patiently he waited, his arm outstretched, hoping she had the courage to overlook his ill-tempered stupidity.

Though distinctly hesitant, her hand reached out. Now he shuddered, but from relief. A relief so sweet and hopeful he had to blink back the glaze clouding his vision.

She took them and clutched both to her chest. Her lips trembled as she attempted a smile. A feeble one but, nonetheless, a smile. *Yes, there is a God.*

Her eyes took on that special glimmer. *That-a-girl.* If nothing else, she'd developed a backbone since coming west.

"Does Lucy know about me? That I'm your mock wife?"

Her question threw him for a moment. The reason for it eluding him.

"Yes. She thought it a wise idea," he answered honestly.

"Well, if when you write to Lucy you've mentioned my other disasters, this one will surely make her laugh, don't you think?" Her smile became infectious.

Her ability to laugh at herself instead of wallowing in self-pity pleased him. Too much.

"I believe you're absolutely right." He laughed, leaning a hip against the divan. "And, yes, I've written to Lucy about your baking and cooking, but not to complain about it, mind you. I only thought to make her smile, as I figured it would. Being a woman who is…was…proficient in the kitchen, she can appreciate the hilarity of it, just as we eventually did."

Her grip on the clothes tightened, her cheeks flushed. Instantly, he rued his words. Damn, he'd meant to keep the mood light, not embarrass her further.

"I think maybe you and Lucy would like each other. You two are very much alike."

"We are?" she asked, surprise arching her brows.

Good, she'd lost that crestfallen look. He found it just as surprising to find how very much he wanted to keep her happy and smiling.

"Yes you are. Oh, not in appearance, not by a long shot. She's a few inches taller, five-foot-eight, actually. Her hair is light blonde, and her eyes are bright blue. But your quick wit and your love of life are quite similar, though I believe she's a tad more shy than you."

He had to hide his grin as he noted how intensely she listened to his words, as if absorbing each one and weighing their measure. "You both give one hundred percent of your energy—or at least she did when she could—to whatever you're doing. And though you two are both quite soft-spoken, most of the time, and have an easygoing nature, you possess the tenacity and resilience to hold your own no matter what."

She laughed at his praise. "You make us sound like paragons of valor, vigor, and..." She stifled another laugh. "I don't know what all."

When her eyes twinkled like they were doing, when that bright smile all but took his breath away, he longed to grab her, crush her within his arms, kiss those delectable li-...

Sweet Jesus! He fought back the powerful tug of his heart, the raging emotions that coaxed him to lose control. Leaning further into the divan to ease the growing discomfort below his belt, he hoped she wouldn't notice how much control he'd lost.

"Not paragons, by any means." He chuckled, feeling anything but virtuous at present. "But can you deny you wouldn't do anything in your power for your friends? Or that once your mind's made up to do something, by God, you give it your all?"

Her lips quirked, and amber chips—warm and glowing—danced in those mahogany orbs. He fought to look elsewhere; his gaze clung to hers.

"I may try to give my all, but the results aren't always the way I intended. You know that first hand." As if just realizing she still clutched the ruined buckskins, she shook them out, folded them, and smoothed a hand down their length.

"No, they're not. But you heed your errors and then make the best of it. You neither cower nor give in or give up. You do what's necessary and go on. Just as we'll do this time."

She glanced at the two articles folded over her forearm, then at him. "Do you know any young boy who could wear these? And I do apologize. I didn't know they would shrink."

"I know you didn't. I can't think of anyone off the top of my head right now. Put them aside, and I'll ask around."

Passing the pile of clean clothes, she headed for the trunk at the end of the bed. "I'll put dinner on the table if you're ready," she said as she lifted the lid and stored the buckskins.

"That'd be fine. Smells good."

Nodding, she proceeded to the kitchen. He knew he should call an end to their discussion. She might have forgotten his temper, but he hadn't. No way could he let the issue rest until he said his piece. Had she cringed, fearful his temper would become physical? Had she suffered at someone's hand, expecting the same from him? The thought of her being abused formed a cold knot in his gut. He only needed a name and he'd fix the bastard.

"I'd never hit anyone for any other reason than defense."

She spun around from the counter, silverware and two plates gripped in her hands. "I know that. You might bellow down the rafters, but I know you'd never do more."

"Your eyes spoke another story a few minutes ago. I thought maybe you'd suffered from someone's anger before." He watched for any expression that might indicate he'd struck the mark. He knew so little of her past. He'd tried to make her open up, but she'd been vague, offering generalizations, for the most part.

"It's true you did startle me for a minute. You looked angry enough to throttle me. But then I realized you'd never do harm to any woman—or man—unless, like you said, in defense." She stepped to the table and set their places neatly, appearing unruffled by his insinuation.

"And no. I've never endured any physical harm. If you thought my father hit me, you are very mistaken." She gathered the salt and pepper and the crock of butter from the counter. "He shook his fist, or pointed an accusing finger enough times, let me tell you. When I failed to measure up in his eyes, he'd rant and rave till my ears rang. But he never wasted energy to hit me. I can honestly say I only wish he had cared enough to want to." Her voice fell away as she positioned the condiments just so.

Her words hit him like a hard right, square in his chest. How cruel a father, how ignorant, not to have seen how much his daughter needed attention. His full attention, his devoted love.

His mind's eye saw the slump-shouldered little girl. One with sorrow in her heart, trembling lips, and tears spilling from her woeful, anguished eyes. Huddled in a corner, feeling unloved and unwanted. He heard her mournful sobs as she cried a river no one cared to heed. Her father might not have harmed her physically, but mentally he had caused a far deeper wound. A wound Luke found he so desperately wanted to soothe.

The scrape of the large spoon hitting his plate brought him back to the present as she dished up the servings. He'd been so lost in his rattled musings, he hadn't realized she'd brought the simmering pot to the table.

"Please, sit. I'll cut the bread from here."

He sat, feeling as if his knees had turned to water. Their gazes met as she placed the spider kettle on the trivet. He wanted to say so much. His tongue felt as useless as his legs. He'd never experienced such deep-seated distress over anything or anyone as he did now. Not even when Lucy had been given her death-sentence diagnosis. The force of his emotions shook him, frustrated him to the point of not knowing what to say.

Did she know how out of sorts he felt? Could she read the utter dismay he'd experienced at hearing her words, his confusion over his reaction? The turmoil he fought within his heart?

"I feel as if I already know Lucy." She sat down joining him. "And I know I'd like her. She sounds like a wonderful lady. And—" her voice caught—"and I still think she's very lucky to have you. Tell me more about her." Her meek smile seemed forced.

Was it his imagination, or were her eyes as tormented as his? Was it merely because of memories of her uncaring father? Or more?

He ached for the latter. Joy warred with stark logic. If indeed she felt more, he'd have no choice but to run like hell the other way. For her sake, for his own. He'd thought his headache had lessened, but now it returned full swing.

Chapter Fourteen

As Morgan cleared the edge of the towering pines, drawing closer to town at a steady pace, she glanced upward. Cumulus clouds, pure white, domed and piled one upon the other to curtain the overhead sun's bright glow. Yet somehow heated rays snuck past the fleecy puffs and through the sparse patches of delft blue to bake the air and raise the humidity.

She paused at the end of town and looked across the wide expanse of the road. "What a blasted fool." She'd ended up on the opposite side from the store. Three men talked and laughed in front of the saloon, their backs to her. Another man sat on a stump—a makeshift chair, if you had imagination—outside the store as he whittled on a piece of wood with a small knife.

Morgan inhaled deeply, lifted her skirt as much as prudence allowed, and painstakingly began her precarious trek over the menacing ruts. Though eager to mill over Mr. Turner's herbs and spices, she scrutinized each step as she dug her shoe into the next valley. No way would she repeat her first night's performance. Of course, today she wore flat shoes.

After countless labored footfalls, she lifted her gaze. Only halfway. The men remained as they were, either unaware of her or not concerned. Luke had explained he had two shifts working. Obviously, these men worked the late shift.

One shift worked from sunup to sunset, the other started an hour before the first left and worked until midnight. The second crew finished what the first had started, rechecked the chutes, dam, and equipment, and prepared for the next day, then slept at the site. They were a means—an extremely costly but necessary means, Luke felt—to guarantee no one tampered with anything.

Trudging the rest of the way, she caught herself fuming once again at how, three days after the fact—three days, mind you—Luke had sheepishly divulged that much of their equipment had been ruined. Her hands fisted within the folds of her hiked-up skirt. She simply couldn't imagine why he thought her too fragile of mind to explain such happenings the minute it happened. Mere decency necessitated he tell her sooner.

Gingerly, she took a few more steps, glancing up to right her balance. She noted the fierce scowl on the man sitting down. Oh, he tried to be non-suspect, but that dark glower riveted directly on the other three. It was one thing to dislike someone, another to glare such pure hatred. A shiver crept up her spine despite the mugginess. Whatever reason the man had for his contemptuous glare, it certainly wasn't her business. She focused on progressing to the store.

As she drew closer to the man, he peered her way. Though his scowl evaporated when he nodded, his eyes remained dark, cold. An equal match to his blank expression. She stifled a shudder. Returning a brief nod, she clutched her skirt tighter and entered the store with as quick a step as she could take. But not before she'd noticed his eyes squint and his lips tighten as the three laughed heartily while walking the other way. And all the while his knife sliced faster. She closed the door behind her, thankful for the barrier.

****

Delighted with her purchases of basil, sage,

rosemary, tarragon, cinnamon, nutmeg, and whole cloves, Morgan had cut her return trip to half the time it had taken her to reach town.

Now, with just bits of basil and tarragon sprinkled over the roast, savory fragrances perfumed the cabin by the time Luke entered. His broad smile turned her insides all warm, soft, and mushy. Much like the applesauce she'd painstakingly created.

"Smells great in here," he said, leaving the door ajar as it had been, and hung his hat on the peg. With the humidity high since early morning, he'd not worn a jacket.

Morgan noted the dark patches of perspiration at the underarms of his shirt, across its back and collar. He'd rolled the sleeves to his elbows and had most buttons undone. Though his shirt looked rumpled and soggy, he exuded raw sensuality. She quivered from its potent force.

She tried not to boast. Tried harder to avoid gawking. "I went to Carl's and bought herbs today. I think they make a world of difference."

He grinned. "I believe you're absolutely right."

When he wiped his brow with the back of his forearm, the shirt gaped further, and she noticed a lot more than before. Her eyes followed the cords in his forearms as they tightened and flexed, anchored on the dark curly mat across his chest. Each spiral of hair glistened with moisture. What would it feel like if she ran her hand…

Oh, saints above! She had to swallow the lump stuck in her pulsating gullet. Inhaled deeply to cool her heated response. How many times had she forbade herself to react this way? But God only knew how much any woman could withstand. And when faced with this rugged, all-too-masculine appeal, she became as vulnerable as the next female. More so since her heart had become involved.

What a mess she'd gotten herself into. And all

because she had wanted to prove someone might desire her. All she'd done was find someone to whom she definitely felt drawn. For the first time she had discovered what the simple word "attraction" meant. Full force. Unfortunately, she now knew what love felt like, as well. And the torment of having to bury that love behind a cool facade.

His smile widened. Her heart nearly thudded out of her chest. "I'll go out to the pump and clean up a bit. I smell worse than a dead animal lying in the sun for a week."

He unbuttoned the rest of his shirt. Her woeful musings erupted into a rapid-firing pulse. She couldn't have pulled her eyes away from watching him hike out the shirt from beneath his belt and wiggle out of it even if someone had yelled fire. His golden skin gleamed, biceps bulged, and taut cords across his chest flexed with every movement. She trembled with wanton desire.

She cleared her clogged throat. "You don't have to hurry. I can hold dinner as long as you like." She knew he'd already taken care of the animals. He always did so upon arriving. He did the necessary tasks, took his meal, then tackled anything else that needed attention. Only then did he sit down and enjoy his pipe. Oh, but evenings were becoming too familiar, all too enjoyable.

"No need. I'm starving after smelling that roast. I'll be back before you know I've left." He balled up the shirt and swabbed it across his chest. Heaven preserve her heart, those dark coils of hair sprang to and fro. Her blood surged faster; the heat of it almost buckled her knees.

"Whew," he laughed, shaking his head. "Glad you're doing the wash and not me. Maybe I should leave this outside."

Nerves strung taut, she chuckled. "Just hand it over. It can't be that bad."

His brows rose as if amazed by her words, but he handed it over. "Maybe you've had a problem smelling when things are burning. Your nose can't be working right if you can say that."

With a grin full-blown, he darted out through the door. Did he think she'd throw the sodden shirt at him for that wisecrack? His joking always surprised her when she least expected it. Oh, how she liked his light clowning.

Curling her arms around the damp ball, she hugged it to her chest as if it were a treasure. When she heard the squeak of the pump handle and the slosh of the water, she lifted the garment higher. It definitely reeked of sweat and toil. But not so offensively that it masked the familiar scent. Horse, tobacco, and man. More specifically, Luke Kincaid.

"Holy heavenly days." She had it bad. How would she ever manage to conceal her feelings for the duration she'd be here? Disgusted that she'd added fuel to the flames that ran rampant too often of late, she sent the shirt flying toward the basket in the far corner.

"Think of Lucy, for heaven's sake, or for your own sanity," she sputtered as she charged across the room. With agitated hands she ladled broth from the roast. Better to cook than to think.

For the next five minutes, she concentrated on preparing thick gravy. She stirred so vigorously it soon turned as smooth as molasses.

****

Luke doused his upper torso and arms with water, soaped up till thick white lather frosted his skin. The water cooled his heated body, but not as much as he would have liked. Or needed it to be, if truth be told. He'd be better off taking a quick dip in the pond not far beyond the cabin.

Frustrated, he scrubbed harder. His groin still pained, achingly so. Thank God he'd been close to the door. Able to turn in time before she saw the bulging evidence of his desire.

Splashing water from the bucket, he rinsed off. With long sure strokes, he pumped the handle harder than necessary, leaned over and immersed his head under the steady stream. The chilled blast cooled his loins in a flash. But what would happen next time? And there would be a next time. Just as physically painful. Just as emotionally frustrating. Just as utterly useless.

Flustered, he curled his fingers tight into the towel as he dried himself. God almighty! She'd had a look in her eyes that mirrored his own feelings. Intense desire, overwhelming need. He'd been shocked to see such a reaction. And dammit, for one moment, just as pleased by it. Thank heavens, common sense had hit him over the head and he'd made a safe exit. Oh, yes, her response, her eyes all soft and heated, had fed his male ego tenfold, triggered his full arousal, and warmed his vulnerable heart. But any way he looked at it, it also spelled double trouble. Now, knowing she harbored an attraction to him would make it twice as difficult.

What a helluva mess.

Chapter Fifteen

The next morning as Morgan stood at the counter kneading dough with painstaking care, Sarah greasing the pans with confident ease, their nonstop chatter about everything and anything hummed throughout the kitchen. Well, maybe not everything, Morgan reflected with a renewed pang of guilt. Anticipation of Sarah's arrival had fueled her until she'd buzzed through the cabin's morning chores. They'd planned this day several days ago. The day she would again attempt her bread-making skills. A day way overdue. She'd been eager to do it right all morning. Still was, even now with task at hand.

Yet incessant regret that she'd deceived Sarah about her true relationship with Luke gnawed deep in her gut. Thank goodness she had the older woman to rely on, to call her friend. Heaven only knew what Luke might have suffered had she not had Sarah's guidance in so many areas. But she couldn't divulge the truth. Not until he said she could. She'd promised him.

Her perfidy slammed in her chest like a solid punch. She'd downright lied by omission regarding her high-society upbringing. Guilt weighed heavy upon her rotten soul as she realized just how deceitful she'd become. Never before had she abided lying. Now her tongue wagged its tall tales to Sarah, Luke, or whoever. She could only hope for forgiveness in the end.

As Morgan relayed her latest calamity, with

Luke's buckskins, Sarah laughed so hard she had to wipe her eyes with her apron.

"Saints preserve us," Sarah chuckled again as she lined up the six pans in a neat row on the table. "God love the man for not wringing your lovely neck."

Remembering how hard-pressed Luke had been to tamp his temper, Sarah's words hit deep. Yet she too chuckled now that the incident lay behind her. "I'd say I came mighty close. Closer than I ever want to be again."

Sarah ambled to the metal dishpan to wash the lard from her hands, her laughter recommencing as if another joke had been told.

"I can't say if my Tom would have resisted. He might love me with all his heart, but I'm not sure he'd ever sweep something like that under the carpet without some kind of retaliation."

Sarah's eyes twinkled as she dried her hands on the towel. "Think I ought to try something like that and see just how much he really cares?"

Morgan grinned, mounding the last batch of dough on the counter before she covered it with a towel. "If you ever need ideas as to what to botch up, I can give you all you want. Believe me."

Their giggles danced off the walls as they sat at the table, drank coffee, and waited for the dough to rise. Not one to sit idle for long, Sarah cunningly used the time to show Morgan how to tighten and straighten stitches on the quilt Morgan had haphazardly tried to repair.

By the time the bread's succulent aroma filled the cabin, they'd rectified the quilt and visited the pond so Morgan could watch the loons she so loved. Some had settled in their nests, while others enjoyed gliding in the sunshine. The women had even picked bouquets of early wildflowers, interlaced with feathery ferns, to brighten their homes, and cleared more than a few pesky weeds from the bed of new seedlings.

Just as Sarah wrapped the third loaf for herself in a towel and Morgan reached for it to set it into the basket, galloping hoofbeats pounded the hard ground, growing louder as they neared.

Morgan's heart skipped a beat. Had Luke been hurt?

A fine sweat pearled her forehead as her imagination ran wild. Her mind's eye pictured Luke injured, lying helpless after being felled by a toppling tree. No, he was far too cautious, she assured herself. But had the saboteurs uncovered Luke's identity and retaliated? Her heart beat like a drum roll against her chest. How foolish to think the worst, yet lately the possibility seemed to lurk in the back of her mind. Now it seeded itself front and center. Her blood ran cold.

Without sparing Sarah a second glance she tossed the wrapped loaf in her direction and scurried to the door on shaky knees. She paid no mind if Sarah questioned her exaggerated reaction. She opened the door to the creak of a saddle, the whinny of a horse. Her mind spun with a hundred gruesome thoughts.

As her pulse bounded in fearful anticipation, a tall, lanky man dismounted and removed his wide-brimmed hat. Even with his brown shaggy hair askew, his face crusted with dirt, she recognized him. He'd worked the logs with Monk.

"Afternoon, ma'am." He nodded, swiping his forearm across his sweaty forehead.

"Is Luke all right?" she managed, past the lump in her throat, before he'd even brought his arm down to his side. She heard Sarah come up behind her. Morgan focused on the man as he nodded to Sarah, then turned his attention back to her.

His grin showed white, crooked teeth. "He's jist

fine, ma'am." He removed his gloves, flexed his fingers. "Didn't mean ta startle er scare ya none. Jist sent me with a message, is all." He fingered the rim of the faded hat with his dirt-caked hands, as if uncomfortable to be here.

"Name's Les Purdy. Work the river and dam with Monk and the others, so I didn't git ta meet ya the other day." He shuffled, leaning his weight from one foot to the other.

Relieved to hear of Luke's well being, Morgan disregarded the man's grimy hands. She held out her hand in welcome. Hesitantly, he shook it. His hand felt dry and cracked, much like tough leather. She noted how his cheeks above his straggly beard hued pink.

"It's a pleasure to meet you, Mr. Purdy." She smiled, shaking his hand, hiding her grimace as the weather-roughened, work-toughened palm scratched hers. Hopefully he'd feel less embarrassed by her hospitable gesture. He smelled of horse, sweat, and dirt.

As their hands fell to their sides, he nodded to Sarah. "Ma'am." He turned his attention back to Morgan. "Luke wanted ya to know he be stayin' the night at the site. Seems some bast-, uh, somebody tampered with the dam during the night. Damn thing almost gave way before we got it fixed. Lucky for us Luke makes us double-check everythin' every mornin', else we mighta had a mess on our hands, 'n' some of us injured, besides."

Her throat felt parched. "He thinks whoever did it might try something else tonight?"

Her face undoubtedly showed her concern, or maybe her voice had quivered. Either way, Mr. Purdy grinned. "Now, don't you go frettin' none, ma'am. There be enough of us stayin' that if any vermin shows up, we'll have him cornered without a blink of an eye."

His reassurance should've slowed her heartbeat, offered relief. Instead, a sense of foreboding consumed her. She wanted to run to Luke's side, to simply be with him. Of course, she knew she could neither defend the site any better than the men could nor run to Luke's side like a scared ninny. He'd not look favorably on her fretting like a distraught wife. Actually, she mused, he'd most likely think her quite silly.

She'd stay put, keep a level head. He'd expect her to. But she didn't have to like it.

"Thank you for coming to tell me. I'll say a prayer for all of you to stay safe through the night." She forced a smile while worrying her hands together. "Can I offer you coffee, or something cold, Mr. Purdy?" God only knew she needed something.

He shook his head while replacing his hat. "Jist call me Les, ma'am. And I thank ya for the offer, but I best be gettin' back. We got us a pot o' stew on for later, but...we might welcome some of that bread I smell. With all the goin's on, Monk ain't had time to bake none."

What a fool for not realizing the men wouldn't be home for dinner. "How silly of me. I hadn't thought about the long evening you men would have there. Please, Mr. Pur...Les, give me a minute, and I'll pack up some bread and dessert. What about something to drink?"

"Got plenty of water and coffee. Bread'll do jist fine. Much obliged."

Morgan turned and hurried inside to gather food. She left the door open so she might hear any further conversation.

"I'm Sarah Hellman, Mr. Purdy. Is Tom staying, too?"

"Good thing you told me who you be, ma'am. I be jist about to go to yur place. He be stayin'. There be six of us stayin' fer the night. Like I told Luke's missus, ain't nothin' to worry about. We can handle any trouble comes our way. You mark my words, ma'am."

Morgan prayed the men were as tough as the man's confident words indicated as she packed two loaves of bread around the spice cake in the shallow basket. Wedging a small crock of butter into the corner of the basket, she laid a towel over the top, tucked it in securely, and rejoined the two outside.

"There's two loaves of bread, butter, and a spice cake, Les. I hope you enjoy them."

"Thanks, ma'am. We'll all be enjoyin' all of it. Much obliged." When he took the offered basket, his smile vanished, and was replaced by a scowl and a shake of his head.

"Almost forgot to tell ya ladies. Luke said to tell ya Hank's goin' to be right fine. Doc sent word by way of Curtis, when he delivered goods to the store this mornin'. Gonna take some time, but his bones're gonna mend up jist fine."

"Oh, thank the good Lord," Morgan said as she beamed. "Thank you so much for telling us, Les. All the men must be so relieved."

"Yes, ma'am. We be hopin' he can join us again after he be back in shape." He secured the basket, remounted, and nodded his farewell. "You ladies have a nice day, and don't ya go worryin' none. And thanks again for the vittles, ma'am."

****

Hours had passed since Morgan walked Sarah halfway home. They'd shared the evening conversing over dinner, never lacking for subjects. As she blew out the lamp, Morgan grinned at the memory of their talk. She'd hoped Sarah might spend the night yet could appreciate Sarah's desire to go home. Sarah had her own fire to tend and most likely would be more comfortable in her own bed.

Curling up into a tight ball under the covers,

Morgan felt more than the loneliness of the empty cabin. She missed Luke's smiles, his conversation about the day's work, the loggers' progress. Would she ever respect, admire, and, yes, love another man as much as she did Luke Kincaid? *Highly doubtful,* she thought, as she drifted into a deep, troubled sleep.

****

A loud thud, then a scraping noise brought Morgan to a sitting position like a jack-in-the-box. Had the sounds come from the door? Why hadn't someone called out? Could it be an animal? No, there'd definitely been some kind of scraping, metal against metal. Her mind fumbled to comprehend what she'd heard. Fearful, she gripped the quilt to her chest. Had she been dreaming? Could it have been distant claps of thunder?

As her mind toiled to sort out the confusion, she heard a distinct *glug-glug,* like liquid being poured from a spout. Wide-eyed, wide awake now, she listened more closely. The glugs seemed to track the front of the cabin. No, no dream. Thank goodness she'd bolted the door. But what in heaven's name had she heard? What was she listening to now?

An eerie suspicion crept through her that she need not worry about having secured the bolt. Fear shivered down her spine, bristled the hairs on her cold arms. Heavy footsteps thudded from one corner to the other.

A splash hit the door.

Dear God, if only she could call this her wild imagination. But she couldn't. Someone was outside. But what were they doing, what did they want? And what the devil…

An odor, faint but nonetheless pungent, curled her nose. She sniffed. Sniffed again. *Fuel oil?* The bizarre mystery unraveled as if someone had written it down on paper. Someone, several someones by the sounds, had poured gasoline or kerosene on the cabin. Had they actually barricaded the exit? No. Surely no one would…

"Who's there?" she called, bolting from the warm bed. She made a beeline to the door.

A subtle boom rent the air outside. Instinctively, she jerked back two steps, away from whatever screamed its warning. But she knew without doubt what that something was. Fire.

Certain her efforts would prove useless, she nevertheless threw the bolt and tugged on the door. It rattled, groaned. Its hinges creaked. All to no avail. Crackles and snaps mixed with roaring whooshes just beyond her reach. She envisioned tall flames licking the outside logs. She'd asked Luke if the logs had been debarked just to make them look prettier. Though he'd laughed, he'd explained bare logs, debarked with a tool called a spud, burned more slowly than ones with bark. Debarking was a necessity for log cabins, especially in these forests. Now she wondered just how long it would take these spudded logs to burn through. *Dear God in heaven!*

A glow, gold and menacing, danced at the window to light up the room. She'd never been in a fire before but realized she needed to think logically, remain calm, form a plan. She couldn't just break the glass, then easily slip out the small window and leap through those flames. She'd have to squirm through, most likely get stuck for a minute, and she'd be burned to a crisp. And it wouldn't take long before the glass shattered, allowing the flames to leap inward.

Feeling the intensity of the fire, she closed and latched the shutters, knowing once the glass broke the flames would devour the shutters' wood much more quickly than the thick logs. Smoke would soon seep inward from around the door and shutters. She already smelled it, the pungent stench of it. Taking a deep breath to gather her courage before she lost all sense of reason to panic, she contemplated her next move. She needed to see, to figure out a way of escape and to deal logically with this outlandish nightmare. She couldn't allow any hysterics to waylay her. She'd already been foolish to close the shutters before locating the lamp.

With arms outstretched, she felt her way around the divan, then darted to the stove. Her hands trembled as her fingers gingerly explored the warm edge of the stove and scanned the wall behind for the potholders. She said a silent prayer when her fingers curled around the sturdy pads. On shaky knees, she tore open the doors so the dying embers would offer light. She now cursed the sunny spring day with its warm air that had allowed her to let the coals simply smolder. She'd have preferred to have a blazing fire in the stove about now. At least the dwindling golden glow shed enough light for her to locate the oil lamps.

"Damn you!" she bellowed at her trembling fingers as she fought to strike a match. It took three tries before she managed to light two lamps. Grabbing the quilt from her bed, she raced across the room and stuffed it along the base of the door. Uncertain it would do any good, she prayed it would at least buy her time to think.

She heard ringing. Did her fright make her ears play games? At that same instant, she thanked God for some kind of hope. Not ringing, but the distant gong of a bell.

Already smoke seeped in around the edges of the door. Should she open the small window on the back of the cabin? Indecision warred with caution. If they'd torched the entire perimeter, then she'd only let flames in. No, she had to try to get out. Eyes tearing, she scanned the room in indecision as to what course to take. Wiping the sting from her eyes with the sleeve of her nightdress, she scanned the room for a weapon. Anything to beat down the door.

She eyed the woodpile for Luke's ax. No ax. He'd left it outside. Her hopes sank.

She coughed. Though the smoke snuck in slowly, its harshness caught in her throat. As soon as she gained a few short inward breaths, she again swiped at her smarting eyes. They shed tears as if floodgates had been opened wide.

What had been crackles and whip-like snaps outside now sounded like thunderous roars of swirling wind. The cabin had ignited as easily as a dry haystack.

Trapped like a tiny rabbit in a snare, her natural instinct for survival nevertheless sprang forth. "You bastards, whoever you are, I'll not go down without a fight." Her screech of fury left her throat raw, dry, and tight. She grabbed one of the two buckets of water by the counter and heaved its contents over the door. She wasn't sure if it would slow down the flames from burning through the thick planks, but anything seemed worth trying.

Determined to break down the barred door, she grabbed the largest log she thought she could handle. With both hands she wielded the log like a bat. Adrenaline pumped full force through her veins; rage and conviction stiffened her stance. She swung with all her might.

She rammed, bashed, slammed. Relentlessly she continued the process over and over with brutal force she'd not known she possessed. The door shook as chips of wood flew in all directions—most from her club, mere splinters from the door itself. She doubled her efforts. Crash after crash reverberated within her skull until her eardrums rang painfully like cymbals clashing overhead. But the solidity of the well-built portal withstood her vigorous attack as if made of the finest crafted cast iron.

She had to pause in her death-defying pursuit of escape to take a deep breath. Her hesitation cost her dearly, she realized. The log suddenly felt like a gigantic anchor in her sweat-slick palms. Dear God in heaven, she had to get out. Somehow, some way. The heat—now at an unbearable height—seemed to envelope her, crush her. She felt…she felt…

"Dear God!" Stunned by horror, sweat running in rivulets over every inch of skin to soak her nightgown, she watched thicker, more noxious smoke snake between logs, curling and spiraling like long, threatening tentacles. Rising heat transformed the small confines of the cabin into a blazing furnace. And she knew Hell could be no hotter.

"Oh, God, I…I can't breathe."

Resolved to fight until her last breath, she sucked in a well-needed breath. And wished she hadn't. An attack of gagging assailed her. She heard glass shatter and knew it wouldn't be long before the flames ate up the shutters and smoke and fire would pour in. Yet she eyed the window. No, it hadn't been the way before, and it was now definitely out of the question.

Smoke, the strong stench of it, clogged her nose, tightened her throat. She labored for air, only to choke on it. Her eyes, scratchy and dry, stung as if the fire flamed inside them. She fought to focus on the door mere inches in front of her. Only then did she realize tears no longer blurred her vision, no sweat poured from every pore as it had seconds ago. Her skin felt dry, tight under the warm, wet fabric that clung to her.

Had all liquid inside her been boiled out of her system, draining her strength along with it? Her arms grew weak and limp, yet jerked in spasm as they screamed their exhaustion. The room spun unmercifully. Fearing she bordered on the verge of collapse, she let the log drop from her grasp. She braced her hands flat against the door to gather strength.

"I won't give up. I...won't." As she issued her faltering whisper, the wood, hot as a sizzling skillet, seared her palms. Instantly, she drew back, snarling as stinging pain lashed through fingers and palms. Nausea barraged her gut, curled upward to her throat. She thought she might vomit. She coughed until she sank to the floor.

She thought she heard splintering wood, her name being called. But from where? Was this what dying felt like? There, again—she did hear her name. She dragged herself to the back wall, listened more carefully, tried to block out the roars from the front of the cabin. And realized it had been easier to breathe along the floor as she'd slithered along.

She barely heard her name, fragments of muffled words, but thought possibly they said, "...get you out." People were here, trying to get to her.

But would they reach her in time? She had to make sure she could still breathe by the time they got her. Consciousness teetered, yet she fought to keep her wits. She wouldn't give up, not yet, not with help so near. Her skin felt on fire, and she knew, even along the floor, the smoke would soon rob her of her last breath. Feeling helpless as a lamb lying ready for slaughter, she wished she could just burrow under the ground and wait for her rescue.

Sweet heaven. The pit. It lay even lower than the floor. It would be cooler, maybe. It might be her only salvation. With renewed hope, she crawled to the pit on forearms and knees.

As she passed the remaining bucket of water, she had enough sense about her to lean over and slurp water to replenish what she'd lost. Oh, if her mother could see her now. Her oldest daughter lapping it up like a horse at the watering trough. But she didn't give a damn, at the moment. Survival called for drastic measures, and she'd done what needed to be done. With swollen fingers and palms throbbing in protest, she lifted the vessel up and overturned it above her head so the remaining water drenched her. It prickled her skin, made her shiver, yet rewarded her with the briefest respite.

She heard thuds across the back of the cabin, shouts mingled with the fire's roar. Through the gray cloud, she saw the first golden tongues lick their way across the ceiling and through chinks. The acrid odor triggered another spate of coughing, easily assaulting her after her effort with the bucket. She curled into a ball till she could breathe more easily.

With one last surge of energy, she used the empty bucket's rim to slide the metal plate back and grabbed the towel above her head, hoping it might filter the air she breathed.

Hands screaming in anger, she managed to pull vegetables and meats from the pit.

As she burrowed herself into the hole, she felt the coolness of the ground and had but one regret.

She'd never told Luke how much she cared.

Chapter Sixteen

Luke swung the ax as if possessed by the devil himself. Palms slick, his clothing drenched with sweat, fury and ruthless determination drove his ferocious labor. Inside he shook with fear such as he'd never known before. They'd made an instant decision the minute they caught sight of the thick iron bar through the flames. It had been wedged through the door latch. Someone had set the fire.

At his right, Monk swung his ax against the back of the cabin just as fiercely. Luke halted long enough to swipe his forearm across his face, then resumed attacking the only wall not engulfed by shooting flames. Thank goodness only the front had been torched. Yet his rage flared to match that of the flames. Only the west wind from across the pond had held the tall flames from igniting the roof before they arrived. But now the roof was engulfed. They needed every precious minute they had.

Tom and Hans stood at the ready. As soon as Monk and Luke took ten swings, the other two would take the same count. They'd quickly set up the regime to avoid hitting each other, to take a breather to regain strength, but foremost to allow wider swings to inflict more powerful hits.

Others heaved water from pails—what water had been brought in barrels by wagon or was now being bucketed from the well or from the pond hand-over-hand in lines—over the roof's edge and against the back wall to lessen the heat, to push the flames back as the four hacked away. Flames from the rest of the structure, plus several lit torches, gave ample light to their task.

They had to get to Morgan in time. They had to. Mixed emotions swirled through Luke's mind as he swung the ax in a wide, descending arc. Splinters of wood flew in all directions. He'd counted on her to help with his role as logging camp boss, he looked upon her as a friend, he enjoyed her company, he relished the times he'd watched her grow as a person—learning skills she'd lacked or had no knowledge of previously.

As the ax's hit vibrated up his arm, he admitted he'd become more than attracted to her beauty, her easy wit, and her eagerness to help as well as to learn. Her sincerity, that deep abiding care for others, had touched him more deeply than he'd wanted. More intimately than he could allow.

And yes, dammit, he was falling in love with her. But now he couldn't take the time to analyze if he'd fallen completely. He needed all his logic, all his strength, to reach her. He'd deal with his misplaced feelings later.

"More water to both the corners!" he shouted, refusing to let useless thoughts deter him from gaining access to the structure before all became lost.

Lost. He shuddered at the possibility of losing Morgan. He'd never forgive himself for placing her in harm's way. He'd known better, yet he'd given in. Because of those damn tempting lips, those big, round, mahogany eyes that drew a man in like quicksand when they pleaded. That shimmering mass of hair he so painfully longed to thread his fingers through, to feel its silkiness.

Water splashed over the steaming logs from his right, his left. He paid no heed as it doused him. Just hurled the ax as if to break through the logs with one mighty swing.

"Give, you bastards!" His bellow tolled with the next pealing blow.

"Change." Hans's order barely rose over the cacophony of roaring flames, sloshing water, the vibration of the back wall of logs. Luke, relieved to rest his arms, yet eager to continue, pulled his weapon out of the wood and stepped back in unison with Monk as the other two moved into place. Thuds echoed while splintering wood flew amidst the steady crackles and whooshes of flames. Smoke—pungent, unbearably smarting to one's eyes—billowed skyward in thick black clouds, while curls of it snaked through the crowd and the clearing like soupy fog.

While he focused on Tom and Hans, one of the women handed him a cup of water. Ax in one hand, the cup in the other, he gulped the water with greed. Mechanically, he handed back the cup with a quick thanks and took the towel offered to swipe his face. As he mopped his neck, someone laid a hand on his right shoulder.

Luke glanced to his side. Charlie Miller held an ax in his other hand. No way in hell would he let him take a turn. The man neared fifty, maybe closer to sixty. And Luke needed to be in the swinging soon.

"This one's good and sharp, Luke. Use it next," Charlie said as he handed it over and took the other from Luke. "Got one for Monk, too. Least the rest of us can do is supply sharp ones." Charlie smiled, obviously pleased to be of service. "We'll sharpen these for the next go-around."

Despite the gruesome fear of not reaching Morgan in time, the back-breaking immediacy of the task, Luke smiled. He scanned the area for the first time since they'd started their hacking.

It seemed the entire little community had come to help. Thirty, maybe forty, men and women passed pails of water up the line. Others showered water on the cabin's backside. Screeches and grating, barely audible, rent the air as men off to the left sharpened the ready supply of axes on grinding stones. Only then did Luke realize how busy the others had been in retrieving all the necessities to see this mission through. A group of women hovered nearby holding pitchers and mugs of water, towels to offer when needed.

He glanced left, taking in needed gulps of fresher air. Sarah and a few other women stood by a stack of blankets while they ripped and rolled bandages. A blanket had been spread open on the ground. A portion of it housed several bottles, small round tins and squares of gauze neatly waiting. The four men he'd sent to haul the thick log he'd downed weeks ago stood in readiness near the women. The ten-foot log lay at their booted feet waiting to be used to bash through the notched-out door. It seemed like an hour had passed, yet he knew all this had been done in a matter of fifteen to twenty minutes.

The togetherness, the outpouring of concern and effort of this small camp-community gathered here, brought another sting behind his eyelids, a tightening of his throat due to far more than the smoke-filled air, he knew.

He fingered the ax, weighed it in his hand. "Thanks, Charlie, you're doing a great job. And that goes for everyone here. Much obliged," he said, raising his voice loud enough for all to hear. Later, he'd make sure everyone had received proper thanks. Right now he had a job to do.

With his focus on Tom and Hans, he turned to Charlie. "I'll need water to wet me down, and a soaked blanket, to go in when we're ready."

"Ten hits," Monk said, accepting the ax from Charlie with a brisk, impatient nod. "Change."

"Let's try ta ram it now, Luke," Hans suggested as he quickly stepped back, wiping his brow across his shirtsleeve. "Looks ready, don't it?"

Luke kept his arm at his side, his fist gripped tight around the ax handle. Studying their progress, he felt reluctant to stop. They couldn't waste time trying to ram through if not ready. Time was too precious. Morgan was way too precious.

They'd axed a four- to five-inch deep groove in two vertical lines from one chink downward approximately three foot to another chink. It would be like a window. That's all they'd need to get in and get in quick. God knew how much he wanted to try to ram it. Was it too soon? Would they lose valuable time in an unsuccessful attempt? Then after more hacking away, break through to find they'd lost something far more…far more…

He refused to think of the possibility.

"Luke?" Hans eyed him anxiously.

"Let's do it. Roll down your sleeves." His deep, barked order set the four at the log into motion, though a lump in Luke's throat nearly choked him on his words. *And God have mercy on my soul if I've made the wrong decision.*

Luke yelled to the women, "Be ready with a bucket of water to douse me, and a water-soaked blanket."

The four men discarded their axes and rolled shirtsleeves down to protect their arms as they prepared to join the stronghold on the weapon. The four others hauled the battering ram until they stood in position approximately fifteen feet in front of the door. The eight joined ranks along the long column, each one wrapping an arm securely around the missile, their stance ready to charge, all wearing an expression of tenacity and sheer purpose.

Luke, on the very end gave the command. "On the count of three…"

"One...two...three. Charge!"

They vaulted as one. As if the log weighed no more than a twig, they lunged as fiercely as an angered bull. The wall splintered, its logs partially cracking and weakening upon impact. Luke felt the collision's jolt clear down to his toes and wondered if his teeth had loosened. He had to readjust his sore arm in order to hang on. Every muscle in his body ached, screamed in protest. He watched the others flinch, roll their shoulders, reposition their arms.

"Back up. We'll try again. And this time make it count, dammit."

Rather than protests, the men—in unison—gave hale and hearty whoops of agreement.

"Let's break those fuckin' logs."

"Ram the hell out of it."

"Try, hell! We'll do it!"

For the first time since being alerted to the fire, Luke grinned. They were a determined force. They gave him hope.

Repositioned about twenty feet back, their arms locked in place, feet braced for attack, Luke sent out the command again.

"On the count of three. One...two...three. Charge!"

Again the propulsion drove swift and mighty, a powerhouse not to be denied. The makeshift window had no hope of survival.

Logs and chink cracked and snapped, howling in defeat to match the roar of the flames consuming the other walls. The carved-out barrier gave way, crumbling and falling inward with a resounding crash.

A blast of heat—confined within far too long—belched outward with the force of a spouting volcano, so torrid and pungent it brought all eight men to their knees like felled saplings.

They had no choice but to retreat while the

heated air swept past in its fury. Men scurried out of its path, scrambling over each other in dire need to escape. Luke's face, forearms, and hands were singed. He wondered if his arms had any hairs left on them. Time demanded he check later. Seared skin and a few lost hairs seemed insignificant at this point.

Morgan. Dear God! Morgan. He had to reach her.

With renewed vigor, he gained his footing. He wiped the sweat from his face with his shirtsleeve. His clothes stuck to him. He still needed to be soaking wet.

He turned just as Les picked up a bucket. "Here ya go," Les said and poured water over him. He barely had time to shut his eyes.

As he swiped his hand across his face, Lila wrapped a soaked blanket over his shoulders. "God be with you, Luke." They'd done it in record time, yet his apprehension mounted. Would he reach Morgan soon enough?

The blanket draped around him like a cocoon, wrapped close to his face with only his boots protruding, he darted to the entry.

He paused before the small portal, said a silent prayer, then filled his lungs with needed air.

"Be right behind ya," he heard Hans from behind him.

Luke turned to order Hans to remember their plan that he and he alone would venture in when ready. He stopped short. Already hands were busily wrapping Hans in a like fashion. He might need all the help he could get. He nodded.

They levered themselves through the opening.

Smoke, bellowing out the new-made opening, stung Luke's eyes until his vision swam before him. He held his breath, bent over at the waist to avoid the thicker smoke above, and cautiously made his way through the thick, heated fog. He decided to do a left sweep first. Around the bed, past the divan.

His eyes burned, his lungs begged for release, yet he pulled the blanket across his mouth and pushed on. Through the kitchen. Searching. Not finding. A beam groaned and then squeaked overhead as thundering flames licked and gobbled at the front wall. Frantic he would have to retreat, his entire body shuddered. He'd thought fear had gripped him before. Now, near frenzy, sweat pouring into his stinging eyes, he expelled a long shaky breath.

How much longer could he stay before he had to retreat outside? He knew the answer all too well. He fought to keep his breathing shallow. He coughed, his breathing heedless of the wet blanket. He righted himself by leaning a hip against the counter, then realized he needed to again crouch down so he could breathe better. He heard Hans' deep coughs from behind and knew his friend fared no better. Flames, like long angry talons, stretched outward as if to snag him with their fervid claws. He pulled away, choked, had to fight for air. Any air.

"Luke," Hans gasped, his gloved hand reaching out from the blanket and grapping Luke's shoulder. Hans coughed till he swayed from it. "I can't…can't…breathe." Hans' raspy voice turned frantic. Another choking fit bent the man over.

Luke blinked to clear his watery vision. Then he heard it. A series of raspy coughs to his immediate left. He bent down, cocked his head, and listened. And stared at a mound in the pit.

Were his eyes playing a game? But that coughing hadn't been his imagination. Relief such as he'd never known nearly toppled him. His heartbeat was beating a hole through his chest. By God, the woman had curled up in the pit. That was his Morgan.

"Get out. I see her…can manage," he forced out between coughs. "I…can't drag you…both."

Hans hesitated. Luke pushed him. "Go!"

Without waiting a second longer to see if Hans obeyed, Luke raised his arm and wiped the blanket across his face. Then, down on his haunches, reaching, his hands encountered a pile of debris. No, meats and vegetables. He pushed them out of his way and reached again, ran his gloved hands over what appeared to be a pile of clothes. And prayed.

Even through tough leather gloves he felt the searing heat of her clothing and skin, as if it were about to combust. The air had thickened to an opaque haze of gloom, making visibility almost nil. But there was no doubt as to the feel of her. Curves, legs, arms, hair, a face.

"Morgan. Thank…God." Elation poured over him, through him.

He pulled the towel from her face. With rapid purpose, he scooped his hands beneath her, slid her out of the dugout, and cradled her against him.

"Morgan, can…you…hear me?" Another round of coughing attacked. He fought to catch his breath. His lungs ached. The intense temperature sizzled his skin. He had to get her out.

He pulled off one glove long enough to press his fingers to her neck. Weak, thready. But a pulse. *Thank God.* He could have sworn he saw her eyes blink open for an instant. As he stood, readjusting her in his arms, a loud squeak rent the air. The building shook. He heard splintering overhead. Instinctively, he cradled her tighter, and hunched over her.

A beam gave way, descending with a deafening crash, barely missing them. Sparks and balls of fire sailed past them. Flames leaped to the blanket. The smell of charred wool blending with pungent smoke curled Luke's nose. Frantically he brushed at the flames clinging to his protective wrap while he tried to survey the immediate area. He could see nothing beyond the tip of his nose. Nothing but thick gray swirls. Blazing gold beyond. All around.

He dared not waste another second. He could feel weakness setting in, as if all his strength and energy were being sucked out of him with each guarded huff of breath. Clearing his throat, he again repositioned her in his arms, held her tightly. He battled to keep the blanket around them. No way could he bend low and carry her. Hell, it'd make no difference if he stood upright, he thought with a peculiar giddiness. The smoke lay as thick at his feet as it did six feet up. He hadn't a clue if the blanket was on fire or not.

Dizziness swamped him for a moment. The entire cabin went black before his eyes could again distinguish walls of bright light through the unrelenting dense gray. He stumbled, bumped into what he presumed to be the divan. Keeping his leg against its back for guidance, he made his way along it. His hip collided with what must be the fallen beam lying across it.

Flames shot up before his eyes, the heat forcing him to retreat a step. Struggling to keep his wits, he prayed his sense of direction wouldn't falter. He moved several feet to the right, to where flames glowed lower as they ran down the slanting barrier. In one fluid motion, he high-stepped over the beam. The blanket snagged on the flaming wood.

Dammit, not now. We're too close. Frustrated, he gripped the edges of the smoldering cape in an iron-fisted lock, his other arm clutching Morgan tight against his chest. Twisting his body, he gave a vicious yank. Mercifully, he pulled free of the menacing beam. He shuffled a few steps before his knees hit against an immoveable object. He faltered, had to readjust Morgan to keep from dropping her.

Was it the bed? He blinked, trying to see where the hell he stood. Damn, too far to the left. He'd have to skirt around it. Unconsciousness baited him. He fought it with every sense of determination he possessed.

His lungs burned, threatening to double him over with another fit of coughing. Yet he held his breath, fought his way around the bed, knowing the next few steps would either save them or leave them to be charred along with the rest of the crumbling logs.

A few more steps should do it. Please. Damn. He couldn't see a blasted thing. He dared not breathe. The roar, so thunderous only minutes before, faded to a dull rumble. But the intense heat hadn't lessened. He wanted to scream in agony. Instead, he staggered, clutched his precious parcel more tightly against his heart. He had to get her out. To safety.

Voices. He could hear murmurs, hear his name being called. Off in the far distance.

Distance? The damn cabin wasn't that big. Was his consciousness ebbing so fast? As his legs wobbled, he willed his weakening limbs to obey, just a few seconds longer.

He fell to his knees. Thick dun turned inky.

God forgive me for failing her.

Chapter Seventeen

Barely conscious, Luke gasped, coughed. Shoved the hands in front of him away. Good God, didn't they realize they were choking him?

His throat hurt like hell. Raw, dry, burning. His chest felt tight, as if it were banded in steel chains. His stomach heaved upward as he took in a breath, so he pushed up onto his elbows. Pungent odors of smoke clung to him, lay heavy in the air. Any minute he'd puke.

He blinked to clear his hazy vision. How the hell had so much sand got in his eyes? Tears smarted before spilling down his cheeks in a warm trail. Just the effort of bracing himself up left him weak as a kitten, so he let the tears flow rather than wipe at them. His vision cleared enough to see Rosie's dour face swim before him. She sat at his side, holding something.

"Here, now," Hans said, coming up behind his wife. Luke's vision started to clear. He watched as Hans affectionately squeezed Rosie's shoulder, a small crowd gathered around him.

Hans ambled past Rosie and knelt down on his shins behind him. Luke's shoulders protested as Hans raised them before inching closer to support Luke's back on his thighs.

"Now then, don't ya be givin' my Rosie such a hard time. Ya let her get that water down ya. Yur plumb dried out. Yu'll feel better once you've got some fluid back in ya."

Water would taste mighty good, Luke realized.

Morgan.

"Mor…gan? Where…is she?" He had to swallow back bile as it rose to sting his scratchy throat. "Is she…" He could neither form the words, nor bear the thought that… *I've got to see her.*

"She's bein' tended to."

Han's gruff answer failed to reassure him. Luke dug his right palm into the blanket-covered earth and pushed upward. "I've got to go to her. I…"

A beefy arm wrapped around his midriff, pulled him back against steeled thighs. His lungs threatened to burst.

"Yur not in any condition to do anyone any good right now. Least of all her." Hans's usual placating voice held too much clip to it. Had he evaded his question?

"I…got to see her." He struggled in vain against Hans's bear hug. "For myself. She's my…wife, dammit." Just raising his voice, uttering those few words, sent fire to every raw nerve in his throat. He tried to wiggle free. What a pathetic effort.

"Yu'll see her. As soon as Rosie gets water down ya and treats yer burns. *Ja*, I promise. I'll help ya over there myself. I didn't drag yur sorry ass out to have ya die on me now."

Disgruntled, Luke ceased his struggle. He let out a long sigh, a snarl to let Hans know just how much he detested compliance.

"*Ja*, go ahead, Rosie. Do yur work. He'll hold still for ya."

Luke sensed Hans's smile of triumph. He'd like to spin around and land a good facer into the giant's mug. His stomach chose that moment to wage battle inside. If he spun around, he'd most likely only heave his guts out. It would serve the smart-ass good if he did spew his bile all over him. Obediently, he took a sip of offered water. The coolness soothed. It left him wanting.

He needed to see Morgan. To see her breathe, touch her, stroke her delicate hand, hear her speak. Hans was right, but he didn't have to like it. He shook with a restless apprehension.

He swallowed each time Rosie tipped the mug. Grimaced at the tightness in his chest as he coughed after each and every gulp. His eyes surveyed the remains of the cabin. Its roof had caved in, leaving walls barely half standing. Gone were the violent flames that had roared like thunder. Now almost gentle flames lapped peacefully as they consumed their final feast.

Just knowing Morgan survived, Luke felt peace settle within him. He didn't care about any of the destruction, only Morgan's safety. But had Hans been truthful?

****

Rosie, now assisted by Lela and Roberta, finished applying soothing salve to Luke's face and neck, wherever his beard had failed to protect him. As they painstakingly spread the salve over his forearms and began to wrap bandages around his arms, he glanced back over his shoulder.

"How bad is she?"

Luke wished he hadn't craned his neck so far. The anguish that flashed in Hans's eyes tore at his heart. Apprehension knotted within his yet churning stomach.

Hans cleared his throat, met his gaze directly. "I won't lie to ya. You'll be seein' for yurself in a few minutes. We reached her in record time, but she inhaled a lotta smoke, Luke. She's...she was lucky to be still breathin' when ya found her."

Desperate for reassurance, yet uncertain he could lie docile while hearing the list of her injuries, Luke faced the women again. Rosie and Lela's diligent hands wound white strips around his forearms while Roberta cut away his charred left pant leg to the knee. He ground his molars as he fought the fiery sting in his arms and on his left shin. Funny, he couldn't remember acquiring any burns. They'd heal soon enough. He'd take on more if necessary, if it meant saving Morgan.

A vacant, almost forlorn feeling washed over him; he felt numb. Morgan was far from being out of the woods, if Hans's tone and few words told true. Far from it. A fist tightened around his breastbone, left him quivering inside. Aching for her in a way he had no right to feel.

When Rosie tied a knot securing the wrap on his right arm, he craned his neck to the side so Hans could hear him. "Will she make it?" He held his breath while that fist gripped harder.

"God's the only one who can answer that. The women be doin' everything they can. We'll all do anything to help pull her through, ya know that."

Luke nodded, too choked up to say his thanks. "How bad is she burned?" He winced as Roberta cleansed his tender shin.

He felt Hans stiffen. "Tell me straight out, Hans."

Hans sighed, leaned back a bit. "Her clothing protected her some, but most of her skin be scalded from the heat. Her hands be pretty blistered."

Luke grit his teeth, fought back tears. "Go on."

"Sarah made us men leave so they could undress her. Rosie can tell ya more."

Trembles shook his entire body. He loathed the thought of her suffering, the agony she yet had to endure. If he could have spared Morgan any of it, he would gladly have done so. Would do it now, if he could. *If only I had been here. If only I had reached her sooner.*

He lowered his left arm as Lela finished, felt the cool soothing of his shin as Roberta applied the salve. Yet rage exploded within until he thought he'd go mad from it. He'd find those responsible for this. Their deterrents and the problems they'd caused at the site all seemed insignificant to the callous horror they'd done tonight.

He gritted his teeth as Rosie lifted his lower leg and Lela wrapped.

Oh, yes, he'd see each and every man responsible pay dearly for what they'd done to Morgan. With each of their lives, if he had anything to say about it. And he sure as hell would.

"That should do it for now." Rosie nodded her satisfaction as she set his leg down. "You keep drinkin' all you can for the next few days. Gettin' that dried out ain't no good for you. I'll change them dressin's every day for you. You're lucky those burns are all surface and not deep."

"Thanks." He'd drink. To recover and go searching. A case of whiskey sounded damn good right now. He'd drink the whole lot in one quick swallow. Just as soon as he saw Morgan.

Hans pushed him up to a sitting position, then levered himself onto his feet. He held a hand out and clasped his other on Luke's shoulder to assist him up.

Luke took his friend's hand and let himself be pulled upward, thankful for the support when his knees went limp. He clung to Hans, planting his feet wide for balance, grimacing from the stinging bite in his limbs. Yep, weak as a kitten. And sore, to beat all time. The ground tilted, spun for a moment, then righted itself. His stomach did a flip-flop before leveling down to dull queasiness. He shook his head to clear the cobwebs, inhaled a deep breath, then let it out slow to get a stronghold on his equilibrium. To settle down the apprehension of what he would see shortly.

"Feel better?"

"Yeah. Just great. Just hunky-dory, asshole.

How the hell do you think I feel? I feel like shit. I'll probably feel worse after I see...after..." A coughing jag gripped him till he had to bend over, gag, cough, spit, and gasp. Finally he caught his breath. When he felt he could again breathe halfway normally, he straightened and gave Hans a tight-lipped smirk.

"Sorry. Guess I'm a bit out of sorts."

"*Ja.* Ya was only in there a short time, but ya went through hell, all the same."

He fisted his hands at his sides. He'd go through hell and back again if it meant Morgan's life. "Yeah, I guess so."

Hans was grim faced, his eyes narrowed. "She be a sweet lady, Luke. One of the best. Got spunk and grit enough to help with yur scheme. But she's not yur wife. Ya need to remember that."

Luke winced at Hans's careless words. He darted a glance to ensure no one stood close by. "Yeah. I know."

Scowling, Hans nodded, obviously satisfied he'd made his point. He placed an arm across Luke's back, a sure grip on his shoulder. They crossed the clearing toward the group of women.

Oh, yeah, he knew she wasn't his wife, all right. But he regretted that fact every minute of every day. He wondered if Hans sensed just how much he cared. How his thoughts, each day and half the night, drifted her way. May God forgive him—Lucy, too, if she ever knew.

The women broke their huddle as they drew near. Luke held his breath as he took in the scene. A sheet covered Morgan from neck to knees. Two women knelt at each side of her legs, ever so cautiously applying salve to her lower limbs. Morgan's head lay propped up on a pillowed blanket. Sarah sat on bended knees, spooning liquid into Morgan's mouth. Several lanterns placed at the corners of the blanket offered muted light. Between the sprawling shadows and Sarah's body shielding his view, he couldn't see Morgan's face clearly.

That was okay, though, he reasoned, as he halted his approach not five feet away. He'd take in her injuries slowly so he didn't entirely come apart. Yet, as his eyes fastened on the exposed limbs, Luke had to swallow down a roar such as he'd never known. Morgan's feet and part way up her calves were definitely scalded, glistening from the salve melting and dripping from the heated skin. The ache in his chest intensified. How she must be suffering. Lord, how he wished he could spare her this agony.

God give me strength. God give her courage and relief.

Hesitant yet determined, he raised his gaze to her face. Sarah, for the most part, remained in his line of vision. Leery, he took a step closer, veering to the left to gain a better view. He took another step and another until he reached the edge of the blanket Morgan lay upon.

Sorrow, regret, and anguish rushed him until he could barely breathe. Good Christ. He swallowed down bile before it erupted, thankful Hans had a grip on his shoulder. Her face resembled the worst sunburn he'd ever seen, reddened, but no visible blistering. At least not yet.

He inhaled, swallowed back not bile but tears clogging his throat. Her face shimmered in the lanterns' glow, and he realized they'd coated it with the soothing salve, too. Hopefully it soothed. Her hair resembled wet tangled ropes, some shortened and frazzled by singeing.

Luke closed his eyes, swaying, as he dug deep to gather needed strength. His once beautiful, sweet Morgan, so full of life, so eager to please and learn all, had survived. But at what cost? Would she be maimed, so scarred by blisters on her scalded skin that others would turn away in repugnance? Would she possess the fortitude to view life with such vigor and zest as she had, or become a recluse, lonely, bitter, and resentful?

He opened his eyes and watched as, half conscious, she accepted another spoonful of liquid. Presently, she bore the will to live, to survive any way she could. Thank God for that.

He smiled, knowing she'd never be lonely, never give up without a fight. Not his Morgan.

She would bounce back, scars, or no scars. Rally to overcome any disabilities that might persist. Others would flock to her because of the way she was. All spunk and spirit, determined to live life to the fullest, with that sweet charm that could knock the socks off the hardest of hearts. And he'd be there to see it through, too. If he couldn't be more to her because of Lucy, he'd always be her friend. No matter what.

God knew he wanted more. And at that very moment he knew he'd take her to wife if he were free to do so, scars or no scars. A swelling deep within his heart expanded until he thought it would burst his chest wide open. Devotion, so powerful, so fervid, nearly knocked him to his knees. His love was that strong, by God. Nothing would ever change that fact. He might not be able to act upon it, but it lay there, deep-seated, imbedded for life.

She'd always be his Morgan. Maybe not physically, maybe not emotionally on her part, but she'd be in his heart forever.

"Ya okay?" Hans put his other hand on Luke's shoulder.

"Yeah. It's a bit of a shock, but I'm fine. I'm more than fine just knowing she's alive."

When Luke met Hans's gaze, he almost laughed. He did smile at seeing the incredulous look on his friend's face. Priceless. Had Hans thought he'd turn tail and run from her blazing tissues, from a woman who possibly lay at death's door? A woman who had stuck by him and helped him in this rotten scheme?

"You think a few burns will stop her for long?"

"Guess yur right there. Let's hope she hops back easy enough." Hans's face held a wariness that belied his eager answer. But Luke would cling to hope that all would be well soon. Her recovery would take time, but, all in all, he prayed his Morgan wouldn't let him down.

Luke grinned. "Although it pisses me off to be beholden to you, you big ox, I probably should thank you for pulling both of us out. I could hear my name being called, but I couldn't think straight. So thanks, Hans, from me and from Morgan."

Hans returned his grin. "Beholden, huh? Well I'll be damned. And yur both welcome."

"You can come closer," Sarah offered.

He nodded, took the few steps across the blanket to reach Morgan's side. Bending down on his haunches, he rested his palms against his thighs.

Her face somber, Sarah placed a comforting hand over his. "She's somewhat awake. Took down more water than I had hoped for. I've been giving her broth Tom fetched for me, to replenish what nourishment she lost."

The woman looked as bedraggled as Morgan. Dark gray half-moons lay under each eye, in a face white as paper. Her hair looked as though a bat had got caught in it and fought its way back out. She'd had it rough, helping her friend cheat death's knock.

"She doesn't look very awake. Can she hear me if I talk to her?" This close to Morgan, he felt helpless, useless, scared he'd disturb her or cause her more harm. She looked so…so lifeless.

"She was awake a little bit ago, but I gave her some laudanum. For the pain as well as to sedate her. Quiet's what she needs. That's what you're seein', besides the burns and inhalin' that smoke.

She'll be pretty tired from all that for some days, I'd imagine. But she'll hear you. Most likely needs to hear you. When she first woke, screamin' in pain—if you could call those hoarse whispers screamin'—she kept saying 'Luke?' It was her way of asking if you were all right."

His chest tightened at thinking of how incredible the pain must have been, how much more she'd have to suffer before relief finally came her way. Yet he smiled to think Morgan had thought of him at her worst hour. His Morgan. And he'd almost lost her. He shivered.

"Sarah, I don't know how to thank you, to thank everyone for everything they did here tonight. I—"

"Don't you go getting all soft-like just now, Luke Kincaid." Her raised voice had Luke leaning back just a tad and raising his eyebrows in surprise.

"Morgan's alive, but not out of the woods. To tell the truth, I thought she'd be much worse. The worst of the heat and smoke must have been when you got inside. Her hands are burned and blistered; God only knows how that happened. I put salve on and wrapped them the best I could. Her arms, legs, and feet are only scorched, but that's a lot of heated skin and can be mighty serious, if not handled right. Didn't wrap them, so they'll stay cooler, and the bandages might chafe, and that'd do more harm. If they blister, then we'll have to." She set the cup of liquid to the side, stretched her back, then stood.

"She's been breathing real good, but after someone inhales that much smoke, they might get all kinds of lung problems. We'll have our work cut out for us come weeks from now, if we're not careful. So I need that confident man who gives orders and sees things done. That's the man I'll be needin', and so will she. Mind you, I'll give every extra minute to this wife of yours. I love her as if she were my own child, I do. And I can rightly speak for all the others that they'll be pitchin' in when needed. You got the power to make her fight, to keep her sights on the bright future ahead. That girl loves you somethin' powerful, she does, otherwise she might have just laid there and taken her last breath."

Oh, if only it were so. To have Morgan's love would be a gift from heaven, would be…

What the hell am I thinking? It would only complicate matters more. It would be disastrous for both of them. And Lucy. How could he be thinking such thoughts? It was a wonder God hadn't let him die in the fire for being such a sinner. Only mentally, but a sinner, nonetheless.

"You seem quite knowledgeable at tending the sick, Sarah. I'm mighty grateful for that, as I am for all you've done. And that is plain thanking you. I'll not let you or Morgan down when the time comes. I promise," he said with a grin and a wink.

"You men are all alike," she laughed, blushing like a young girl. "You think your handsome faces, those rogue smiles, and flirting will get all of you into our good graces, don't you."

"Why, Sarah, the thought never occurred to me. You wound me."

"Pooh and stuff it, young man. Save it for your lady fair here." Despite her reprimand, she gave a hearty laugh. "I can see why she took to you right from the start." Hands on hips, she studied him. "I do believe it's those eyes of yours, or maybe that smooth talkin'." She laughed.

How I wish that were true. Luke chuckled as she went on.

"I don't know as much as some about doctorin', but I did help a doctor back home for a while. He taught me a few things. I took care of some bad burns, let me tell you, and praise be to God I did. And I thank the good Lord Lela and I had the salves we brought with us. Otherwise you might've seen me come unglued tonight rather than being any help to this poor young'un."

"I don't believe that for a second, Sarah."

She looked ready to become unglued, if her eyes told the story. The talk had shifted back to serious. They didn't need that right now. He turned his attention to Morgan.

"Morgan, honey, can you hear me?" He would have liked to reach under the blanket, to take her hand in his, but no way would he cause her more pain. So he opted to brush the side of her head with his fingers, ever so careful not to touch reddened skin on her face or neck.

"Can you hear me, sweetheart? It's Luke. I'm safe and you're safe. You're going to have a harder time than I, for your skin's scorched like a bad sunburn, your hands are burned, worse than any of my burns, and you inhaled a lot more smoke. But in no time we'll have you up and at 'em." His endearments had come readily, before he'd thought twice about them. If Morgan should ever question them, he'd say they'd been for Sarah's benefit. After all, they were supposedly married. Yeah, that sounded good.

Her lips parted, curved upward, though not more than a fraction. The lantern flickered, sending slanted beams and shadows dancing to and fro across her face, but he thought he saw her eyelids ripple. He couldn't be sure. Yet her lips had said enough. She'd heard him. It stamped down his alarm a degree. She was a determined lady, a fighter. She'd make it. She had to. He'd damn well see she did.

"I know you can hear me, Morgan, so listen carefully." He curled a stray lock of hair back from her cheek and tucked it behind her ear. "We'll find those men, and when we do, they'll pay for what they did to you. That's the promise I'm making to you. I'll..."

"Ah, Luke?" Monk said in a hushed tone as he drew near.

Luke glanced to his left as Monk knelt down. The man's eyes widened as he stared her.

"Jesus." He frowned, and crossed himself. "Is…is she gonna be okay?"

"She's going to be fine. It'll just take some time."

Monk's skeptical gaze met his. "Sure am glad to hear it."

His eyes swung back to Morgan. "Luke says yur gonna be right as rain, ma'am. We'll hold him to that, an' we'll do our part, too. Yep, ya betcha."

That this man of so few words offered encouragement and help to Morgan impressed the hell out of Luke. Sure, Monk worked from dawn to dusk as a helluva monkey and was a mighty fine baker of bread, besides. But who would have thought the man could say so many sentences in a row? Morgan had life pegged right.

Life was good. With all its ups and downs. It was damn good.

Swiping his beard with a hand, Monk met Luke's gaze. "Come to tell ya, I be movin' in with Les for a bit, so yous and yer missus can take my place till ya got a new one. Ain't clean as she'd probably like. Ain't got no fancies the womenfolk fuss 'bout. But it got a good roof overhead. Mattress ain't the best, but it be thick tick. Ain't no bugs, I tell ya. I make damn sure of that."

The man's solemn face looked set in stone. He'd said his piece and that was that. How many sentences had he issued in a row? Monk's face might be granite, but his heart sure overflowed with sunshine.

His offer left Luke temporarily speechless. Hell, he hadn't even thought that far ahead.

He swallowed down the huge lump in his throat. "I'm mighty obliged by your offer, Monk, but I can't put you out of your…"

"Ya might be boss, bull man, but ya ain't got no place to go, do ya?"

Dumbfounded by the man's sudden bravado, Luke shrugged.

"Ain't no hardship fer me ta leave that place fer awhile. If'n I can't stand Les's snorin' and fartin', I can jist skedaddle. Shared plentya nights with them stars afore. Wun't be the first. Sure as hell wun't be the last."

Luke bit back a bark of laughter at the man's vehemence. Monk would take offense if he let loose his mirth. The offer rose from pure sincerity. He'd not look a gift horse in the mouth, as the saying went. He'd not offend such an offer of friendship.

"I'm mighty obliged, Monk…" Morgan's moan interrupted him from embellishing his thanks. Hell, it'd be better not to get too lavish with any gratitude. They'd both be choked up by that time.

He turned his attention to Morgan, stroking her hair. "It's Luke, sweetheart. I'm here. Do you need something for the pain?"

Christ, he felt helpless. He needed to see her comfortable, not lying on a blanket on the chilled ground. He wanted to offer reassurance, unsure how to promise such a thing.

Guilt riddled his gut for having put her in the direct line of fire. Fire! The mere word sent fury spiraling through him as he contemplated who could have done such a violation to such an innocent.

He'd never felt so inept, at such a loss as to what to do next for someone, as he seemed to be now. It gnawed at him, left him in a quandary. It damn well didn't sit well at all.

"Here," Sarah offered, coming to Morgan's side. She knelt down, a bottle in one hand, a spoon in her other. "I'll give her a little more laudanum. Just enough so she'll sleep and won't be in pain. That's what she'll need for the next few days. Rest and comfort will heal her faster."

Removing the top of the brown bottle, she handed it to Luke. He accepted it and watched her pour a few drops into the spoon.

"Couldn't help but overhear you two," she said, easing the liquid between Morgan's lips. "It's good of you, Monk, to offer your place. Morgan'll surely thank you when she's able. Won't be far to go for any of us to watch her while Luke's workin'."

Had everyone figured out what had to be done so quickly? He'd not thought past the fact that Morgan still breathed.

Get hold of yourself. He'd always been one to take charge. Yet here he sat, a tortoise on an eggshell, a dunce without direction. He bade the cobwebs haste from his befuddled mind.

Okay, Morgan had suffered. Badly. But, with God's will, she'd soon be well. As her husband, he had the duty to see she recuperated readily. He had trees to fell and move down the river. He had men to apprehend. He needed to take charge.

"That should be plenty for now." Sarah reached over, took the cap from Luke, and screwed it on the bottle.

"How long will that take to work?"

"Just a few minutes." She rose and dusted off her skirt.

Relieved, Luke nodded. "Good, I'll make a litter and be back before it wears off. It'll be more comfortable than the buckboard, and I'll be able to go through the woods instead of around."

"I'll help," Monk eagerly offered.

Chapter Eighteen

Luke cautiously sat down on Monk's bed and scrutinized Morgan as she slept. Minutes ago Sarah had given her another dose of medicine. Two pillows lay under her head, while others supported each arm and one under her knees kept her legs from touching.

Sarah had indeed acted like a mother hen, assuring her charge was well settled before leaving. Like an army general, she'd issued instructions. When to give the laudanum, when and how much liquid to force down her, to keep only a thin sheet over her so as not to hold in heat from the wounds, and to keep the fire banked to prevent her taking a chill.

With a satisfied grin and a heavy hand, Luke swiped his face as the entire night took its toll. He'd need to trim his beard, come morning, he realized, as his hand brushed over charred ends. Right now his mind and body needed sleep.

Wishing the bed wider so he could be close to Morgan yet not crowd her, Luke scowled at the floor, since Monk didn't own a couch. Damn, he'd become soft. No, it'd been a long, back-breaking, terrifying night. His wounds screamed. Bloody drainage colored the bandages.

He'd been obstinate, unduly willful, when he'd insisted he help make the litter. He shouldn't have. But he'd felt the need to take care of her. Now he paid. It'd been worth it.

Resigned to having no other choice, he gathered

a few worn blankets, stretched them out beside the bed, and balled up his jacket into a lumpy pillow. Sarah would bring more pillows.

He turned down the wick in the lamp on the crude table, set the spoon and medicine on the floor by the bedside so it would be handy when she awakened, and lay down on his humble bed. Unable to find a position to ease the stinging in his arms, he rolled over, unscrewed the top of the bottle and took a small sip.

It wouldn't hurt to gain just an hour or two of good sleep before having to tend to Morgan. Yes, just an hour would help.

****

"N-, n-..."

The whispered cry roused Luke from his drugged snooze. The moan, more a whimper, had him blinking to orient himself.

Morgan.

Instantly awake, he squinted through the muted daylight at the clock on the table. "Shit." He'd slept four hours. Four friggin' hours. Two hours longer than she should have gone without water, an hour longer than the medicine could hold her.

"Damn idiot." He sat up, rubbed his hand over his hazy eyes.

Before he could haul himself up, he had to flex his arms, shoulders, and legs to ease out the tightness in his muscles.

"I'm here, sweetheart. I'll get you some water. You'll feel better with some water and medicine." He touched her shoulder, hoping the contact might soothe her.

Her eyelids twitched, her long lashes fluttering like a butterfly's wings. A wonder she still had lashes. She opened her eyes, looked up at him. They were clouded from the laudanum, glassy from discomfort. His heart constricted at knowing he'd again caused her to suffer.

"Good…morning," she mouthed, not even a whisper leaving her lips. The fact that she tried to speak, with a smile, in spite of her obvious raw throat nearly ripped his heart in two.

"Shh, don't try to talk." He sat down beside her. "Sarah said you might not be able to speak for awhile. The heat scorched your throat, plus you inhaled a lot of smoke. Just nod or shake your head so you won't irritate it more."

She nodded, turning her head to scan the room.

He read her weary-eyed question. "It's Monk's cabin. He wouldn't take no for an answer. He's bunking with Les till we build a place. Sarah'll be here soon. She appointed herself your personal guardian." Her eyebrows rose.

"She tended your burns. Wouldn't leave till she knew you were well taken care of. You have another mother, who loves you very much." *As much as I do, though I know better.*

Again a faint smile curved her lips, yet her eyes clouded over with pain. Damn, she needed liquids and relief.

He strode to the table, poured water from the pewter pitcher into a chipped mug, grabbed a towel, and returned to sit by her side. The mattress dipped under his weight as he leaned to position the towel like a bib under her chin. Reaching down, he took the spoon he'd left with the laudanum, wiped it clean with the corner of the towel, and dipped the spoon into the water.

"Here you go. It's bound to taste good." He smiled at her eagerness to accept the offering. She swallowed with much effort, but her eyes glinted appreciation.

"That's good, huh?" He gave her a smile of encouragement.

She nodded, her smile barely visible. His heart

sang.

He repeated the process over and over again, allowing her an interval to gain enough strength to try again. He poured half a teaspoon of laudanum, and brought the spoon to her lips.

Her eyes rounded, then she shook her head.

"Oh, no, you don't. Doctor Sarah said you need this every three hours. It's way overdue."

When she shook her head again, her eyes now sharp and determined, he laughed at her stubbornness. Ah, a good sign, indeed. Yep, his Morgan was one tough lady. A fighter. She'd pull through this. For the first time in nearly twenty-four hours, since finding the dam tampered with, after fighting the blaze and being near frantic over her injuries, he felt his heart lighten.

Elated, he leaned back. "If you think I want Sarah's wrath on my shoulders, young lady, you're mighty mistaken. No way am I going to get in her line of fire. She may be soft-spoken and good-natured most of the time, but I've seen her in action. And I have a sneaking suspicion, if push comes to shove, her claws can be as deadly as a mama bear's."

Her eyes twinkled in delight. Yes, the world was good indeed. "You think it would be amusing, do you? For me to take her heat? I don't think so. Not me. I learned years ago a man had best watch himself when it comes to crossing a woman on a mission."

She bit her lip lightly and he knew she fought the smile that would cause her face agony. He'd best get to business.

He leaned closer, brought the spoon to her lips, and met her gaze. "Be reasonable. I could deal with Sarah's wrath, believe me. I'd rather listen to her ranting than force you to do something you didn't want. But you need this to keep the pain under control so you can rest."

She held his gaze. Looked unconvinced.

"Please, sweetheart." He watched her eyes soften as defiance fled. His pulse flitted at realizing his endearment had caused such a response. He shouldn't have said it, hadn't meant to, really. It had slipped out easily from mind to lips. He'd have to watch himself and his words from now on. For both their sakes.

"Take it. It's the only way I can help you right now. I won't be able to sleep knowing you're suffering because of me."

She frowned, her eyes darting to his bandaged arms, his face. She drew in a quick breath, winced, then quivered.

"I fared much better than you. I may have pulled you out of the fire, but I blame myself that you were there in the first place."

She tried to pull an arm from under the covers, shaking her head back and forth.

Placing his free hand lightly on the covers, he halted her movement. "Don't use your arms. It'll cause more pain to your hands. I'm to blame, and for that I'll never forgive myself. If you want to help me deal with that, you've got to take this. Please."

He knew he played dirty pool, working on her sensibilities and compassion. It could be his only means of breaking through her determination. And if that's what it took to get her to comply, so be it. He'd play good and dirty.

"Please. For me."

Her lips thinned. She knew exactly the game he played. And she didn't like it one bit. Their gazes locked. He knew the instant she relented—saw it in her eyes.

She parted her lips in silent acceptance. A jolt of desire ran through him from head to toe. He yearned to toss the medicine aside, lean further down, and taste the delectable sweetness.

Forcing irresponsible longings back where they belonged, he brought the spoon to her lips. Lips that looked soft as a rose petal kissed by sunshine. *Stop.* He spooned in the laudanum.

"You won't regret it, sw…Morgan. You need the rest."

Her smile turned so pathetic, so defeated, he felt his heart lurch. Felt the bite of pain from it. Damn, if she didn't resemble a doe that knew she'd been bested. He shook, battling the urge to take her in his arms, to reassure her, to hold her against his chest. All warm and soft and…*Christ!*

He felt anything but warm and soft. His blood flowed hot and rampant; his groin ached. Hell, he was hard as a rock. Shifting to ease the discomfort, he bent down, retrieved the bottle, and strode to the table. He set down the laudanum and went to the counter to start coffee, all the time keeping his back to her so she wouldn't see his despicable reaction.

With his back to her, he set the pot on the stove. "Sarah and the others should be here shortly. I need to go outside for a few minutes. Is there anything you need before I go?" He prayed she needed nothing.

When no response came, he looked over his shoulder. What a jerk. She could utter not a word. Had he thought she would?

She shook her head slowly. Good, the drug had begun to kick in.

"I won't be long."

****

After relieving himself, Luke stared up at the sky, reluctant to go inside quite yet. What a coward he'd become. No, sensible, logical. No use playing with fire when a flame tempted you.

Wagon wheels clattered close by, along with the plod of heavy hooves. "Thank God."

He needed to go to the site, assure himself

everything had gone well for the duration of the early morning, and that work had resumed as usual. He needed to distance himself from Morgan. From the temptation of making the biggest mistake of his life.

After extending his heartfelt thanks, he'd issued orders before leaving the destroyed structure that had been his home. Of course, orders hadn't been needed, as the men who'd accompanied him to the fire planned to return to the camp, to pick up where they'd left off. He felt confident those left behind to guard the dam and camp had done their part while the others had battled the blaze.

Tom's wagon crested the small knoll, breaking free of the surrounding forest. Luke noted how Rosie sat thigh to thigh beside Hans, obviously unembarrassed that Sarah and Lela were perched in the back. Luke sighed in relief as they neared. He'd be able to leave shortly, to go work off his frustration. Some of it, anyway. He needed to focus on work, make plans for a new cabin. He needed to think of Lucy and forget his attraction to Morgan.

Yet the thought of leaving Morgan all day sent his mind into turmoil again. The women could take care of her. Bandages needed to be changed, broth simmered, her body bathed. She had needs he could hardly meet.

He felt his face blush. He'd relieved himself without giving thought to her personal need. This situation of her being bedridden could never work. How would he meet her needs, decently, when alone with her? Everyone except Hans believed them married. They'd assume he could handle her elimination problem. *Damn.* He swept a hand over his face to rid the perspiration. What if she had her woman's time and he needed to assist her with changing of her…

"Christ. What the hell am I to do?"

Hans drew the wagon to a halt in front of the cabin, none too soon. Shaking off the disturbing questions, he ambled across the clearing toward them. He'd figure out something for dealing with the future awkward situation. Something that had better be good.

"Thought you'd still be catching a few winks," Hans said, looping the reins over the brake, his expression full of razzing.

"When have you known me to laze in bed?" He could give as good as Hans shelled out. He lowered the tailgate and reached up to assist Sarah and Lela out.

Hans laughed as he leaped to the ground, then swung Rosie down. "Ya got me there."

"Good morning, how's Morgan?" Sarah frowned at Luke's soiled bandages.

"She had several hours of peaceful sleep. Just gave her some more medicine. She took a fair amount of water, too."

Sarah nodded, then joined the others at the back of the wagon. They gathered baskets of what looked to be salves and bandages. Lela stuck a pillow under her arm and handed over a mounded basket of food to Hans.

"Where's Tom?" Luke asked, as Hans adjusted the basket.

"Rode out first thing this mornin'. Said he'd get a few things done before we got done here." Hans reached for a sack.

Sarah pulled a basket to the end, bounced it through the air as if judging its weight, and turned to Luke. "Here, you take this one. I don't think it's too heavy."

"Too heavy? For me? Hell, woman, I could lift and carry you in without giving a second thought." Her words cut deep.

Her eyes twinkled, a light chuckle escaped her

lips. She knew she'd gotten his goat.

"Not today or tomorrow you won't." With hands on hips, she plastered on a look of disapproval. "Just look at those arms." He glanced down at the sloppy, soiled bandages, feeling like a little boy being scolded.

"You wouldn't take 'no' last night, would you. No, sir. You had to help with that litter, ride through the woods, then carry her in. And what for, I ask you? All to start those burns to bleedin' is what for." It was a wonder her loud, annoyed huff didn't blow the wagon ten feet ahead.

Sheepishly, Luke looked over at the others for support. All were straight faced. Straight faced? Hell. They were having a helluva time holding back their mirth. No help there.

Hans's brows arched as he shook his head. "Glad yur the one at the end of her tongue." Hans didn't even try to hide his irritating grin as he shifted the items in his arms.

"A good friend you are," Luke retorted, but found the woman's ire just as amusing.

With a basket in each hand, Sarah tipped her head toward the cabin. "Let's get you in there so I can see to those arms." She made a beeline for the cabin before he could counter her demand. They all fell into step—workers following the queen bee.

Entering the cabin, Luke set his light parcel on the table. "Sarah, I've got to get to the—"

"I tell ya, girls, ain't no use talkin' to a barn door." She deposited her baskets on the counter. "It just don't listen." She eyed a sleeping Morgan, the covers up to her chin, her face laced with a dusky tinge of fatigue despite her ruddy cheeks. Sarah frowned as she surveyed the make-do bed on the floor.

Luke spit out what he hoped sounded logical. "I didn't want to crowd her in the bed."

Sarah whirled around to face Luke, her brows arched. "That was very thoughtful. But you'll sit down and let me tend those wounds. That camp's not goin' anywhere."

"But—"

"No ifs, ands, or buts about it. You just sit yourself down. The sooner you do, the sooner you can go. Them bandages need changin'. If we don't, you'll end up with a ragin' fever and festerin' that'll smell like a pig's droppin's. We got us one bedridden patient. We don't need two."

His brows rose this time, at her vehemence. She was right, but, dammit, it didn't sit well, taking orders. He had a hundred things to see to, and he usually gave the orders. Women. They could drive a man crazy.

He glanced at Morgan. She looked so sweet, so very fragile. When well, she grabbed at life, so ready to please, so determined. His chest swelled with memories of their shared time together. Women. They could also make a man's life heaven.

"Might as well do as the harridan says, Luke." Hans laughed. "She be determined as you when ya got a mission."

Luke eyed Hans's fresh bandage over the gash on his forearm, then peered at Sarah. She stood with hands on hips, eyes unwavering. He'd not win the skirmish against such a general.

"Sit."

Yep, the woman had a mission, all right. Luke grinned, sat, and let her do her worst.

****

Luke issued orders and instructions as if he were captain of a ship that was going down. They'd lost precious time since yesterday, what with repairing the dam and fighting the fire. Hell, by the time he'd got there, half the morning had gone by. He pulled a branch aside so the men could lead the oxen through. His arms burned as if flames stirred under the wrappings.

"Glad Sarah isn't here to see that," Hans said from behind.

Luke nearly jumped at his words. Wouldn't surprise him if she lurked nearby. Wiping the sweat from his face with his shirtsleeve, he swallowed, praying the white-hot sting would vanish.

"I can't sit back when work has to be done."

Hans nodded. "*Ja*, we both know that. But I want to be there when she sees those bandages tonight."

At Hans's smirk, Luke glanced down at his shirtsleeves. Already spots of bloody drainage had seeped through the gauze to discolor the plaid. He looked down at the pant leg that had started to tug. Dark areas marked where the buckskin adhered itself to the bandage.

"Shit."

Hans grinned.

"Don't say it. I'll get enough when I get back."

"*Ja*. And I'll be there to hear it." His grin grew.

"Maybe you shouldn't. You promised her you'd see me not raise a hand today." Luke chuckled as Hans's face blanched.

"Shit."

The two laughed throughout the rest of day each time the bleeding restarted, knowing he'd pay for it later. Only Luke knew he gritted his teeth more than not when burning jabbed his arms or flamed up his leg, nearly buckling him to his knees.

By sundown, Luke, ready to drop to the ground where he stood, called it a day. It'd been a long two days, not only for him but for the others, as well. They all needed rest.

He left a handful of men—those who'd not spent half the night battling the blaze—to man the site throughout the dark hours. Tom tied his horse to the back of the wagon, Hans took the reins of the team, and Luke sacked out in the back, wanting peace and quiet, and a blanket to rest his exhausted body.

****

"Never in my born days have I ever seen the likes of two more pig-headed, stubborn imbeciles."

Luke swayed, leaned against the counter, and listened to Sarah's wrath. God, he'd love to just slither to the floor. If she'd just let up, do her thing, and be done with it. But oh, no, she had to say her piece first. She had for the last ten minutes.

Fiery hot and sharp as a new ax, her tongue-lashing persisted. He'd never received so many derogatory names in his life. He deserved them. He braced himself against the counter more heavily so he wouldn't crumble before she had the last say.

His gaze drifted to the bed. He'd checked Morgan's condition upon arriving. She'd fared well through the day, thank God. If from nothing else, his heart had lightened at knowing she'd rested comfortably. Hopefully, her recovery would progress.

Right now her eyes twinkled and her lips just barely curved. He knew she laughed a good one inside. At least Hans wasn't laughing this time. Yep, Hans got as good as he did.

When his bandages had been changed, his stomach filled, and a dose of laudanum taken to ease the burning, Luke watched Tom bank the fire for the night and said his good night as they all left. He nearly crawled across the room. Damn, but his ears still rang.

Quietly, so as not to awaken Morgan, he turned down the wick till its glow bathed the room in a soft glow, pulled back the top blanket, shucked his shirt and buckskins, and sank down. Blessed be the comfort of warm bedding and a soft pillow.

"Lu...ke?" Her wispy whisper pierced the silent air.

Instantly alert to anything she might need, he popped upright to a sitting position.

"I'm right beside you, sw-…Morgan."

"N-…"

He scrambled out of the covers, sat down by her side. "Don't try to talk. Sarah said it would do more harm to stretch those cords too soon."

Through the dim glow he saw her smile, so sweet and so pleasing it seemed to feed his tired body with a heady calm.

"Flo…or." She shook her head.

He barely managed to decipher her mumbled word. "What…what is it you want?" Floor? Floor no? No floor. As understanding hit, he smiled. "You don't want me on the floor?"

She nodded, her concern evident.

He chuckled. "Believe me, I've slept on much worse. And the way I feel tonight, it feels like a king's bed."

She shook her head, more adamant this time. "Work, to-…mor-…" she coughed and her eyes clouded. From fatigue? From pain? It tore at his innards.

"Shh." He brushed back a lock of hair that had slipped to her cheek. "Yes, I have to work tomorrow. But if not the floor, the only other place is here in this narrow bed. You and I both know I shouldn't do that. I'll crowd you too much. I—"

She shook her head, issued a moan. He watched her lips quiver, her breathing accelerate. How could he deny her anything?

"You sure? I don't want to compromise you more than I already have, or crowd you and rob you of needed rest."

She nodded, though a frown furrowed her brow, and her eyes conveyed she'd overexerted herself just by trying to talk.

Only then did he realize he sat clad solely in

thin drawers. Damn, his buckskins needed to dry out so he could brush out the soiled pant leg in the morning. Aw, hell, he wasn't up to rummaging to find the pair Hans had loaned him.

"Ple-…ju-…b-…ne-…me…"

Please just be near me. The words gut-punched him. His heart turned over, leaving him breathless. Oh, Morgan, sweetheart, that's all I want. If only you knew what you ask. His vision swam in front of him. He had to blink, to will the moisture away.

He stood, crossed the room to fetch the laudanum and spoon, then returned to the bed and placed them on the floor. Knowing it foolish to grant her request, he nonetheless reached under her and gently slid her over in the bed. His heart lurched when she shuddered from the movement; it righted with her relieved sigh.

Easing in beside her, he turned on his side and extended his arm above her pillow to give her more room.

"This what you wanted?"

It seemed forever as her eyes scanned his face in the muted light. The thin sheet rustled as her arm moved beneath it. She took hold of his right wrist and brought it over her so his arm lay across her at her waist. He nearly leaped off the bed.

Their gazes met, held. A lump in his throat rose, grew enormous. His arm, where it rested across her, heated, but not from the burns he'd obtained.

Here they both lay, he thought, in turmoil. She with a gamut of painful burns and barely able to whisper, himself tired beyond belief, with burns more than discomforting, and he could only think about how soft she felt through the thin nightgown Sarah had dressed her in. How clean and fresh she smelled after Sarah's efficient ministrations. How much their warm contact mimicked an aphrodisiac, with only thin garments as barriers against any…

Damn! Settle down, you fool. She only wants comfort. Get your thoughts in the right frame of mind. But another part of him refused to overlook her nearness. The mere touch of her incited a fire deep inside.

"Feel better?" he asked, wondering if she detected the huskiness of his voice.

"Mmm."

She slithered over a fraction, snuggling closer, resting her head in the crook of his arm. Wherever her body touched him a flame sizzled, heating his blood, scorching his skin.

He fought the trembling that threatened. It would do no good at all for her to suspect the effect she had on him. He listened to her sigh again. At least *she* lay content. He wanted to grunt. Sleep would elude him for quite some time, he reasoned. It would most likely take all night for his rock-hard arousal to dwindle.

He held her lovingly. "That's right, sweetheart, go to sleep." *Before this bed ignites.*

Chapter Nineteen

Wheels clamoring like thunder, hooves plodding the earth to match the pounding beat of a bass drum, and a booming “whoa” that echoed within the four small walls jolted Luke awake. It damn well put him in a sour mood. It had been one hell of a night.

Sleep deprivation had his eyes burning, while his muscles begged for more rest. Yet he levered himself from the bed, cautiously, so as not to awaken Morgan. He snatched the blankets off the floor, plopped them over a chair, and darted across the room to don his pants. Voices rose in volume as the sun, barely rising, dove through the cloudy windows.

He had but one button fastened in his fly, his belt hanging loose, when a light knock came and the door swung wide. Sarah burst through the open doorway as if propelled by a whirlwind. A basket in each hand swung with equal fervor.

She cleared half the room before skidding to a dead stop. Her mouth fell open. Her eyes looked ready to pop out of their sockets. In one breathless second, her face paled, then flushed.

“Oh, my, I’m so sorry,” she stammered, averting her eyes to the bed. Despite her flaming cheeks, the mother hen’s smile mirrored her satisfaction that her chick remained safe.

Her gaze roamed everywhere but toward him, while the baskets slowed their swinging. Luke, now very much awake, secured the buttons, pulled the belt buckle tight, and slipped into his shirt. He didn’t know if he should be embarrassed or laugh at the silly woman's mortification.

Instead, he crossed the room, relieved her of the baskets, and deposited them on the table. Only then did she dare a glance at him. Though her face looked sunburned, she appeared to be recovered from the awkward scene.

"I never considered I'd be intruding. I don't know where my mind is today. I..."

"Don't give it another thought, Sarah," Luke cut in, offering a welcoming smile. Astonishingly, or maybe not so astonishingly, his sour mood had vanished, he realized. Yes, it was all he could do not to laugh at the woman's sincere urgency to see to Morgan's needs.

"No harm done. But maybe, in the future, give me a minute longer to answer the knock."

Her face flamed to match the linen covering the baskets, her hands kneading each other.

Tom's voice rang his censure from the doorway. "Woman, you ought to have more sense than to barge into a man's home first thing in the morning."

Lela and Rosie peered over Tom's shoulder with mischievous grins and eyes glistening. Luke caught the softening of Tom's eyes as he peered at his wife. Though he'd said his piece emphatically, this man was obviously wrapped around a woman's finger.

"I'll not do it again." When Sarah's gaze locked with Tom's, Luke felt a swift kick to his innards. Love, true and devoted, poured from each of them. A deep and potent longing ached within his chest. If only he had the right to look at Morgan with such emotion.

Aw, hell.

****

Luke worked like a man possessed from their arrival at the site until dusk, when he called an end to a day's good work. There'd been no havoc at the site during the night. None today, either, thank God.

They had cut far more than the day's anticipated allotment, and had the logs bobbing in the swollen river's jam. He'd worked off some frustration concerning his feelings for Morgan. He and Hans had even made time to search for possible clues at the charred cabin. And, by God, they might have a lead. A long shot, maybe, but something. He'd had a good day.

Now as he and Tom rode over the bumpy terrain to Monk's cabin, the sun tucked behind the mountain peaks, while muted ribbons of red and orange skimmed the summits. Luke contemplated the night ahead with both eagerness and dread. He needed to see Morgan. Just being away for so many hours had him restless, concerned over her comfort. Yet he wondered how he'd survive another sleepless night if she insisted he again stay close. And more importantly, he needed to put their relationship in perspective. Proper perspective.

He had a fiancée—ailing, yes, possibly nearing death in the coming months or year. No one knew for sure. The thought of losing her, no matter if his heart belonged to another, pierced deep down inside, plagued his conscience with guilt-ridden disgust. He did the heartfelt affinity, the passion-driven longing he felt for Morgan, but he did love Lucy. Had loved her for who and what she was from early childhood. Owed her his devotion, pure and steady. And he'd honor that devotion no matter how hard, how heartrending it might become.

He owed Morgan, too. Owed his gratitude for fulfilling her end of the bargain, for offering her assistance and advice when he needed it the most. He vowed then and there he'd see her safely back with her family if she so desired, or wherever she might wish to settle. She deserved to go on with her life without having him shatter it in a million hopeless pieces by his lust, his foolish, wayward desires.

But how much could one man take before he cracked, before he illogically submitted to those tortuous yearnings? God, he ached. Ached simply picturing her sweet smile, those big compassionate eyes, thinking of how gentle her voice. How soft, like rose petals, her skin when he touched her. His chest tightened as if compressed in a vise and with every breath someone gave it one more turn.

"We can have a cabin up in that clearing by the pond in two days flat." Tom's comment brought Luke back to the present. "Just like Hans said, if we take one day to fell those trees just north of the site, they'd be perfect size."

"It's not right we take two whole days away from our work for my benefit. We'd not…"

"Who the hell ya kiddin'?" Tom snapped before clucking to the team to get them moving up the gradual slope. "We're ahead of schedule even with the fire and the damage to the dam. Ya just hired those three yesterday, so now we got extras to man the trees while we raise the cabin."

Luke looked out over the land, inhaled the clean, fresh, pine scent as he wrestled with his options. Hans, Tom, Monk, and several others had needled him all day to pick a day this week to start. The air had cooled in the last hour as the sun receded, leaving the temperature now in the comfortable seventies. He seemed to think better without the heated rays hammering his skin.

Monk certainly didn't seem to mind being put out of his cabin. But could he ask him to give up his home for however long he'd be here? If it were a sure bet it'd only be two or three more weeks, he'd stay put. But any longer wouldn't be right. And the situation between Morgan and himself would only grow more awkward unless he had a bigger area in which to distance himself from those tempting lips, those dark eyes that beckoned him to pull her into his arms.

Christ, why did he torture himself with thoughts of her throughout every stinking minute of the day? Why couldn't he sleep at night instead of conjuring up silly hopes for the future that could never be? How the hell could he resist her closeness, the heat and feel of her soft skin, the shapely curves nestled against his side as they lay in that narrow bed?

"Give it up, Luke. Ya know we can do it." Tom pulled back on the reins in front of the cabin. "Whoa." The horses dug their hooves into the loose soil and shifted their weight to a stop.

"Monk's cabin's no place for your wife. Ain't big enough, for starts. You'd do the same if one of us got burned out."

Tom's belief that Morgan was his wife left a bitter taste in Luke's mouth. He'd never liked outright lying, especially to a friend. What a helluva mess his life had become.

"I'll think on it tonight."

Tom scowled, obviously dissatisfied by his answer. "Yeah, ya think about it long and hard." With that, Tom leaped down and strode to the cabin. He felt hollow inside. He'd placed Morgan in danger, and now she suffered for it. He'd lied to everyone but Hans while acting his part. Mentally, but still shamefully sinful, he betrayed Lucy each time he yearned for Morgan's love.

Yep, my life is one fucking mess.

He had not the foggiest notion how to correct it. But he did know one certainty. He had to keep his distance. While Morgan slept, he concentrated on shaving off the shaggy mess of his mustache and beard. It felt better to be clean shaven again.

****

Only a saint could withstand Morgan's pleading eyes. And Luke was far from being a saint.

He'd taken laudanum to get some much-needed sleep for his aching muscles, respite from his willful libido, and relief from an agonized heart. Adjusting the covers, he wrapped his arms around the major source of his agony. Sleeping contentedly, she nestled against him, her head on his shoulder. He held her tightly, yet gently, as if she were a precious porcelain doll.

And all the while he berated himself for dishonoring Lucy with lascivious thoughts of another woman, betraying her by giving his heart and soul to that very one. For taking advantage of Morgan's naivety, so eager he'd been to share her nearness for all the wrong reasons. For lying to ninety-five percent of the camp regarding his true identity and his fake marriage, and for refusing his friends' well-meaning goodwill to the point of provoking their anger. Just what had he become?

****

Morgan settled within Luke's warm embrace and cursed her selfish, childish behavior. What had she been thinking? If Luke ever knew why she craved his nearness, he'd be appalled. He'd think her no better than a loose woman. She'd lose his respect as well as her dignity. Oh, but she'd had the strength to caress his face—clean shaven, high cheek bones, square chin. She knew her eyes had mirrored her thoughts. How shameful.

She never should have insisted he join her. She shouldn't have snuggled up to him last night. Or now. But God help her, she could have no more resisted urging him to do so than to take the very next breath. She'd thought if she couldn't have any other part of him at least she could glory in their shared closeness. Or at least she'd convinced herself that would be enough.

Now, however, she paid dearly. Longed for his kiss, the touch of his large, calloused hands upon her breasts. Wickedly yearned for his hard-muscled body to press against hers.

Could he hear her heart hammer, feel the heat of her body as her blood raced like molten lava through her veins? Did he know it took most of her energy to curtail the rapid breathing threatening to give her away? Dear God, how she ached, how she yearned for so much more.

Sinful is what she'd become, a disgusting, sinful Jezebel. What other logical woman would share a bed with another's fiancé? Wish for him to turn his devotion from his intended and offer it to her?

How had she sunk so low as to use her injuries to gain a mere embrace? Her wanton behavior sickened her, its disgrace ringing more pronounced as she realized she did, most assuredly, glory in the feel of his warmth and strength, the gentle yet steel-armed embrace.

When recuperated, she'd have to pull in her reins and bury her feelings in order to survive.

But how did one live with a heart broken in two? Or face a future that held nothing but yearning and dread?

Chapter Twenty

It took Luke only two days to concede defeat. Lying next to Morgan each night, hard as a rock, praying for salvation, generated his decision. Of course, those sleep-laden eyes each morning as she bade him farewell had him yearning to taste those pouting lips, and equally boosted his acceptance of a new cabin. He needed more space. Before he lost his mind and any honor he had left.

****

The new dwelling rose, steadfast and spacious, within three days' time. Another week before it could be furnished, time for the chink between logs and the mortar laced between the fieldstone wall to set. Now, with that accomplished, Luke surveyed the finished project, marveling at all the long, grueling hours everyone, including the women, had put in.

By day, sexually frustrated, he pushed to see the end in sight. At night, he lay moody, guilt-ridden, and disgusted at his lustful thoughts while Morgan snuggled trustingly against his heated skin.

He owed a world of gratitude to the handful of women who took turns during the day and into the long evenings seeing to Morgan's needs.

As dusk crept in, the forest grew quiet; birds nestled in for the dark hours ahead. He carried the last load of wood inside and stacked it along the front wall. Tomorrow he'd bring Morgan to her new temporary home before setting off to the log site.

"She'll love it, Luke. It's a fine cabin," Sarah said, carrying in a vase of purple wildflowers and feathery pines.

He brushed chips of bark from his shirt as Sarah set the vase in the center of the kitchen table, fussing over its arrangement. The table, one of many donated items, though marred and battered had been given in friendship. He felt humbled by the town's generosity. The town he lied to. About himself, his purpose, his so-called marriage.

"Yeah, I think she will." His mouth went dry; he felt every bit the imposter.

"And just think." Her eyes beamed brightly in the lantern's glow. "This is a bit closer to the pond. Oh, how she loves those loons."

Luke smiled, reflecting how every evening previous to the fire Morgan had excitedly described their various trills and tremolos, how they'd swoop under the surface, swimming faster than a bullet, then bob up on the far side. Yes, she loved them. So much that every day, with help, she'd trudge to the water's edge and lie on a blanket to study them.

Sarah bustled across the room to where a threadbare couch faced the woodstove. There she unfolded a quilt of maroon and deep green that she'd brought in earlier. Giving it a shake, she opened it halfway and draped it across the back of the couch.

"Adds a nice touch, Sarah. Thanks." *It'll come in handy for sleeping right there.*

Relieved he'd have more space, so he could keep his lust under control, he experienced a sense of loss at the same time. He loved the feel of Morgan's warm, slim body against his, to hear her light breaths as she slept, to inhale her clean, sweet scent...*God grant me some peace of mind.*

****

Morgan stood in the doorway speechless with awe as she gazed at her new home. Dismayed that it might be more temporary than she'd like, she wisely pasted on a bright smile. No sense in showing her true colors to either Luke or Sarah and Tom.

"Oh, my." She swallowed and cleared her throat of the annoying phlegm that so often persisted before she could utter a few words. But at least her voice, though husky and raspy, had returned enough to speak above a whisper. "It's…so much bigger than…I expected. So new…"

"I know, sweetheart," Luke said, placing a hand at her waist to guide her farther inside. "Don't talk too much at once. You don't want to lose it again."

Morgan felt a warmth curl through her, slow but heady, irresponsible yet satisfying. Whether due to his steady hand against her waist or his tender endearment she couldn't be sure. Hell's bells, probably both. Even knowing his endearment had been meant for Tom's and Sarah's ears, she basked in it. She could pretend, just for a minute.

And the cabin's spaciousness, the beautiful rock wall behind the stove, the way the sun's rays poured through the wide windows to fill the room with a soothing glow added to her contentment. By New York City standards, the opinion of those equal to her parents, the cabin would be considered crude, or worse. It was the loveliest home she'd ever had.

"Where did you get..." She cleared her throat. "The windows?" It amazed her how excited she felt over something so temporary, not really hers to keep and cherish. And oh, how Luke's grin sent that warmth scurrying rapidly through her veins.

"Seattle."

"Never thought he was a foolish man, before," Sarah huffed as she toted a basket through the doorway and placed it on the counter. Tom followed suit, depositing his parcel next to hers, a wince on his face at her blunt words regarding his boss.

Sarah spun to face them, her hands on her hips. "You got a right to know how careless he can be with his money, honey." Her gaze shifted from Morgan to

Luke and back again. “He paid top dollar, he did. Said he had to have the best glass and the finest hinges made. Why, he paid twice what he should have for some man to fetch them quick-like. For that woodstove, too.”

Morgan had to fight down laughter at Sarah’s outrage. When a needle stuck in the woman’s side, it undoubtedly poked true and for a long time. Shocked at Luke’s frivolity, Morgan glanced sideways to see if his scowl matched Tom’s embarrassed one.

Luke wore a grin a mile long, his eyes glinting amusement at Sarah’s bluster. Was there a better man on the earth anywhere?

“Now, Sarah, give me a little credit.” He smiled as Sarah frowned, her foot tapping her exasperation. He turned to Morgan. She felt her heart tweak.

“This cabin wasn’t built just out of logs and clay. It’s fortified to last a good many years—by the strong bonds of friendship, by long hard hours of devotion by a concerned and caring community. How in God’s name could I not complement the beauty of such a treasured gift with anything less than perfect glass and hinges that allow windows to open and let the gentle breeze flow in? Anything less would have been an insult.” He gave her a sheepish shrug as if he regretted being so vocal about how touched he’d been. No wonder she loved this man.

“And I needed the windows and woodstove in a hurry.” That boyish grin flashed again. Morgan’s heart thudded in her throat.

Morgan’s excitement pleased Luke to no end. Yet frissons of heat shot from his hand, where it still caressed her waist, up his arm and to a directly plotted conspiracy in his loins. He wrenched his hand away from the source of his dilemma. *Good God, I can’t even touch her innocently and not be affected.* What the hell would he do for the duration of their remaining time together?

He watched her, pleased as punch, as a kaleidoscope of emotions crossed her face, her wide eyes devouring the cabin's entirety. Thank God, they'd have more space, a separate bedroom. Though that thought offered some salvation, he knew no amount of space would be enough to keep his growing feelings at bay. Yes, it would take more than added roominess to keep his distance. It'd damn well take a will of steel. Did he have that kind of will power? She still bore a few scabs on her face where the skin had blistered. She'd have slight scars, one on her forehead, another on her chin, but nothing that wouldn't fade in time. She'd still be his lovely Morgan. Hell, who did he try to kid? She'd be lovely even if she'd been left with deep scars.

Morgan's frown halted his troubled thoughts. Had the ride overtaxed her? He nearly panicked.

"Where…did all this…"

"Why, honey," Sarah offered, "your friends and neighbors."

"But—"

"Never you mind, now," Sarah insisted, striding to Morgan's side to place a loving arm around her shoulder. "There ain't nothin' here that's gonna be missed by any of us. That's the God's honest truth. Accept it for what it is. Plain neighborly love. Yep, plain neighborly love."

Morgan's eyes turned to shimmering pools as they darted to him. Their soft warmth twined around his heart; their rich darkness held him spellbound. Were those tears of sincere gratitude, or dismay that they continued their deceit? Most likely both combined. No matter the reason, they pierced his very soul. *Added space sure as hell isn't going to do it for me.*

He cleared his cotton-filled throat. "Sarah's right. No one donated what they couldn't do without."

She blinked several times, and smiled. *Yep, it's not going to be any easier living here.* Her eyes scanned the room, full of wonder and obvious gratitude. Had he expected any less?

****

As dusk settled over the land, dots of sparkles and a glowing crescent overhead lighting the sky, Luke stood at the edge of the small lake. A lake so small some would refer to it as a natural pond. Silent, with Morgan contentedly sitting a few feet away, he watched two loons glide effortlessly across the water. Water so still it looked like a mirror, images of surrounding trees reflected in its glass-like surface. Only tiny ripples that gathered, fanned out, dissipated, then rose up again behind the coasting birds gave evidence the surface was truly liquid.

He canvassed the birds' journey while his mind rustled in turmoil. A turmoil so hopeless, so unsettling, he felt as if the earth had tilted off its axis.

He'd put in a backbreaking day's work and had been only too happy to say goodnight when Tom had fetched Sarah and departed for home. He'd thought he would welcome a pleasant dinner, prepared by Sarah and shared with Morgan in their new home.

But pleasant it had not been.

It had been more than awkward. Frustrating and mind-boggling, to be exact. And irresponsible. Forbidden, unintentional, yet compelling sensuous glances by both of them, tension-filled air laced with musk-scented heat. Hell, he couldn't even remember what they ate. Every bite had stuck in his gullet like a stone. That had been dinner.

Dessert had been the luscious locking of gazes until they both trembled from the magnetism between them.

He'd needed air. To breathe, to cut the tension, to stop himself from feasting on what would be the biggest mistake of his life. Had he not suggested they come watch the loons, he would've gathered her in his arms. And he wouldn't have stopped there. If he'd touched her they both would have been doomed.

Why the hell had he asked her along? He should have come by himself, to calm his rattled senses. Who was he kidding? To calm his damn arousal. He couldn't think straight with her so close. Why hadn't she parked herself anywhere else than by his side?

A yodel, full of arrogance, rose up from one of the birds. "Must be the male trying to impress the lady by marking his territory," he said before thinking. *Damn foolish bird.* Did males always fall prey to a pretty female?

The other answered with a short exhilarating wail that turned soulful. Had she given her acceptance? If it were only that easy, that simple, between himself and Morgan. He'd stake his claim and she'd accept. But that could never be.

He'd hoped his feelings were one-sided, for if they weren't, it would be much harder to resist her charm. But over the past several weeks he'd caught her shy glances when she thought he wasn't watching, had seen her eyes reflect her growing feelings. *God help us both, sweetheart.*

And now what were they to do? How could they both battle the tug that pulled so potently, so fervently that they couldn't look at each other without their hearts tattooing in their chests?

There was only one solution. He'd openly acknowledge the fire in order to snuff it out. Then and only then could they prevent any rekindling that might ignite into a major blaze. Without analyzing how he'd accomplish such a feat, he dove in.

He lowered himself to the ground, sitting close to her so as not to chase her friends on the pond away with his voice. Stretching out his legs, he leaned back on his elbows, kept his vision focused on the mysterious couple swimming with ease.

"I have something I find difficult, but necessary, to say."

With knees bent, bandaged hands encircling her legs, Morgan looked at him. "Go ahead."

Straightforward, that's what she liked. He'd caught her glance out of the corner of his eye. Knew he should look at her. Instead, he focused on the lake in order to say what he must.

"I thought we could share a cabin, accomplish what I came here for, then move on, no strings attached, no regrets. I was wrong. I find myself…drawn to you more each day. I admit it because I know you must realize that by now. I thought I could hide it from you. Thought I could divert my feelings by working harder at the site. But I think about you while I'm there more than I have a right to. I find myself looking at you with eyes that should only be for Lucy."

He paused, took a needed breath. Had he rambled on like a total fool? He needed to keep talking. To lay it on the line. Before he had the chance, she spoke.

"What do you expect me to say? That I'm sorry you're attracted to me, that I promise not to compromise the situation?" He heard dismay in her quivering voice. He wanted to take her in his arms, hold her, crush her lips against his. *Jesus!*

"I don't expect you to say anything. Just let me finish. We're sensible adults. We can work this out. We have to." He waited. She said nothing. *Damn.*

"I vowed long ago I'd never be unfaithful to Lucy. Integrity forces me to keep the vow sacred. Unfortunately, I've already marred that integrity. If only in my mind, I've betrayed that vow and her. It nauseates me to know I've let her down. But I can't let my feelings for you go any farther. There's no future in it. For either of us." He cleared his throat.

"It'd not only be unfair to Lucy but lecherous of me to take advantage of your innocence. I'd leave you soiled with no benefit of any future commitment. As for me…I'd feel guilty for betraying her, ashamed I'd ruined you, and most likely more…" He bit back the word heartbroken. "...frustrated than I am already."

He hesitated, allowing her to speak. Nothing.

He kept the cruising birds in sight. "I need your help. I can't fight this desire without someone pulling in my strings. Unfortunately, it has to be you. I can't explain our situation to anyone and not unveil my cover. Of course, the fire clearly shows someone's onto me. But we—"

"Hans knows," she interrupted. "He could keep you…in line." Her soft voice quivered.

"Hans isn't around when I'm alone with you." He regretted his bark when the loons scooted across the water to the other side as fast as their webbed feet would propel them. Morgan jerked a bit more upright.

"I don't…know if I can do it, Luke. You've come to mean a great deal to me also." Her extended words induced coughing. After a few hearty clearings of her throat, she breathed more easily.

Luke had no choice but to look her way. "It tears me up inside every time I think how you could have perished in that fire. A fire meant to destroy me. I—"

"Shh…" She reached over to gently place her covered palm on his forearm. "It's over. Done with. You had no control over what they did." She swallowed, took a deep breath. "You saved me, Luke, and for that I'll always be grateful."

Their gazes locked. Moonlight shimmered, bathing them in silver. A caw sprang from a treetop as a parent said its final good night to its nested clan. Grass and pine pleasantly perfumed the air.

A powerful yearning threatened to dissolve his

logic. Her eyes lured him to submit, her touch inflamed his blood, her lips begged to be kissed. Her expression—innocent yet hungry—drew him. He read it, felt it, matched it with his own, and longed to fulfill her wish, his greatest desire.

It would be so easy to give in. He wasn't sure how not to. It became sheer torture to fight against its pull. He shook with need, trembled from restraint. Sweat beaded his forehead, coated his palms. He'd faced many a peril, temptation, and challenges, but none had proven as difficult to conquer as battling his emotions for this woman.

Her hand remained on his arm, featherlight, smoldering. Covering it with one of his, he gave a light squeeze. "I thought discussing this might dampen the fire. Obviously I've added more fuel."

She smiled shyly. "I don't think anything can change the attraction we feel. But I *will* promise to also honor your vow to Lucy." She cleared her throat, went to a whisper. "I knew from the start you couldn't offer more than friendship. It's my fault I let my feelings grow."

Luke listened to her heartening words, studied her composed face. She would hold strong through coming years, no matter what she faced. Every day since arriving here she'd matured, excelled in talents she'd never before attempted. And she'd done well at all them, maybe not at first, certainly not mastering them without turmoil, but she'd persisted, until she'd met each challenge and conquered. Yes, she was a fighter, determined to live life to the fullest. No wonder he loved her so.

"It doesn't make it any easier for either of us, but thank you for understanding. I wish I could offer more. If there were any way possible...Hell, let's leave well enough alone."

Realizing he'd best keep his hand where it belonged, he withdrew it. The air crackled with precarious tension. If he wasn't careful he'd be touching far more than her hand. He took a step back and her hand fell away. It was for the better.

He'd wanted to tell her that if anything did happen to Lucy—inevitable death lurked, after all—that maybe...Hell, maybe what? That he'd come find her? That she should wait, possibly years, for him to declare his love and make good on it? Hell, maybe her affection stemmed more from gratitude or friendship. She hadn't exactly declared anything stronger. He had no right to ask such a thing. More importantly, he'd never wish for Lucy's health to decline faster just for his benefit. No, never that. He loved Lucy too much to ever wish for her death.

As one loon spread its speckled wings, propelled itself upward, and thrashed its feet, Luke turned his attention toward the interruption. Its wings flapped and fluttered, sending it into a furious dance, barely skimming the lake's surface. He remembered Morgan saying loons did that dance accompanied by a yodel to ward off intruders. This time the bird most likely courted the female at his side, marking his territory. Definitely the male.

Just then, that lovely lady softly wailed. The majestic yet haunting melody floated through the still air. Undoubtedly satisfied with her answer, the male glided to her side. Though the evening had grayed, moonbeams illuminated the red of their eyes as they turned and headed to the far side of the water.

"They're almost eerie, so mysterious, but so lovely," Morgan whispered as they retreated.

"Yes. And unfortunately only when the loon truly sings could I offer you more."

Her head snapped up from her fascination with the birds. Her gaze searched the face he fought so hard to hold blank. Christ, how he wanted to enfold her in his arms. To say words he longed to say. To kiss her into submission.

His heart felt torn to shreds.

Would he have any heart left, upon returning home?

Chapter Twenty-One

Sleep evaded Morgan. Lying in bed, she glared at the ceiling. A gentle breeze ruffled the thin curtains, while starlight tweaked through to send shadows dancing across the slanted planks above. She felt as restless as the haphazard images scurrying over the ceiling.

Lord, she wished she dared be that aimless. If so, she'd jump out of bed, fling the door open and leap into his bed on the divan. Bed? Not hardly. She'd seek his arms. Plain and simple, that's where she wanted to be. That's where he wanted her to be. He'd said so, hadn't he?

Only when the loon truly sings could I offer you more. Luke's words repeated themselves in her mind. Their acidity churned in her stomach until she thought she'd heave up dinner; the bittersweet sentiment they were meant to impart tore at her heart, leaving an unbearable ache in her chest. A loon didn't actually sing. It wasn't its nature. Never would be.

How could she ever look at him again and not want more? Lately she'd felt his heated glances more than not, noted the husky voice with an endearment. She'd tried to convince herself that all had been for the benefit of others.

They'd both been tiptoeing over a wobbly stone path, hiding their pent-up emotions, unaware of the other's true feelings. Now she knew his most secret desires. She might have held back the intensity of her feelings for the sake of sanity, but how would either of them keep their footsteps from faltering? If they were able to keep walking the straight, narrow path, both would walk away frustrated, with longings unfilled. At least their pride and integrity, as he'd put it, would be intact. But if they slid off that path, even for one split second, they'd be forever... Forever what? Guilt-ridden? More frustrated? More disheartened than if they'd not sated their hunger? They might end up pining for more. That could be far more painful.

There was only one acceptable answer. At all costs, broken hearts be damned, they had to bury their feelings, honor his vow, remember Lucy, who lay suffering at this very moment. They had to walk with even strides, sure feet, no matter if they'd walk away to a lifetime of regret.

With that disturbing acknowledgement, she tossed and turned, tugging at the quilt as if it might help soothe her cursed soul. And as she digested what she had to do, she prayed sleep would overtake her so she could escape the heavy burden on her tender, wounded heart.

"You may belong to another, but I love you, Luke Kincaid, with all my heart, and will forever," she whispered the forbidden words into the starlit room. With that final acceptance, her heart shattered, the sharp shards of regret piercing her unmercifully. Curling into a tight ball, she burrowed her face into her pillow to muffle the gut-wrenching sobs that tore from her lungs.

****

Even at five in the morning the sun rose strong, polishing the greenery and bathing the multiple colors of wildflowers near the forest to brilliance. A cool breeze blew through the open kitchen and living room windows carrying gathered scents of pine, clean and fresh, the sweet bouquet of blooms, full and robust.

Morgan inhaled the lovely fragrances as she set Luke's breakfast on the table. Her hands remained tender, but, while she had to apply salve twice a day, it pleased her that Sarah had declared the bandages could be removed. Returning from the barn, Luke closed the door, strode to the table, and pulled out a chair for her. As she sat, her nerves got the best of her.

"It looks like it'll be a gorgeous day," she said as Luke skirted the table to take his own seat. Did she sound like she was rambling? Oh, Lord, she only sought to lighten the awkward tension strung tight as a bowstring between them this morning. And, damn, if his shirt pulling taut across his broad shoulders and steel-muscled chest as he sat didn't set her pulse to bounding.

As he adjusted his long legs under the table, pulling his chair closer, his gaze met hers. She felt a fiery current streak through her blood. She fiddled with the napkin on her lap. If she ever confessed how deep her feelings were, it would sign both their heartbreak warrants.

"It's about time we had most days this good," he said with a smile. "Longer days, better days, mean we'll get a lot more done." Breaking eye contact, he took a long slow swig of coffee.

She exhaled, relieved the tension had lessened, somewhat, as he focused on his food. "How many logs do you have to have before you open the dam?"

She followed suit as he picked up his fork and began eating the fluffy eggs she'd so painstakingly prepared. They hit her stomach with a thud. She discarded her fork and concentrated on her toast and coffee.

Obviously he didn't have any problem with eating this morning. She watched as he shoveled potatoes and eggs down as if he'd been starved for a week. A warm glow of contentment settled within her at knowing she could at least offer him some satisfying meals now.

"Another twenty or so should do it." He paused, leaned back against the slats, and sipped his coffee as if he had all day to sit and relax. "What are you going to do today? Any big plans?"

Thank goodness he kept the conversation going. It broke the awkwardness.

"Oh, I'll go water what's left of the flowers and vegetables, clean a bit in here, get supper going. Maybe go see Sarah. I need the exercise and should take advantage of the nice day."

His brow furrowed, his frown deepened. "Sure you're up to it? You don't want to overdo too soon. Sarah will have my hide if she thinks I let you do too much. And I want you to be cautious when you're by yourself. You take that gun I showed you how to use. Don't forget it."

His concern wove a warm path through her. She laughed at his worry over Sarah's wrath. She didn't laugh at the reminder someone might try to harm her. "I promise I'll take all the blame if she starts spitting fire. And, yes, I'll take the pistol with me, though I pray to God I never have to use it."

His grin nearly took her breath away. She wanted to wrap her arms around him so badly she almost threw caution to the wind.

"Sure, you say that now, but how do I know Sarah won't come after me waving her rolling pin? She just about did before."

"I promised, that's how. I said I'll take all the blame." She laughed. "I…"

The sound of horses' hooves out front had them both rising to their feet. Luke placed a hand on her forearm. "Stay here till I see who it is." The implication of his words froze her to the spot. Seeing him retrieve his handgun from its holster hanging by the door tripped her pulse.

He made a beeline to the living room window, peered out. His shoulders relaxed. “It’s Tom and Hans.” But she noted his scowl as he crossed to the door and swung it wide.

“Weren’t you to pick up them this morning?”

“Yeah.” He strode outside without a glance her way, pushing the gun into his waistband as he went. She scurried to catch up with him, seeing his tension in the way he fisted his hands, in his purposeful strides.

Dismounted and leaving the horses to graze freely, Hans and Tom met them in two strides.

“What’s happened?” Luke asked, his voice brittle.

“Les spotted the boot print,” Hans said, his voice gruff, his body stiff and taut to match Luke’s. “Thought we better come over and talk some, maybe make some plans before we got to the site.”

Boot? What boot?

A twitch worked back and forth in Luke’s jaw and the sides of his cheeks. Chilling claws of apprehension dug into the back of Morgan’s neck as she watched his shoulders square, his eyes turn dark with rage.

“Where?” Luke asked, steam nearly rising from his pores.

Hans glanced her way, then back to Luke. Luke’s lips compressed.

“Morgan, you need to go inside. We men need to discuss something.”

She saw *red!*

“I don’t need to go anywhere, do anything. Unless it’s to clobber you over your head.” She had to inhale to catch her breath, to stop her shaking from outrage. “I’ve no idea what’s going on, but I’m assuming it has to do with the fire. Or maybe the vandalism. And if that’s the case, then we’ll all go in, have coffee and talk. Me included.”

"Now, Morgan, honey…"

"Don't Morgan-honey me, mister. I'm in this for the long haul. That was the deal. Stop trying to protect me. I'm made of sturdier stuff than fluff. I need to know as much as you do."

Luke looked like he'd bitten into a sour apple. Hans and Tom appeared to be holding back laughter. She held hers back, as well. "Come along, gentlemen, we can discuss this inside."

****

"Okay, spit it out," Luke said as they sat and he watched Morgan gather cups. Hans's mouth opened, and she held up a hand.

"Back up for a moment. And start with the boot."

Hans grinned at Luke. "She been takin' lessons from Sarah?"

Luke scowled at Hans. Frustration gnawed at him, but he figured it better to bring her up to date fast so he could find out what the hell they had.

"Hans and I left the site the other day and searched around the cabin for any clues. We knew it'd be a long shot, but we checked anyway. Though there were lots of people at the fire, none of them ever got close to the front wall till the fire was out. We found boot prints with a deep score across the middle of the right boot along the entire front."

She paused in pouring coffee into the third cup. He saw her hand shake. "Go on. I'll put another pot on."

"When I looked at them closer, I realized they'd been made before the fire, because debris had fallen over some of them. Deep prints left in moist soil. Moist from when you'd watered your flowers or when kerosene was being poured. If they'd been made after the fire, that ground would have been dry from the heat."

She set the pot on the stove, turned and gave

him a blank look. He knew she hurt. Her eyes said it all. He hadn't shared that information with her. Hell, she'd been just getting back to feeling well; he hadn't wanted to burden her with a long shot. He could kick himself now.

"Please, continue." She came to the table and sat in the chair by his side.

"Hans and I decided we needed to recruit help, to have more eyes watching for that boot. We told Tom and five others we trust implicitly. That's it. Hans?"

Hans cleared his throat, looked at Morgan. "Les and some others been sleepin' at the site." His gaze flew to Luke. "When he got up this mornin' he saw boot prints with that marking near the oxen pen. That ground's pretty moist, and he said the prints were as plain as day."

Luke heard Morgan's gasp, closed his eyes, and took a deep breath. His insides shook with blazing fury. He wanted to jump up, go get the bastard. But the trained investigator in him held him back, kept him rational. He knew he couldn't go charging off half-cocked and kill the son of a bitch. But whoever wore that boot would pay.

The fact the culprit worked their site had steam nearly rolling out his pores. Either he had a group working for him or he worked for someone else, most likely the latter. He didn't believe any of the men, especially the ones who worked the night shift, had enough balls or brains to mastermind a scheme of this magnitude. So that meant he'd have to flush the boot man out and make him talk. Oh, yeah, that'd be the easy part. And he'd enjoy every stinking minute.

Luke rubbed his hands together, as eager as a child for recess. "What'd Les do?"

Hans laughed. "Since it was an hour before startin' time, he told 'em he had the trots, needed to ride to his cabin, grab some medicine, and be back before they missed him. Came to my place since it was closer. He figured we'd need to talk before gettin' there."

Morgan cleared her throat. "How will you find out who it is?"

Luke looked into her questioning eyes, and gave her a big smile. "That, my dear, will be child's play. We'll look at every boot, starting with the night crew." The men rose from the table.

Her eyes rounded and he read the fear. "Believe me, it's nothing we can't handle. We have the element of surprise. But we need to get there before that crew leaves."

As Hans opened the door, Luke cinched his holster, grabbed his jacket. "I'll saddle my horse. It'll be quicker."

Halfway through the doorway, he looked back over his shoulder. "Lock the door and keep your gun handy. And stay inside until I get word to you."

Morgan sat glued to the chair. Her heart seemed to have lodged in her throat. She should be angry at him. She wanted to run after him, throw her arms around him and beg him to be careful. But she wouldn't. He—they—had a job to do. He didn't need any more delay. And though her fears screamed to run after him, she inhaled, folded her hands on her lap, and prayed.

****

Haste being paramount, Luke readied his mount in record time. Yet the three cantered their steeds while planning their strategy, then spurred their mounts through the dense trees. They arrived none too soon. Seven of the night crew were mounted and ready to leave. Damn, the other three had already gone. He'd deal with them later, if need be. Yet an uncanny suspicion pierced his mind that this wouldn't be as easy as he'd told Morgan.

He scanned the men, trying to see who had left,

and decided to deal with it later. He nodded to Tom and Hans to be ready. “I want no questions. All of you dismount.”

Frowns and grumbles followed, but all seven dismounted and gathered in front of him. In unison, still mounted, Luke, Hans, and Tom pulled their guns and aimed them at the men. Fourteen eyes widened. Others on the day shift milled closer, most likely shocked to see the drawn guns.

For safety, guns weren’t worn while working, but a few had already put them on. “I want those wearing gun belts to drop them and kick them behind you. Now.”

His face must have said, “Don’t tempt me,” for no one said a word. Just stared, dropped the belts where they stood, and kicked them back. No one batted an eye. Either the man could act, or he wasn’t here. Luke didn’t let his guard down for one second.

“Now, all of you sit down, and I want all you others, except those who know what’s going on, to join them on the ground.” With that done, without a peep out of anyone, he smiled.

“Now show us the soles of your boots. Put your legs straight out, and do it nice and easy, ’cause us three have itchy fingers today, believe me.” He kept his eyes on the group while they did as told. “Les, Peter, and Monk, join those fellas and see what you can find.”

While he watched the three do a thorough inspection, he searched the faces for Hicks, the man Morgan had told him about, who worked the night shift. He’d had him watched with a keen eye since she’d voiced her concern. He wasn’t here. Damn. This didn’t bode well.

When they finished they turned toward him. All three shook their heads. *Shit.* Now they had their work cut out for them.

****

Realizing one or more of the men inspected could be in cahoots with the boot man, whether they were in the day or night group, Luke ordered everyone to stay put. He couldn't take the chance one of them might warn the others. He promised they'd all get a day's extra wages for the inconvenience, along with an explanation for his actions, but he expected them to work. He left Les and three others wearing their guns to guard the rest while his party left.

Luke rode to the edge of town, Tom, Hans, Monk, Andy, and Peter at his side. "We'll split up here," he said, reining in behind the tree line. "Tom and Peter, you two circle through the trees to the far end and make your way to Mort's cabin. If he's there, check him out. If he's our man, bring him to me, if not, tie him up, then join Hans and me as soon as you can."

"Monk and Andy, go left to Derk's place. The same goes. Hans, you come with me. Two to one, that's Hicks sitting on that stump in front of Carl's, and I think he might just be our man. Hans and I'll wait here, say, ten minutes, to give the rest of you time. You four be careful. If Mort and Derk aren't there, then they could be around town anywhere, and Hans and I might need your help if they're involved with Hicks. But before you ride through town, make sure Hans and I are already approaching Hicks. I don't want him running and shooting up the town. Good luck."

The four nodded and rode out.

Luke sat in silence on his horse alongside Hans. Impatience gnawed at his gut. Determination had him chomping at the bit. Remorse ate at him like a jaundiced viper. He'd known Hicks could be his man, yet he'd waited. He should've plowed through him before but had hesitated, waiting for the proper time, a safer time to do so. He should have known better. He thought of how others had suffered, how Morgan had suffered, how she could've died… God forgive him. He'd waited.

"You chewin' yurself up, or are ya just plannin' more of yur strategy?"

Luke glared. "Yeah, I'm doing both. You want to make something of it?"

"Whoa!" Hans laughed. "I'm yur partner, remember? I'm also yur friend. Don't eat me alive. Save that for Hicks."

Luke settled back in the saddle, only then realizing how stiff he'd held himself. He shook his head. "I never should've waited. I should have approached Hicks two days ago, looked at his damn boots then."

"Oh, *ja*, and if his boot had been bare? What then, bucko? It would've sounded the alarm, for sure."

"That's not the point. The point is I waited and I shouldn't have. I could've figured out something if I'd been wrong."

Hans snorted. "Let me tell ya somethin'. Ya been workin' as hard as any of us. Been doin' a helluva job, besides. Ya got more schoolin' than any of us, and the brain to use it well. This be the closest anyone's come ta findin' out who wants ta harm us and the railroad. And if it ain't Hicks this time 'round, we'll all stick by ya till we find him. Ya got my word on that. The others, too. Ya waited till ya thought it could be done safe-like. So don't go beatin' yourself up."

He shook his head and smiled. "You're a good friend, Hans. The best. Thanks."

"No thanks expected. But yur welcome. Has it been ten minutes? 'Cause I'm chompin' at the bit here, just as much as ya are."

He laughed, checked his watch. "Five more minutes. Then let's go kick his ass."

****

They rode into town slow and easy, scanning the wide road for the others, keeping their focus on Hicks. He sat alone, whittling on a long stick, his back against the porch's pole, his long legs stretched out in front of him. He looked as though he hadn't a care in the world.

When they came within twenty feet of him, he looked up at the approaching horses. He stopped his whittling, smiled his usual smirk that failed to reach his eyes, and nodded. His obvious lack of respect should have sounded warning bells long ago.

Cold-hearted bastard, Luke fumed. *Never did like the man.* Hicks, never one to do more than he had to, or to give more than a smug nod or a few sarcastic words, was about to find out just how cold, smug, and sarcastic his foreman could be. Luke gave a curt nod.

They drew up in front of Carl's, dismounted, and were tying the reins to the rail as Luke caught sight of Tom and Andy coming from the far end of the road. Good.

Luke ambled in front of Hicks, Hans at his side. He prayed Carl wouldn't step out the open doorway before they finished their business.

"I'd think you'd want to catch some shuteye rather than whittling."

"Yeah? Well, now, my time's my time, boss man," he said, slurring the "boss man." He ignored them, looked down, and whittled again on the long, thick cane in his hands.

Luke wanted to shove the man's teeth down his throat. "Well, now, I don't think so, because I need to interfere with your time." He drew his gun. "I believe I'll ask for only a minute, just long enough for you to show me the soles of your boots. Actually just the right one will do fine."

Hicks's fingers froze, one hand on the wood, the

other clutching the knife. He raised his head and glowered. Eyes blazing hatred to a depth he'd never seen sent a chill down Luke's spine. He stiffened it.

"Hey, Mort," Hicks yelled. "Need a bit of your persuasion here."

He'd not counted on one of Hicks's buddies being here, but hell, a good fight between four seemed only fair. Luke glanced at the doorway just as Hans flung him back against the wall.

Luke felt the cane slash across his face, hit his right hand. His gun went flying. His face and hand burned as if he'd been whipped. Pure rage had him ignoring the scuffle behind him. Hans could hold his own.

Hicks leaped up, both hands gripping the cane's ends to try and topple him. Luke dodged, bent low, and dove into Hicks. Drove his left fist into the man's gut. Pain ricocheted up his arm. Hicks fell to his knees with a whoosh. The cane thumped in the dirt. Luke landed a swift facer with his right. Arms and legs tangled as they rolled across the ground, scrapping like two vicious dogs.

"Luke, you'll kill him! Back off."

Only then did he realize hands gripped his shoulders, trying to restrain him. He sat back on his haunches, took a deep breath, and wiped the sweat and blood from his eyes with his aching right hand. Hell, his entire body felt trampled by a herd of wild horses. He stared at Hicks's almost pulverized face. The man breathed, but was out cold. He peered over his shoulder at Tom's scowling face. And grinned.

"Check his fucking boot."

****

By late afternoon, Morgan had worked herself into a dither. It had been all she could do not to run to Sarah's to see if she'd heard any news. When she heard a horse gallop up, out front, she ran to the living room window. Seeing Luke, she sighed in relief, yet flinched at the sight of his bruised and battered face. *Dear God in heaven.* She raced to the door and flung it open.

Tears sprang, blurring her vision, as she watched him cradle his right arm while he dismounted. She ran to his side. “Here, let me help you.”

He looked down at her and gave the best lopsided grin she figured he could manage with that split and swollen lower lip. His left cheek and eyelid didn’t look any better.

“I’m fine, just a few cuts and scrapes. But we got the bastards. A… Sorry.”

She laughed, overwhelmed with joy at having him all in one piece. “You can tell me all about it after I take care of your horse and see to your battle scars.”

His brows rose. “Appreciate the offer, but I can take him to the barn, if you’ll get me some warm water and towels. Wouldn’t mind some coffee and food, too. Haven’t eaten all day.”

“But your arm, you’ll need help. I…”

“Believe me, nothing’s broken, just sore, and I need to work out a few kinks before I settle back. It’s been one helluva day.” His shoulders slumped, and she knew better than to push it.

****

“Mostly just scrapes and scratches, thank God. I think Hans made out a little better with Mort than I did with Hicks. When Andy and Monk didn’t show in town, we went to Derk’s place. Andy had taken a knife in the gut when Derk put up a fight. He’s not doing so good. Carl fixed him up the best he could. He thinks he’s holding his own for now. Stew Hansen and Harley Burdett offered to wagon him to the doctor outside Seattle, if needed.”

She listened silently as Luke relayed the past morning, watching him eat the stew and guzzle his coffee. She'd cleaned the wounds on his face, hands and arms, applied antiseptic salve, and covered them with bandages. His left hand now soaked in the basin of warm salt water. A hot compress rested on his right shoulder. Chills still ran up and down her spine each time she thought of Willis Hicks. Derk Thomas. Mort Harris. How much worse it could have been for Luke and the others.

"Monk's got a few broken ribs, but he managed to knock Derk senseless enough to have him tied by the time we got there. He'll be hurting for awhile, but Hans and I bound his ribs, and he felt better."

He pushed his bowl away. "But I regret Monk and Andy got the worst of it. And that Hans, Tom, and I aimed our guns at the others at the site. I'll need to apologize to everyone tomorrow." He rolled his shoulders, flexed his hands. "You know, I think I feel much better now."

"You'll soak the right hand now that you've finished. Let me just change that salt water so it'll be warmer."

"I think Hans was right. You taking lessons from Sarah? You almost sound like her."

Setting the coffee pot on the stove, she added another log to the dwindling flames, then gave him a perturbed scowl as she carried the kettle to the counter.

After making the fresh batch of salt water, she took it to the table. "Now your right hand."

"Yes, ma'am." His eyes twinkled, and his smirk had her heart doing a somersault. Even with his bruised and swollen face, he took her breath away. She smiled, knowing he would be all right.

She watched him flinch as he immersed his left hand. "So where are they? And now what happens?"

He sighed, leaned back in the chair, then grinned. "You could say it took some more mighty powerful talking before they spilled their guts. But all three are nicely bundled up like lassoed calves at Carl's store, ready to greet the law in Seattle. I've got two men guarding them."

She eyed his hand and then the slight bluish hue now appearing just above his left eyebrow. "I'm wondering if all your bruises came from your fight with Hicks, at Carl's, or if some came from your powerful talking."

He shrugged his shoulders, gave a meek little-boy kind of smile. "Like I said, some mighty powerful talking."

Oh, how she loved to feast on his bright smile, gaze into those expressive eyes. Eyes so green they matched the new moss along a riverbank. Lord, have mercy. She'd made a vow. But how did one stop those heartfelt feelings, those heated stirrings? How did one simply cast away the love that burned so intensely way down inside? He'd said he was attracted to her. What would he think if he knew her attraction went much deeper? She couldn't let that happen.

"Were they acting alone, or were they hired?" Did she have to coax every answer now?

"They were hired by the prominent and wealthy but not so honorable stagecoach owners Bass and Wheeler. Seems they didn't like the idea of losing their lively income. So they hired thugs. The law will catch up with them real soon. Just as soon as we take the three in."

"I'm going to have some more coffee. Would you like more?"

"Yes, please." He looked down at his left hand in the basin. "I'd love a smoke. Would you mind getting my pipe, too? "

"Of course not." The distraction would settle her nerves. She retrieved the pipe, tobacco, and can that served as ashtray, then assisted him in lighting the tobacco. Once she'd filled their two coffee cups, she sat and sighed in relief. She could do this. She had no other choice than to simply remain friends. The term seemed to burn an ulceration in the pit of her stomach.

"When will you have them taken to Seattle? Or will you do it?"

"I want them under lock and key as soon as possible. Most likely tomorrow or the day after. And yes, I need to be the one who takes them in. I'll take Hans, and maybe Tom, too, with me. The rest of the men can work the site now that the culprits are no longer a problem."

Luke flexed his fingers, wincing as the bruised and swollen knuckles rebelled. He didn't want her to know how severely he'd beaten two of the vandals. He'd been vicious. A man possessed, to punish the ones who'd caused so much injury and chaos. And he wasn't sure how much of his brutal vengeance had been payment for harming Morgan. But, oh, yes, he'd given extra blows for each and every second she'd suffered. Had absolutely no regrets on that score, other than his men pulling him off the foul bastards before he'd finished them off.

****

Three days later, morning brought warm sunshine, gleeful songs from the treetops, and a gentle breeze to ruffle the thin curtains drawn back at each window. But to Morgan, as she gazed out the wide pane of glass over the counter, the world seemed anything but sweet and promising. Lurking like a nasty prowler were the frustrating, heartrending questions regarding the future. Her future. She'd find happiness only one way. Yet that way was as impossible as flying off to the moon. She wiped the last dish from breakfast as Luke returned from the barn. He'd been gone only two days to Seattle, and she'd missed him terribly.

She felt nervous as a mouse cornered by a

calculating, ravenous cat. He'd be handing the job of foreman over to whoever qualified. She'd have no purpose here. She couldn't stay here, unmarried, without protection of a mate. All the men were spoken for other than those choosing to remain bachelors or widowers. Besides, she had no desire to start any kind of relationship. Not yet, anyway. Her heart lay bruised and battered; it had suffered enough for the time being. Maybe someday she could look at another man, possibly open her heart, if she could bury the ache, the agonizing pain.

"We'll finish the first quota of logs today and release the dam," he said, swiping his forearm along his brow. "May take a day or two to ensure their collection downstream."

She wiped her hands dry on the towel, thankful to have something to hold onto. "What will the men here do after that?"

"Oh, they'll have plenty of work here, if they want. Some might pick up and follow the intense workload farther south. Those logs have to be milled, hauled, and laid out for track. That's where the big money is. If they opt to stay, they can keep felling trees. There's another quota for the railroad due in a month. Their jobs aren't done here, by a long shot. And there's hundreds of others needing logs for furniture, homes, paper, whatever. This dense forest will be a prime site for logs for a long time coming."

"Do you think most of them will stay here?" Both she and Luke skirted the main issue. She leaned a hip against the counter for support.

He shrugged. "I'd say at least half. It's not a bad little community. Most of the men are pretty happy here. Seattle's not so far they can't get what they need from time to time. This camp could become a good-sized town someday. Some of the couples are bound to start expanding their families soon. And that'll encourage others to come."

Her heart contracted. Would she ever be able to love another, want to have children by another? She took a needed breath, plunged forth. "Your job's done. Will you go home after the logs are sent?" *To Lucy?* Her heart hit her feet with a staggering thud.

He braced a hand on the door jamb and met her gaze. His eyes sent her a silent message, one neither dared verbalize. Her world careened, tipping on its axis, nearly shattering her emotions. Her pulse thundered in her ears.

She pushed her hip farther into the counter to resist throwing herself into his strong arms. Silence hung heavy in the air. A wounded, pained expression crossed his face, and she realized her own eyes must mirror all his emotions. She turned, praying he didn't read the depth of her despair.

"Yes, I'll leave…but most likely not for another week or two. I've done my part. At least I think I have. Am damn proud of it, if I say so myself. But I'll need to make sure the law has apprehended Bass and Wheeler, and there's no more vandals in the area, before I can say all's safe. I can't stay any longer than that. I'm needed…at home, at my office. Hans can easily take my place now. And do a fine job, I'm sure."

What to say? Oh, mercy. She clutched the towel harder, gulped down threatening tears.

His expression turned intense as if something weighed heavy on his mind. "Will you go back home?"

No. She would not run back home like a naughty little girl who'd made a horrible error. At least not yet. She was far from ready to endure her parents' wrath. It would be all she could do to mend her broken heart over the next decade.

She turned toward him, avoiding eye contact. "No, no, I won't. I came this far to find a new life, and I'll not give up that dream unless I have no other choice." *How will I ever make it through the first day, the following week, without him, wondering about him, yearning for him?*

Again she relied on the towel, twisting it now to steady her trembling hands, to fight the weakening floodgate in her eyes. Anguish hit her heart like a hurled cleaver.

He nodded, almost complacently. "Have you thought where you'll go, what you want to do?"

"Not yet. But I'll think of something."

He scowled, pushed away from the doorway, and took a step toward her. "We can talk more when I get back. Maybe we can come up with a solution between the two of us."

She wouldn't burden him. "Thank you, but it's my problem. I'll think of something."

He chuckled, his eyes bright with merriment and possibly a bit of respect and admiration. "I'm sure you will. You think hard and long, and we'll see what we come up with. Deal?"

"Deal," she said, nodding with a smile that felt as tight as an overstretched bowstring.

****

Dusk covered the land by the time Luke arrived for supper. Sarah, having borrowed Carl's wagon, had gathered Rosie, Lela, Roberta, and Morgan to go watch the big event at the site. It'd been wonderful chatting nonstop to and from, spectacular to see the dam blasted open, feel the earth shake under one's feet as the previously calm, dammed water surged forward like a tidal wave upon its release. A thousand or so tremendous logs had rushed downstream to their new destination. Atop the mountain, she and the other women had waved to their men down below before returning home.

Now, after Luke had assured her there had been no mishaps, she encouraged him to expound further on every detail of his day. She listened intently to his jovial recounting of how well the release went, how the timbers had obediently plunged down the river to be intercepted at the other end, where the sawmill's crew claimed their plentiful bounty. Not one reasonable, logical idea regarding her relocation had sprung to her mind. Mashed potatoes, squash, ham, and buttered biscuits stuck in her throat with each and every small bite.

A deafening quiet gave her pause. She glanced up, meeting Luke's bemused smile. Only then did she realize he'd stopped talking, had even stopped eating to watch her trail her fork through the knoll of potatoes. A hundred thoughts had vied for consideration in her mind, all being ruled out the minute they surfaced.

"Not hungry?" His grin, as always, set her pulse to humming.

She shrugged. "I'm sorry. My mind wandered, but I'm truly pleased everything went so well. And I'm happy Sarah came to get me and the others. We had a wonderful time being together, and it was exciting, all that powerful water, those huge logs moving so fast. The entire camp should be proud of their accomplishments. Especially since the sabotage is over."

"I agree. Got word today Bass and Wheeler are behind bars. And since there's been no more trouble here, Hans can take over easily." He nonchalantly leaned back, sipping his coffee, his gaze scrutinizing her. It made her downright edgy. God forbid he knew how devastated her thoughts were. Or why.

Clearing the lump in her throat, she set her fork down. She avoided making direct eye contact. "Do you still plan on leaving in three days?"

"Yes. But that depends on how long it takes you to answer some questions."

Her gaze flew to his. "What…what questions?"

His features softened, his eyes became less

penetrating. "I've not pressured you, and I've tried not to probe until you felt comfortable telling me more of your past. But you've deliberately withheld anything more than the story of your fiancé."

Talk about being in a corner with no exit in sight. She inhaled to calm her jitters. What could she tell him? What should tell him? Taking a sip of her cooled coffee, she shrugged so he'd not know just how threatened she felt.

"I told you before, my life wasn't exciting. I lived in New York, had nothing in common with my family, and when Bethany and Malcolm betrayed me, I simply left to see other parts of the world. I…I'd hope to find a husband, build a life, start a family. It's all quite simple."

He laughed so hard he had to set his cup on the table. "You are anything but simple, Morgan. Believe me, you have sides to you I've yet to uncover, if my hunch is correct."

She felt the heat of a blush race across her cheeks and down her neck. "I don't know what else you want me to tell you. My life was plain, sim…"

"Don't." His fingers splayed over the table's surface as he glared at her. "Don't make another mockery out of what we have here. We've both lied to everyone except Hans, but we've never lied to each other. At least not openly. You've kept secrets, and I honored your privacy. But now I have to deal with what's right for you, see to your well being…"

Now she needed to interrupt. "You don't have to do any such thing. I'll manage on my own just fine. It's simple. You go your way and I'll go mine."

His brows rose at her vehemence, the crowfeet crinkling as he smiled. She'd expected a whoop of laughter. "I've had all I can take of your 'simple.' Nothing's been simple since I met you. Not our scam, not the running of the site, not our attraction that grew despite our intentions otherwise. And I highly doubt you led a simple life before. Have I got that right?"

At the mention of their strained relationship, emotions they now knew he restrained and—with any luck on her side—her feelings he could only suspect ran deeper than friendship, her mouth turned dry. He was right. Nothing had been—or, it appeared, would be—simple ever again.

She fingered her napkin with agitated fingers. "I…"

"I want the damn truth!" His bellow rekindled memories of the very first time he'd ranted with frustration. His dilemma now obviously posed no less a problem.

Well, she'd earned his friendship, his respect, and, God have mercy on their sinful souls, his love. And, by God, she'd done it all on her own merit. For, yes, *simply* being herself. She'd tell him what he wanted to hear. She owed him no less.

"What do you want to know?"

His eyes rounded, obviously astounded she'd been defeated so easily.

"Well? Ask away. I'll tell you whatever you what to know. It won't make any difference. We'll part, and that will be that."

He nodded, with a smirk of satisfaction. She felt tempted to button up her lip to erase it.

"Where do you hail from?" He eased back, his eyes gleaming with eager curiosity.

"New York."

"Not good enough. The town."

"Not town, city. New York, to be exact."

His brows arched more than a notch at that one. "In the city or on the outskirts?"

She had to laugh. "Oh, right smack in the heart of it. With all its flair and fanfare. All the elite doing their best to impress anyone they could." She met his gaze with a sneer, unable to hide her disgust. "To save you the next question, yes, my family included. Excuse the cliché, but I was born with a silver spoon in my mouth, attended the most elite schools, had the best upbringing. My father is president of one of the largest banks. Actually he holds the most stock, so he just about owns it. I should be honored, don't you think?"

The smile, the laugh she'd expected, failed to surface. Instead his shoulders tensed. He went back to studying her, only this time his perusal lacked criticism; it merely sought.

"I take it that kind of life didn't appeal to you."

Her anger dissolved with his concerned tone.

"Hardly. I never want to be that rich again. I guess my mother hit it on the head. I'm cut from another mold. I only sought a happy, honest life—a life where family and friends meant more than social status. One that I could be proud of, maybe even make some small contribution while I was at it. Whenever I helped others less fortunate, whether they were sick at the hospital or sheltered by the mission for the poor, my reward was an inner peace I can't begin to describe. And I loved planting flowers, bushes, trees, nurturing them like infants until they'd bud and blossom, pleased that others enjoyed their beauty, as well. My family disapproved of both efforts."

She paused, noting how his eyes had turned gentle, understanding. That was all the incentive she needed to continue.

"And you could say my worst fault was, and still is, my craving for knowledge. I always had my nose stuck in a book. I swear my mother has nearly expired from apoplexy a thousand times. But I love learning about the sea, the land, people in far-off places, world politics, even industry with its buzzing business world."

She'd not expected any reprehension from Luke

over her last confession, but she nearly swooned as he successfully disarmed her with his smile of approval. Elation tore through her, while a sudden vulnerability warned her to resist his magnetic charm. If she failed to hold strong, she'd forget they had to part in a few days. Then where would she be?

"You're one amazing woman. I think I knew it the minute you hit the ground with your skirts flying high." They chuckled together at the recollection. Gazes locked, held. They both swallowed, and she knew he too felt attraction escalating. The room became too hot, too confining. If she didn't pull her gaze away, they'd cross a line on the path that would lead only to more heartbreak.

Nervous, frustrated, and anxious to break the emotions storming the room, she broke eye contact, pushed her chair back, and began gathering dishes.

"Not so amazing." She laughed, the stack of plates wobbling as she went to the counter. "I have a thirst for learning, for enjoying the—I know you loathe the word, but—*simple* joys in life."

"And you loathe the posh, pretentious, high society life." He joined her at the counter, where he set the cups and the salt and pepper down. Lord, he stood much too close to calm her nerves.

"No, no, I don't. But I had my fill, thank you very much, and now I'll enjoy life."

"You come up with anywhere to go to enjoy those simple joys, Miss Inquisitiveness?" He brought more from the table.

She poured hot water into the basin as she shrugged her disappointment. "No, not so far."

"I might have an answer."

Interest rallied, and she glanced over her shoulder as he stirred the fire and added more wood. "Any suggestion would most likely be ten times better than anything I've come up with."

"You could go with me to San Francisco. We'll

get you a room at a hotel or a boarding house, and I'll make a few inquiries. There's always someone looking for help of some kind."

Hopes soaring, she scrubbed the pot with more vigor. "I'm willing to do just about anything that will pay money and still be respectable at the same time."

As she dried the last dish, he lit his pipe. "Why don't we sit in front of the fire, and you can tell me what sounds appealing for work." He sat down in the big chair.

Eager as a child for a piece of candy, she marched to the divan. She began listing her abilities, ranging from bookkeeping and filing to caring for the sick to tutoring in most subjects.

Luke listened with an interested ear. God, she was gorgeous. Not just her outward beauty, but her inner spirit, her drive, her fresh outlook on life in general. He didn't doubt for a minute she could do anything tossed her way if she set her mind to it.

He'd pegged her right. She heralded from the elite, had an upbringing to equal his, maybe better. Yet here she sat, babbling like an excited child. He couldn't blame her. Though possibly temporary, he'd found an answer, given her direction. And for that he was immensely satisfied.

But what would happen when she found out he planned to stop before arriving at San Francisco? Not just a stop, but most likely an extended stay, if Lucy had anything to say about it. And what the hell would she think when she found out he led the kind of life she wanted to avoid? The shit would fly higher than a racehorse could kick it up.

And he'd be at the receiving end.

Chapter Twenty-Two

Morgan roused from a doze as she felt the carriage turn off the main thoroughfare. She glanced over at Luke. He sat opposite her, deep in slumber, his long legs stretched out to his left. She craned her neck out the window as the two-horse vehicle rolled smoothly over a long, curving, well-packed drive. Tall shade trees lined each side like sentinels guarding acres of well manicured verdant lawn.

Should she wake him? He'd told her they'd stop briefly before going on into the city. Surely he'd want to wake for a few minutes before their arrival.

He'd been the best traveling companion she could have asked for, pointing out various points of interest along the entire steamer trip from Seattle and explaining how different towns had cropped up and why. She'd learned the lay of the land and how nature had played its role in determining where people located and established their communities.

"Luke." He didn't bat an eyelash. "Luke," she repeated, gently nudging his forearm. "Wake up, we're here." She frowned, realizing he'd never actually said where he planned to stop. Most likely an inn, or possibly a friend's home for a respite.

He blinked, and stretched his shoulders. He gave her a lopsided grin. "I didn't mean to sleep so long. We're here?" Would she ever get tired of feasting her eyes on him?

"Yes, wherever here is. You never told me."

He dazzled her with another one of those incredible smiles. "You'll see."

She wasn't sure she liked his secrecy. But as the carriage pulled to a halt, her inquisitiveness leaped forth and she glanced out the window. And gawked at the elegant white mansion.

Long-paned windows graced the ground and upper stories. Four huge columns supported a second-story veranda, giving it a dramatic and stately appearance. Yet the two-step portico, its huge cement urns overflowing with multicolored flowers and flanking an intricately carved door, beaconed welcome to all. The polished brass-and-glass, gas light fixtures added to its charm.

She held her tongue as they descended from the carriage and strode across the portico. She'd find out soon enough who owned this, she supposed, yet Luke's obvious omission stymied her.

The door swung wide before they reached it. A stout woman, possibly in her sixties, with a graying upsweep and a wrinkled face beamed from ear to ear. Morgan immediately liked her.

"Why, saints preserve us." She clasped Luke's hands in hers as tears glistened in her eyes. "Thank the good Lord you're all in one piece, Mr. Luke. Welcome home."

Luke released her hands and embraced her in a hearty bear hug. "You had a birthday while I was away, Melinda, but you still don't look a day past thirty. It's good to be home."

Welcome home? It's good to...? Her breath caught in her throat, her stomach twisted. *No.*

Rattled, overwhelmed, she inhaled deeply, praying the vertigo wouldn't send her to her knees. She canvassed the dark wood staircase that swept past a gallery of gilt-framed portraits, the cut-crystal chandelier overhead. Not gaudy like that of her parents, but equal to it in size.

She took it all in: the spacious foyer with its polished marble floor, the maroon velvet chair, a small ornate table under a gigantic oval mirror, an Oriental rug, intricately carved moldings. Lord have mercy, he was possibly richer than her parents.

No longer stunned, she battled the hurt and humiliation setting in. How dare he not tell her. Yet how long had she kept her secrets? She had no right to be annoyed. What difference did it make? She'd be leaving shortly. She'd hardly be a part of his life.

Keeping that in perspective, she turned back to the two who eyed her as she took in the surroundings while in hushed tones they discussed Lucy's condition. Their conversation ended as she met their gazes, but she'd caught the word "nap." Melinda's motherly smile warmed her. Luke had more than a sheepish look to him.

"Melinda, I'd like you to meet Miss Morgan Prescott. She hails from New York, and was my partner, quite an instrumental one, in achieving my goal. Morgan, this is Mrs. Elliott. Without her, I couldn't run this home."

More like your partner in deception, but you do well enough on your own. Lord, had she ever been this miffed? But, remembering her manners, she held her tongue.

Melinda stepped past Luke to clasp Morgan's hands between her two warm ones and give a hearty squeeze. "You don't have to tell me who she is. I read each of your letters to Miss Lucy and would know her without you telling me. Welcome to Eden's Glen, Miss Prescott. And I thank you from the bottom of my heart you were there to help. And I thank the Lord every day that you've recuperated so well from that horrible fire. We all prayed for you, child."

So touched by the woman's concern, praise, and genuine welcome, Morgan found her temper at Luke's deceit being replaced by a feeling of satisfaction she'd not felt in a long time.

"Thank you, Mrs. Elliott, for the welcome and

for all your prayers. They indeed helped." Morgan cleared her throat when the phlegm accumulated. She'd been able to talk sentences for some time now, but the blasted phlegm still persisted at times.

"Gracious, where are my manners, and my duty? You two make yourselves comfortable, and I'll get you some beverages and food. You must be famished after your carriage ride." Mrs. Elliott nodded and turned to fetch her offerings.

"A cold drink would be welcomed, I'm sure, but no need to hurry, Melinda. On second thought, bring Morgan a cold drink, and I'll fix me something from my study." The woman nodded again before sashaying through the far door.

Luke glanced at Morgan, scowled, then stepped toward the door to their left. "Maybe I should offer you something stronger, too. You look as if you might need a more potent kick."

She followed him into an elaborately decorated study. Definitely his room, of course. It was masculine, businesslike—posh, as he'd say. "No, thank you, I fear the only kick I need is toward you. Why didn't you tell me we'd stop at your home? Why didn't you tell me you're rich as sin? You could have, when I confessed all."

He seemed to mull that over for a moment as he lifted a decanter from a shelf and poured two fingers of what she assumed to be whiskey into a glass. He took a long, slow swig. "I could have. But if I had, you'd never have accompanied me here, knowing I was rich as sin." His smirk at repeating her words made her bristle. Did he think this a joke?

"Would that have been so bad? We could each have gone our own way. Neither of us would have been worse for the wear. Why did I have to come here? Why didn't you simply tell me?"

He cleared his throat, got that sheepish look about him again as he swirled the amber liquid in the glass. "I thought if I told you of my wealth, you might run. And Lucy wanted desperately to meet you. If I'd asked you to meet Lucy, you might have run even faster. I also wanted to insure you found employment and a respectable place to live."

"You selfish oaf! You're right. I would have run. Not so much from you being rich, because I've seen a side of you that says you're not like the self-centered, society-climbing frauds like my parents. And you're right—I can't face Lucy. How can I look at her, when I know you're as…as attracted to me as I am to you? Don't ask me to face her. Please."

He stared at her, and for the life of her she couldn't imagine what churned in his mind. And, good God, she'd nearly blurted out just how much she did care. Stupid, stupid girl. He simply stared. No regret, no sheepishness, no narrowing of the eyes at her plea. Just a total concentration on her face. She squirmed, feeling self-conscious, as if she'd committed a crime by asking to be let off the hook.

The awkwardness broke as the door opened and Mrs. Elliott entered carrying a large glass and a plate of bite-sized cookies upon a silver tray.

"Here we are, now, dear, a nice big glass of lemonade to sooth that parched throat. I squeezed the lemons myself, just this morning."

Conscious of the fact that Luke continued to gaze at her, Morgan's hand shook as she reached for the glass, yet she returned the woman's broad smile. "I'm sure it will be wonderful, Mrs. Elliott."

"No 'Mrs. Elliott' in this house, my dear, just Melinda, to you and everyone else."

"Thank you, Melinda," she said with a nod and took a sip. "This is just what I needed. It's delicious."

Melinda beamed. "And here's a few sweets to tide you over till dinner." She set the tray down on the low table before turning back toward Luke.

"Dinner will be at six, if that still suits you, Mr.

Luke. Alfred put your bags in your room and has put Miss Prescott's in the blue room as you requested. Can I get you anything else before I check on Cook?"

Morgan opened her mouth to deny she'd be staying, but Luke cut her off. "As always, you're on top of everything, Melinda. No, there's nothing else for the moment. Thank you. I believe I'll show Morgan around the Strafford estate and then go visit Lucy, if she's awake."

The woman nodded, with a broad smile, and swept past them.

As soon as the door closed, Morgan glared daggers at Luke. "I'm not staying. You should have made that clear. I thought I made that clear."

"You did nothing of the sort." She wanted to wipe away his smirk by throwing the lemonade at him. Right smack in his face. But the thought of wasting all Melinda's diligent efforts—and Melinda's swoon at such a waste—curtailed her physical response.

"I said I wouldn't face Lucy. I thought you understood I'd not be stay—" A cough cut her rebuff short. She had to take several sips of lemonade before she could breathe easily again.

"Let's take our drinks with us while I give you a quick tour." He came to her side, took her elbow with his free hand, and led her to the door. "I'd like you to see the grounds out back. Just down the knoll is a lake, much larger than the pond, and there are always loons." She opened her mouth again to tell him she didn't want any tour, but he shook his head.

"Hear me out. It's late, and I'm not thrilled at the thought of venturing into the city this evening to find you suitable lodgings after the long trip. If you're still determined to leave tomorrow, we'll go first thing after breakfast. Fair enough?"

She felt a defeated foreboding at his insistence. Did she have any choice? "All right. But I plan to leave in the morning."

He led her to each of the doors off the main hall, allowing her to look into the library, dining room, parlor, and kitchen. The servants' quarters were housed beyond the kitchen, he said. Every room was enormous, decorated elegantly, yet each had a homey, welcoming effect rather than the starched atmosphere of the home where she'd grown up. It seemed to suit him.

"Your name is Strafford?" she queried as they ascended the sweeping staircase.

"Yes, but my given name is Mathew Lucias. I've always gone by Luke because my uncle's name was Mathew." At least one thing rang true.

When at last he led her to the blue room, she scanned it, feeling breathless, awed. Light blue walls displayed still-life pictures galore. Flower gardens, mountainous landscapes, all breathtaking in soft watercolors. Floor-length white brocade curtains were pulled back with royal blue satin ties to match the rich Persian carpet. A white plush comforter covered the fourposter bed, while a mound of deep blue velvet pillows at the head invited one to lie down. He'd requested this room for her. She should still be angry at him, shouldn't she?

"It's lovely," she said in whispered wonder.

"I'm glad it meets your approval. I'd hoped it would." How could he doubt anyone would marvel at such a delightful room, she wondered, as he ushered her down the hall.

When he opened the next door and motioned her in, she eagerly anticipated its splendor, though she knew she should still be miffed at his deception.

She'd taken three steps into the dimly lit yellow room before she halted in her tracks. Her mouth agog, struck stone-still, she stared at the woman in the bed. She lay propped up on two pillows, her eyes widening slightly at their entrance. Morgan's mouth went dry; a fist twisted in her stomach, her palms moistened. She'd kill him. The first chance she got.

Diverting her eyes from Lucy, she scanned the room. A cot stood in the far corner, an ornate armoire in the adjacent one. A dresser, a dressing table, and a chair lined the wall to her left. Her gaze flew back to the bedside and focused on the rocker. A plump elderly woman, dressed in black, her graying hair pulled severely back in a tight bun, slept with her head tipped down and her wrinkled hands resting in her lap.

The silence roared in her ears until Luke spoke. "I'm glad to see you're awake, Lucy. I was eager to see you and to introduce you to Morgan."

Feet glued in place, Morgan heard the click of the door latch followed by Luke's muffled footsteps against the Aubusson carpet as he approached the bed. Her gaze darted back to Lucy.

Morgan recalled Luke saying Lucy's eyes were always full of warmth, blue as the sky on a clear day. The room held such gloom she couldn't see the color of her eyes. But what she did see made the backs of her eyelids burn.

A slight twitch in Lucy's right shoulder as if she wanted to raise her arms in greeting. Her lips seemed to strain to part. Her lids dropped half-mast as Luke took her limp, thin hands in his.

"Welc-…ho."

That soft, whispered voice nearly broke Morgan's composure. She'd wanted to hate this woman. Well, maybe not hate, but simply dislike her. Lucy had the man she so desperately wanted and was the blockade to Morgan's happiness. But seeing this feeble woman, so thin and frail, extinguished any venomous thoughts. Morgan gave thanks for her own health at seeing how easily it could be taken away.

"Shh…" Luke whispered. "Don't try to talk. It'll

only rob you of energy. It's good to be home, to see you again. I've a million things to tell you, when you're up to it." He sat down, the bed dipping from his weight. Tenderly, he fingered back her hair to behind her ears, leaned over and gave her a gentle kiss upon her lips.

Morgan had to blink back tears. Should she leave this heartrending scene? Just as she started to turn, to give them privacy, Lucy glanced her way.

"Pl-..." Her whisper came out in a whoosh, causing Morgan to wince. Lucy's left hand rose from the bed an inch, only to plop back onto the coverlet.

The woman in the chair nearly bolted from the chair. "Oh, Mr. Strafford, I…I didn't hear you come in," she stammered, coming to stand by his side. "You really shouldn't be in here now. Miss Melford needs her rest. I'll not have you wearing her out."

The woman's commanding voice to her employer shocked Morgan. And she'd called her patient Miss Melford. Instantly, Morgan took a dislike to the haughty face, pinched lips, and cold dark eyes. Never mind the bold stance with fists dug into her hips.

Luke slowly raised his head and glared at the woman. Most people would have cringed. The woman didn't flinch one bit.

"I've been away far too long, Mrs. Aueteby. If I've a mind to say hello and check the well-being of my fiancée, I've every right to do so. Anytime. You may be in charge of her and feel you must protect her while I'm gone, but never—and I stress, never—tell me not to enter her room." His words, direct and curt, hissed through his teeth. Morgan was glad she wasn't on the receiving end of such a speech.

"Why, I never! I…"

"If you would leave us for a few moments, Mrs. Aueteby, Miss Prescott and I would like to visit with Lucy. We'll not stay long. You have my promise."

Morgan nearly giggled at how well Luke managed to keep his voice so controlled. His nonchalant tone seemed to bite the woman more than if he'd ranted. *That's the way, Luke.*

"But..."

"Thank you, Mrs. Aueteby. That will be all for now. I'll call you when we leave."

The woman left in a huffed snit. Morgan wished she could follow.

Chapter Twenty-Three

“Morgan, come over to the bed so Lucy doesn’t have to strain to see you.”

Luke’s request didn’t surprise her, but she hesitated to obey. Yet there seemed no way to avoid this meeting without causing Lucy undue upset. And she’d never do such a thing to anyone.

With leaden feet and a heavy heart, Morgan approached the left side of the bed, where Luke remained. She forced a smile as she met Lucy’s gaze. Her face felt pinched and tight.

Luke graced Lucy with a boyish, affectionate smile that seared Morgan’s heart with new anguish. “Lucy, this is Morgan, previous novice at cooking and mending, burner of bread, scorcher of shirts, shrinker of clothing, and the best undercover partner I could have asked for.”

His gaze lifted to her. “I…we appreciate your taking time to meet Lucy. I know it means a lot to her, because in each letter she had written to me, she begged me to bring you here.”

Well, if that little speech didn’t make her feel like a heel, nothing ever would. Oh, yes, she’d wring his neck when she got the chance, wring it until he cried uncle. Maybe longer.

Feeling guilty and selfish, Morgan plastered on another smile. “It’s so nice to finally meet you, Lucy. I’ve heard so much about you I feel as if I already know you. You have a wonderful fiancé.” *Just let me get my hands on him, and he’ll know just how wonderful he truly is.* “You should be very proud of him for the magnificent job he did."

Lucy's eyes went from dull, glazed-over gray to an ever-so-slight twinkle of the sky blue Luke had mentioned. Morgan watched her swallow as if it were a struggle, knew she would try to whisper, and leaned closer.

"Than…y fr com…in'."

The effort it took Lucy to utter those simple whispered words, to force that wan smile, went straight to Morgan's heart. She felt the strain within her own chest. Selfishly she'd entertained thoughts of avoiding this meeting. Yet here Lucy lay, ill, having to exert enormous energy to offer a feeble attempt of welcome, while appearing to gain joy from doing so. Morgan had never been so humbled in her entire life.

Without hesitation, she reached to gather Lucy's hands in hers and give a heartfelt tender squeeze to their coolness.

"The pleasure is all mine. Luke told me what a wonderful person you are, how courageous you've been, how you keep up your spirits. I'm not sure I could ever be so brave."

Regret surfaced the minute she'd issued the praise. Would her words dampen Lucy's spirits?

"Y…wou…be."

Though it pained her to see Lucy labor so, Morgan's heart swelled at hearing the woman's murmured words, at seeing her lips grapple again to smile. Their eyes met and held, and once more Morgan witnessed the blue glitter overtake the gray. She felt a bond, true and steadfast, blossom between them, more binding than any she'd ever experienced with her own sister. By Lucy's expression, she also perceived the potent connection.

Morgan had but a second to wonder how she could be so drawn to a woman she'd intended to despise, and then Lucy's eyelids drooped and her face turned white as the sheets.

Panicked, helpless, more than speechless, Morgan's eyes flew to Luke for help. She didn't understand this illness Lucy suffered.

His lips thinned with obvious concern. "Lucy, I fear we've tired you, and I promised not to. Though it irks me to summon Mrs. Aueteby, it's best you nap, and we'll return later."

Lucy's eyelids struggled to lift as if she wanted to voice denial.

Morgan's spirits sank lower as she watched him take Lucy's hands in his, his calloused thumbs tenderly stroking pale skin.

"No, don't argue. The excitement of my return and meeting Morgan has clearly taken its toll. I'll show Morgan the grounds while you rest. We'll return before you've missed us."

With an affectionate squeeze to her hands, he stood, leaned down, and placed a kiss upon her expressionless lips. She appeared to relax instantly as she drifted off.

Turning hastily, Morgan choked down the bitter lump in her throat and headed for the door to escape such an intimate scene. She needed air.

****

They strolled across the sprawling lawn with its tall shade trees and down the gradual knoll. Six wooden chairs faced the lake, set back several feet from the azure water's edge where wildflowers, bright and vivid, swayed their heads sedately as if welcoming their visitors. It was peaceful here, silent except for the faint rustle of overhead leaves and an occasional warble from treetops. She felt anything but peaceful inside, tormented by a maelstrom of confusing thoughts and emotions.

She cleared her throat and leaned against a chair for support. "It's beautiful here." She wished she were a million miles away.

"The minute I saw the property I knew I had to have it."

She wanted to scream at him to let her leave. Leave now. "The lake's bigger than I thought it would be." She watched the sun dip farther down. Dusk started to cover the land.

"Yes, much larger than the pond by the cabin. It's a mile wide and five miles long, fed by a stream at the north end." He took a few steps and stood a foot to her left.

No way could she continue this walking on broken glass. He talked as if nothing was wrong. But everything *was* wrong. "I can't stay here. You know that. I..."

"She needs you."

What did he want from her? "Oh, God, don't say that. She doesn't even know me. Don't ask me to stay longer. Don't ask me to talk with her as if I'm her friend, as if I don't..."

Silence strung out between them. Her chest ached with the heaviness of her heart, with a pent-up breath she found difficult to release.

"As if you don't what? Want her fiancé?"

Her breath exited as if someone had smacked her back. She gripped the chair until her knuckles turned white. Her pulse beat a thunderous roar in her ears from holding back the myriad mismatched, careening emotions.

She turned to him, determined to have it out. She'd like nothing more than to punch him, right square in that handsome face of his.

"Why are you doing this? What do you want from me?"

Their gazes locked. She recognized the longing and loneliness, the turmoil and torment of raw emotions she herself fought. He shrugged, his eyes full of defeat as he shook his head.

"I don't honestly know." Hearing his dismay, she

longed to reach for him, stroke his cheek. Whisper that all would be well. Instead, she turned toward the lake and watched four loons glide close by. Lovely, regal, free, serene. She couldn't even force a smile.

"Come, sit for a minute, enjoy your friends, and then we'll go back. I've no right to ask, or to think you'd want to stay longer. I'm sorry. First thing tomorrow I'll take you to the city."

If he'd ranted and raved, begged her to stay longer, she'd have been able to fight him. But this disheartened man, who now sat with his shoulders slumped in despair, tore at her very soul. Damn, she'd done that to him.

She skirted the chair and sat in the one next to him. "I'd stay and help if I thought it would do any of us any good. And eventually I'd have to bid Lucy goodbye, and the parting would be all that much harder. You have to agree."

"You're right. It's just..." He watched the loons duck under the water. "I thought maybe you'd be so good for her. She craves people. Not like Mrs. Aueteby but someone younger, someone who'd care what mattered to her. I wanted to give her that."

"I do like her. Very much. She's as lovely as you said."

He shook his head, glanced at her. "She was lovely. Now, she's just a shell of who she used to be. I wish she could enjoy the days she has left instead of being cooped up in that dreary room, having to put up with that old...biddy."

For the first time since stepping foot on his property, Morgan laughed. A good hearty laugh. "Oh, she's all of that. Wherever did you find such an old, starched, offensive hag?"

His eyes danced as he chuckled at her colorful description. "Doctor Giles, Lucy's doctor and our mutual friend, recommended her. Guess I should have hunted for someone else when I saw she wasn't what Lucy needed. But I was in a hurry to go north. I thought at least she'd be in good hands. I can see now I should have searched longer, tried harder."

His expression turned serious. "Someone like you would have been ten times better for her. God only knows where I'll find someone younger and strong enough to care for her. The ones I did interview lacked either compassion or the knowhow, or else didn't want the job."

If she'd felt low before, when facing Lucy, now she felt selfishness wrap around her as if it might strangle her. It swept through her, sorely testing her conscience.

"You couldn't find anyone else?"

He leaned back. "No, I tried several times, but no one wanted to take on such a burden. She requires a lot of work and time. I offered top dollar, but still no go. I thought about caring for her myself, letting my business slide for a bit, but I knew she preferred and needed a woman to assist with certain needs. Then the job in Washington popped up, and that was that."

It would be best if she let his words go by the wayside. He'd paid her well. She could easily settle in San Francisco until she found gainful employment. She should leave tomorrow, not think of the man she'd be leaving, or the woman she shouldn't give two figs about. Yes, it would be wise to go her own way, forget his problem of finding someone for Lucy, to overlook the fact Lucy lay at the spine-curdling mercy of that old shrew. Why in heaven's name did she even let the notion she could help cross her mind? Silly. Stupid. Illogical. She should, and rightly so, be furious he had dragged her into this dilemma. She still hadn't boxed his ears..

"I'm still angry at you for dragging me in to see her. I wanted to scratch your eyes out."

His eyes glittered as he chuckled. "Did you?"

"Yes, damn you." She tried to sound angry, yet a smile surfaced. "I wanted to run from the room, and you know it. Actually, scratching your eyes out never crossed my mind. I contemplated punching you, right square in the nose, if you want the truth."

His grin could disarm the hardest of hearts, and he'd already taken hers. Well, almost, if it could be so. A warm laziness seeped through her as she watched his eyes twinkle.

"You lacked many talents when we met, and you kept secrets, but you were always truthful. So I can believe you wanted to punch me. And I deserved it. Why didn't you?"

"It wasn't for the lack of wanting to." They both laughed.

"Why didn't you?" His voice grew husky, his eyes darkened.

She pulled her gaze away, afraid of what they might say or do if she didn't. "Lucy. She looked so thin, so fragile, so very pitiful, as if that big bed would gobble her up any minute."

Stealing a glance his way, she watched his face sober. He nodded solemnly. "She is pitiful, but don't ever let her hear you say it, or let her know you think that way. It'd crush her."

"I'd never be that cruel. To anyone. I didn't want to like her; I wanted to run away and not talk to her. But I'm truly glad I met her. And I do like her."

"I wish you could've known her when she was well and happy and exuberant. You two would have been like sisters. Your spirits are much alike."

Once more, Morgan found her mind toying with the idea that maybe she could benefit Lucy in some way, her heart tugged by the friendship offered in Lucy's eyes. Insane. Pure insanity is what it would be to stay.

"Were you really sleeping in the carriage, or

playing possum to avoid my questions?"

He looked like a little boy caught robbing a sweet from the candy jar. "Like I've said before, you're one smart lady." His tentative smile successfully disarmed her.

"At least you're being honest." She threw him what she hoped was an exasperated scowl. "Will you go back to your business right away?"

His eyebrows arched. "Why do you ask?"

She felt uncomfortable, probing into his affairs, but she needed some answers before she stuck her foot in her mouth.

"You purposely withheld that we'd stop here so Lucy could meet me. You even planned on me staying, most likely thinking I might help, didn't you?" She cleared her throat, then continued before he could interrupt. "For all that you owe *me* a few truthful answers."

Their eyes met, and he hesitated while she coughed and caught her breath.

"Yes, I'm needed there. I've left too many things to slide while I've been away. As I said before, if I thought my caring for Lucy would be sufficient, I'd do it, but she needs a woman."

She toyed with the fold in her dress. Poor manners be damned. She needed personal questions answered. "And, because of the workload, you'd be at your office a great deal? Or is it money that's the issue?"

His eyebrows did more than arch at that one. Oh, how could she have been so brash?

"My dear Miss Prescott, I have no idea where this is leading, or why, but let me clarify a few things. I own, as I've told you, a thriving investigative business. I have four others working for me, but it does demand many hours of my time. So, yes, I'll be away from home most days and many evenings. As for the money..." His frown crinkled his forehead. "...my business is most lucrative, as is my forty-five percent of shares in the railroad."

She sat up straight, her mouth agape. She'd thought possibly, even with such a grand mansion, he might be hurting financially. What a fool. "You're a stockholder? You never said you were one of them. You...you said the stockholders were concerned about the sabotage."

His eyes went bright with merriment. "Me included. What better person to see the job done? I told you I had an avid interest in seeing the railroad built."

"You didn't say you had an *invested* interest."

He rested his elbows on the chair arms, steepled his fingers in front of him. "Guess I failed to clarify that. Does it make a difference?"

"You purposely lied. You profess to value my honesty, so how can you be so smug?"

"My, my. You do give as good as you receive, don't you? You know, when I first met you I thought you fairly meek and mild. But as time passed I grew to appreciate the passionate, spirited side of you. Do you realize you actually swore at me a few minutes ago? You're full of surprises too, Miss Prescott."

"Oh!" She jumped up and stomped her foot on the ground, glaring at him. "Do you know that sometimes you're the most caring, understanding person I've ever known, and other times the most infuriating man I've ever talked with? And stop calling me 'Miss Prescott.'"

His roar of laughter sent the loons skimming across the water at full speed.

"You oaf!"

"I've been called worse." When he attempted to mask his grin, it nearly sent her into another tongue-lashing.

"Morgan, please sit down. My neck's getting sore looking up at you." At her hesitation, he patted the chair she'd vacated.

"Besides, now I have a few questions of my own."

She really should be annoyed with him, but she wasn't. She found their banter uplifting, to say the least. How very handsome he was when somber. How devastatingly appealing when he laughed, or smirked as he did now. Oh, she wanted to always see him like this instead of down and depressed over Lucy. Lord, it always came back to her, didn't it?

Sitting down, she folded her hands in her lap and prepared for his inquisition. What would, should be her answer?

"All right. Now, why all the personal questions? It's not every day someone asks me about my finances, though I don't try to hide anything. But what are you up to?"

"I, well... Oh, pooh. I thought maybe being away had set you back some. I simply needed to know if you still had enough money to hire someone better for Lucy."

He rubbed his chin. "I see." If his scowl said anything, it clearly said he didn't see. "And since I have money to hire someone, do you have someone in mind?"

She would have stayed simply as a favor, but she needed him to view this as a simple business deal. It could be nothing more. Then she could walk away, pleased with what she had been able, hopefully, to accomplish with Lucy, as well as more financially ahead. God only knew how long it might take to find employment. Well, the die had been cast. She'd made up her mind, it seemed. She surprised herself that she'd already made that decision. Would she be satisfied with it? Only time would tell. *You may live to regret it, Morgan Prescott.*

"I may." She watched as realization entered his eyes. He had such an expressive face. Bold lines, square jaw, softly intriguing eyes. She could stare at him for endless time and never tire. The cautious curl of his lips sent her blood rushing through her veins as if a dam had burst.

"Are you applying for the job?" The tension within him became a tangible force between them. She felt it, saw it revealed in his questioning gaze.

"Yes. But only if you understand the rules."

He frowned. "The rules." He let the words roll off his tongue as if tasting their bite.

"You paid me very well before, and for that I'm more than appreciative. But it certainly can't hurt to have more, just in case I need it after I leave here."

"Of course. You've developed a good business mind." He nodded for her to continue.

"Since you can well afford it, and I need more money, I'd be willing to help care for Lucy while you find a replacement for that witch you call an attendant."

Had it been anyone other than Mrs. Aueteby caring for Lucy, she'd go her merry way. But the woman simply rubbed her the wrong way. How could she leave Lucy in her clutches? Not without having a guilty conscience.

Guilty conscience? What was she thinking? She coveted Lucy's fiancé. Had felt remorse, guilt, you name it, for how long? Did she think any of those feelings would vanish just because she'd be caring for Lucy? What would she be getting herself into?

He rubbed his jaw, all the while watching the loons drifting farther out toward the middle of the lake. The breeze ruffled the hair at his nape. She longed to stroke its softness.

"So the rule is to pay you for temporarily filling in."

"Yes, but I'd need to work with Mrs. Aueteby for a short while until I know what Lucy's needs are. It shouldn't take long, since the old…witch obviously doesn't do any more than she has to. But I could start taking over during the day so she wouldn't be with Lucy so much."

"And what I paid you in Washington, is that reasonable?"

"Very." She'd argued he was overpaying her, but had taken it when he refused to budge.

"It's an easy rule. I'd expected something of more magnitude."

"I said rules. Plural."

"Ah, now for the kill."

"It's quite simple, really."

"I shudder to think what it is, when you say simple. You've used that word several times today, and you only use it when you're nervous and out of sorts."

He laughed at the indignant glare she sent him. "Go ahead, state all the rules."

"Promise me you'll diligently pursue someone for the job and not simp—not just sit back in order to prolong my stay."

He dramatically crossed his hands over his chest. "I'm shocked you'd think such a thing."

She glared at him through narrowed eyes. "I'm serious."

"So am I. So I'll say right now that I'll actively search for someone. But you must realize it may be a while before I do find someone." At her nod, he added, "Any other rules?"

"One more. You said you're away most of the time. That's a must." She peered at the lake, too embarrassed to look at him. "We've admitted we're attracted to each other, and we know we can't let it go further, ah, since nothing can come of it. It'd be too difficult if you were around too much. I'd never want her to suspect how…I'd never want to hurt her that way."

Dear God, had she said too much? Would he

realize she'd already fallen head over heels in love? She couldn't let that happen. She'd have to watch her p's and q's every step of the way.

The breeze seemed to vanish, the soft rustles ceased, not a bird chirped. Time stood still as she forced her knees to stop shaking under her skirt. Staring down at her clasped hands, she heard him swallow. Or had it been a gasp?

"You're right. It'll be very hard indeed. More difficult since we're both aware of our…attraction. I, too, would never want Lucy to sense we've betrayed her in any way. We may find it impossible. It might…be best if I keep Mrs. Aueteby at our beck and call. The two of you can divide her care between you. I know you'll be good for Lucy, but if we find ourselves being torn, then I give you leave to pack at any time. I won't stand in your way."

She dared a glance his way. He looked as distraught as she felt. His eyes held a weary sadness, his mouth a line of tightness that matched the strings of her heart. Could they manage this escapade they were venturing into? Or would the strained atmosphere, the strain of love withheld, weaken them, break them until they shattered?

"I think that's a good idea, though I'll not enjoy working alongside that…woman."

He grinned. "Like I said, you can take turns, actual shifts. You won't have to be around the 'old hag' longer than to change places. But if you do need any assistance, promise me you'll call Melinda, or Alfred. He tends the lawn, does maintenance, and helps Melinda, Cook, or John at the stable, if necessary."

She nodded as the sun dropped lower and a breeze nipped with a sudden chill.

"Come." He took her hand and brought her to standing. "It's turning cool. We'll have time to visit Lucy with our news before supper's served."

Chapter Twenty-Four

Morgan vowed she'd ignore the hag's indignant attitude, abrupt movements, and rigid, thin-lipped silence as the woman undertook the task of administering Lucy's morning bed bath. But it wasn't easy. Mrs. Aueteby hadn't taken Luke's announcement well, two nights ago. The gimlet-eyed glare, almost savage, she'd focused at Morgan had told the severity of the woman's scorn. Still did, for that matter. And she wasn't even aware of the possibility she might have been replaced instead of given an assistant.

Determined to mollify the pinched-faced old coot, to learn how to best care for Lucy, Morgan held her tongue and handed her the towel. The woman grabbed the towel—none too gently—while her contemptuous turtle mouth withheld even the slightest curl of lips for her patient. Bitter distaste swamped Morgan as the harpy flung impassive words at Lucy rather than to her. The surly attitude and broad-shouldered, long-armed, stocky stature reminded Morgan of a nasty, temperamental warhorse she'd seen once.

Strong and overwhelming protectiveness toward Lucy surged through Morgan at lightning speed. She didn't like this woman. She despised how she treated and spoke to her charge and had to bite her lip as the witch manhandled Lucy's frail limbs. It would be only a matter of time before she could no longer keep back words that begged to be voiced.

Thick drapes were drawn closed—supposedly to

keep Lucy calm and restful, to create a subdued atmosphere. Last night Morgan had almost gagged as Mrs. Aueteby spooned down gruel—a sick, pathetic version of a watery mess—so revolting it had been a wonder Lucy didn't puke. This morning Lucy had paled as soggy milk toast was forced past her lips.

"The bath always tires her out." Morgan flinched at Mrs. Aueteby's gruff voice. "She'll sleep for a few hours," her so-called mentor continued, fluffing the pillow and laying Lucy's head down more roughly than Morgan thought necessary. The woman hadn't even propped Lucy up, as yet.

"I'm done for now. You go hang the damp towels on the drying rack in the laundry room, then sit here while she sleeps. And don't dawdle. My back needs a break from standing."

Morgan's nerves threatened to explode as she watched the woman dab Lucy's sweaty face with the damp cloth, then throw it on the towels and nightgown she'd discarded on the floor.

She forced calm to her voice. "I'll help you change the bed so I can take the linens, too."

The old hag snorted as if her offer disgusted her. "I don't change the bed but once a week, unless it gets too soiled. No sense in breaking my back if it's not necessary."

Heaven forbid you'd be expected to go out of your way. Morgan strove to keep her voice congenial. "It'll certainly be easier with two of us doing it together from now on. I…"

"No need for it today," Mrs Aueteby interrupted in a snit. "Just take the laundry and hurry back. I'll take the basin down when I go to eat. You can empty the slop bucket later, after she's asleep."

Oh, Lord, just give me strength to hold my tongue a bit longer.

****

For four more long days Morgan, tight-lipped, her temper near cresting, scrutinized Mrs. Aueteby's routine—what there was of it—silently declaring a monkey could have been taught to do the tasks more efficiently and much more pleasantly. When Morgan tended Lucy, she disregarded what Mrs. Aueteby might think. She drew the curtains back and opened the French doors to the veranda to let the pleasant outdoor air and sunshine soothe and brighten her spirits. With Lucy comfortably propped up against several mounded pillows, Morgan brushed her hair, filed and polished her nails, related all her past calamities, and read novels Lucy might enjoy.

When the witch retired for the night in Lucy's room, Morgan worked quickly and furiously in the kitchen, straining or pureeing vegetables and fruits, simmering broths nutritious and rich with flavor from a beef shank or chicken. By the third night Melinda and Cook had wholeheartedly joined forces with her, promising to prepare all she'd need during the day so Morgan could sleep.

Now, on the seventh morning, as the light breeze soothed Lucy into a peaceful nap, Morgan wrote commonly used words on a large cardboard. Having herself been unable to speak after the fire, she thought this might make it easier for all of them. She'd shown Lucy the chart of letters and words, completed last night, and the long knitting needle Melinda had donated as a pointer. Lucy had welcomed the new and much less tiring means of communication.

As she dipped her pen in the black ink, then retraced the word *pain* in bold block letters, she wondered if Luke would be as enthusiastic about her new idea.

Luke.

She regretted her demand of a wide berth between them. She missed his banter, his pleasing smile, the approval that made his eyes sparkle when she accomplished something meaningful. True to his word, he stayed away during the day, returning late in the evening. He'd visit with Lucy, take his late dinner in the dining room, then go to his study before retiring. Only once, the night before last, had they come face to face in the hall.

They'd spoken briefly, politely and impersonally. She'd updated him on Lucy's status, the changes in Lucy's care during the day, and how pleased Lucy seemed by it. Oh, yes, his eyes had twinkled. Had her pulse beating like a drum as he'd voiced approval. And that broad smile had nearly sent her leaping into his arms. Thank heaven Melinda had come upon them to tell him his dinner awaited. Again, as last night, the pain in her chest, tormenting and visceral, squeezed and twisted. Yet she had to remind herself she'd actually demanded it be this way. It just might kill her before she finished. She concentrated on the lettering of *open* to rid her mind of such torment, the many days ahead of yearning for something so unattainable.

"What in the world?" Mrs. Aueteby's shriek sent the cardboard tumbling to the floor, the pen flying across the room, and Lucy's eyes springing open with a look as frightened as a mouse facing a starving cat. Morgan hadn't thought the woman could move so fast. But her brisk march toward her didn't compare to the fire flaming from her eyes.

Morgan braced for inevitable war. This was her time with Lucy, and she'd damn well care for her charge—her friend, she corrected—the way she saw fit. To hell with the old incompetent hag. A quick glance at the dark pool of ink on the carpet heightened her mounting ire.

"How dare you scare Lucy awake like that!" Morgan rose and stepped to the bedside to give Lucy a reassuring smile and pat on the hand. Then she turned to glare at the red-faced beast.

"We welcome visitors, *pleasant* visitors. So I must remind you to keep your voice at an even keel. We're enjoying the lovely day, and if you don't like it, go crawl back to your cave where you came from." Morgan clutched her sweaty palms together to stop their shaking. She felt her face flush, yet refused to give an inch. She couldn't believe she'd just voiced such words.

The woman's cheeks darkened to almost purple, her lips thinning to a fine line surrounded by white. By gosh, if she didn't resemble a turnip. Morgan hid her grin.

"This is not allowed, Miss Prescott," the woman huffed as she stood stiff-backed, hands on hips, her eyes dark and menacing. She started to cross the room, obviously to close the French doors and pull the curtains shut.

Morgan lost her composure.

"Stop right where you are, you old hag." The woman froze as if struck dumb. Dear God! Had she just uttered those insulting words? The shame of it, the gall. Nevertheless, she burrowed her fists into her hips and glared at the woman pressing hand to chest, mouth agape.

"Lucy loves the fresh air, the day's brightness. It has to be ten times better for her to feel uplifted and happy than to be in such gloom as you gave her all day. It's a wonder she hasn't lost her spirit."

The woman flinched. "Just who do you think you are? You have no training in these matters. Why, you're no more than an addlebrained young girl. How dare you give me orders? How dare you call me names, when I have complete charge of her care? I..."

"Let's get one thing straight, Mrs. Aueteby. You no longer have complete charge of Lucy." Morgan smiled, sweetly, feeling as wily as a fox, content as a cat lapping warm milk. "By Mr. Strafford's own words, we share her care. Do you know why?"

The woman's eyebrows rose with an indignant scowl. Morgan continued before she could say yea or nay. "Because you're incompetent. You think you give good care? You *don't.* Lucy perspires and needs a bath and her bed changed more often than once a week. She needs a good massage with oils and lotions at least once a week to keep her skin intact and her circulation flowing. She has enough to face each day without you adding gloom to it. She needs to enjoy life in comfort." She bit back the words "for as long as she has left." Mrs. Aueteby stood stone still, her eyes round as saucers.

"And she needs hearty food for strength, fresh air to fill her lungs, and to see the pleasant days to brighten her spirits. She needs people to talk *with* her, not *at* her."

The woman's anger oozed from every quivering pore. Morgan rushed on before she could counter. "I've offered her soft, pureed, nourishing food, not tasteless mush. I've simply opened the doors to let her hear the birds sing and smell the fulfilling scents of flowers. She can see the pleasing day, feel the warmth and freshness of the soft breeze. I talk to her, read to her, share in her wants and needs. I offer her care, not a dominating dictatorship."

Morgan turned, gestured with her hand. "Look at her. *Really* look at her. She may not be physically able to smile, or voice how she feels, but her eyes and the pink glow in her cheeks shows she feels one hundred percent better, healthier, than she did under your austere thumb."

Oh, the woman looked, all right. She scowled, and tightened that thin-lipped face. She looked as if she might scream the house down.

"Her pink cheeks are most likely due to too much sun, or a chill, or fever. And foods hard to digest aren't good for the bowels. Why, she's so sickly that the bright day you brag about will for sure cause her blindness on those worn eyes. She..."

As if a bedeviling banner waved in front of her, Morgan saw red. Her friend lay in dire need of rescuing, and presently she was the rescuer. Tit for tat. Morgan knew she'd be the one screaming the house down, literally. She couldn't have lowered her voice if she wanted to.

"You, Mrs. *Aueteby*, *ought-to-be* shot, or put in an asylum. How can you think such things? She's happier and more comfortable because she's able to enjoy each day rather than feeling as if she wears chains. If you had any compassion for her, you'd clearly see that. I want you to leave this house immediately. You've shown you care nothing for her feelings, wants, or needs. Pack your things and leave, or I'll have Alfred escort you from the premises. I'll see Mr. Strafford pays you your due."

"You have no right, you have no authority."

"That's where you're wrong, you old battle ax. I have the right because Lucy is my friend. Therefore, I'm obligated to protect her at all cost, especially from your vicious, selfish claws. I'll give you a half hour to pack, or I'll make good my words. You're a witch in disguise, and she'll not miss your ruthless manhandling one bit." *And neither will I.*

The woman stomped out of the room, leaving the door wide open and a foul taste in Morgan's mouth. Eyes round as saucers, Melinda and Cook peered around the door casing.

They remained silent, concerned query in their eyes. Morgan smiled, betraying nothing of her inner turmoil. And felt the first shudder roll like a punch through her torso. Heavens above, she'd just fired the woman as if she had every right in the world to do so. What would Luke say? What did poor Lucy think of her thunderous ranting and crazed raving?

"Everything's fine now, ladies. Please come in." As they cautiously entered, she silently praised her own composure in light of what she'd just done. Well, she'd answer their questions and face Luke's inquisition later. Right now, she needed to console and rectify the situation with Lucy.

She turned, bracing herself to encounter a frightened and possibly angered Lucy, if any emotions could break through the limp facial muscles. She paused, her heart warming more toward the remarkable woman who surprisingly wore admiration across her face.

"Oh, Lucy," Morgan sighed, taking her hands. She blinked past tears as the wonder of Lucy's reaction sank in. For days Lucy's features had been void of any expression. It had been a feat for her to turn her head, to whisper the slightest audible sound. Yet now, though fleeting and minuscule, a twinkle lit Lucy's eyes, the corner of her lips curled slightly with approval.

"I feared you might want me to leave right along with that hateful harridan, but I think I see your approval." Lucy gave no visible sign of acquiescence.

Morgan squeezed Lucy's hands. "Wait." She bent down, retrieved the cardboard, and held it up in front of Lucy.

"Remember how we did it last night? When I come to a letter or word you want, you give a good blink. Okay, now, did I see your approval?" She pointed a finger to the word "no."

Lucy just looked at the board. Morgan slid her finger to the word "yes." Lucy blinked. Not just an involuntary blink, but an intentional one. Morgan beamed.

"That's remarkable," Melinda said, as she and Cook drew closer to the bed.

"I'm…we're hoping the board will make it easier for Lucy to convey her wishes or needs."

Resting the cardboard against the bed, Morgan took Lucy's hand again. "You may approve, and I'm ever so grateful you do, but I'm truly sorry for exposing you to such a wretched scene. If I had held my temper this time, I would've had it out with her elsewhere. Unfortunately, my tongue got to lashing before I thought of the consequences. I hope you can forgive me for my reckless outburst."

Lucy's mouth thinned as if struggling to communicate.

"Don't try. Please. I simply had to say it." She took the weak movement of Lucy's hand within hers as answer, realizing in amazement a bond of friendship had flourished right from the start. Mutual respect and admiration had drawn them further together. They were, simply put, kindred spirits. And Morgan's heart ate it up like sugared candy.

"I've some custard with just a touch of nutmeg cooling," Cook said, her eyes darting from Morgan to Lucy. "I can bring it right up, if you'd like."

Morgan smiled at Cook, whose real name, she had learned, was Phyllis but who insisted on being called by her official title. "I think that's an excellent idea. But let's see if Lucy agrees."

Eager to again test her new device, Morgan positioned the chart upright on Lucy's lap. Melinda retrieved the knitting needle from the table and handed it to Morgan. As the needle pointed to "yes," three sets of eyes watched in anticipation.

Lucy blinked. Blinked again with what Morgan believed to be more enthusiasm than Lucy had shown since they'd met. Morgan's heart swelled at Lucy's accomplishment, at witnessing the pride in the pale face that lay upon the soft maize pillow.

Cook laughed. "Why, I do believe custard will be just the ticket. Come, Melinda, grab that slop pot, and I'll get that custard."

****

From Lucy's window, Morgan marveled at the beauty of the blue sky turning to pink marble as the sun started its descent on the horizon. Stretching out the stiffness in her back, her pulse quickened when she spied Luke's horse cantering up the drive.

She went back to the bed, more than a bit apprehensive to face Luke. Her nerves felt as if nettles scrabbled under her skin.

"Lucy, are you awake?"

Lucy opened her eyes slowly. How utterly devastating to be unable to smile, to easily express yourself.

"Luke's back, so I'm going downstairs." She forced a grin. "Not that I want to. Heaven only knows how he'll react when I tell him what I did." She found it impossible to hold back a chortle, remembering all she'd done in Washington.

"Of course, he's used to my blunders by now, don't you think? And he always took them better than I'd ever imagined. But I do need to discuss what happened today."

She wondered if she should call Melinda. But the woman always seemed so busy.

A faint twinkle lit Lucy's eyes. Morgan studied Lucy for a moment before leaning over to kiss her forehead. "You know, even though it's been only a few days since we've changed your care, you definitely have more facial expressions. And at times, like now, your eyes speak for themselves. I do believe we've made some headway. I promise I'll be back shortly."

At the door she glanced back. "That's if he doesn't throw me and my big mouth out the front door." Laughing despite her mounting tension, she went downstairs fortified by altruistic pride in her accomplishments with Lucy, more so by knowing Lucy had felt her own pride this afternoon.

Chapter Twenty-Five

Morgan knocked on the study door, then opened it with trepidation at Luke's call to enter. She'd hurried straight to his domain, knowing he always took a moment to sort through his correspondence before visiting Lucy. She didn't feel as confident as she had a minute ago. Slick-palmed, her hands trembled as she took a step inside and closed the door.

His devotion to Lucy was apparent by his visits every morning, again before his dinner, then once more, usually longer, just before retiring. Morgan found she admired him all the more for that devotion. Yet at the same time her selfish ego and yearning heart cried a thousand bitter tears. She always left during his visits, not only to allow them their due privacy but to be able to breathe past her languishing torment, to escape possibly witnessing their tender byplay.

With emotions rioting, she forced a smile, willing her voice to remain steady. "Before you visit Lucy, I'd like to discuss something, if you have a few minutes." *I hope.*

"I've all the time in the world." He smiled, set down the envelope he'd been opening, and came around the desk. "Please have a seat." His gesture indicated the leather chair in front of the desk. His smile twinkled in his eyes. She could easily drown in them.

Taking the seat, she wondered if *he'd* scream the house down when he found out what she'd done.

Well, it was up to her and her alone to tell him. She folded her hands on her lap to quit their trembling, bit her bottom lip, and took a deep breath.

He frowned, folded his arms across his chest, and leaned against the desk to study her. *Oh, this isn't going to be easy.*

"Can't be that bad. Melinda said Lucy had a good day. You're good medicine for her."

She read admiration and more in his sultry gaze. She shouldn't feel the tingles she felt when he looked at her that way. She felt her face flush. Would he say the same when he knew she was her only medicine at the moment?

He chuckled. "Now I've embarrassed you, or…my God, Morgan, are you afraid of me?"

She bit her lip harder. He raised his voice. "Have I ever given you any reason to think I'd bite your head off? I might have lost my temper when you shrunk my buckskins, but I'll remind you how short-lived my anger is, and it's never physical."

Realizing how foolish she'd been—she knew him better than that—and now she'd not only wounded him but insulted him, as well, she cleared her throat. "I'm not afraid of you, Luke. And God only knows I've given you enough things to test your anger. I apologize for even thinking the worst of you. But this time you may want to bite my head off."

"Really?" His eyebrows arched and that boyish grin tickled her heart. "This must be something to surpass everything in the past. I can hardly wait."

His playful ridicule made it easy to simply blurt it out. "I fired Mrs. Aueteby." Relieved she'd said it point blank, she sighed.

He held his position, a dumbfounded look on his face if there ever was one. Then he pushed away from the desk, unfurled his arms. "What?"

Oh, dear. She flinched at his bark. He'd settle down after shouting, she reassured herself. She admired that controlled quality. But how long would it take this time? "I said..."

"I know what you said," he replied, his tone subdued rather than explosive.

Was this the calm before the storm? She swallowed.

"What did she do?"

He hadn't asked why, or what the hell she thought to accomplish. He merely wanted to know why she'd had to take such drastic measures. How could she not love this man to distraction?

"She was sim-, incompetent."

"I see." Again he leaned back against the desk, rubbing his chin as if analyzing the situation further. "At least I think I see. Can you be more specific?"

Morgan was thankful he seemed more inquisitive than furious. She disregarded his effort to hide the grin most likely due to her almost saying "simply" again. She relaxed, inhaled.

"Oh, I can be very specific." She sat up straighter, intent on saying her piece now that he'd asked. "You know she didn't do any more than absolutely necessary, and what she did do was done roughly and...incompetently. Lucy could hardly breathe in that closed-up room. It was so gloomy it's a wonder Lucy didn't suffer eyestrain or become totally depressed. The slop that woman fed her wasn't fit for pigs. She never even held a conversation with Lucy. She gave orders like some sanctimonious army general." She took another deep breath to continue. "She..."

She saw his broad smile, watched him silently chuckle. *Good Lord.*

"I apologize. I didn't mean to run on like that." Her dander had her all but shaking.

"Please." He grinned, shaking his head. "Don't apologize. Everything you say is true. I should have set her straight the first night back, when I suspected she was 'incompetent.'"

He boosted himself up on the desktop. "The only thing I really want to know is, ah, when have you ever heard a sanctimonious army general?" His chuckle finally escaped to fill the room.

Not for a moment did she take offense but grinned along with him.

"You wouldn't have to ask if you'd ever met the headmistress at the second finishing school I attended. She would've made Grant and Lee both turn and run with their tails between their legs, had they faced her on the battlefield."

They shared a smile. "You are indeed the best medicine for Lucy. And I've no regrets you fired the woman. But how did this all come about?"

She proceeded to give him an exact and verbatim account of how things had materialized. He howled when she related how she'd said the woman ought-to-be shot. They discussed the charts she'd made and how well they were working. When their sides ached from laughter, their gazes met and locked, and silence filled the room. Tension rose like steam from a kettle.

Morgan felt the pull, knew he felt it, too, by the way his eyes darkened and smoldered, the lids lowering a bit. Her pulse quickened and the longing she'd tried so hard to suppress and ignore stirred within her. She ached from want. Before either of them could act upon their wayward emotions, she turned her head to study the many books lining the far wall.

"I told her you'd send what she was owed."

"Thank you. I'll make sure she receives it tomorrow."

Morgan stood and faced him. "I'd better go so you can visit Lucy before dinner."

"Take your dinner with me, if you haven't

already."

Oh, how she wanted to say yes. But at what cost? They'd pay dearly for a few stolen moments. Neither one of them could afford the sorrow, the anguish that would eat at them for having to deny more than words over a hot meal. She studied the books on the shelves.

"Thank you for the offer, but I planned to have a quick meal in the kitchen with Cook, to discuss more dishes for Lucy, and then finish the word chart before morning."

"For God's sake, have dinner with me. It'll be harmless. I need to talk to you, anyway."

Her head swung back to him, her eyes met his squarely. "It would be far from harmless." *More like harmful and heartbreaking, to say the least.* "And you know it as well as I."

"Morgan..." He slid off the desk to stand, reaching out to her.

She stepped back. Shook. She couldn't help it. Her nerves scattered; her senses swirled. She yearned for his touch, to touch him. His virile appeal, potent magnetism, intoxicating musk, the kindling flames in his eyes—all converged on her while her heart leaped perilously.

"Don't. Please." She felt the blood surge from her fingertips to her toes as her passion intensified. "I need to go," she said, as she turned to flee.

It took a moment before Luke could think. He wasn't often rattled. It had taken every bit of willpower to resist hauling her into his arms before she strode across the room.

"I may have found someone for Lucy." He watched her stop and spin around, her eyes wide with surprise, full of questions, yet leery.

"I'd intended to tell you after I saw Lucy. I would have told you over dinner. Since you're here now, we can discuss it, if *you* have a few minutes."

"How long have you known about this person?" Her frown said a thousand words.

"Don't get your dander up. Just since today, or actually yesterday. Please, sit back down, and I'll tell you." He watched her walk to the chair, sit, and clasp her hands on her lap, her frown still doubting his truthfulness. He again leaned against the desk.

"Yesterday my partner, Ben Randolph, suggested it might be good for his recently widowed niece to care for Lucy instead of dwelling on her recent loss. She took it pretty hard. She's twenty-nine and has just started to look for work since her husband didn't leave her with much. Her name's Diana Tompkins. She cared for her parents before they passed, then cared for her husband till he died two months ago from a lung disorder."

He hiked himself up to sit on the desk. "Diana sold her small home and has been living with Ben and his wife for the past month, till she could get both feet back on the ground. I asked Ben to have her come today and talk to me, which she did. She's intelligent, pleasant, and I think she'd be good for Lucy. Hopefully the job will be good for her, too."

He watched Morgan. She'd listened intently and now looked speechless. He knew if Diana proved worthy, Morgan might leave. And then where would he be? With a knife in his heart.

"Are you willing to give her a try? Train her to your liking?"

She swallowed, looking dazed. His heart felt that knife pierce deep. Did she feel it too?

"When do you want her to start?" Her voice sounded forlorn. He wanted to say, "Never."

"Thinking I had to fire Mrs. Aueteby first, I told her two days. I did suggest she try it with you for a few days to make sure she and Lucy would suit. What do you think?"

Morgan smiled, but he noted the smile didn't

sparkle in those eyes as usual. "Since I saved you the trouble of firing that witch, I suppose that's good."

"I want to thank you for saving me from her wrath, but I apologize for you having to bear it full measure. So, thank you." Did she find it as hard to converse at this point as he did?

"You're welcome. And now I need to see Cook. Tell Lucy I'll see her after your visit." She stood, her smile beaming somewhat brighter. "Thank you for keeping your word."

She turned and left him in the empty room with an equally empty heart.

****

From day one, Morgan found Diana delightfully spirited, warm, and sincere, and very conscientious about Lucy's needs. And Lucy took to Diana, as well. Over the next week, they gave quality care to their patient. Lucy responded well to Cook's new menu, the daily routine of being wheeled out to the veranda to bask in the sunlight, to lie in bed eager to hear another story read.

Contentment filled Morgan as she watched her charge enjoy the afternoon's soft breeze caressing her cheeks. Lucy appeared more relaxed, listening to musical chirps high above the sprawling lawn as they harmonized with the gentle rustle of leaves. There wasn't anything more rewarding than offering a friend help and witnessing the benefit of such a small effort.

Morgan basked in the growing bond between them, formidable and endearing, and knew she'd cherish it forever. As she scrutinized Lucy, she prayed her health would remain stable for a while longer. She'd deeply regret leaving if she decided to leave her solely in Diana's care.

She reminded Lucy she'd intended her stay to be temporary. And Lucy didn't like that idea at all. But Morgan made a point of saying that by meeting Lucy she realized how quickly life could change, the importance of family, and that she needed to decide if she should go back to New York. Oh, yes, Lucy had accepted that as gospel, and, though she'd miss her, she had wished her well. It broke Morgan's heart.

Unwittingly, her thoughts turned to Luke. By evening, when he arrived to sleep at Lucy's bedside on the narrow bed, her emotions had twisted in all directions. She fought the desire that leaped within her at seeing him—his warm smile, handsome face and magnificent physique—and the way he gently ministered to Lucy. Oh, they could speak politely, laugh over the day's events, conspire ways to better meet Lucy's needs and improve her care. All the while her heart was torn in two.

Now, as she watched her friend, her guilt at coveting her fiancé rose to such proportions it nearly gagged her, twisting in her chest until it felt ready to burst through skin and bone. How could she remain loyal to Lucy and yet go on yearning for his touch when she saw him every evening and greeted him in the morning before he left? She had no choice but to leave. Diana could well manage Lucy's care.

Agonizing over a love lost was one thing. Having to face that forbidden love day in and day out was totally another. And how much longer before Lucy suspected? Morgan had sworn she'd never let that happen. Oh, how sinful, how selfish, to think of baser desires while Lucy struggled each and every minute to simply take the next breath. It surprised Morgan God hadn't struck her or Luke down with a bolt of lightning.

Pulling her gaze away from the lawn and her mind from agonizing distraction, she noticed Lucy's eyes had opened. Lacking the ability to produce any facial expression, Lucy simply stared intently. At her. Could she see deep down inside her, read her darkest, unruly thoughts? Did she read the longing, the heated sensations she'd felt, thinking of Luke? Dear God in heaven. The hair on Morgan's nape prickled.

"Well, now, I think it's time I took you inside." She found it easy to give a bright smile to someone she loved. And she did love Lucy dearly, with a deep-seated devotion that still surprised her. She cringed at thinking Lucy could have discovered her secret.

"This fresh air is good for you, but it tires you out. And that was a measly catnap you had, if I ever saw one. I've done enough lollygagging, so I'd best get to doing something constructive."

Morgan wheeled the high-backed wooden chair to the bedside. She locked the brakes, braced her feet wide apart, threaded her arms under Lucy's armpits, and planted her hands on her back to hug her tight. In one clean swoop she transferred her onto the bed. It had become old hat to swivel her into a prone position smack in the middle of the bed.

Straightening, Morgan stretched out the kinks in her back, then pulled the sheet and the down comforter up to Lucy's chin. "There now, easy as pie." She laughed at her own joke. "Of course, making a pie wasn't always so easy, especially for me, let me tell you." She knew she rattled on but couldn't help it. She forced a smile to cover her self-consciousness.

"Would you like some tea? Maybe one of those scrumptious molasses cookies Cook baked yesterday? I could dunk it again. I know I'd love one, and Diana most likely would, too. She'll be back in a minute." *Had* Lucy picked up on why she babbled?

Pointing the knitting needle to "yes," she frowned when Lucy failed to blink. She pointed to no. Lucy blinked twice before eyeing the bottom of the chart. Since Lucy indicated to continue, Morgan sat down on the bed, and repositioned the chart for easier access.

"All right, let's see what you do want."

For the next fifteen minutes, Morgan scanned the chart while Lucy blinked her answers. The final result amounted to Lucy asking her to stand by Luke when she left this world. And she'd asked her to listen to her heart when she did so. *Dear God.*

A lump the size of an orange lodged in Morgan's throat. Unsure whether Lucy had insight into Morgan's true feelings for Luke or if she'd simply chosen today to discuss her wishes, she questioned how to respond to Lucy's request. She answered as best she could.

"I, like everyone else, hope that day is a long ways away. But you can be assured everyone will stand by him. We'll give him the support he needs, as long as he needs it."

She grasped the chart more tightly so Lucy wouldn't see her hands shake. Discussing Lucy's death—the mere word chilled her bones—tore at her heart. She preferred to not think about it. But it would arrive, all too soon, most likely. And the delicately fine line she trod made it ten times harder to converse with the other woman. Morgan's mind spun with conflicting thoughts. Her emotions roiled inside until she thought they'd erupt as vomit.

"I don't know about you, but I prefer to enjoy the day rather than discuss your demise. You've been doing extremely well lately. Let's focus on that, and treasure each good day as it comes."

It wasn't easy to remain uplifted at a time like this. Pointing to "yes," she prayed Lucy would answer in kind.

She did, thank the good Lord.

"Now how about that tea and cookie? And then I'll let you rest."

Ah, Lucy double-blinked at the right word.

Yes, there is a God.

At least for the time being.

Chapter Twenty-Six

The sun shone brightly, slowly descending the curve of the clear blue sky, the soft breeze pleasantly cool as it sprinkled a light scent, sweet and clean, from the multitude of surrounding blossoms. The lake, blue as the sky, shimmered with gentle ripples. With Lucy in the wheelchair to enjoy the loveliness made the moment perfect, Morgan thought with contentment.

Alfred had carted the chair downstairs while Luke carried Lucy. With a knitted wool afghan over Lucy's lap and a shawl draped over her shoulders, he'd wheeled her down to the water.

Lucy's eyes canvassed the four loons as they glided from the far side of the lake like well-maneuvered boats over each ripple. They drew close to the nearby bank, only to cautiously skirt away when they sensed the presence of humans.

As if a tangible force, Morgan felt the thrill within Lucy at being able to once again enjoy the serenity of nature and its curious yet fascinating creatures. She too basked in the sheer beauty of the picture and could understand how much more this meant to Lucy. It was a day made in heaven, directed and orchestrated by God himself, if she ever saw one. And Morgan thanked her lucky star she could share such a fulfilling moment. The realization this might be the last outing with Lucy, if she decided to leave, threatened to dampen her spirits. She refused to let that happen.

"Do you know loons can dive at remarkable

speeds, and go about two hundred feet in just one dive? That enables them to catch a fish and swallow it whole while they're underwater. Carl—he ran the general store in the logging camp—loaned me several articles about them. Since then, Luke brought a recently published book for me to read. I love reading anything about them."

Lucy watched the birds in fascination, yet Morgan saw she listened closely.

"I itched to know if there was significance to the various calls. I found the wail is their most frequent call. The tremolo that sounds like fluttering usually signals alarm or worry, but sometimes it can be a greeting. I think the tremolo sounds more like a nervous laugh than fluttering. And only the male can yodel and does so to defend territorial boundaries. They hoot to call their mates, or chicks. There's only four calls, but I swear I've heard combinations."

Lucy blinked twice.

"I'm glad you want me to continue. Loons are believed to be one of the most ancient birds, existing millions of years ago. So they're really prehistoric." She paused when Lucy again blinked two times. "So you knew that fact." She laughed in delight at Lucy's eagerness to concur.

"Do you also know that although the male is usually slightly larger than the female both can fly up to a hundred miles an hour? Lord, that's remarkable." Lucy blinked once. Morgan nodded.

"Their average life span varies from fifteen to thirty years. The female lays two large eggs, one day apart, each taking from twenty-seven to thirty-one days to hatch."

Pure satisfaction seeped through Morgan as she noted Luke, leaning nonchalantly against a big sycamore tree, seemed as thoroughly engrossed in her information as Lucy.

"You've probably seen them thrash those webbed feet and beat the water while they hold their bodies stiff and upright. I love to watch that. It's to tell intruders to stay away. I just recently discovered it can be very dangerous for them, because some may do it until they're so exhausted they can die. Not very smart on their part, I think."

"You must be studying that book as well as reading it." Luke laughed as he eased down the tree trunk to a sitting position. He leaned back, stretching out those long, solid legs. Morgan's pulse skipped. "I'll have to find another for you."

Watching the sinewy muscles flex under his well-fitting trousers, Morgan replied, "I'd appreciate that." She hoped neither he nor Lucy had caught how winded her breath had become. God help her, she'd nearly panted. "I'm almost finished with it."

A part of her reveled at his admiration, another part girded itself with resolve. It would not be good if she allowed herself to be influenced by romantic notions.

For the next half hour Morgan related any and all facts regarding loons. She focused on Lucy, avoiding any scrutiny of the tantalizing physique under the tree.

It was a long, nerve-wrenching afternoon, to say the least. Only the satisfaction of knowing they'd pleased Lucy kept the guilt of her attraction to Luke at a minimum. When the wind picked up, Morgan eagerly accepted calling a halt to their outing.

****

Over their first few days together, Diana and Morgan developed a well-paced regime. They worked side by side when lifting or turning Lucy. Other times, they alternated. Morgan welcomed the hours when Luke was at work or cloistered in his study. It had become a mind-boggling effort to totally avoid him. His scent alone, that subtle woodsy fragrance, nearly drove her to distraction. As soon as he came to visit Lucy, she'd leave the room.

Lucy seemed to be holding her own, though her body continued to wither. Watching Lucy's eyes close as slumber took hold, Morgan's tears escaped. She gathered the soiled laundry, then quietly shut the door behind her as she headed downstairs. How would she ever endure leaving her friend? Or Luke? But Diana was a capable, caring caregiver. She had to keep telling herself that.

"Is everything all right?" Luke asked as she cleared the last step and he pulled the study door closed. She had no right to wonder if his concern was for Lucy or her. No right at all.

"Yes. Lucy's sleeping like a lamb." She wiped the wetness from her cheeks with the corner of a sheet and fought for composure. "It's just…I thought she'd been holding her own fairly well, but I just realized how much thinner she is. And how much more easily she tires."

The silence hung like heavy, thick fog in the high-ceilinged entrance for what seemed to be minutes rather than mere seconds as both dealt silently with their own troubled thoughts. She didn't want to deal with this right now. Not with him present to distract her, to witness her faltering strength. She needed to deal with possibly leaving, to form a plan of how to remain strong until she walked out the door. She couldn't do that with him sending her pulse fluttering and her heart yearning.

"Let me take those," he offered, coming to her side in a few long strides.

As he reached out to relinquish her burden, she pulled back. Oh, how she wished she had the right to say, "Just wrap your arms around me, and I'll be fine."

His brows arched, yet he lowered his arms to his sides.

“Thank you, but I can manage. I need to keep busy. Otherwise it will get to me.”

He nodded, obviously understanding her need. Their gazes met, held. The usual magnetism played tug of war between them. He felt it. She could see it in his eyes, the quick breath he took. She leaned toward him, needing any consolation he could offer.

Thank heavens, logic sprang forth as Lucy’s nightgown began to slip from her pile. Straightening, Morgan readjusted her load and stepped back.

“I’d like to talk to you after I’m rid of this laundry.”

His face solemn, he nodded again. “When you’re done, just come to my study.”

****

The study door stood open. Luke sat at his desk reading a piece of paper. “Luke?”

He looked up and smiled. “Please, come in and have a seat.”

She crossed the room and sat in the leather chair. Her pulse hammered, her heart heavy as a stone. Would he accept her leaving? They had no choice. She girded herself with resolve. She would give him no time for small talk. She’d say her piece and be done with it.

“As you know I’d planned to stay only a few days, and it’s turned into much longer. Diana is now more than capable to manage Lucy’s care. I’d thought to leave soon, but I won’t leave until Lucy starts holding her own again.”

His expression went grim. He leaned back in his chair, his shoulders stiff.

“And you think you can just walk away from Lucy and not look back?” His eyes smoldered; his voice was clipped and harsh. He made her sound so callous. She blinked several times to check the swimming tears.

"I have to leave. You know that. It's not fair to any of us if I stay. It's too hard. And you certainly don't need two of us. It's a waste of your money. And I believe Lucy already senses there's something between us."

He frowned, leaned forward. "Why would you think that?"

"She...asked me to stand by you when the end comes." Tears slowly spilled down her cheeks, and she swiped at them. "I told her we'd all stand by you. But Luke, I never want her to think we've been more than good friends. It's too hard to stay and not give her more to suspect. When...I told her I needed to go see my family, she accepted that."

She watched him steeple his hands against his chin, his face tight with strain. "Do you really plan to go to New York, or did you just tell her that?"

"I think I need to go into the city first. I'll most likely stay at the boarding house you told me about, for a little while, until I decide if I really want to go back to New York. But I'll not leave while she's so weak. She's hardly taken down enough nourishment today to keep her going."

He looked her straight in the eyes. "I understand the strain between us. I also understand you may want to eventually go back and mend fences with your family. But I can well afford and would like nothing better than to have the two of you care for her. I hate the thought of your leaving. And I appreciate your waiting till she's doing better. Thank you for that."

"You're welcome." She managed to lift her voice above a whisper.

Luke watched her leave. He'd noticed Lucy deteriorating even while she emotionally thrived on having Diana and Morgan care for her. He sighed, wondering just what the next few weeks would bring. Knowing he'd have to let Morgan go if Lucy stabilized, he prayed with all his heart she'd rally again. At least he had time to accept Morgan's departure. But when she left, it'd likely kill him.

****

Four days later, the funeral, as Lucy had long ago requested, consisted of only the household members and Luke's business associates. The service was held at the house, somber and simple, with the usual meal following.

Morgan, with the others, offered Luke condolences, yet yearned to comfort him within her arms. But she couldn't. They owed that much to Lucy. They needed to grieve. They needed another long talk in his study. But this time she'd really dread it. Because she'd be leaving.

****

The next morning, Morgan knocked on the study door.

"Come in," Luke called, and Morgan reminded herself to stay strong.

She opened the door and pasted on the best smile she could give to the man behind the desk. "Good morning. I'd like to talk to you before Diana and I leave. How are you?"

His smile stilled, his face grew serious. "Please have a seat. And how am I doing? Fine, considering I've just buried my fiancée and the woman I want is leaving."

This was harder than she'd originally thought. She hated leaving. "I can't stay here, even with the others present. You know as well as I it wouldn't be proper."

He eased back, his eyes narrowed suspiciously. "And what would be proper? That I venture to the city and properly court you?" His smile lacked humor.

Her anguish almost overcame her control. She had to do this. She focused on the wall. "Proper would be mourning for a year, but at least six months. We owe our respects to Lucy, and we both need time to mourn. I feel guilty as it is. I'm sorry, but I do need time."

"So you want me to let you go on your own and not give two hoots? Do we see each other at all, or maybe you're planning to go to New York fairly soon?"

His sarcasm bit hard. "We can't see each other at all for at least six months. It would be too hard. Who knows, we may have gone down other paths by then." The lie stuck in her throat like a stiff nettle. Her insides shook while she swallowed tears. "I appreciate your offer to help me find work, but I need to do it on my own."

He cleared his throat. "It'll drive me crazy not to check on you."

"I'm sorry for that, and it's going to be just as hard for me, too, but it has to be."

"So this is it? Just a quick goodbye, and I'm not to seek you out until after six months?"

Oh, God, she hadn't wanted to hurt him. Didn't he know she suffered, too? Her gaze shifted to his green eyes, and she sucked in a breath. "Yes," she managed to choke out. And watched his expression turn to mute wretchedness.

Silence hung in the air, bitter and lonely. Had she been right to demand this? But if she faltered for one moment, they'd be doomed.

"Six months it is," he said, his expression taut and derisive, his voice terse.

What should she say? If she offered any apology, she'd shatter. "Thank you."

She stood, turned, and fled the room, away from those compelling eyes, those arms she sought to hold her yet had to deny. And wondered whether she'd made the right decision or the worst mistake of her life.

Chapter Twenty-Seven

Luke watched the carriage roll down the drive, his heart empty. Fisting his hands, he struggled against the urge to haul her back by the hair on her head. How could she just leave? Walk out of his life? For six damn months? How could he wait that long? He slumped onto the step, bowed his head, and prayed she'd be all right, that his sanity would hold.

Well, hell, he was an investigator. He'd keep tabs on her. His passion stirred just thinking about making love to her as he had yearned to do for almost as long as he'd known her. He hadn't been celibate before proposing to Lucy. But he had been since. For two long years. What was another six months? They did need to properly grieve, to take time for her to deal with her guilt. And they did owe it to Lucy. He prayed he wouldn't lose Morgan along the way. He'd make certain to play his cards right. And he always played his cards well. He felt better already.

****

Morgan knew it would take almost an hour to reach the boarding house. But the time seemed to fly by as she and Diana talked nonstop about what they each might do when back in the city.

"So after I sold the house and paid off his debts, I thought I had enough money. But I needed a little bit more to buy the large ovens, so I had to go to the bank for a small loan."

"Oh, Diana, I'm so happy you'll finally have your dream. A bakery will be a little gold mine, especially since there isn't another one. You'll be raking in the money in no time."

Diana frowned. "I think so, too, but I didn't have any equity to back up a loan, and the bank wouldn't take a chance on a woman without collateral."

Morgan's heart ached for Diana. It seemed all her dreams were ended before she ever got started. First her marriage, and now owning and running a bakery. Two to one, had she been male she would have secured the loan. Oh, the gall of that banker. What an injustice.

"Could you ask your uncle for the loan?"

Diana shook her head, her lips thinned. "No, I don't want to ask him. Oh, he'd probably give it to me, but if the bakery flopped, then I'd be indebted to him, and I never want to be indebted to anyone again. My husband was, and I can't let that happen to me."

Morgan's mind whirled a mile a minute. This could be her answer. *Oh, by golly.*

"You know, I've thought of something, if you'll hear me out."

"Certainly, I'd welcome any ideas," Diana said, with a hopeful expression.

"You know about all my catastrophes with baking and cooking, but I did finally conquer baking quite well, if I do say so myself. Not as well as you or Sarah, I'm sure, but I'm eager to learn perfection and I'm a fast learner. I need a job. I have more money than I'd thought to have from playing the mock wife and from caring for Lucy. Luke paid me very well."

Morgan's heart lit up at seeing Diana's grin. "I could be a partner, a small partner, since you'd be putting up most of the money. But I could work with you and be very happy doing it."

Diana actually beamed as she clasped Morgan's hands in hers. "Oh, Morgan, that sounds so wonderful. My goodness, yes. I'd love you to work with me, to be my partner."

"This sounds too good to be true, for both of us." She squeezed Diana's hands in return. Her decision to avoid Luke still weighed heavy on her heart and would for the next six months. Yet, for the first time in days, she had a plan, a purpose, happiness in her heart. And oh, but it felt good.

"Now, just how much money do you need?"

****

"What do you think? Does it look appealing?" Diana came from behind the glass display case to view her work from the front.

Morgan finished loading the cash register, closed it, and joined Diana. "Everything looks scrumptious. I like how you grouped the items. It's perfect. The whole place is perfect."

"I couldn't have done it without you. Thank you so much, Morgan," she said, embracing her friend in a crushing hug. With tears in her eyes and a grin of pure satisfaction on her face, Diana stepped back. "But let's do one final inspection before we open the door."

"All right. One last look." Morgan backed up and leaned against the front door to examine the hours of sweat they'd poured into the place over the past two months.

They'd bought the building and shared the apartment upstairs. They'd had carpenters insert two picture windows, build a wall to separate the shop from the kitchen, and construct a three-tiered display counter encased in glass, as well as the cash register counter. In the kitchen, the workmen had built shelves and huge counters and had installed the ordered ovens just two weeks ago.

The rest we've done ourselves, Morgan thought with pride. They'd scrubbed and varnished floors, painted walls a soothing gold, hung pictures and decorations, and set up a kitchen any baker would give his eyeteeth for. They'd clustered three tables, with chairs, on each side of the entry door. The display case paralleled the left back wall, and the checkout counter stood to the right. Diana's idea of a wooden chest full of toys and a shelf with children's books along the left wall was brilliant. The ivory tie-back curtains Morgan had just finished hanging gave it a final touch.

She smiled and saluted Diana. "Looks magnificent. Open that door, partner."

Eight hours later, Morgan felt ready to drop. But a good drop. There'd been a steady flow of customers since the first one entered. When things slowed, Diana had gone back to begin the baking for the next day. It had been a very good first day.

Morgan glanced at Diana to see her wiping out the nearly empty pastry case. "Can I lock the door now? I don't think I can take another chime from that bell you hung over the door."

Diana looked up and grinned. "Yes, lock up. And that bell will be very handy after things settle down and we're both in the back. But let's count the money before we go up."

Morgan knew how she felt. "This is your big day, so the privilege is all yours. I'll go wash the coffee pot and last cups. We make one helluva team, you and me."

Diana giggled. "We do, at that."

****

Luke scrutinized the newly famed bakery from across the wide street. He grinned at the big wooden sign. It was an eyecatcher, painted sky blue with bold gold swirling script declaring *Delights*. Two women exited carrying cardboard boxes.

He walked across the busy thoroughfare, reminding himself to relax. Yet eagerness rode him as if he were a charging bull. Three months ago he'd asked Diana for Morgan's whereabouts, but she told him she'd vowed secrecy for six months. She hadn't even mentioned to Ben that Morgan had partnered her. He'd only had to dig deeper to locate her. Well, he'd waited her damn six months, actually a few days past, since he'd been out of town on business.

The bell clanged as three people exited, and he stood aside for them, then entered. He took in the surroundings. Very classy, yet nicely cozy. The aromas of baked goods, cinnamon, apples, and coffee permeated the entire room. His mouth watered. They'd named it well.

His gaze locked on Morgan. She was behind the display case, retrieving a pie for an older woman in front. He listened to them chat as she placed the pie into a box. His pulse ran a mile a minute, and he took a calming breath so he wouldn't rush over and swoop her up into his arms.

Would she feel the same emotions when she spotted him? Or had her feelings changed? Confidence was what he needed. He nodded to four ladies at one of the tables to his left as they conversed over what looked like turnovers. Nodded again at the two sitting to his right.

As Morgan and the customer made their way to the cash register, Morgan looked his way.

Her mouth formed an O as she halted. "Luke. It's so good to see you." Her voice sounded winded. The glow of her smile warmed him across the room.

He strode to the counter, returning her smile with what he hoped was one equally intoxicating.

"Hello, Morgan. It's good to see you, too. Please, finish your business with this lovely lady. Then I'd like to talk to you, if you've got a minute."

He watched her swallow. "Of...of course." He noticed how her hand shook as she worked the register. *That-a-girl, right where I want you.*

"Thank you, Mrs. Dilion, and enjoy," Morgan

said, handing over the woman's change and the box.

"Thank you, Morgan, and good luck." The woman grinned at Luke, obviously enjoying the electricity in the air, then meandered over to talk to friends at the table of four.

"Have dinner with me tonight."

Her smile vanished and her eyes saddened. His heart plunged more quickly than a sinking ship.

"Oh, Luke, I'm so sorry, but I can't tonight. We'll be baking a cake and other pastries for a wedding tomorrow. We'll be up half the night, as it is."

His mind churned. His heart leaped with hope. "Do you have to work all day tomorrow?"

Her eyes gleamed. His pulse raced. "Why do you ask?"

"I thought if you could leave early, we could go see the loons and then have an early dinner at my home. I'd bring you back before it got too late. The last time I asked you to have dinner with me, you turned me down. Please. I've waited your six months. Don't turn me down again."

She eyed the customers, then her face brightened. "It sounds lovely. Diana's in the kitchen, so I'll ask her later if our part-time woman can help out, but I'm sure it'll be fine. What time?"

Their eyes locked, and he wasn't sure he'd ever breathe again. "How about three?"

She offered a sudden, arresting smile. "That'd be fine."

"I'll be here." He gave her a wink, watched her grin, turned, and strode two feet away before he stopped in his tracks. He hadn't seen her for six months. He'd be damned if he'd just leave.

He spun around and stalked back. Disregarding the astonished look on her face, he cupped her face between his hands and drew her lips to his. He kissed her with all the tenderness he possessed, fighting the urge to devour. His mind reveled at the softness of her lips, her eager response. He heard sighs, *ohs*, and *oh, mys* from the nearby tables.

With sheer willpower, he pulled away. "Till tomorrow, pretty lady." He turned, his footsteps light, having witnessed Morgan's eyes full of passionate wonder.

****

As they rode to Luke's home they related their childhoods. He was an only child. His father, a successful carpenter, hadn't been rich but had provided well, and they'd been a happy family till both parents had died six years ago. Morgan told of years of trying to be herself yet constantly at odds with her parents, since she refused to be a snob.

Now, after tearful greetings for Morgan from Melinda, Cook, and the others, they leaned back on the bench by the lake, sipping wine, fascinated with watching the loons glide across the rippled pond. A soft breeze gently rustled the leaves overhead.

She thought of their sweet, potent kiss yesterday yet tried to relax. But how would she ever push aside the strong bond she'd shared with Lucy, forget that she'd betrayed Lucy by loving her fiancé?

"Talk to me, Morgan. When we were up north, you did everything in your power to keep most of your thoughts, especially your past, a secret. And since Lucy's death, I feel like we've stepped back to square one." He sighed, stroked her hand. Tiny goose bumps ran up her arms. His touch always affected her, no matter how hard she fought her feelings.

"We don't talk like we did. You don't even look at me the same way. We lived together for over two months. I'll be damned if I know how we didn't either lose our sanity or end up in bed together. And yet we still don't really know each other."

How closely his thoughts mirrored hers. His growing frustration brought a smile to her lips. He looked like a little boy, all frazzled and at a loss for the correct words. Oh, but he wasn't a little boy, no, indeed, and they were playing with fire, drawing closer to it minute by minute.

"We did end up in bed together, several times." Her grin grew, despite her awareness she should change the subject. She was tempting fate and those flames that would singe and burn.

He threw her a stern, exasperated look. "You know what I mean. We didn't make love, and therefore didn't betray Lucy, at least not physically."

She sighed. "No, we didn't, thank God." She saw him wince as if she'd slapped him. "I couldn't have faced her if we had. I wouldn't have had the opportunity to get to know her, to love her, or to help her in any way, if we'd betrayed her."

He nodded, though his eyes looked tired, discouraged. "I know. I feel the same way. I'm thankful we didn't. You made a big difference in Lucy's last days. You've made a bigger difference for me. I'm not certain I could've gotten through her last few weeks had you not been by my side. And now that Lucy's gone we need to talk—about our pasts, our thoughts, our feelings. And what we want in our future."

Was she ready to bare her soul? She'd missed him, had been heartsick with longing for him, but she still felt she'd be betraying Lucy. So she answered his original question, giving a bit more from her unspoken past.

"My father was never satisfied with anything I did. I tried to be prim and proper to win his affection, agreeable when he insisted, and astute, self-motivated, and self-reliant when he commanded it. It wasn't good enough. And my mother wasn't much different. They were both happier when I was away at a boarding or finishing school. I could never please them. Since then I've betrayed my friend by coveting her fiancé. I'm not sure I like me at this point. How can you possibly want someone like me?"

Luke felt the chill radiate down his spine as she spoke in that passionless voice. Would she forever hold her feelings within that protective glacier? Not if he could help it. She had to be on the edge, tempted, vulnerable. And he wasn't about to look a gift horse in the mouth, as they say. He'd take up an ice pick if necessary to chip away her defenses. Hell, he'd use an auger, if need be. He wasn't about to lose her before he ever had her.

He held her gaze. "I'm in awe, if we're being truthful. How you ever turned into the warm, sensitive, unselfish, and caring woman you've become while you had such an insensitive and cold-blooded family is beyond me."

Tears pooled in her eyes and glistened on her dampened lashes as a ray of sunlight kissed her face. It was all he could do to hold back, to not take her in his arms again. If he was to break that formidable barrier, she'd need to take the first step. He wouldn't force her. If he did, she might flee and never return. He couldn't take that chance. Not after all they'd been through.

Her shoulders slumped. *That-a-girl.* He stifled his grin. Waited.

"My family isn't entirely cold-blooded, Luke." She sighed, shook her head. "I guess I never tried to look at them from a different perspective. But now I can. And I really believe they meant well, in their own way. But money and prestige clouded their priorities. They forgot how to let themselves truly care, or at least how to let down their guard long enough to show it."

"I believe you're being too generous." He'd push her to see things in a different light. At least he hoped he could. If he riled her, it might work. She was one helluva passionate woman. And he craved that passion for himself.

Her shoulders squared like a general's. *That's it, get angry.* He almost laughed out loud.

She stood. "Do you think my sister intentionally meant to hurt me with Malcolm?"

He raised his brows. "Do you mean to tell me she didn't?"

She huffed, stamping her foot against the hard earth. "Of course she didn't," she fired back. Her mouth opened, snapped shut. Her eyes rounded as if only now realizing what her words truly meant. Lowering her tone, sounding almost amazed, she said, "She was simply naïve. All she wanted was to catch a man's eye, to call him her beau, to be the belle of the ball. She wanted to please our parents, impress others. I don't imagine she ever thought about what it would do to me personally. At least not…intentionally."

She stared at the ground. Did she find solace in hearing her own words? It took every fiber within him not to offer comfort, verbally or physically.

"Is that what you truly believe? That she gave no thought to what she was doing to you?"

She raised her head, gave him a smile that dazzled the sun. "Yes. She's fickle, ruled by money as much as my parents, but I can honestly say she'd never have thought about how she'd hurt me."

Her eyes sparkled as she laughed. "She knew I didn't love him. Maybe she thought I'd be relieved she'd taken him. I should've thanked her instead of screeching at them like a shrew."

"You've forgiven her, then? And Malcolm?"

She nodded. "Yes, I believe I have. Lucy's death showed me life is too short to hold grudges, especially if things aren't always what they seem."

"You could write her a letter."

She grinned. "I believe I will. It's crazy, but I miss my parents. I might write them, too."

"Yes, I believe you should." *Now for the auger.*

Chapter Twenty-Eight

He stood, keeping his movement slow, fluid, and calm as he took a step closer to her, so she wouldn't retreat. Took her hands within his and held them gently.

"I love you, Morgan. More than life itself." She turned her head to look at the pond. He felt the faint tremble of her hands. He wouldn't give up his pursuit. Not now, not ever.

"Don't turn away from me. Not now that we can finally be together. You've dealt with Bethany's betrayal, your parents' disregard, a grueling time up north, and Lucy's death. Now you need to listen with your heart. Think of Lucy's request."

Her head jerked around. He saw a pensive shimmer in her eyes, then a shadow of alarm, or was it confusion? She pulled out of his grip, turned away, and peered again at the lake.

"You said she asked you to listen with your heart and to take care of me when she was gone. She wanted that for you, for me. For her, so she could rest peacefully, knowing we're happy."

Her shoulders began to quake, her small sobs sounding like smothered gasps. He'd not meant to cause her such anguish. Only to win her acceptance. Guilt and selfishness clutched at his stomach; defeat and agony twisted deep within his heart like shards of glass.

He couldn't stand it another second. Wrapping his arms tightly around her, he covered her cold hands with his. He laid his cheek against the top of her head and held her back tightly against his chest, then rubbed his hands up and down her arms to warm and soothe her.

"Forgive me. I didn't mean to make you cry. I only wanted you to reach deep inside for what you used to feel for me. At least, I…thought you had felt the same as I." His words nearly ripped his heart from his chest. Had he been wrong?

"Luke, I…"

"No. Don't say anything until I finish." He swallowed down the lump that threatened to gag him. He'd say his piece, then let her go. He had no other choice. "I mistakenly took your attraction for me to mean you loved me every bit as much as I love you. I see now that though you felt attraction you obviously don't share my deep feelings. Not enough to overcome all that's happened around us. I apologize for my error."

Holding her against him was the worst torture he'd ever endured, now that he knew he couldn't have her. "I'd hoped all this would work out, but I won't fight you on this any longer. Your happiness is all that matters to me. I love you enough to want that happiness for you, no matter how hard it is for me to let you go." He felt the hot sting in his eyes, had to blink to prevent tears from spilling. "I…"

He stopped when he felt her quake within his hold. He'd been torn to shreds by her sobs, knowing he'd caused them. But as chuckles bubbled forth, he became totally perplexed. "What the hell?"

She swiveled within his arms, laughing outright now. "Oh, do stop. I can't bear it."

He must have looked as befuddled as he felt, for she smoothed gentle fingertips over his furrowed brow. Her laugh had left him raw inside. He'd laid his heart out on the line. And lost.

Morgan watched his glistening eyes turn rich jade as if seeking answers to a thousand questions.

It had been quite amazing to hear him humble himself. But now those dark eyes spoke hurt. She'd wounded him severely, painfully so, and knew she needed to allay his fears immediately.

She took his face between her hands, held his gaze, and allowed her deepest-felt feelings, her pure unconditional love, to pour forth from her eyes for him to see. "I love you with all my heart, Luke Kincaid Strafford. I've loved you for a very long time and I will love you forever."

This big, strapping man, possessing enough ruthlessness and brawn to storm and conquer the wilds of the cruel north, ample finesse and intelligence to live the life of the elite, smiled a smile a mile wide. And, unabashed, let the flood dam open until tears ran freely down his cheeks.

"You're one exasperating woman," he chided while his hearty laughter and whoops sent the loons zooming across the pond to safer waters. She yelped as her feet left the ground, his excruciating bear hug threatening to cut off her next breath as he swung her around.

"L...uke, I can't breathe," she managed to squeak out. He immediately loosened his hold, though her feet remained a foot or so above the ground. He swung her around once more.

Her laughter joined his. "Have I made you happy, or are you trying to kill me?"

He stopped his swirling to peer down at her. She still dangled from his arms like a rag doll. "Ah, my love, be assured now that I've heard by your own words that you're mine, I'd not let anything or anyone harm a hair on your head. And, by God, I'll never ever let you go."

"It must have been a moment of insanity that made me say such a thing," she laughed.

His eyes twinkled above his mischievous grin. "Then let's be insane together."

His mouth captured hers, his arms tightening their stronghold. It was a greedy, starved-for-too-long kiss. It devoured, claimed possession. It careened down to her suspended toes, sang through her veins, and scalded her skin. She wanted it never to end. So she reciprocated with equal zeal, her hands caressing his sinewy back as his hands ardently explored hers.

Through hazy consciousness, she felt her feet touch solid ground, his arms loosening their hold. He withdrew his lips, gazed into her eyes. Shocked at her own eager response to his fervor, she nonetheless had no desire to pull out of his embrace. And, heaven help her, she felt dismayed that his lips had abandoned hers. A warm glow ebbed through her as she read the love and potent desire in his eyes. She smiled, knowing the dark jade was now from passion.

He returned her smile, his hands casually roaming her back, his labored breath warm against her face. Her pulse bounded, hammered in her ears. When he brushed a gentle kiss across her forehead, her knees weakened. She leaned into his solid strength, her head against the hollow of his neck, chest to chest, thighs to thighs. Her heart galloped, emotions spun in delight.

His one hand buried itself in her hair while the other rested at the small of her back. "I fear I may never want to unlock my arms from around you, sweetheart, yet if I don't go slower and settle down, we may embarrass ourselves right out here in view of all those in the house."

She nuzzled her face against his steeled chest, reveled in feeling the taut, corded muscles across his back, and rested her hands at his waist. The mixture of his own scent, soap, and that faint clean aftershave she'd always found so appealing became intoxicating. This felt so right.

"Mm… Do you really think they'll look out?"

His laughter, rising into the tree limbs, sent more birds to flight. "I'd not want to give them anything more provocative to see if they should. We may have already shocked them."

"Is anyone in the stable at this hour?" Her cheeks burned at her words. For shame.

His deep chortles swirled around her like the sweet music. He stepped back, holding her at an arm's length, and she felt her face flame more, if that were possible.

"You little minx. I believe your lust is as potent as mine. And if it is, it's remarkable, in fact quite unbelievable, we've been able to hold off this long."

"You can believe it, my love. I'll have you know I lost many a night's sleep in our cabin as well as here, sir. It was all I could do…"

"Jesus, woman, enough," he growled, an animal lust glazing his eyes. He literally dragged her by the hand toward the stable.

She had to almost run to match his long determined strides. Her breathing hitched, her heart drummed, and not from the strident walk. Anticipation? Excitement? Pure lust? All three of them, to be honest. She felt a fervent need, a long-awaited craving to feel his arms around her, his hands upon her, his lips seeking hers. A tightness in her lower abdomen screamed for release as her footsteps quickened. Oh, yes, she'd welcome any advances he might make her way. She was ready to show her love. It had been hidden way too long; revealing it was now way past due.

The hinges squeaked as he opened the door. They'd pledged their love; now they'd act upon it. Oh, yes, she was ready. She might be naïve as to the whole gist of lovemaking, but she had no doubt he'd guide her, show her the way. Her eagerness had her trembling.

Releasing her hand, he allowed her to go in first. She took several steps inside. Though he left the door ajar, she had to squint against the darkness. After a moment, her eyes adjusted to see the many stalls. The smell of leather, hay, and horses filled her rioting senses, potentiated her already aroused state. He wasn't the only one feeling animalistic.

He spun her around and crushed her against him, his lips claiming hers. Wrapping her arms around his neck, she returned the kiss full force, molding her body to his. Her mind spun. Only the two of them existed. And she reveled in it.

With one hand on her nape, he ravished her lips while his other hand slowly kneaded her breasts. She responded to his magical touch, the small buds swelling and hardening to an almost painful ache, the junction between her legs growing warm, pulling taut.

When his lips left hers, she sighed her dismay. Fiery passion blazed in his eyes. "Come," he said, taking her hand and leading her to an empty stall.

A horse whinnied from a few stalls farther down. Morgan paid no heed. Not when her soon-to-be lover led her to a safe haven for their lovemaking, not when her blood pounded in her ears and the fire under her skin had her anxious to rip off his clothing.

He stopped in the center of the vacant stall, her hand still in his. His hot gaze swept the length of her as if he wanted to gobble her up. She felt no embarrassment at his perusal, only more feminine and aroused than she'd ever experienced before. Boldly, she let her gaze match his, surveying him from head to toe. Her heartbeat skyrocketed as the air thickened.

When he reached out a hand, caressed her cheek, her breath caught from its reverence. When one finger gently skimmed her lips, trailed down her neck, she shivered from its heat.

"You're so beautiful, so sweet. I want to make love to you, here, now." His eyes bore into hers as he waited. He was giving her the choice. And the beauty of realizing he wanted it to be her decision, as so often in the past her parents hadn't done, had her knees nearly buckling.

"Yes," she whispered past the lump in her throat.

Without further hesitation, he unbuttoned her blouse and pushed it off her shoulders. She shrugged it off, allowing it to fall at her feet. Her heart hammered as his eyes widened and his lips curled upward as he gazed at the revealed cleavage her chemise allowed. He unfastened her skirt, let it join the blouse. Her satin chemise barely reached mid-thigh and his eyes raked over her exposed legs. At his silent, intense inspection, her breasts swelled, becoming acutely sensitive to the soft fabric against them, as if his hands were stroking them to life. Her core, like smoldering embers, begged to be stoked. This prolonged anticipation was becoming unbearable, yet she craved the emotional high, wanting the tantalizing sensuality to go on forever.

"God, you're fire in my blood." His approval stirred *her* blood until she nearly swooned.

With her whole being waiting, wanting more, begging for his touch, she reached out with trembling fingers and undid the buttons of his shirt, one by one, as he'd done to her. Only she did it slowly, to tantalize, to hopefully inflame him to match her burning desire. When her hand lightly brushed his chest, she felt him shudder, saw his eyes darken. She'd not known his nipples would be as sensitive as hers. Eagerly, she became more determined to give him the same heady pleasure that consumed her. But how much longer could they play at this teasing game?

He helped her pull the shirttails out by unfastening his belt buckle and the top button of his pants. Just that simple act, of his fingers touching hers during the process, of him allowing her to undress him, had her limbs aching, her blood coursing through her veins like a surging river. As the shirt joined her discarded clothes, her fingers itched to run a trail through the dark mat of hair on his chest, to see if it felt as soft and springy as it looked. Her eyes followed the line of dark hair from belly button to below his underwear, the bulge that strained against his parted pants, and realized he too had little control left. Her reaction hit swift and potent. Raging lust grabbed her, shocked her. She had to fight back the wild, storming urge to literally rip his pants off, then and there.

She glanced upward to see if he'd heard her gasp, seen her reaction. His smirk held a spark of eroticism, his eyes glinting with bright, flaring desire, his breathing as labored as hers. She felt the heat of his gaze seep into every pore. Her hands shook as she undid the rest of the buttons, it not being an easy feat over the heated bulge.

"Let me help you," he said, his grin mirrored in his eyes. Obviously, he sensed her awkward shyness in trying to avoid touching that part of him. Could he also sense another part of her that wanted to feel that growing staff? As he took charge, pulling the pants down farther, she placed her hands on each side of his hips, eager to assist. Her heart galloped like a horse determined to win the race of the season as her eyes became glued to the part of him she longed to—God help her—have inside her. Before the pants even crept past his underwear he covered her hands with his own to glide the pants slowly, so frustratingly slowly, downward and over his narrow hips. Through the undershorts she felt the hard muscles of his hips, his thighs, the curling of hairs that covered his skin. *Oh, my.*

"I…can't stand this." Her husky tone sounded foreign. Her heart thrummed, sweat pearled across her brow, dampened her palms, warmth flowed between her legs. Dizziness threatened.

"I love an impatient woman." He laughed, grabbing a blanket draped over the side of the stall. "I can't wait any longer, either." With one flick of his wrist he had the blanket flaring open and settling over the hay-covered dirt floor.

"Our bed awaits," he said, his grin devilish as he bowed and gestured with a sweeping arm. She laughed at his antics, her heart swelling with a love so intense it left her speechless.

She felt no shyness as she sat down on the middle of the brown wool. Oh, no, she'd waited too long for this moment. He followed suit, seeking her lips as soon as he reached her side, tilting her back so they lay side by side on their newly made bed.

Flames that had calmed now rekindled. His hands seemed to be everywhere on her, touching, kneading, massaging, firing her skin, and turning her blood to molten lava. Her lips clung to his, her tongue followed his lead, then took command at tasting, laving. Her hands roamed, touched, and stroked all that heated skin, the sinewy cords, the silky hairs on his chest, abdomen, muscled thighs, and calves. She didn't intend to miss touching one inch of him.

Only dimly aware of her surroundings, she felt hay prickle her back through the blanket as he rolled her over and covered her body with his. And when skin touched skin, every inch of glorious heated and sweat-covered skin, she vaguely realized he'd removed their last clothing. Sensations, mind-boggling and tingling, raced rapidly. She wanted him—now.

His lips roamed down her neck as his hands

caressed each breast before sliding across her belly to tease the fine hairline below as his kisses trailed in their wake to lave, then suckle her breasts. She arched off the blanket as delicious currents, half ice, half flame, soared through her.

Unable to reach him with kisses, she boldly encircled the engorged part of him she so diligently had avoided minutes before. Its satin feel surprised her, fascinated her. Its pulsating hardness, its size, had her groaning with heightened impatience.

Instinctively, she stroked and caressed him in a rhythm that seemed totally natural, exhilarated by his passionate moans. His lips trekked a heated path down and across her stomach. His fingers feathered through damp hairs to massage the aching mound that begged for release. Then his finger was inside her, matching the rhythm of her hand. Swift, potent fire shot through her. Her back arched as she felt the overpowering need for more. And she begged.

"Please."

"Oh, but there's more, my love, so much more, before I claim you as mine."

She had no idea what he meant. She wanted him to join them as one. Now. But when his lips kissed her there, where juices ran like a spring stream, when his tongue worshipped the very core of her, she gasped, called out his name, and shuddered with violent explosions.

Still quaking in the aftermath, she felt him cover her body with his. He kissed her forehead, eyelids, cheeks, nose, and finally, with the taste of her essence on his lips, he placed a gentle kiss upon her mouth. She trembled from the sheer sweetness of it.

"Look at me, sweetheart." His warm breath fanned her face, his fingers splaying through her hair, the tip of his shaft nudging at her entrance.

She opened her eyes. Their gazes locked.

"Look into my eyes as we join together, and know this is meant to be, for the rest of our lives. I love you with all my heart, Morgan. And I always will."

Tears rushed her eyes as she read that love, the deep commitment they'd share in the future for all time. "I love you, too, Luke. With all my heart, and I always will."

He laced his fingers with hers as he brought their arms out to each side. The intimacy of their threaded fingers had her breath catching once more. Palms to palms, fingers woven in a lovelock. Then he was inside her. Sliding, just barely inside. Ever so cautiously.

The prolonged anticipation became unbearable. Their gazes melded. Flames soared. She tilted her pelvis upward, felt him slip in farther. But more incredible was the unconditional devotion she felt transfer from him and to him with the mirrored feelings she read in his eyes. "Now?"

"Now," he whispered, covering her lips with his. She felt one faint smart. Then heaven was handed to her. She accepted it willingly, with a greediness she had no desire to deny.

She rocked, he thrust, she writhed, he pumped, their tempo surging. She panted, gasped as she sailed through a million glimmering stars to sweet ecstasy; he groaned, mumbling erotic words that had her crying her release. She felt him tremble, stiffen, and collapse against her.

Love flowed through her like warm honey as she lay cradled within his arms, their heated, drenched bodies too exhausted to move. An amazing sense of completeness settled within her, and she knew their love was meant to be.

They lay silent, content to catch their breaths, to return to earth. She listened to Luke's heart gradually slow to a normal pace. She loved the feel of his solid chest against her cheek, the satiny texture of sweat-covered skin under her fingertips. She smiled, recalling Lucy's words.

"Are you laughing?" Luke asked, sounding incredulous, yet he didn't move to look at her.

"I didn't realize I'd actually made a noise. I thought I was simply smiling."

"Oh? And what has you actually giggling, when I haven't the energy to do more than *simply* breathe at this point?" She heard the laugh in his voice.

"I was thinking of how Lucy asked me to take care of you."

He did move then. Only far enough to cock his head to see her face. "And?"

Though his face was shadowed, he had the most handsome scowl. With a boldness that surprised her, she grinned. "I believe I've taken care of you quite well, at least on one level."

His roar of laughter shook what little hay rested peacefully on top of the rafters down upon them like dandelion whiskers floating on a breeze. She remembered their cabin, how she'd thought his roar would shake those rafters down around them. My, they'd come a long way.

"I believe you're absolutely correct," he said, returning her grin.

Taking her hand in his, he kissed her curled fingers. Her throat constricted from the tenderness of the gesture. His eyes met hers, his face more sober than she'd expected.

"She knew what she was about, what we were about. It was her last hopeful wish that we'd share a life together, a long-lasting life filled with love. The kind of love that was long denied—or, I should say, the passionate love that could never have existed between Lucy and me."

Tears pooled in her eyes as sorrow gripped her chest in its tight vise. Sorrow for the young woman, much too young to die, who had indeed said her farewell to the cruel world. Sorrow for the mismatched alliance both Luke and Lucy had realized should never have been. Sorrow for both Luke and herself in losing such a dear and sweet friend.

Such gloom after such ecstasy made her restless. The barn suddenly felt stifling. Her deeply imbedded guilt at coveting Lucy's fiancé for so long reared up to sink its unforgiving tentacles into her until she felt suffocated. Unwilling to let him see her remorse, she rose and strode to the door. She grasped the door's casing, hoping to find solace for the confusing past.

Taking a deep breath, she tried to be logical. They loved each other; they were meant to be together; Lucy wanted that, she knew. Yet how could she ever forget she'd betrayed her?

Hay rustled, followed by Luke's bare footsteps padding over the packed earth. As he came closer, she stiffened, expecting—what? His anger? A reprimand? His plea to forget?

Instead, he rested his hands, gently, on her bare shoulders, his chin on the top of her head. He remained silent. His tender touch, his understanding silence, seeped into her pores like warm, soothing oil. As a faint breeze fanned her nakedness, she shivered. Luke slid his arms around her waist, and she savored the coziness of the cocoon he offered.

A dozen or so loons had gathered on the pond. Flocked closely together, they glided to the middle, painted silver by the three-quarter moon. They stopped their leisurely paddling to float on the gentle ripples as if without a care in the world. Oh, to be that lucky.

At first, only one called, its softness stirring the quiet air with beauty and mystery. Another, farther out, offered a hoot, both intimate and calming. As the two persevered, now almost in unison, others offered soulful wails and variable tremolos. To Morgan's surprise, a haunting yodel joined the delightful symphony.

She smiled, wondering why that yodel had been added. Just weeks ago, Lucy and she had laughed at how even loons showed their arrogant virility by yodeling to warn other males to stay away from their own.

"If you listen, really listen, you'll agree they're definitely singing," Luke said, his breath tickling her ear and causing her to shiver.

But she did listen. To the various sounds, the sheer beauty and magnificence of the strange, primitive birds she'd come to admire and love. And, glory be to God, she'd thought their combined vocals had been more like an orchestra, but now as she truly lent an ear, possibly with a deeper desire to hear a melody, it sang clear. Would wonders ever cease to exist?

The loons were singing. Even the yodel accompanying the chorus? Oh, yes, he was the tenor. And it was the sweetest harmony she'd ever heard.

Morgan turned and wrapped her arms around Luke's waist. Through her eyes, she bestowed all the love she felt for this man. His eyes sparkled with the love he freely offered in return.

"I think it's fate, sweetheart," Luke said. "Tonight, of all nights, when you question what's right or wrong, your fine-feathered friends are giving you a sign. They're telling you to listen with your heart, as Lucy and I both have asked you to do. Listen, and let love in, and let it grow. How can you argue with Mother Nature at her best?"

The loons continued to harmonize as she smiled up at the man who held her heart. He smiled, but she felt tension in his arms, saw wariness in his eyes. And all the last nagging doubts flew. It seemed so clear now. Why hadn't she seen the truth before? Accepted what was right?

"I'm only human, so I don't suppose I can fight Mother Nature. And I've just realized how blind, how very foolish I've been." He remained quiet, allowing her to say what she needed to say, obviously knowing she needed to say it. Oh, how she loved this wonderful man.

"Lucy had your friendship and love throughout childhood. She was blessed by both in your engagement, though you both knew and accepted your love for each other was…more platonic. You stood by her, gave her your devotion and the best possible life she could've asked for till the end. And now, I think—no, I believe..." She met his gaze. "I truly believe it's my turn to accept the love you offer me, and to return to you all the love I have for you. I finally realize she was happy for us and she could die in peace knowing we'd be together." He offered her a smile that sent her heart racing.

"If you'll still have me," she added with a mischievous grin.

"Is that a 'yes' if I ask you to be my wife?" His eyes twinkled.

"Are you asking?" A glow flowed through her. Their lives would always be full of happiness now that they'd made their commitment. She no longer had to hold back her thoughts, her actions, her desires. He loved her for herself, the way she thought, how she acted.

He raised his brows, grinning. "I guess I'll have to, in order to make an honest woman out of you." His hands drifted down her back to settle on her hips. The path his hands had taken left flames along her skin. Was he as affected by his touch as she was?

"Oh? Is that so?"

"Yeah, that's so. I know you're as ready to go

back to that blanket as I am." His hands lowered to her bottom, his fingers slowly kneading each round curve. Her breath caught, her pulse took to galloping. She fought the impulse to lean back. She avoided looking into his eyes.

"I could resist you if I had to." She had to fight to hold back laughter. Lord, he was right. She felt the passion stirring deep within. Her blood was ready to boil just from his teasing.

With one curled finger he lifted her chin so their eyes met. "I'll tell you why, if you don't realize it." His voice had turned husky and his eyes now smoldered to match the fire growing in her lower abdomen. "When I first started rubbing your back, your breasts swelled before my own eyes and the nipples turned to little pebbles. I believe, my teasing one, that you're highly aroused, and you have set me on fire all over again."

"I..." She had no recourse, she realized, her face feeling as it were engulfed by flames. He was absolutely right. She'd not paid any attention, but her breasts and nipples were "ripe for the pickin'," as some would say.

He hugged her in a tight yet loving bear hug, all the while laughing at her embarrassment. "Don't fret, sweetheart. Your eager response pleases me immensely. And believe me when I say I'm just as ready as you are."

Oh, she knew *that* for a fact. She felt his readiness against her. Oh, and if that didn't send the excitement through her to no end. She was panting like a dog after a tasty bone.

"Neither one of us has any shame," she said with a giggle. "Here we are, standing in the open doorway, both as naked as the day we were born. Lord, have mercy. You've not only made me a dishonest woman, you've turned me into a naked harlot, as well."

Luke hugged her tighter, devouring her lips with his. It nearly sent him over the edge. Reluctantly, he drew back, unable to know which of them was trembling more. But he had one important matter to settle before their world spun out of control again.

He loved her little pout, the wide-eyed surprise at his withdrawal from her lips. "Will you let me make an honest woman out of you? Will you do me the honor of becoming my wife? I love you, Morgan. I've told you that today, and I meant it. I'll always mean it, no matter what."

Her smile was radiant. Her eyes had turned dark brown, glazed with passion, with chips of gold dust sparkling. "I love you, too, so much it nearly scares me. And I'd be proud to be your wife, even though you are stinking rich and have turned me into a corrupt, insatiable hussy."

"Thank God. But all I wanted was your *simple* 'yes.'" His hands caressed her shoulders, his fingers stroking across the nape of her neck. He loved to make her shiver with his touch.

"All right. Yes, but only under one condition."

He stared at her, baffled. "What condition?"

"You take me back to that blanket and keep me warm this very minute. I'm chilled out here with no clothes on." She laughed. "Are you going to expect this often when we're married?"

"Every wonderful day we share, maybe more," he informed her as their laughter trailed them back to the blanket.

"I guess I'll have to be the devoted wife and endure your demands."

"Absolutely." He was a very happy man.

He led her to the blanket. They never heard the loons begin their second round of chorus.

Not over the singing of their hearts.

A word about the author...

Beverly Wells, an award-winning author, is a Public Health Nurse and part of Homeland Security's Medical Reserve Corps. She read only medical books until her friend introduced her to romance novels several years ago. Now, she can't get her nose out of them, whether historical or contemporary.

She lives with her husband and rescued dog Jamie in the Finger Lakes Region of New York State. She enjoys nature, all animals (especially dogs), being in or on the lake, cooking, flower gardening, but especially loves visiting with her son, daughter-in-law, and her lovely two granddaughters.

Visit her at her website
www.beverlywellsauthor.com
or email her at
bev@beverlywellsauthor@gmail.com

She'd love to hear from you.

CPSIA information can be obtained at www.ICGtesting.com
Printed in the USA
BVOW010552070512

289402BV00004B/1/P

9 781601 549860